THE DARK LANTERN

THE DARK LANTERN

HENRY WILLIAMSON

This edition first published in 2010
by Faber and Faber Ltd
Bloomsbury House, 74–77 Great Russell Street
London WC1B 3DA

Printed by CPI Antony Rowe, Eastbourne

A CIP record for this book is available from the British Library

ISBN 978–0–571–27003–3

CONTENTS

Part One

CAMBERWELL BEAUTY

Part Two

HETTY'S BIRTHDAY PARTY

Part Three

NEW HOME

Part Four

WINTER OF 1894-95

Part Five

DEATH AND RESURRECTION

Part One

CAMBERWELL BEAUTY

Chapter 1

A JUNE EVENING

OVER THE Hill at night shone the stars of heaven; but they were seldom observed by those walking there, for northward lay the city of London, with its street lights seen on a clear evening winking away into the haze by the river; while to the east and south of east lay the high roads into Kent, the vegetable garden of London, marked by the diminishing gas-flares of the borough. Turning towards the west, where the last of the sunset was lost in the smoky dew, the solitary walker pausing in his constitutional beheld here and there in the dark spaces below him steady points of light which were windows of farm-houses lit by oil-lamps, and weather-boarded labouring men's cottages showing a glimmer of dip or farthing candle. Arable farming was, towards the close of the nineteenth century, still being carried on in the fields yet unbuilt upon south of the Hill.

The gentle winds of evening in May, eddying from the chalk downs of north-west Kent and pushing back the smoke of London across the marshes of the river, brought the cries of owls, and sometimes, when the scents of lilac and hawthorn blossom were in the still air, the voices of nightingales answering one another across the moonlit spaces of the night. Occasionally when the wind was from the south-east the chatter of warblers could be heard among the reeds of the Randisbourne brook beyond the railway station half a mile away.

Upon the acid pastures of the Hill, clover-diminished owing to the steady descent of soot, an occasional straying hare was to be seen, uncertain and depressed of ear, as though having heard the rumour that the forty acres of immemorial glebe land were to be sold, and to that distending and *parvenu* county whose only claim to arable and pasture, beyond its city parks, was by its suppression of farmlands under the weight of its burnt subsoil, a clay variously yellow and umber, made into brick houses in rows—the county of London.

A certain young man, solitary of condition rather than by nature, was frequently upon the Hill at night. A countryman by birth, but working in London by necessity—put into a private bank through the influence of a connection of his father's—he went there to be alone in his pensiveness, to share the darkness with the cries of night birds, and the flutter of moths which found their ways thither with the rising warm airs of early nightfall from the orchards below and the reeds of the brook beside the hamlet of Randiswell. He looked upon the Hill as a friend, after the constrictions of work at a sloping mahogany desk, in ledgers and parchment-covered pass-books: a friend that was somewhat sad like himself, in that it was neither one thing nor the other, neither of the true country nor of the fashion called the Town.

To others in the neighbourhood—generally the older people—the Hill at night had another aspect. It was said to be a place neither safe nor nice to venture upon in the darkness, whether of summer or of any other season. The reason lay in the extension of the county of London into the county of Kent, and the adventuring thither of thieves and other blackguards. The Hill after dark was declared to be the haunt of those two menaces to an orderly life—lovers and footpads.

The term *lovers*—a term of deprecation, of course—included all couples seen to be moving on the various footpaths leading up its grassy slopes, whether the observed approach be made by couples whispering with elbows linked, strolling slowly with arms cross-laced behind the back, or proceeding unspeaking and a little apart as though intent upon business. Young servant girls, especially those with rosy cheeks, fresh come into service from the remote country, were warned by their mistresses never to speak to strange men, and certainly never to go with any man, whether young or old, anywhere near the Hill after the sun had set.

As for the footpads, they were a figment of the mind echoing from past danger, rather than from present reality. The body of a sailor from the docks at Deptford, a Royal Navy man too, had once been found there, garotted by a bow-string; and farther back in time, Dick Turpin had hung out in the woods then at the southern base of the Hill, near the Great Field which was now the cemetery. Nevertheless, screams were still to be heard upon the grassy dark slopes at night, cries soon stopped by a covering hand indifferent to, indeed enjoying, the virgin's tears. The warnings to adolescent female loneliness had some basis in reality.

True love was there, too, among the rye and timothy grasses of the blackened pastures, seeing through the benison of conjoined thought the scintillating wonder of the heavens, or watching, arms about one another's necks, the remote fiery breath of railway engines approaching or leaving the metropolis; love in sweet silence listening to the bleat of lambs in the fold beside the dark building of the grammar school, and when the air was still, to the rumble of waggons loaded with vegetables and corn for the London markets upon the cobbles of the distant high road.

True love, absorbed in its own feeling, had no thought for youths or men who might be creeping and spying, hoping for a share in lust; nor were such concordant couples of any use to the peeping toms. They were attracted to the hard-eyed fornicators, and calculating seducers, the cowards who fancied themselves as toughs—tortured products of the dark and narrow streets and ways of London—who were ready to thresh, and even to kick to death, anyone creeping to spy upon them.

One evening in late June of the year 1893 the solitary young man who regarded the Hill as a friend was walking up the western slope to the elm trees upon the crest, to visit some strips of cloth, impregnated with a boiled mixture of foots sugar and beer, which he had pinned upon the bark an hour previously, for the purpose of luring moths thither. He walked with some elation, owing to the exaltation of his thoughts. Upon his return from London at a quarter past seven that evening he had found a letter beside his plate, a letter which, after a period of dread—as one awaits an alternative sentence of life or death—he had, when the landlady was gone from the room, begun to open with the aid, or encumbrance, of an ivory newspaper-cutter. This object, fitted with a handle consisting of a deer's slot and pasterns—the forefoot to the ankle of the beast—was fully two feet in length; and as the tip of the cutter was about two inches in width, the insertion into the flap of the envelope, without breaking the paper, was a matter of some care and trepidant slowness. At last it was achieved, and the letter drawn forth, carefully, tremulously; and to his relief he saw that the young woman, to whom he had written after an interval of three weeks' silence, was coming to meet him and his sister on the morrow, at the rendezvous he had suggested by the Observatory in Greenwich Park.

Since the previous April the landlady had known that something was wrong with her favourite among the young gentlemen she looked after in her apartment house. During the five years she had been doing for him, never once had she known him to behave other than as a perfect gentleman, she told her friend and near neighbour, Mrs. Birkett the midwife. He had never been late for his meals—except when delayed by fog at night on the line, and fog was something no man could control, the river Thames being where it was. He always got up as soon as called in the morning to do his exercises with dumb-bells and Indian clubs. Afterwards he took his cold tub, sponging himself all over, including his head, winter and summer, and never making any splash on the floor. When he went for a ride on his safety bicycle, which he kept beautifully clean, he never forgot to dust the wheels first before bringing his machine into the house to stand against the wall in the space under the stairs, where Mrs. Feeney the charwoman's carpet-beater, broom, brush, pan, and pail with hearthstone slab and swab for the front steps were kept. And in five years he had never missed a payment for his bed-sitting room and weekly board of eleven shillings: and certainly never once during those years had he ever come home the worse for liquor. Indeed, he seldom took a glass of anything except water, lemonade, ginger-beer, or perhaps lime juice sometimes in the hot summer weather. He was most reserved, never speaking about himself; and he seemed happiest when he was looking at his collection of moths and butterflies in the big wooden boxes that opened wide to reveal the winged creatures pinned in rows within.

Mrs. Cummings was a little sorry for the lonely young fellow who wore a beard: indeed she felt some concern for his solitary condition. He never went to the theatre, not even to a music-hall, and certainly never to a dance. Looking at his butterflies, riding his bicycle out into the country, and playing his 'cello, always with a mute on the bridge—and a blanket hung over the door inside his room—were hardly her idea of a gay life; still it seemed to satisfy him, so perhaps, as she told Mrs. Birkett, that was all that mattered. But it was not natural for a young fellow to avoid making friends in the neighbourhood. His only visitor was a younger sister who sometimes came to see him of a Saturday or Sunday afternoon.

Ah, Miss Theodora Maddison had quality if ever a young lady had! They were a rare sight, seen together, Mr. Richard and Miss Theodora, both tall and slim and smiling, so good-looking with their blue eyes and fresh cheeks and fair hair, always so considerate and friendly towards everybody, high and low alike.

Mrs. Cummings, elderly childless widow of a sea-captain, and Scots, was fond of her young man, as Mrs. Birkett the midwife pleasingly spoke of him to her. Mrs. Cummings had known for a long while that Mr. Maddison had a sweetheart somewhere, by the way his face altered whenever he received a letter in a certain handwriting, with a post-mark in Surrey; and afterwards, when he opened his boxes of butterflies, and started to tell her about them, and where he had got them, Mrs. Cummings knew that he was in good heart with his young lady. She was most curious about this unknown personage, as she thought of her. Who was she? By the good quality of the envelope, she was one of his own class, probably living in a big villa, with a carriage and pair. But why did she never come over to see her Richard?

Mrs. Cummings was content that nothing very serious had so far appeared to upset the young man's living; for of course, like everyone else, he had to make his way in the world before he should think of getting married.

One Saturday afternoon during April of that year Mrs. Cummings had been sure that something was afoot, as she put it to Mrs. Birkett: for after his dinner on coming home at two o'clock from the office, he had spent a long time polishing his boots with a velvet pad, and then in brushing his best frock coat and smoothing his silk hat; after which he had played awhile on his 'cello, the strains of the tune being audible in the kitchen below—played without the mute this time, so something obviously was in the wind. Drawn by the sounds, Mrs. Cummings had gone upstairs to listen on the landing, for her young man was playing *Loch Lomond*.

When he had come downstairs, all togged up, as she told Mrs. Birkett, he had said that he might be late that night, and telling her not to wait up for him, he had returned to the station, wearing a new pair of dogskin gloves and carrying with his 'cello a bouquet of roses set in maidenhair ferns. She had expected him back about midnight, deeming that he had gone down into Surrey to be with his friends; but to her surprise, and even consternation, he was back again after little more than a couple of hours, and she guessed by his face what had happened. He had gone to his room and shut himself in, and was so quiet therein that after an hour she had crept softly up the stairs to the landing and listened outside the door, prepared to say, should it be opened suddenly, that she had come to ask him what he would like for his supper. Listening intently, Mrs. Cummings had heard the sound of sobbing.

"Yes, Mrs. Birkett, it looked as though his 'cello had known more of what was to come than he did: whoever it was who took the high road, our Richard was on the low road that night."

That had been in the early spring, when the elms along the high road were coming into leaf. He was drawn-looking for some days afterwards, and right off his feed, she told Mrs. Birkett; but about a week later, after reading a letter placed beside his plate on the table laid for supper when he returned from the City at a quarter after seven o'clock one evening—the same Surrey postmark, but the writing was that of an older woman, Mrs. Cummings decided—the lines of care had vanished off his face, and he had eaten two platefuls of mulligatawny soup, followed by two helpings of steak and kidney pudding flavoured with oysters, and a large portion of treacle tart; and once again, the muted strains of the 'cello were audible from his room.

Letters in the same thin and sloping handwriting followed at about weekly intervals, in nearly transparent envelopes, each bearing a twenty-five *centime* French stamp. About a month later the Surrey post-mark reappeared, and Mrs. Cummings deduced, with some certainty, that the young lady had returned to England again, accompanied by her mother, who had been writing those letters to him.

By this time both she and Mrs. Birkett, cronies over a pot of tea, and always popping in and out of one another's side-doors, were most interested in the romance, both agreeing that the course of true love never did run smooth—particularly after the babies started to arrive, added Mrs. Birkett, a trifle sardonically, but nevertheless considerably intrigued by what she had, on so many occasions, been told by Mrs. Cummings.

Now it would soon be midsummer: the grey dust on the dry surface of the high road was beginning to settle upon the lower leaves of the elms: the cuckoo had stopped singing: fish in the shops would soon be unreliable, though fresh-boiled crabs were safe, and made a nice change for her young gentlemen, served with a salad of lettuces, spring onions, radishes, and new potatoes grown by the very old man on the railway embankment, and brought to the door by his granddaughter on the barrow drawn by a donkey.

The last two weeks in June were to be Mr. Maddison's holiday, and he was thinking of spending it on a bicycling tour all by himself down to the West Country to visit the place of his boyhood, Mrs. Cummings told Mrs. Birkett. But then—a letter came by Special delivery! In the young lady's handwriting, and the right Surrey post-mark! When he had read it, and had had his supper, Mrs. Cummings went down five doors to Mrs. Birkett, who was preparing to go out on a case that night, and told her the latest news: he had put off his bicycling tour one day, as on the morrow he had to go to Greenwich Park with his sister, to meet a very special friend.

"Let's hope the Old Man doesn't appear upon the scene, with a horse-whip," remarked Mrs. Birkett, who from her favourite reading knew all about the ways of the supposed wealthy in such situations. "They do say some of them chestnut trees in Greenwich Park are hollow, and an irate parent might easily conceal himself in one of them."

Such was the power of popular print upon Mrs. Birkett the midwife, so realistic in other ways concerning the matters of life and death. She knew the ways of men, having seen them at their best, and worst, in the homes she visited. Without children herself, she professed a mild contempt for the idea of parenthood: but perhaps her real feelings were indicated in the fact that she regarded all those she helped to bring into the world as partly belonging to her; and this feeling of aloof protectiveness was extended to the mothers themselves.

"Your young man must be in high feather tonight, Mrs. Cummings. A nice holiday in front of him, and the Belle of the Ball in Greenwich Park tomorrow. Where is he gone tonight, after more moths? That stuff you were boiling on your range this afternoon—what does he call it, his concoction?—fair gave me a headache. Fancy wasting good rum and beer on moths. Camphor is more in my line, the horrid things."

"His are real wild moths, not the kind that nibble, Mrs. Birkett. The kind you put in rows, on a pin, in wooden cases. You ought to see his collection, it's a tribute to the Almighty's wonderful variety, all gaudy colours they are, you'd never credit it."

"So he catches them with demon rum and beer, does he? Not the kind that nibble, but the kind that tipple. He ought to drink some of his concoction himself, dear, it would give him gaudy colours—the stench of the stuff! Why don't you suggest that he take a bottle of it to Greenwich tomorrow, to give to the Old Man in case he pops sudden-like out of a hollow tree with that whip of his?"

"It's a shame, Mrs. Birkett," exclaimed Mrs. Cummings, laughing, "the way you guy the poor young fellow. His butterflies and moths are a hobby that keeps him out of mischief anyway. You know what that Hill is, after dark. He's up there now, to see what luck he's had with his strips. Off he went with his lantern and bottle of crushed laurel leaves, to pop in what he catches, and stifle them, before I came in just now." She finished her cup of tea and remarked as though suddenly, "Goodness, I must be getting back, it's young Milly's night off, and I don't like to leave the washing-up for her when she returns! She's gone to the Penny Reading at St. Simon's Hall."

"Well, anything so long as she keeps off that Hill. Your young man sounds a proper bodysnatcher to me, dear," was Mrs. Birkett's parting remark, delivered with mock dolefulness. "Mind he don't pop Milly in that bottle of his, Mrs. Cummings." And in good humour the two women bade one another good night.

Mrs. Cummings's words to her friend Mrs. Birkett, that her lodger's hobby kept him out of mischief, might have struck her (had she possessed that kind of mind) later in the evening as ironic, could she have known what happened by the row of elms on the Hill, a few minutes after he had returned to her own kitchen.

As Richard Maddison walked up the grassy slope to the dark masses of the trees before him he was being watched by three men, or rather, by one man and two youths lying hidden in different places upon the grass.

His step was light, he was buoyantly happy after the weeks of anxiety and depression, during which he had often doubted the loyalty of the girl he loved, and hoped one day to marry. It had never occurred to him that she, who was loyalty itself to him, would not therefore be disloyal to her father, to whom she had given a promise that, while she was abroad with her mother in the south of France, she would not write to Richard Maddison. His sister Theodora had more than once put this aspect to him, but his feelings were such that he had seldom been able to keep his mind in balance. Now for the time being doubt was gone from his mind; and he was master of himself.

He reached the top of the slope, coming to the row of elms, where he paused to look around him, while feeling for his lucifer matches in a waistcoat pocket. The sky was starry, the wind warm and gentle, a good scenting night for moths.

Squatting on his heels, he opened the front of his lantern, turned up the wick, and struck a match. The phosphorous head gave a little cracking noise, and spluttered into flame which soon crept along the wick, the colza oil giving a clear yellow light. He turned the wick down, then closed the door, so that the beam was enclosed. The metal slide had to be moved round before the light was visible through the bull's-eye lens. With the lantern in his left hand, and a small net, shortened on its telescopic handle held in his other, he moved to the first of the strips pinned to the bark of the nearest tree. Three woodlice and an earwig on that one.

He moved to the next tree. As he shone the beam upon the section of old trouser-leg saturated with foots, or coarse sugar, boiled with a pint of ale, he saw what looked like two little fireballs glowing there. It was one of the Sphinges, or Sphinx moths, popularly called Hawk moths; but before he could determine whether it was Lime or Privet, or perhaps Convolvulus, it had gone.

He waited for it to return, holding the lantern steady to attract it by the beam, while resting his forearm against the bark. A small white Phantom fluttered to the light, followed by a Yellow Underwing, an Angle Shade, and a Cinnabar. They were small game. He hoped for something splendid, like a Death's Head, which laid its eggs on various plants such as jasmine, snowberry, or tea-tree, but more usually on potato leaves and the relative deadly nightshade. The Death's Head had once been fairly common in the district. Pooley, the market gardener with the donkey barrow who "farmed" the railway embankment, an old man of nearly a hundred years of age, when speaking of them had called them locusts. He was afraid of them—the black skull on the thorax, the mouse-like squeaks if alarmed or seized. The Death's

Head sometimes crept into straw honey-skeps, and the bees covered it with wax as it drank from the cells: to be found in the autumn, an entombed grey mummy, by the cottager taking his honey after a sulphur candle had stilled for cver the winged gatherers within their straw-bond home set in the alcove of a cottage wall.

Other eyes, beside the lambent orbs of Sphinges, had seen the light-rays from the lantern among the trees. One of the men lying on the grass had raised himself on an elbow and was staring up the slope and muttering angrily, not so much to his companion, a fourpenny-bit picked up outside the Jack earlier that evening, as to the tormented figments of his mind. He wore a jacket of wincey cloth black with coal dust over a ragged shirt equally grimy, and a choker round his neck. After the day's round he had called in the Jack for a quart of porter, leaving his horse and cart hitched to the staple in the tree outside the pub. There he had stayed, drinking, until shortly after ten o'clock when, driving home past the cemetery, he had picked up one of two women loitering near a lamp-post. Two youths had seen the accosting, and had followed what they called among themselves the buck navvy and his tom on to the Hill, to creep as near as they dared in order to enjoy the preliminaries; with the intention, at what they reckoned to be the moment of sensation, of getting up and passing as near the feet of the prostrate couple as they dared, caps well pulled down to hide their faces; and in passing to shout taunts and then to flee in wild and thrilling excitement into the darkness, away from murderous imprecation.

The passing of the stranger over the grass between them and their quarry had interrupted the sport, and now they were watching, from a distance of fifteen yards or so, the dim figure of the buck navvy raised upon an elbow and staring at the light moving among the trees.

They saw the buck navvy rise to his feet, and watched him walking up the slope. They followed at a safe distance, hoping to see some sport.

The coalman unfastened his belt with the big brass buckle as he strode forward in a crouching position, intending to come unawares upon the man with the light.

Richard Maddison, having moved to the fourth tree, was gazing with unbelieving amazement at what he beheld in the circular and wavering beam of his lantern. There upon the strip of damp cloth was clinging a butterfly whose colours and shape at first perplexed him; and moving slowly towards it, in his astonishment forgetting to hold his net in readiness, he saw that it was one of the Vanessas; but the colouring was unfamiliar. It might have been Polychloros, the Great Tortoiseshell, with its rich mottlings of chestnut-brown and black; but the wings of this insect, vibrating ever so slightly as it sipped the concoction, were edged with yellow-white. Was it a variant of Atalanta, but if so, where was the scarlet on its wings? It was not a Red Admiral: nor was it Vanessa Cardui, as the Painted Lady had deep black upper wings with five chalk-white spots near the tips. Certainly there was a white scalloping also along the edges of the Cardui's wings: but it was an August butterfly: whereas the insect feeding on the strip had definite deep brown wings shot with purple, as he saw when he moved to within a foot of it. By Jove, it was—could it be?—yes! it was exactly like the coloured woodcut in the old book given him by his grandfather—it was a Camberwell Beauty! Last seen in England nearly a hundred and fifty years ago, three of them being recorded as taken at Camberwell in 1748!

A Camberwell Beauty! He gazed without power of movement.

"What's the gaime, eh? Oo d'yer fink yer are?"

"What? Who's there?" Startled, he turned round, shining a light into the direction of the voice.

"You 'eard! Oo'r' yer insultin' of, wiv that bull's-eye?"

"Well, you startled me." Richard lowered the beam. "What do you want? I'm not interfering with you. I'm looking for moths."

"You're a——flycop, that's your bleedun gaime. I knows yer! Comin' 'ere, spyin' on honest men, you stinkin' long streak o' hosspiss dahn a drain! I'll larn yer to come pokin' yer long snout into my —— business!" The words came to Richard out of the darkness in a deadly rasping monotone. He could see the outline of a man, and of others approaching. It was a gang.

He shone the beam again into the man's face, whereupon he said in the same deadly tones,

"Put that bleedun glim off o' me, or you'll never see daylight no more, you sodden Judas."

Richard's heart seemed to be beating violently in his ears. As three other forms approached up the slope, one to the right and two close together, he drew a deep breath to steady his voice before speaking, and said, "Who are you, to dare to use such language to me? Do you want to be given in charge?"

"Oh, so that's yer tone, is it? Well, you've arst for it!" Richard saw the glint of the buckle as the fellow fingered it in his left hand.

Bracing himself to receive the assault, he moved to have his back to the tree, while wondering dispassionately what Hetty would think, and Mr. Turney, if his body were found there in the morning, battered about the head and face. Mrs. Cummings had warned him about the Hill at night, and of the garotted sailor found there. Well, he would sell his life dearly, as befitted an enrolled special constable.

Putting the lantern at the base of the tree, he said, "I told you I came here to find moths, which I collect. Look, here is the net!" and he held it low in the rays of the lantern.

The conciliatory attitude had an opposite effect on the other man. "God A'mighty, I'll give you bloody net! I'm going to mark you so you'll never forget! I'll teach you not to go creepin' and crawlin' after honest men!"

"That's right, paste 'im, guv'nor, we seed 'im crawlin' about on 'is 'ands and knees in the grass, arter lovers, di'n't us, Ginger?" exclaimed an adenoidal voice.

"Yus, we seed 'im, wiv 'is lamp an' all," said the lesser of the two shadows.

"I tell you I came straight up the hill here, to my lures on the trees! Anyway, you have no right to threaten anyone like this, particularly a special constable!" And picking up the lantern, Richard shone the beam on the strip, to which the butterfly was still clinging. At that moment, it took wing into the darkness.

The coalman spat violently; and declaring to the others that the man before them was a copper's nark, suddenly shouted, "'Ere, cosh 'im all together, boys!" and took two turns of the leather belt round his right hand in preparation.

The coalman by nature was not combative. Bandy-legged through lack of proper food when a baby, beaten and bullied as a small boy, the coalman would never have dared to attack the stranger, whom he regarded as a dummy from an unreal world, had he not felt that now was a chance to prove to himself his fighting prowess under favourable conditions. With eyes closed, breath held, and head low, he rushed forward; Richard side-stepped, with the result that the coalman, flailing the buckle past his shoulder, bumped head-first into the tree and fell to the ground, groaning and whimpering.

The two youths, coming at Richard on one side, prepared to add their kicks and punches while the buck navvy did the fighting, got a fright as the enemy ran at them, caught one by the shoulder and flung him with a violent twist to the ground, then sprinting after the other, bore down upon him and caught an arm and flung him down likewise.

"Come on, get on your feet, both of you, you dirty little cowards!" cried Richard, in a rage. "You ruffians, you have spoiled my chance of getting a Camberwell Beauty! Come on, get up, if you have got any manhood left!" The youths ran away silently. "Blue funks, both of you! Next time I will haul you to the police station!" He felt a wonderful exhilaration, and wished that he had given the ring-leader a straight left to the jaw.

The fourth figure was standing by, hands in pockets of a man's cast-off overcoat. "Blime, you didn't 'arf give it to 'im, dearie," she said. "I saw it all, and it wasn't your fault."

"Well, thank you for what you say," said Richard, in a voice higher-pitched than usual. "I was only looking for moths. And now I have missed the catch of a lifetime—a Camberwell Beauty!"

"Well, dearie, you found a sweetheart instead. Come on, leave the bloke up there, 'e ain't 'urt. Serves the bleeder right for interferin' wiv a gentleman like you. Come an' 'ave a bit wiv me, dearie. You give me what you like."

Richard was frightened as she approached, a bulk of dark clothes moving over the grass. As he edged away she said, "Come on, old cock, don't be shy." Trembling now, Richard picked up the lantern, turned the wick down so that the light within died, and saying "I must go now. Good evening," he moved away in the opposite direction to which he had come, hoping thereby that his identity might be concealed. The other, however, was not deceived; she recognized him as one who lived in the high road and went about on a bicycle; and as his pace quickened she said in a voice deadly with contempt, "Go and —— yourself, you Jesus Christ on Tin Wheels!"

Chapter 2

QUARTET

As Richard returned to his lodgings by a circuitous route—walking between rows of dark houses, all their front or best rooms being unused—his footfalls echoing from the big paving stones—he felt much jubilation. What an adventure, and what an escape! And although he had been greatly afraid, no one could say that he had shown the white feather! If only he had been in a position to use his straight left! Many times in his bed-sitting room he had varied his morning exercises by boxing an imaginary opponent, for just such an emergency; but until now he had not been called upon to defend life and limb "with his dooks." It had been one of his ambitions since being bully-ragged at boarding school to be the envied possessor of a powerful straight left; and now the opportunity to prove it was gone. That rough deserved a good thrashing, if ever a man did. And the horror of that woman—if she could be called such, with obviously all womanly qualities debased beyond redemption.

His rapid striding echoed from the flag-stones. By now he had turned downhill towards the station and was passing the dark bulk of St. Simon's church on his right. Another turn to the left, and he was in Twistleton Road, with its avenue of limes murmurous in the breeze of the summer night, its large houses set back from their carriage sweeps. By returning this way he hoped to reach his lodgings in the high road without being noticed.

All was well: no figure was waiting to waylay him: no beastly taunts by wretched boys, no crying out of that odious nickname fastened upon him by the cads of the gutter. He reached No. 220, and let himself in by his latch-key.

Mrs. Cummings greeted him at the foot of the stairs. "Did you have any luck, Mr. Maddison?" she enquired. "Anything in the bottle tonight?"

"Nothing tonight, for my pains, Mrs. Cummings." He went up the stairs two at a time.

"Would you like your saffron cake and cocoa now, Mr. Maddison, or later?"

"Now, if you please, Mrs. Cummings. I think I shall retire to bed early. I have a long day before me tomorrow."

"Does that mean you intend to keep to your original plan, and make your start for the West Country before sunrise?"

"Oh no," replied Richard, "I shall start on Sunday, if all goes well, Mrs. Cummings." He shut his door behind him. He had a dread of encountering one or another of his fellow lodgers.

Within the safety of the familiar room, his oil-lamp turned down to a glimmer on the table—there was a gas-jet, but he preferred the softer light of the lamp—he lay back in the armchair, stretched out his legs, closed his eyes, and with a deep sigh let his thoughts range away from the present. This was what to himself he called the Camera Obscura of the Mind.

There were many scenes he revisited by this practice, seeing them in sudden illumination, and always fragmentary. Many of the fragments seemed to strike direct into his breast, transfixing him with poignant longing for that which was gone for ever and ever. Usually the scenes were sunlit, murmurous with summer, of ripening corn in the fields below the downs, of finches and butterflies in the cool breezes of the upland slopes, of sunlit faces of boyhood friends, his brothers and sisters—and then the vision of his world became dark, with thoughts of his mother. Pain darkened the remote enchantments of the summer sun, so that he could scarcely stifle a groan, as he drew up his legs and clenched his hands, while he fell into the abyss of humiliation or despair. Only Love could save him, blissful and radiant Love to dispel all longings of the past, to restore all broken hopes of a home gone for ever.

Hetty, Hetty!

Mrs. Cummings knocked on the door, with a lacquered Japanese tray holding a cup of cocoa, and a slice of yellow cake on a plate. He took it with his usual slight bow, bade her good night, and closed the door softly again.

As he munched the saffron cake and sipped his cocoa, he reflected that surely it had been the hand of Fate that had led him, on the very evening of mother's funeral, to the Round Pond upon the edge of the Heath. Ah, but the terrible sequel! No matter, let the scenes be recalled again in their right order: let the Camera

Obscura of the Mind reveal what had happened, in chronological sequence. Calmly now! And feeling content with the warm fluid inside him, Richard settled down into the armchair, which was both stuffed with, and its fabric woven of, black horsehair upon the upright wooden frame, and covered his eyes with the long and thin fingers of his left hand, while resting his head on palm and elbow, preparatory to finding, by reflection, the proper course to pursue in his present dilemma. Now to begin again from the start:—

Was it not indeed Fate that had impelled him to leave Father, brothers, and sisters immediately after the funeral, to return to London, and then, upon arrival in the chill twilight at his lodgings, to spend but a moment there before departing for the crest of the Hill, to be nearer the eternal stars: and then, as though drawn by some mysterious call, to walk down to Pit Vale and up to the Heath? Why did mother's face accompany him always, to regard him sadly, as though asking him to go to her in the darkness, to be united again with her for ever? Mother's face, wasted and worn, called to him from the coffin: then her face suddenly was that of a harpy. Oh, what terrible thought was he thinking? Mother, mother, you know I love you, I would give my life to bring you back again—her face regarded him steadily, calling him.

So desperately appealing did her gaze appear to be upon him from the depths of the grave, that as he crossed the Heath towards the lights of the village in a hollow, an involuntary groan was wrung from him, and he cried aloud to her in the night, "Oh, why do you not leave me alone?"

In the cold clear March night, hung with crescent moon and evening star upon the west, the cry was heard by two young people standing beside a stationary pony and trap by the round pond. They could see but one dim figure walking against the sky, faintly illuminated by the reflected lights of London in the far distance. Perhaps the other was walking away from the man who had cried out?

"Shall I ask him, Hetty? He sounded like a gentleman."

"Yes, Hughie, do. There can be no harm, surely?"

Drawing a deep breath, the youth called out, "Hi there, I wonder if you would oblige me with some information?"

It was Richard's turn to hesitate. The Heath at night was no place whereon to get into conversation with strangers: yet the voice appeared to be that of an educated man. After a brief pause he said, "Were you speaking to me, sir?" and walked towards the pond, in relief from his thoughts.

"Yes, sir, if you will pardon the liberty. I find myself held up for want of a light. I told m' groom to put new candle-sticks in before we left Surrey this afternoon, and deuce take him, he left in the stubs of the old ones, and now they're burnt down to the springs. Do you happen to know of a chandler's near here?"

Richard walked down to the white posts and railings enclosing the pond. He saw the eyes of a young woman upon him, softly. At his approach, her companion moved up beside her, he noticed. He had exchanged his frock coat and silk hat for a Norfolk jacket and deerstalker cap before leaving his lodgings. No doubt he looked to be a questionable character.

"There is a shop in the village below," he said. "But I ought to warn you that the constable here is somewhat officious concerning the law of lights on vehicles at night."

Had he not been shouted at one evening as he had passed by on his new Starley Rover: and alighting, when most men would have pedalled away rapidly, been told, for his pains, that the next time he would find himself in Greenwich Police Court?

"The constable has his duty to do, of course," he went on, "And so it will be entirely at your own risk if you decide to move on the highway without lights."

"Well, if m' sister and I leave the trap, the pony might bolt, or be stolen."

Richard saw the gentle eyes regarding him steadfastly. He was impelled to offer, beyond his sense of discretion, "Would you care for me to look after it for you, sir?"

Surely the eyes had an eager look in them, due to his presence?

"I could not trespass on your kindness to that extent, sir."

The eyes seemed to reflect the light of crescent moon and planet.

"Well then, if you like, I will go down and buy you a box of candles."

"That's most civil of you, but I cannot allow myself to impose upon a stranger's kindness."

Did they think he was imposing himself on them? He was about to move away, telling himself that he was the last person to remain where he was not wanted, when the young woman said, hesitantly, "Hughie, if you lead the pony on the grass, well away from the road, perhaps——"

Raising his cap, Richard turned and walked away.

Alone once more in the darkness, he felt regret that he had departed so abruptly. He continued slowly over the gravelly common, feeling the young woman's gaze to be upon him out of the night, in the soft darkness about the starlit level spaces all around. He looked back at the pond and the trees, at the wavering beams of reflected gas-light on the surface of the water. There was yet hope: she was the young fellow's sister. Who was he? Some wealthy young puppy, no doubt, with his affected way of speaking. Quite-the-chap-don't-you-know sort of fellow. Well, that appeared to be the end of a romantic encounter.

As he walked on aimlessly, his mood changed to one of self-scoffing. There were such things, after all, as traps set for idiots. One had only to read the Adventures of Sherlock Holmes to know that. He recalled the visit with Theodora to Madame Tussaud's Waxwork Exhibition in Baker Street, and the tableaux there of a young fool's ruin through women, wine, and cards.

Perhaps after all it had been but a case of genuine forgetfulness. He stood irresolute upon one of the greens which had been made for golf. A wild idea came to him. Should he go down to the village, and chance meeting them again? Oh no, no! whatever was he thinking of? It would be akin to an act of that dreadful object, a masher.

He stood still for a few moments, his eyes closed, thinking of the scene in Rookhurst Churchyard only that morning—and yet how far away it seemed. Well, that part of his life was ended. Oh, why had he left so soon? Father had asked him if he must leave at once, would he not return with his brothers and sisters to luncheon at home? And now it was too late.

Irresolute, Richard Maddison looked about him on the Heath; and then, turning about, he set off in the direction of his lodgings.

During the weeks that followed, when he was living a normal life of routine again, the eyes of the young woman often recurred to his mind at odd moments. It might be as he walked across London Bridge; or sat at his sloping mahogany desk in the Shop—as the main room of Doggett & Co. was called—entering in his meticulous hand items of debit and credit, of mortgage interest and dividend per centum, in ledger and pass book; or while eating luncheon in the Golden Grain Teashop in the Strand. He became romantic about the Unknown Inamorata, as he called the figment to himself. She was rare and aloof, infinitely tender; she understood his every secret thought. Vanessa inamorata!

At night, in his bed-sitting room behind the muffling blanket and with muted strings of violoncello, the reading-lamp turned low and the sheet music illuminated only by the beam of the dark lantern, he expressed through his bow and strings his feelings of secret love and tenderness. The blanket was hung over the door as a protection, as a security against the coarse thoughts of others; for there were three other lodgers in the house, and one, in particular, fancied himself as a comedian. In Richard's eyes he was a rather vulgar fellow, ever since the occasion when he had described 'cello music as a noise varying between the grunt of hungry hogs and cats calling for unborn litters on the tiles. This fellow also derided the collecting of butterflies; to him, Richard's appearance fitted with a stereotyped joke of the comic papers—the bearded eccentric with a net, on summer evenings setting forth awheel in knickerbocker suit, the paraphernalia for "bug hunting" slung across his back.

Lying in the armchair, Richard recalled the wonderful afternoon when he had discovered the herb fields to the west of Croydon. Here amidst the variegated scents and colours covering hundreds of acres under the North Downs was an Entomologist's Paradise. And how very nearly had he missed meeting the most wonderful butterfly of all to be found in that district, Vanessa Inamorata! For when his sister had suggested to him that he accompany her on a visit to some friends of hers who lived in a village in the midst of the herb fields, he had refused. People? No fear, he preferred butterflies, he told Theodora. But Dora had replied:

"They are awfully friendly people, boy, a musical family, you must bring your 'cello. Hetty, the second daughter, is ever so jolly. I met them during May Week last year."

"One of your blue-stocking friends?"

"Oh no, Hetty is not at Girton with me, Dickie. Hughie, her brother, is up at Trinity."

"H'm, an elegant young chappie, I bet. Hughie, did you say? Does he drive a pony and trap? No; such people are not much in my line, Dora."

"Nonsense, Dickie! The brother is a violinist of great promise. Yes, he drives a pony and trap, like most young men nowadays.

We want to form a quartet to play Mozart. Do come. You must not let yourself get in a rut, you know."

"A rut, do you say? I am not likely to do that. Does this Hughie ever go to Blackheath, do you know?"

"I think they have an aunt living at Greenwich, Dickie. Why do you ask?"

"Oh, idle curiosity. Well, I am not a fellow who fits in well with others, you know, Dora. I am not one of the rut-dwellers. Besides, I am right out of practice with the 'cello."

"Well, I suppose I shall have to go alone."

"Do not make yourself a martyr, Dora. There is plenty of time to consider it. By Jove, look at the sun shining on the Crystal Palace over here, it looks to be on fire!"

They were walking on the Hill. The northern face of the glassy building on the far crest and the west tower were flushed in the setting sun.

"A grey mullet becoming a red mullet."

"How graphic a description, Dickie."

"Well, it is only what I have thought at times. It is a queer place, you know. I attended a concert of the *Messiah* there once, and felt that at any moment the entire roof would collapse, under the diapason of the great organ."

"That is what they thought when the Queen opened it during the Great Exhibition, before the royal salute was fired from cannon, forty years ago! I wish I had been alive then."

"Ah, they were the good old days, to be sure."

They came back for tea to his room. Afterwards he played on his 'cello, to prove that he was badly out of practice. His sister said that the purity and tenderness of the tone delighted her. He wanted to ask her questions about her friends; but dared not expose his feelings. Could it be——? But no, he did not want to meet anybody in villadom! He wanted to spend all his free time out of doors—to explore the North Downs, to study in particular the Blue Adonis.

However, curiosity prevailed. The very next Saturday he and Dora had gone together by train to her friend's place in Surrey. How self-conscious he had felt as he walked beside her carrying the 'cello in its canvas case. They had gone only a little way out of the station when they heard the cantering of hoofs, and a landau, its hood folded back, came around the corner with swerving rear wheels, drawn by a fat horse compelled to such unusual exertion by the would-be Jehu on the box waving a whip. For a moment Richard thought its near wheels were going to strike the railings; but the carriage was too heavy to be upset easily. Seeing them, the driver pulled on the reins and the horse clattered to a standstill.

With a shock he had recognized the driver. Theodora was smiling, and waving to the girl seated in the carriage. She wore a fur hat and tippet; the *inamorata*. The sun seemed to have new meaning.

"Oh, Dora dear, we were afraid we would be late!" And the merry laugh, as she jumped out of the carriage and ran to greet them. Her cheeks were glowing, her hazel eyes alight with pleasure as she clasped Theodora. Then she turned and looked at him, surely aware that his heart was pounding audibly through his arm and resounding in the 'cello.

There were unrealized introductions, then they were in the landau, while the horse started off briskly of its own accord, striking out with eager paddock-thoughts. Like old times, to be behind a horse again!

Thus began his associations with the Turneys of Cross Aulton. On the initial visit he felt himself to be happier than he had ever been. Mrs. Turney was so kind, so gentle, so free from all fussiness; and he felt sure that Hetty liked him, perhaps more than liked him. With relief he had learned that the father of the house was not expected home that Saturday afternoon. Under Mrs. Turney's benevolent eye they had a most enjoyable time in the drawing room, Theodora at the piano, Hugh first violin, Hetty second violin, and himself with his 'cello. They played some of *Eine Kleine Nachtmusicke*, with many interruptions, and repetitions of phrases wherein piano, fiddle, and 'cello lost one another, amidst laughter. Hugh, who certainly showed some skill with his instrument, and fancied himself as a virtuoso, grew tired of the musical tangle, and during a pause broke into his celebrated *May I Come over the Wall*?, a dialogue between a tom cat and his lady love in the moonlight. It really was extremely funny. What a wonderfully happy family they were, to be sure.

Trying to live again in the moment, Richard remembered how he had felt at first a little out of it, since he was so much older than the others, six or seven years at least. He had supposed that Hugh and Hetty were about twenty, a year older than Theodora; and his relief had been great when he had learned, on the way back to London, that Hetty was actually twenty-four. Certainly she did not look a day older than nineteen.

At this point in his retrospection Richard turned over in the chair, covering his face with his hands, and uttered a repressed groan; and for the moment the Camera Obscura of the Mind broke down.

On the following Saturday Richard and Theodora had returned to Maybury Lodge, by special invitation, to continue practising as a Quartet. Mr. Turney had been at home. Immediately on seeing him, Richard thought of the Prince of Wales, though Mr. Turney was not so stout. Otherwise the resemblance was remarkable. His Royal Highness occasionally came into the Shop, where his affability to members of the staff was greatly esteemed. Richard was soon to realize that Mr. Turney's likeness to the Prince was but superficial.

Unknown to him, or indeed to Theodora, there had been some talk between Thomas Turney and his wife when he had heard who had been invited to the house during his absence. For various reasons Mr. Turney was prejudiced against the name of Maddison. This attitude showed itself in his remark, made jokingly, when Richard was introduced to him by his daughter. Having watched the tall young man in the cloth cap and Norfolk jacket walking up the steps, carrying the big 'cello in its case, he said, as Richard bowed to Hetty with it under his arm, "Haven't I seen you with that thing beside the pit queues outside Toole's in the Strand? What d'ye do with it when you're not playing it, d'you sleep in it, he-he-he?" To this unexpected greeting Richard had not been able to think of any reply, and thereafter had remained subdued.

There was another guest that afternoon, a young man even more noticeably lacking in ease than Richard. In a stuttering voice, this other young man admitted to Mr. Turney that he had a flute concealed in the pocket of his greatcoat, while hastening to disclaim any skill in playing it. Indeed, he was but learning it, he stuttered in some panic; it happened to be in his pocket by ch-ch-chance. Mr. Turney laughed at his excuse; and again his individual sense of humour met with no response from the young man other than a nervous stare at the pattern of the carpet. Hetty tried to put him at his ease, saying that she too was the veriest amateur, almost afraid to play in the presence of her brother, and her great friend Theodora, who were both so accomplished. Noting this attention to the stranger, Richard became the more silent.

The fact was that the presence of two constrained young men had put Mr. Turney in a mood inferior to his usual jovial self. Also, he liked to be in his own house, at the week-ends, unencumbered with visitors. He was away on the road all the week, and wanted to enjoy his family when he had the chance. His presence therefore dispelled the previous happy spirit between the young people; and soon after tea Hugh made his excuses, saying that he had to go to his study upstairs, to work on a thesis for his tutor; actually to change his clothes preparatory to going up to London in the hope of meeting some 'varsity friends for billiards at the Carlo Gatti in Villiers Street. In the space of a few minutes he had crept down the back stairs, slipped through the kitchen, and run down the garden path to the door in the wall, and so to the lane outside and the railway station.

Meanwhile the guests in the drawing room had risen to pay their respects to Mrs. Turney, preparatory to leaving. Hetty protested that they had had no music, would they not stop for at least a little while longer, and play? Both 'cellist and flautist, eyes upon the carpet, declared that they must go. Thomas Turney acted before there could be further persuasion; he wanted a quiet evening by the fire, in the bosom of his family; and so, going to the door, he held it open for them to find their own coats and hats. Afterwards, when they were gone, he declared that young Maddison was a poor fish, stilted, with no sense of humour, and obviously possessed of a great conceit of himself.

"Don't encourage him to come here any more, I say, d'ye hear me, Sarah?" to his wife.

Whereupon Hetty quietly left the room. Soon afterwards her mother also left, ostensibly to see about supper; and going upstairs to her daughter's room, found her lying on the bed with one of her nervous headaches.

Thomas Turney had known for some time that Hetty's friend Theodora Maddison was the youngest child of a man whom he had encountered at Brighton a dozen years before, when the children had been little and he and Sarah had taken them for August to the seaside. The Turneys had rented a small furnished house in Kemp Town, where they had been going every summer for several years, and the house adjoining had been the scene of a scandal. It was occupied by a man of a class Thomas Turney disliked, an idler who wore a velvet smoking jacket in the evening—a fop in his opinion. His disapproval increased when it was learned that the florid young woman staying with her middle-aged admirer was an actress. At night, and sometimes by day, there were frequent noises of quarrelling, and once a bottle had crashed through the front downstairs window and shattered itself on the flag-stones near where Sarah was standing with Charley her eldest, Dorrie, Hughie, Hetty, and the baby in the go-cart. The younger children had been terrified by the screams of the baggage and her tipsy appearance half-undressed at the open front-door.

Thomas Turney had run down the steps of his house, in case there was trouble. Thereupon the baggage had shrieked to him for help, and when he had turned away, telling his wife that he wasn't going to be such a fool as to get mixed-up in that sort of nonsense, she had started to abuse him, asking him who he thought he was, the tailor's dummy used to measure the clothes of the Prince of Wales? Then she had called him an old Jew and no gentleman to stand there and not help a lady. The scene—which he declared afterwards to be highly amusing—his sense of fun came from an Irish mother—had ended when she had been dragged inside kicking and struggling and biting the hand of her embarrassed companion upon her mouth.

Some time later, when travelling for the Firm in the West Country, Thomas Turney had encountered this individual again, coming out of the office of a solicitor, one of the Firm's customers, in Colham; and in the course of talk round the supper table of his commercial hotel that evening, he had learned more about him; and all this he remembered later on when he discovered that the Maddison girl who had made friends with Hughie and Hetty during the inter-collegiate boat-races at Cambridge was the daughter of the selfsame Captain Maddison whose racketing ways were a scandal in the district where he lived, or used to live, with his wife and family. However, Thomas Turney had nothing against Theodora, a lady-like young person; but this Richard, or Dickie as they called him—a proper dicky-bird so far as he could see, with no more heart than a goose-chick—was the spit and image of his father, without personality or any redeeming feature whatsoever. And the less Hetty saw of him, the better.

"D'ye hear me, Sarah?" he demanded, when his wife returned to the room, quietly to sit in her chair opposite to him across the fire, "I want Hetty and Hughie to have nothing further to do with him, music or no music, it's all the same thing in the end. I am still master in my own house, please understand that."

"Yes, of course, dear, naturally," Sarah had replied.

"You want to nip such things in the bud, 'tis better so in the long run, whatsay?"

Thomas Turney hoped that he had seen the last of the fellow; but when, to his astonishment, he reappeared unexpectedly two weeks later, on a Saturday afternoon, and had the effrontery to ask permission to pay attention to Hetty, disclosing that his only means wherewith to support a wife were a beggarly hundred and ten pounds a year as a clerk in Doggett's in the Strand, the master of the house had worked himself into a rage, shouting at his visitor that he was a fool if he expected to keep a wife on such a wage, and a scamp as well, to have been seeing her on the sly, for he knew very well that the rule of Doggett's was that no clerks were allowed to marry without permission unless they were earning a minimum of one hundred and forty pounds a year!

"What right have ye to pay court to my daughter, without her parents' knowledge, eh? How would ye like it if I were to tell your secretary that one of his whippersnapper juniors had come to me, trying to involve me in a conspiracy to break the rules of his employers? And let me tell ye this! We do business with Doggett & Co., which is one of the Firm's original customers! Now tell me, does your secretary know who you are, and where you come from, eh? Does he know what sort of a man your father is? Put that in yer pipe and smoke it, you niminypinimy dressed-up son of a drunken wastrel!"

The older man was by then in such a rage that he was shouting his reserved thoughts, for which afterwards, upon reflection, he was a little ashamed. But the idea of it, daring to think he was good enough for Hetty!

"Take yourself off, d'ye hear? And never let me see your face inside my house again!"

Richard, who had approached Mr. Turney because he considered it the right thing to do before he spoke of his feelings to Miss Turney herself, remained silent and unmoving during the tirade. His face had gone pale; and upon his dismissal, he had bowed stiffly, still holding his silk hat and bouquet of roses in maidenhair ferns; and leaving the room, had taken his 'cello from beside the coat-rack, and gone out of the front door, hastening down the steps and nearly falling on his face in the gravel. He recovered himself; and was almost running when he reached the chestnut tree which overshadowed most of the front lawn and garden, watched by Hetty and her mother from the sitting-room window, Hetty quivering and nearly unable to breathe for her sobs, and the tears silently running down her mother's face. And watched, too, from a bedroom window on the second storey by the youngest child of the family, a schoolboy called Joseph, and a friend of his of the same age of fifteen. Both boys, knowing nothing about what had been happening, had laughed out loud at the comic spectacle below.

Hetty was pale and subdued for some time afterwards, and one day her father called the doctor to her. That fox-hunting and hearty individual promptly diagnosed chlorosis, a common ailment among young women, he declared, popularly known as the green sickness, and entirely due to anaemia. It could be cured by drinking a tumbler of fresh-killed bullock's blood every day an hour before luncheon. Hearing this, Sarah spoke to the doctor in the privacy of the morning room, and told him of her daughter's unhappiness over a young man. Thereupon the doctor advised, in addition to the daily medicament of ox-blood, a complete change of scene; advice which he evidently determined to follow himself, for glancing at his gold hunter watch, he said he must be off, as the Old Surrey Hunt was having its Steeplechase that morning.

Thomas Turney himself could not spare the time to take his favourite daughter to the Swiss Alps, or to Algeria—he wanted to visit both places one day—so he sent Sarah with her to the South of France. Before they departed he obtained a promise from Hetty that she would not write to Richard Maddison; and somewhat to his surprise, and certainly to his relief, Hetty said at once, "Yes, Papa," and he kissed her warmly, hugging her to him with his sturdy arms around her, kissing her cheeks and eyes and brow while declaring that she was a good dutiful daughter, and no one would ever love her or have her real interests at heart like her own papa. The strength of his embrace alarmed her; she was very fond of papa; but now her hitherto open fondness was partly withdrawn, and fear took its place.

Hetty had been able to give her promise a little less unhappily than might have been, because Mamma had told her that she intended to write to Dickie and any letters from him in reply she would at once read to her. And Theodora wrote regularly to her, saying in the first letter, *Leave off your corset, that symbol of subservience and falsity, and buy yourself some simple cotton gowns, and you will be surprised at your lightness of heart.* So Hetty was occasionally her gay and light-hearted self by the tideless blue and translucent Mediterranean Sea, where from the little quay the fishermen in their white and azure boats with high prows sailed away to drop their trammel nets; and where the fine hot glistening sand of the bay seemed to purr under her bare feet. Above the straight trunks of the palms with their spiky leaves the sun shone bright and hot, and in the afternoon heat she lay on her bed, resting, trying to read, while one thought filled her.

At night during the full moon of May the nightingales sang in the tall reeds by the shore, answered by other birds singing far away up the slopes of the rocky hills covered with wiry bushes bearing such beautiful blossoms. It was a place, so different from England, so bright, so vivid, so beautiful—and yet so empty. The fisher-folk were contented, the children brown and bare-footed, their faces so unlike those of the white-faced ragged waifs she felt so sorry for in the streets of London. And very late at night, or early in the morning, when she sat and thought at the open window of her *auberge*, and the nightingales had ceased to sing for a period, she had sometimes heard across the warm and melancholy silence of the little fields growing vines and aniseed and potatoes the sad cry of what might have been a little bird, calling in its loneliness to another as solitary as itself.. *Honk!* came the sad cry in the darkness, and after a while the cry would be answered from far away, perhaps in a slightly different key. *Honk!*

Hetty thought it might be an owl, or perhaps a water-bird; but a very nice Englishman staying in the same *auberge* with his lady mother told her one day it was a tree-frog, and Hetty was disappointed, but said after a moment's thought that it must be a very nice tree-frog. Her brown eyes looked as she spoke as though they were filling with tears, and the young man's heart was stirred by the sight; for he too loved beauty, and was lonely. On the last night before she left he asked Hetty to marry him, after a rather agitated discussion in private with his lady mother, who having said that Miss Turney was obviously a genteel young woman had added that it could be seen at once and without any stretch of the imagination that she and her people were probably *in trade*. What of it, asked the young man; grandpapa was a tradesman, wasn't he to be sure, how else could he have become Lord Mayor of London and on retiring after his year of office been given a baronetcy? My dear, said his lady mother, that is quite a different thing altogether, he was a *City* man; and you must never forget, dear boy, that you are the heir to the title, with a great position to keep up. And to her relief, mingled with surprise and a feeling of indignation tactfully suppressed, she heard the next morning, after the young woman had driven away in a *voiture* with her corded boxes, beside her mother in old-fashioned clothes of black bombazine, that her son's proposal had actually been refused.

Hetty was sad at the nice young man's distress, but ever so grateful to him for the way he had understood when she had told him that she loved another. She had shown him Dickie's photograph, taken in his knickerbocker suit beside his safety bicycle, and had hinted at Papa's opposition. Thereupon he had begged her to regard himself as being entirely of service to her, declaring that he would be ready to help in any manner possible to him, should she call upon his services. He had given her his card, with an address in Belgravia, and as she left in the carriage, had whispered, as he raised his straw boater, with its black band with the pale blue lines, *Sursum corda, Miss Turney.*

Sursum corda—keep the heart high. How had Dickie been feeling, while she was away? Rather low, it would appear: he was so easily discouraged, so easily made to withdraw into himself. It was because of the sadness of his early life, she knew, as dear Dora had told her.

While they had been on the Riviera Mamma had written to Dickie regularly once a week, and he had replied to Mamma, in his beautiful handwriting, with a quill pen. She had known how he was feeling by the guarded way in which he wrote, ending up always *Yours most obediently to serve you*, and signing his full names. He had mentioned himself scarcely at all, but had described the weather, how hot it was, or how cold, and how the traffic was becoming so congested in the London streets that it was hard to see how in a few years there could be any movement at all upon them. Sometimes he had written of a favourite place of his, the Hill, telling how the young rooks had left their nests for the tree-tops, and how he had seen a pair of partridges under one of the thorn hedges, but so many men nowadays were about with long-legged dogs, that he could not see how they could survive to nest there. One letter was beautiful, it described the nightingales singing and all the countryside black and silvery under the moon with the Crystal Palace, "Sydenham's lunar chrysalis" glinting on the far ridge. This letter had made Hetty weep in her bedroom as she read it again and again, for a nightingale was singing just outside the open window of the *auberge*, but it was not the same moon he had seen from the Hill: now the moon was worn, as though dying, and in her imagination she saw him walking all alone and carrying his hat in his hand, as he did whenever he was away from people. Oh my love, my love, my love. But not one word, in any of his letters, about her; unless the concluding *Yours most obediently to serve you, Richard Edward Maddison*, was a message to her. Ah, why should he love her after what had happened?

And then the journey to Paris, the buying of the brown and purple taffeta *ensemble* with the yellow ruchings—the very latest, Madame declared, in the *Marche:* and to Calais and the awful crossing, rolling and pitching, to Dover; the fast train to Victoria: the old familiar line down to Cross Aulton. How empty the house looked, how vacant the garden! The place was terribly still, even her own bedroom seemed different. Then the postman, and the letter to Mamma which had blotted out the sunshine at once like a fog striking through all her life: the letter saying that he was thinking of giving up his post in Doggett's, and of emigrating to the colonies, perhaps to Australia.

The next day Hetty had one of her nervous headaches, and the sporting doctor, now very busy with his greenheart fly-rod, pronounced that the rich food of the South had clogged the ducts of her liver. He prescribed a spoonful of jollop to be taken three times a day before meals and one extra before bed at night: brimstone, treacle, Glauber salts, and probably a mouse baked in the oven and ground up in pestle and mortar at midnight, Hughie pronounced, after sniffing it and then tasting it. In the morning the stuff was removed by him to the ledge of a bee-hive, to cause a little riot among the busy buzzing proletariat of the insect world, said Hughie. It seemed to have that effect; for after clustering upon it and eating most of it, the bees from that hive started to rob the honey from the other hive at the far end of the orchard, and corpses, said Hughie, were soon lying all over the place, as after a performance of Webster's *Duchess of Malfi*.

Hetty had recovered when Theodora came to see her. On Theodora's suggestion, she sent a letter to Dickie saying that she was writing on behalf of Mamma to ask him to bring Theodora to meet them on Saturday in Greenwich Park, for a picnic luncheon under the trees, and afterwards to go down and see the ships; and she had ended up, after hesitation and some tears, *Ever your faithful friend, Hetty*. But oh, if he should go to the colonies, for ever and ever!

At last Saturday morning, after a night of broken sleep, was announced by the singing of her favourite thrush in the apple tree near the open window.

Chapter 3

BEHIND THE COB'S EARS

THE VILLAGE of Cross Aulton in Surrey was twelve miles from Hyde Park Corner as the coach drove; but ten by way of the London, Epsom, and Dorking Railway. The parish comprised nearly three thousand acres, of which four hundred were meadow land, twenty-four were water—being the river and its many tributary springs and rillets breaking out of the chalky subsoil—and the remainder occupied by railways, public roads, and market gardens. And of these four square miles of arable, lying under the chalk downs, most of the fields were used for the cultivation of herbs, for seasoning and medicinal purposes. It was the variety of the colours and scents of these two thousand odd acres of herbs surrounding the village of old red brick, and bright water running everywhere from the springs—in the gutters, down the shady lanes, along ditches in the woods, through the pond divided by the road—which had given Cross Aulton the reputation among City men of being the jolliest village south of the River. Its numerous brooks held many trout, pink-fleshed and quick-growing from the ample insect and shell food in the glassy waters; a pack of foxhounds was kennelled in the village; there were the beagles, for running after hares across the furrows in winter—"Nothing like it for the liver, old chap"; and above all, there was an express service of twenty-five minutes by train to the City.

If one excepted those immigrants from counting house and factory, the fortunate classes who could afford to live away from the congested surroundings of their work, Cross Aulton was inhabited by country people who got their various livings in the fields, in the mills upon the river bank—grist, corn, and one of them a snuff mill—and in garden and stable. There were the usual trades connected with a village; eight inns and taverns, all of them brewing their own ale; a barber, with his three-coloured pole over the door of his shop, which was also the post-office; a blacksmith, cornchandler, stationer, watchmaker, joiner, tailor, pastrycook and baker, draper, saddler, physician and surgeon: and as there were several wealthy houses in the parish, Cross Aulton had a Gas House, and near it, a Fire-Engine House. There was an Ordnance School, where orphans and foundling boys with close-cropped heads and wearing little black jackets and short trousers to below the knee were trained for the artillery branch of the Army. There were two Board Schools, one for boys and the other for girls; and a Liberal member of Parliament.

Such was Cross Aulton, with its meadows and herb fields, its woods and parks and downs, its airs aromatic in summer from blossom and leaf within the surrounding hills; a place so esteemed by its inhabitants that the testimony of the local doctor, in a letter to *The Times* some years previously, had been endorsed by all who read it in the locality. Cross Aulton, he declared, was the healthiest and warmest place in England, its climate kept equable in winter by the temperate waters issuing everlastingly from the chalk in a hundred springs; while consumption, ague, fever, "and all affections of the air passages were of trivial severity." The doctor had married a wife of means, and being much interested in hunting, shooting, and fishing, found it "a very genial climate" in which to practise.

The place had other literary association, in addition to the encomium in *The Times*. It was mentioned in Domesday, when the Conqueror, having hanged or otherwise slain the Saxon families which owned them, had given the five manors to the Norman nobleman who became Constable of the Tower of London. Evelyn, visiting the place before the Great Fire, had recorded that it was "excellently watered, and capable of being made a most delicious seate, being on the sweete downs, and a champion about it fully planted with walnut and cherry trees, which afford a considerable rent." Alexander Pope, in his poem *The Sea-born Brothers of the Thames*, wrote of "the blue transparent Vandalis", the river Vandle which in its ten miles to the estuary turned the stones of forty mills by its guided weight of water; while Ruskin, in a preface to *The Crown of Wild Olive*, had recorded the sand bubbling from the springs set about with water-cress and brook-lime, and also the "broken shreds and rags of putrid clothes" cast into the river by the poorer people.

Neatness, order, and natural beauty, so esteemed by the well-to-do, were equally esteemed by the species called lower. The ponds and runners, the brooks and rills, the wells and stone-encircled springs were the haunt of feathered beauty and grace. Kingfishers sped along the skiey waterways, drawing their azure and emerald hues through the reflected clouds. Wagtails, both pied and grey with breasts of daffodil, danced delicately upon wooden pile and willow stump, to take the new-hatched mayflies thick upon sedge and betony: creatures of exquisite grace arising later in the sun's day as water-blossom amidst swallows, chaffinches, white-rumped martins and other birds winging to the early summer feast above the gliding Vandle, the uneven gliding Vandle broken in ring and ripple by the brown nebs of the young fat trout sucking in drake and spinner. To stockbroker and younger city merchant the sight was magic. The mayfly's up!

And so, replacing the herons for a week or two upon the meadow-banks came the anglers with slim hickory rods and varnished lines coiled within brass reels, and gently swishing casts of silkworm gut or plaited horsehair tailed with lure of feather, wax, wool, silk, and deadly barb of steel falling upon the brimming water. The surface flopped with the rolling fish, or threshed with their bubble-shaken terror; while bees laden with honey from the fields of lavender and thyme filled the air with murmurous honey-flow.

Across the waters and through the shade of trees came the smack of willow on leather, and faint clapping from the pavilion under the walnuts as a ball rolled over the boundary and batsmen ceased to cross between the wickets, but turned back to their creases. In the gardens could be heard the gentler knock of box-wood mallet on croquet ball and iron hoop on lawns amidst flower-beds and fruit trees, and hammocks idly swinging in the shade. Straw boaters and short flannel jackets and white flannel trousers with stripes and brown shoes of leather and white canvas, and curling moustaches; for beards were going out with the century, and the future, despite what the guv'nor, or the pater, says, is no longer a denial of beauty, but to the ideals of men like William Morris.

"Meanwhile Hughie, your ideas will have to wait, m'boy, and you must learn to walk before you can run, he he he! Tell Jim to bring the carriage round now, will ye, there's a good fellow. Drive with me so far as the station. I want to talk to you about your future. This period of enforced rustication could be turned to profit, if you'll take my advice. After all, I'm not a wealthy man, and so you may as well face the matter of having to earn your living sooner or later, eh?

"Well, here we are, with five minutes to spare. Better be a little too early than a moment too late. Now look after your mother and sister, won't ye, like a good fellow? The drive will do them good. Here's half a sovereign, you won't want to be beholden to your mother for everything. Now don't go to Quartermain's Ship Tavern for luncheon, it's too expensive, tell your mother to put up a hamper and take your own. For tea, you can go to the Ship Stores, next to the Tavern; it's cheaper; and if you're lucky you might get some fried whitebait, Greenwich is famous for its whitebait, and eaten with cayenne pepper, lemon juice, and brown bread—not this trash they sell nowadays, this bleached white so-called bread—and butter, it's most delicious. Are you listening, m'boy?"

"Indeed, to every word, sir."

"Well, you didn't look like it. If you can't get whitebait, the shoals may not have come up the river yet—they run about the time of the end of the parliamentary session—get shrimps. They're always plentiful. And don't forget to show Hetty the Thames barges, they're a wonderful sight in a running tide and a stiff breeze, sprit-rigged, managed by only a man and a boy. And don't forget to go into the Museum, and see the Nelson relics, particularly the jacket he wore at Trafalgar, when the Frenchman's ball struck him. And go and see your Aunt Marian, and give her my kind regards. Well, here's the train. It's a lovely day, and I wish I were coming with ye: look after the women, Hughie, you're head man now, you know, while I'm away!"

"Yes, indeed sir, be sure I shall exercise my own judgment."

Hughie drove back from the station, lolling in the back of the landau, a dull vehicle. He wished he could have some blood in the shafts of his new painted dog-cart, a spanking turnout in dark brown lined with yellow, and take Hetty up beside him. That would make the fellows turn and look at them! Should he try the old nag? No, it was slow, and too raw-boned for a dog-cart: one wanted a fast-stepping cob, fourteen hands. And with a Dalmatian running behind the tailboard, quite a swell affair!

Well, he would go in this hearse with Mamma and Hetty and make the best of it. What else was there to do? He regretted his premature departure from the 'varsity. Progged; sent down—he had not told Papa all the truth—only that he had been rusticated for crowning a public statue with what to the Warden of his college he had described as an article indispensable to nocturnal semisomnambulistic interruption. That bit of wit had not been appreciated, nor had the jape been interpreted as a gesture to the traditional British freedom of thought in Merrie England. Besides, it would have kept the poor hatless statue's head from contact with rain, should any fall during May Week. Such was the reward of a lack of complacency!

Hugh Turney's wit was of the kind that fed upon itself; he often thought certain things were immensely funny, which no one else except his younger sister Hetty appeared to appreciate.

On the way home he passed the Crown, with its stables and the words LIVERY AND BAIT large-painted on the wall. Stopping the carriage, he jumped out and spoke to the ostler for some moments, and then to another man who appeared with a whip in his hand. He was the owner of a stable of hacks, hunters and ponies, and the short discussion was ended by Hughie producing the half sovereign, spinning it and catching it, then pressing it into the other man's hand.

It was a deal, apparently, for half an hour later Mrs. Turney, with Hughie and Hetty, set out for Greenwich, not in the slow and heavy family landau, but in Hughie's smart brown and yellow turn-out drawn by the fast bay cob who had come second in its class in the recent local Horse and Pony Show. They bowled along the road to Croydon, the two ladies beside Hughie holding the reins, his fawn-coloured bowler at a slight angle on his head, a stock-tie with an opal tie-pin sprouting at the lapels of a lemon-coloured waistcoat and his check coat and pepper-and-salt trousers ending in a pair of yellow boots.

Mrs. Turney had packed a hamper in preparation for the picnic; it rested under the seat. The time for the meeting was half-past twelve o'clock; and as the distance was reckoned to be about seventeen miles, they would have plenty of time for the journey, specially if the cob continued at that pace.

There had been a tenuous mist over the meadows and the village during the previous night, of the kind that foretold a fine day when the sun should rise over the tops of the trees. The morning was already warm, but hung with wraiths of vapour turning into sunlight almost as one wondered if they were really there. To Hetty, sitting beside her mother, the day seemed unreal, as though she were elsewhere, and it could not possibly be happening that she was actually at last on the way to meet Dickie. Her feelings were as the hanging shreds of mist: one moment a chill immobility of hope was upon her: the next moment she felt warm and happy as the sunshine. Her parasol lay furled beside her, for she could not bear the thought of being out of the living brightness of the June morning which was as the thought and image of Dickie, Dickie, Dickie, in her very being.

Hetty was brown of face and neck and arms and legs below the knee from the sun of the Cote d'Azur, from lying upon the white sands and swimming in sea as glassy clear as the spring-water which welled up in the garden from the grotto lined with sea-shells by some past occupant of the house, and now over-grown with ivy. Her thoughts welled up like the water, which was ever shifting specks of gravel and sand before it slid away down the stony runnel and under the arch in the garden wall to the ditch in the lane outside. Many a time brother and sister had put paper boats or twigs personal to each upon the crystal mushroom of the spring-head, and watched them rocking and sliding away down the runnel, and into the ditch through a hole in the wall; and then, dashing through the door, they followed their barques beside the lane and across the road and so to the iron grille leading to the pond. They had to be very small boats to get through the iron bars, and also not to become a nuisance as dirty bits of paper lying on the clear bottom of the pond, where thin shadowy forms of trout could be seen watching the underdrift for any nymph or shrimp brought in the flow.

It was of another age, of a far remoteness, that time when Papa had made her promise not to write to Dickie while she was in the South of France. How long ago, and so dream-like, it all seemed now!

"Are not the herbs beautiful," said Mrs. Turney, having observed the *distraite* expression on her child's face. She laid her hand upon Hetty's, and gave it a reassuring squeeze. At the question, the gentle childlike eyes were turned to her, and Sarah, reading the thoughts upon her daughter's open face, took a resolution that Hetty's happiness should come before all else. Immediately the idea made her afraid, and reflective; and Hetty, seeing the wistfulness in her mother's face, took a deep breath and said to herself, with a quiver of lips and eyes averted to hide sudden brimming of tears, that whatever happened, she must never do anything to hurt her lovely, lovely Mamma.

Then as they turned once again to each other, mother and daughter smiled, and wiping her eyes with a cambric *mouchoir*, Hetty gave the merry little laugh that to Sarah her mother had been the index of the child's nature since before she could talk, and cried out, "Oh Mamma, I am so glad to be alive, and to be me!" and closing her eyes, held back her head and breathed deep to inhale the scents of the air into which she was rushing. It was an old game she had played with herself when alone, or with Hughie and Joey and Dorothy as they went that way in the carriage: who could guess first the colours of the herbs, and the names as well, by their smell, with the eyes shut fast, and no cheating. Hetty and Hughie had been usually the winners, for Dorrie was slower, and Joey, the youngest, who had been dropped on his head by nanny when he was a baby, usually last of all. Sometimes they had pretended not to know, in order to give little Joey a chance of winning. But usually he got all mixed up, not knowing even lavender from garlic. Dear Joey, it was too bad to make fun of him, even in thought.

Abandoning the game, which was no fun by herself any more, Hetty drew the colours through her eyes, filling herself with the massed joy of the flowers. Oh, how beautiful it was to be living in England!

From hedge to hedge in the morning sunlight lay acres of herbs of all colours and hues of the rainbow, from deep purple of lavender to bright yellow of fennel and dark red of valerian. But these colours were more vivid, more familiar and earth-bright than any band of spectrum, whether seen in the sky or on the cloth of magic-lantern. The marine blue blossoms of hyssop lay adjacent to the blazon of marigold, the Herb of the Sun; then came a field of Vatican sage with its heliotrope flower-heads, the Oculis Christi of Gerard; more hyssop, deep blue as the Mediterranean, and then paler blue licorice. And oh, the azure of the chicory, the heavenly azure of the rayed flowers, the very blue of remote sky, far beyond the highest lark. Then a field of opium poppies—she did not like them, they were different from other flowers, livid and fleshy in the midst of wavering cerulean blues and reds and shades of brown to palest pink of centaury. Sweet marjoram with its rose-purple flowers: how beautiful was its other name, mountain joy. And the rosemary! Grey bushes of rosemary as far as the distant hedge, acres and acres of grey-blue blossoms, "dew of the sea", as the Romans called the flower. Colour after colour in succession, scent after scent dashing upon the face out of the morning! Coriander, with flowers of pale mauve; tall angelica clothed in bright green leaves and white flowers; sweet cicely, smelling like myrrh, also clothed in white; tarragon, "little dragon", said to be a cure for snake-bite or wound of wolf in olden time; a field of peppermint, both black and white varieties side by side. And the butterflies among them, thousands of butterflies, attracted alike to tall spikes of mullein with their clusters of primrose blossoms and lowly pale florets of thyme. If only Dickie were beside her, to see them! And now they were come to the big lavender fields, with the loveliest scent of all, her favourite lavender!

"Hughie dear, pray stop a moment. Let us listen to the bees."

Hughie reined up in obedience to his mother's request, and they sat in the shade of a wayside oak and listened. It was as though the sunshine itself were singing. The very leaves of the oaktree above seemed to be moving in response to the vibrations upon the air. A deep note hovered just beyond the ear's acceptance; it was near, it was afar, it was the air itself, or the sunshine, resonant in fragmented acres of transparent and iridescent wings, each a wandering trumpet note in praise of high summer. Hoverflies and wild bees, ichneumons and sand-wasps, coarse-burring beetles and cobalt dragonflies from the watery ditches, green Spanish bottlefly and blue blowfly with globed eyes of emerald and carmine, hive-bees and solitary bees, diptera and ephemeridae, gnat and drifted drake, warble and hoverfly, grasshopper and field cricket—all in movement with hum and whine and whizz and whirr over the heated and odorous surface of the earth.

"A real old-fashioned summer," said Sarah, thinking of her childhood.

"Would you ladies give me leave to light my cheroot?" asked Hughie, a little satirically, as he tipped his hat over an eye dazzled by sunlight piercing the leaves overhead.

"We don't mind, dear," replied Sarah. "But do you think you ought to be seen by others smoking while you are driving with your mother and sister?"

"Oh, I'm known as a confirmed beer and 'baccy chap already," replied Hughie. "But of course, if it is going to upset you, I won't, dear Mamma."

"I do not mind for myself, Hughie, of course not. I am used to it, dear. My mother regularly used to smoke a clay pipe when no one was looking. Only as we are going through Croydon, I thought perhaps . . . gentlemen do not, you know, dear, in the company of women—not their women, anyway. But please yourself, dear."

"I like the smell of a cigar," said Hetty.

"Very well, light up if you will, dear boy."

Hughie lit his cheroot, drew upon it, and expelled a whiff of blue smoke towards a small spider slowly sliding down a line. Frantically the insect, green and pink of body, scrambled up again.

"It should be a good year for honey," remarked Sarah. "Our hives will be full, now that Jim has cut out the young queens. They looked like swarming a few days ago."

Hughie winked under his hat brim at Hetty. She smiled back at him. Then she sighed deeply, checking the sigh as she remembered it was not good manners to sigh audibly.

"Now," said Sarah, hearing the sigh. "I fancy we should be thinking of going on, though we are in good time, to be sure. How are you feeling, Hetty dear? Dickie must be feeling nervous, too. How you will smile at it all very soon! Your Dickie is so trustworthy a young man, and so in need of a good woman's care, more perhaps than most young men."

Sarah had mentioned about moving on for her daughter's sake, knowing how nervous she was, how her imagination made her anticipate events. She was so very young for her age of twenty-four years, a child still, a very good girl, with a capacity for happiness, and unhappiness, beyond the ordinary. How fortunate she was to have Dora for a friend, for Dora, though inclined to be an advanced young woman, was wise beyond her nineteen years, and as true as gold. What a pity it was about her father, for that was at the bottom of Tom's adamant attitude to poor Dickie. It was not fair to blame the sins of the fathers on to the children. It was not Christian.

Hughie looked at his watch, which he had recently got out of pawn, owing to the lucky backing of a filly in the Oaks. The summer Epsom races had recently been run, and to Sarah's relief—for she had the countrywoman's fear of them—the gipsies had gone away.

"I think there will be time to finish your smoke, Hughie."

The spider was venturing down on its line again. A solitary bee was cutting, with just-audible rasping of its jaws, a round piece from an oakleaf above.

"That's the brute that bungs up the keyholes with its nests," remarked Hughie, watching it keenly. "Cunning little beast. Makes a cylinder of leaf sections, gummed together, fills it with pollen, lays its egg, and seals the end up. Next year, another bee. They make their nests in the water-butt taps, too."

"The Almighty has many wonders," murmured Sarah. A whine of sound curved between mother and son, there was a sharp click of jaws, and a small wasp had taken the spider.

"There's one of them," said Hughie, expelling smoke in the direction the wasp had gone.

"Now Hughie, don't be awkward," said Sarah gently. "I believe that is all your college education has done for you—to make you contrary."

"My *university* education, Mamma, if you please," said Hughie, staring before him.

"Yes, dear, of course, naturally. Anyway, dear boy, you should know very well that there is evil as well as good in the world," went on his mother, somewhat lamely.

"Chops and steaks as well as Botticelli and eau-de-cologne, Mamma."

"What a boy you are—you've never changed since you were a tiny tot," said Sarah, recovering herself. "Now my dears, we should think of going on. What a treat it is to be behind such a mettlesome cob for once. It will be nice for you, Hughie, when you can have one of your own like it, won't it?"

This hint came from Sarah's hopes for family harmony: a hint to Hughie to enter the Firm when he came down from the university with his degree. It was Thomas Turney's ambition, often repeated to Sarah, that his second son should follow him into the family business. Charley, the eldest boy, had already proved a disappointment, and taken himself off to what was generally considered to be the refuge of the destitute, the Colonies. Poor Charley, all the winter he had been learning to farm in Manitoba, by loading hundreds of tons of bullock muck from a covered yard on to a sled and hauling it out into the fields to be piled in heaps upon the snow, in the intervals of feeding the bullocks in the yard, whereby the muck was replaced almost as fast as Charley could haul it away. So work never ceased for Charley, according to Charley, to the amusement of Tom when he read the poor boy's occasional letters out loud to everyone at the breakfast table. So now it was for Hughie to make up for Charley's defection in the Firm.

Hughie drove easily, almost lackadaisically, beside the fields and past the woods to Croydon. But after entering the London road he seemed to have assumed a task of honour, that every vehicle on the road proceeding in a northerly direction be passed at speed. The stub of the cheroot projecting under his black moustaches had ceased to burn; and holding it between his front teeth, his light brown bowler tapped more firmly on his dark head by a gloved hand released for a moment from its manipulation of the near-side reins, his pointed shoes placed well apart to assure a balance against any sudden canting of a wheel in pothole or gutter, Hughie was leaning forward, staring alertly into the future, which was bounded for him by the next vehicle to be overtaken by his flashing mustard-coloured and varnished wheels. This was Hughie's normal method of movement when, as he put it in the vernacular, he held the ribbons between his fingers.

The sturdy gelding flung out its feet with the full action of the racing trot, without once over-reaching, for the driver's hands conveyed their sensitivity and respect for the eager animal, which responded perfectly to the wishes of the companion with whom it was sharing its *joie-de-vivre*.

His mother was used to his dashing ways as a driver; and her usual placidity was never disturbed when she was her son's passenger, for as she put it, "I rather enjoy moving about the countryside with Hughie, one sees so much more his way."

Swiftly as he moved upon an ordinary road, Hughie would never be so bad-mannered as to let the ponies he drove break into a canter, much less a gallop, upon sett- or cobble-stones. He had a real sympathy with horses, and would not allow one he was driving to damage its feet. He kept the cob at a gentle trot all the way beside the lines of horse-trams of the borough until they came to the bottom of the hill leading to the Heath, where Hughie pulled up and dismounted, to pat the animal on the neck and flick the flies from off its eyes, mouth, and face with a whisk. He slackened the girth round its barrel-body, and then on foot led it up the steep hill, from the crest of which were to be seen the distant trees of Greenwich Park.

He took the cob on to the grass, where it rested awhile before proceeding at an easy trot along the road to a trough where, after removing its bit, he let it drink. The cob having been girthed-up and cooled off, Hughie mounted to the driver's seat again, and they crossed the Heath, seeing old gentlemen in red coats playing golf, and boys flying paper kites, while others were sailing boats in the round pond where he had first met Dick Maddison, and thought him to be a queer bird. So they came to the iron gates of the Park, and here Sarah clasped Hetty's hand, for her daughter was quivering.

Chapter 4

THAMES-SIDE IDYLL

SARAH TURNEY had not been inside Greenwich Park since she and Tom had occasionally gone down the river from Blackfriars Bridge by boat during the early days of their marriage, when they had been living in a cottage near Camberwell Green. So much had happened since that time, over a quarter of a century ago, that she was surprised to find the place much as she had remembered it. The deer were still on the grass, and there stood the avenue of Spanish chestnuts leading up to the Observatory. Ah, there they were, Dickie and Dora, just getting off a seat. Dora was waving, she had seen them.

"They came early, for it is only now striking noon," said Sarah. "Hughie, pray stop here, we will get down, and walk to meet them," for she had seen that Hetty had lost all colour. "How are you feeling, dear? Now then, where is my bottle of smelling salts?"

"Oh Mamma, please, it is but a momentary giddiness," replied Hetty, with a nervous smile.

Hughie, who with a flick of his wrist had thrown away the stub of the cheroot, felt for his stocktie and pin, and with a tug on the curly brim of his hat with one hand set it at a slight angle. Then he placed the butt of the holly whip in its socket and leapt lightly to the ground. He gave a hand first to his mother, then to his sister. The ladies shook their skirts. Hetty arranged the ruchings on her bodice, and with parasol opened and held with a little slant to the rear, as she had observed to be the correct thing from the fashions in *The Queen*, she went forward beside her mother, while Hughie looked about for someone to hold the head of the pony.

Hetty took a timid glance at Richard, who with a smile was lifting his straw-boater and bowing slightly to Mrs. Turney. He did not look at Hetty as he bowed to her in turn. Theodora with a slight colour of animation in her cheeks took Sarah's hands in hers, and kissed her. Then she turned and kissed Hetty. "Honk!" she whispered. "All is well." At this Hetty's eyes filled with tears, and though she tried to reply with the talismanic "Honk", only a subdued hysterical sob came from her, as she heard Dickie asking Mamma if she had had a good journey, and saying that the weather must have been perfect for it.

"Yes, it is indeed perfect, and so much more temperate than the South of France. We felt the difference when we crossed to Dover, but there is no place like England. Oh Dora, my dear, I have left my purse in the dogcart, will you come with me and help me find it, my eyes are not what they were", and together they went back to where Hughie was standing. "I thought those two might want to be alone for awhile," she explained, when they were out of earshot.

Hughie, lounging by the pony, raised his hat, and looked at Theodora. Her cheeks were pink, her eyes shone, and she smiled with her wide mouth, revealing the strong white teeth of the upper jaw, which were regular, but slightly crowded. It was her voice that Hughie found so soft, so clear, so beautiful in tone and modulation; but he noticed also her slender fingers, the curling of the fair hair behind the ears, the tall neck, the long straight nose, and the deep blue of her eyes. Why had he not noticed these points before? She had been several times to the house when he was at home, and he, who prided himself on a keen intellect and acute powers of perception, had never observed them before. Hughie was a little discomposed. He set his billycock hat slightly firmer on one side.

"Why, Hugh, you have got a new pony," said Theodora. "How well he stands. And what fine cannons, and the strength in those shoulders! I noticed the action as you came along. Those dark tips to the ears, and dark line down the back surely denote a thoroughbred? And your colours match Hetty's dress to perfection! Have you had him long?"

"Oh, I'm just trying out the cob's paces, he's from a stable in the village," replied Hughie, casually. "He got only the red riband at the local show t'other day, most people fancied him for the blue, but the ways of judges are mysterious, like those of the alleged Supreme Authority."

This was a reference to a former argument Theodora and Hugh had had about the novels of Thomas Hardy.

"But surely all judgement is relative to the judge? Don't you agree, Mrs. Turney? The Biblical epigram states this much better, of course."

Hughie felt a slight chill upon his new-found delight in Theodora's person. Why couldn't she forget she was the Girton Girl, of the noble Band of Blue Stockings?

"I'm afraid such things are above my head, Dora," replied Sarah. "Well, Hughie, shall we go for a walk? That man waiting over there looks as though he is expecting to hold the cob's head for you."

A ragged eager man who had been observing the group intently as a means to a meal of pease pudding and boiled bacon hastened forward, cap in hand.

"Hold y'oss'sead, guv'nor? Gimme what you fancy, guv'nor. Long's yer like, guv'nor."

Ignoring the man, Hughie said, "The cob's off-fore shoe is loose, I'll go down to a farrier's I know in the village, and meet you here in an hour's time, Mamma, if that is agreeable to you? I think I should get it clenched, so if you will excuse me——" To the man he said, as the ladies walked away, "I'll see you at one o'clock, if it's worth a tanner to you, and I'll throw in some grub. All Sir Garnet?"

"You're a toff, sir, I knew it the moment I clapped eyes on you."

Hughie looked at the man quizzically as he considered an appropriate bit of wit, but evidently decided not to risk it, the fellow's eyes were hard and dark. While he stood alertly to the cob's head, Hughie got into the cart and with an affectionate caress of the whip on the animal's shoulder drove away down the avenue, his mind set on a brandy and seltzer and conversation with the barmaid of the Trafalgar Tavern. That was more in his line, he told himself.

Richard Maddison and Henrietta Turney were walking side by side over the grass, among the fallow deer and the tall may-trees with their impenetrable ingrowth of thorns. Both were proceeding in an aimless way, scarcely knowing where they were going. There was a subdued look of suffering on both their faces. How different everything was from the imagined meeting! Hetty with her radiant hopes and sudden joys while boots were being polished; hands scrubbed; curls set; hat stared at in looking-glass; set of skirt and latest-style-of-bustle from Paris examined by Mamma; buttons of tall boots of *glacé* kid fastened by button-hook, but not too swiftly, not too hurriedly, lest the buttons come off—and so, disaster! The little perspirations under the arm-pits, oh would they never stop, for there was not time to sew a dress-shield into the gussets of the arms. Richard with his controlled agitation as he changed his clothes after a brisk constitutional on the Hill, his watch lying face up on the table beside the straw-hat cleaned with spirits of salt: trembling fingers straightening yellow shirt and tie: cream flannel waistcoat and tennis trousers with brown stripes searched yet once again for the slightest grease-spot: conscious of Time's rushing silence as white socks were pulled on: of the world standing still while his feet were inserted into brown and white canvas shoes with a feeling akin to terror, lest he be late, and—where oh where was his shoe-horn? Had Mrs. Cummings borrowed it? Had the charwoman Feeney taken it? Desperately he had used the ivory end of the newspaper-cutter, while the bell on the strap-string downstairs announced the arrival of Theodora. And he was not ready!

Now the unrealizable walk to Greenwich Park was over, and Richard was moving in a void of unspeakable anguish with Hetty beside him: Hetty to whom the drive with Mamma and Hughie was already as remote as the Mediterranean, as she ached with a dumb helpless feeling to comfort him, while no words would come to her.

Sarah and Theodora saw them walking side by side, as the two ladies approached the Royal Observatory for the famous view from the terrace. Across the river in dark blue distance could be seen the forests of Hainault and Epping, and the heights of Hampstead to the north; while below, a forest of varnished masts and spars of ships, lying moored along the winding reaches of the Thames, glistened above the waterside houses, with red and yellow funnels of steamers.

As Sarah and Theodora were enjoying the variety of life in the prospect of the calm summer morning before them, Richard and Henrietta continued to move among the trees, heedless of and unheeded by the deer.

Richard gave a long sigh. He looked lonely, so lonely, thought Hetty; and she walked closer beside him; and even as she felt her tenderness and concern to be overwhelming, the terrible thought pierced her that he did not want her any longer: that he had come to tell her that he was going to emigrate to the colonies. And then, as he nearly bumped into the circular tarred railing round a sapling, while she walked around the other side and back again to where he was standing looking at her, she felt it to be coming true, even as she had hardly dared to think: for he was saying in a strained voice that he was thinking of leaving the country and going to Australia to join his brother Hilary. She felt so ill she feared she would faint; she grasped the railings, and stared up at him, her eyes large and dark, her lips pallid.

He cleared his throat and managed to say, "Well, it is—it is—encumbent upon me—I feel—to apologize for any inconvenience—I have caused you and your family." As she could make no reply, he said, in the same strained voice, "Shall we find the others now?" And with a darkness entering upon him for what he had said, thus making the calamity he had dreaded come true, he smiled bleakly at her.

"Yes, Dickie."

They moved away from the caged sapling, in the direction of the Dome; and as they came to a seat he turned to her and said, "You see, I cannot possibly keep on any longer as I have been!"

His unhappy eyes looked for a moment into her face.

Tenderness broke from her as a spring, the tears rolled down her cheeks. She took his hand and held it against her bosom.

As they sat side by side, he could feel upon his wrist the exquisite warm tenderness of her breast under the silk of her bodice; and his words were as though wrenched from him, "I have been through torture! I cannot bear the suspense any longer! I only want to know if you will marry me! I cannot marry you yet—it is dishonourable to ask you perhaps—for my salary is but one hundred and ten pounds a year—no one in the service of the bank is permitted—to marry—under a hundred and——" He gulped; gasped; and continued—"pounds per annum."

"I will wait, dearest."

Oh, the beauty of her stroking his hand, the sweet innocence of her nursing his arm as a baby to her breast. He cried out, "Then you will marry me, Hetty, after all?"

"Of course, Dickie, how could you think otherwise?" she managed to say.

"And you will not mind waiting for me?"

"Of course not, dearest, I love you."

"Do you really? How can you love me, when I am dull—a failure?"

"Oh Dickie, dearest, you are not. I won't have you say such a thing!"

"Then shall we be married, whatever happens?"

"Yes, dearest."

"Will you give me your solemn promise? It will be all of two years to wait, you know!" he said warningly. "On the other hand—but I must not count my chickens before they are hatched—I might get an unexpected increment."

"Yes, dear, I am sure you will."

The morning was become clear and beautiful about him. He was loved, he was loved! Controlling his voice, he said, "Well then, that is settled. Isn't it warm and peaceful here? You look so sunburned, just like a dark-eyed gipsy! Do you know, I cannot understand why you, in that fashionable Riviera throng, should ever have given a second thought to a poor man like myself."

"Oh, Dickie, you should not say such things, even in fun! How I wish you could have been beside me! It was beautiful on the shore, the sea there is so clear, the waves like glass, but it was lonely every moment without you, dearest. Didn't Dora tell you? I hoped she would."

Richard laughed in his relief. "All that Dora told me was that you apparently wanted me to become a tree-frog!"

"Oh yes, dearest, they were ever so sad, crying 'honk' across immense distances, each one so lonely, perched all by itself in the top of a tree! They were only little frogs, too, ever so small."

"So you wanted me to become a little French frog, did you?" he exclaimed, with every satisfaction.

She saw the absurdity of her remark, and laughed merrily. "Oh, how awfully silly you must have thought me! I meant for you to join our Club! The Tree Frogs Club! You will, won't you, Dickie?"

"First you must hear if I am really qualified to be a frog, Hetty. You see, I had a rare, indeed a unique lady with whom to console myself in your absence, or rather, she appeared at the very end of it. But I lost her, owing to the beast! It was, indeed, a case of Beauty and the Beast. She was a Beauty, too, if ever there was one."

"Dickie, have you been flirting?"

"I fed her on beer, too!"

Hetty laughed. Her tears had been wiped away, but new tears started from her eyes, tears of happiness. She knew Dickie's kind of jokes, usually very involved, and you had to give ever so many guesses at the end, before you found out what they were about. They were never unkind jokes, like some people made about others.

"Well, while you were drinking beer with her, I was drinking champagne!"

Richard considered this, and said unhappily, "H'mph. I thought as much. With some fashionable and gilded youths, no doubt."

"No, dear, with Mamma. We drank nearly a whole bottle, with some langoustes, or cray-fish . . . I liked it—but not at first. It was a bit too prickly to drink. The funny thing was, the nightingales sang ever so much better afterwards! But tell me about your beautiful lady. Where did you meet her?"

"On the Hill."

"Someone lonely like yourself?"

"Someone very lonely. She might have come from France, too, by the look of things. Her dress was edged with yellow-white, not with grey-white, which would have been the case had she been English."

"Are you serious, Dickie? Who was she, some ma'mselle, teaching French to a family?"

"She was a demoiselle, I am almost sure. And the funny thing was, that her dress was in the same colours as the one you are now wearing—dark brown shot with purple, and those edgings were yellow, just like yours. In fact, my pretty one, I think it was you I saw, now changed back by a good fairy into my dear little Hetty."

Hetty saw a tear in his eye. She watched him wiping it away with his long slender fingers—her own were short and the fingers not half so nice as his—and then taking his hand she held it for a moment against her cheek. But she must not forget to ask about the end of the story. What could she say? She did not understand it, really, but must pretend she did, lest she disappoint him. A frog who would a-wooing go! A frog with a beard. Poor frog. "Well, Dickie, do tell me some more."

"You were born in Camberwell, were you not, Hetty?"

"Why yes, Dickie."

"Have you ever heard of a Camberwell Beauty?"

Hetty looked modest. "No, dearest, I cannot say that I have."

"Well, I saw one last night. It came to my concoction on the Hill. It is a very rare butterfly indeed, said to be extinct in England since seventeen forty-eight. Unfortunately the cads on the Hill are not so rare; on the contrary, they are coming there more and more from Deptford and other slums. I saw it clearly with my dark lantern before it flew away."

"Oh, a rare butterfly! Yes, I have heard of a Camberwell Beauty, from—from Mamma!"

"Well, I have seen one!"

"Then it may be still alive, dearest; how lovely to think of a rare and beautiful butterfly living amongst us in these progressive days."

"Progressive, eh? Well, I am a conservative in such matters, and do not believe in the spread of industrialism and free trade under the name of progress."

"Yes, dear, I'm sure you're quite right. But I am glad the butterfly escaped."

"So am I, of course! Still it would have been wonderful to have had it in one's collection. Even a rich collector like Mr. Rothschild probably hasn't got one. Well, there it is. No use crying over spilt milk. Some guttersnipe will beat it down, probably, or a bird get it. Whereas, preserved in a case, it would give pleasure and interest for many years to come."

Hetty was glad he had not minded too much about not having captured the butterfly; she had never dared to tell him that she could not bear the idea of one being put in a bottle with crushed laurel leaves, to suffocate the poor thing, just because it was beautiful. She hoped he would say that having lost one Camberwell Beauty he had found another, as in a fairy story; but perhaps she was silly, and vain, to think like that.

As a fact, Richard had thought of it, but had checked himself from saying it, as it might have seemed too fanciful, too far-fetched, as he put it to himself. So he let the thought pass without uttering it.

He sought in one of his waistcoat pockets. He felt a small gold filigree brooch there, which had belonged to his mother.

"Then we are tokened to one another, as they say in my old village?"

"Yes, dear."

"Perhaps it would be for the best not to disclose anything of this to Mr. Turney," he went on. "He comes into the Shop periodically, to see the Secretary about new ledgers and stationery. It might be awkward if the Secretary knew."

"Yes, dear, of course I understand the position. After all, I am of age," she went on tremulously, "though of course Papa's will is law, to all intents and purposes." She looked at him with pleading in her eyes. "Papa just now is much worried about Hughie, after Charley having been such a disappointment to him. Hughie somehow does not seem to be cut out for a business. Joey is still at school, he loves Papa, though he is not very bright, but it will be some consolation when he is taken into the Firm."

Brown eyes looked steadily at blue eyes, which soon looked down and away. She wondered what he was thinking as he sat unspeaking beside her, staring at the ground. Her hand sought his hand and cherished it, and with a sigh he withdrew the brooch from his pocket and gave it to her, saying again that it had belonged to mother, and now he gave it to her, and would she let him have a tress of her dark hair in exchange?

Henrietta Turney felt for Richard Maddison, but not with him. The patterns of their minds were different, perhaps because although both were English, they came of different stocks. Richard was fair and blue-eyed, Germanic not only immediately from his mother, but from a line of tall men from over the sea with fair colouring, settling originally in the north-east of Britain; while Henrietta was dark, britannic, of a stock of small farmers rooted for many millennia in the Midlands, on heavy clay, the most difficult soil in the island to cultivate, to make friable, with a near subsoil of the exacting blue lias which is brought to a proper tilth season after season only by endurance and proper judgment; but to those who farm it with reverence it yields well. The one from dark sturdy stock secure on a dark soil: the other from a fair people sprung out of a sandy earth which will not grow wheat, but only rye; basically insecure upon the "hungry soil" of agricultural classification. So everything must be conserved, nothing must be wasted, for in droughty times the crops wither and the children starve. To conserve is to be meticulous, from which arises the rigid attitude called honour. The migrations of the West Germanic peoples in early history were due to starvation; while the dark, sturdier folk were rooted in their heavy soil with its deep reserves, and knew not the racial anxiety-pattern of the sandy-haired men.

"Yes, dearest, and will you give me a lock of your hair? It is so beautiful, Dickie. I wish my hair were like Dora's."

Sarah saw the two young people approaching the terrace under the Observatory some while afterwards. By their faces she knew what had passed between them. She liked Richard, and thought that marriage would bring him out; he was so reserved and shy. But he was a dear boy, and trustworthy. He was loyal, too, for he would never utter a word against his father, not even to his favourite sister Theodora. What was it Dora had said of Dickie? *He is narrow in his outlook, Mrs. Turney, but within his limits my brother is the soul of honour.*

"Well, you are just in time to see the Ball go down," Sarah said, with a smile. "I wonder where Hughie can have got to?" To herself she said, a little sadly, that she was only too well aware where Hughie had gone. "It is almost one o'clock."

There was a clock in the face of the wall by the terrace which told the time at Greenwich for the entire world, its face being marked with the twenty-four hours. Masters of ships in the river below watched for the coloured ball to descend in order to adjust their chronometers; while precisely as it descended on its pole the time was telegraphed to the most important towns and cities in the United Kingdom.

The Red Ball fell. At once Richard consulted his silver timepiece and noted it was seven seconds in advance of the hour; Hetty looked at the small Waltham watch which had been her twenty-first birthday present, pinned with its silver bow to her bodice, and remembered that it had stopped some days ago at half-past nine and no amount of shaking could start it going again. Theodora said her clock was the sun, while Sarah replied that she had never known her to be unpunctual. But where was Hughie? The naughty boy had the hamper with him.

They went to look for Hughie, and the hamper. They found him, waiting for them.

"Oh dear, and I called him a naughty boy!" murmured Sarah.

Smoking a cheroot, Hugh Turney was pacing up and down with profound thought written in the lines of his brow, and swishing at flies with his whisk. The ragged man with the dark, hard eyes —time-expired soldier from India—was dutifully holding the cob's head in the shade of a Spanish chestnut tree, ready to touch the forelock pressed on his forehead with water. As they approached, Hughie's face broke into a broad smile. He greeted them with an exaggerated sweep of his light brown bowler, as though fancying himself as a cavalier with plumed hat. The temporary groom touched his forelock dutifully.

"Ah, back from the Temple of Time, and Sir Isaac Newton's popular demonstration of the Law of Gravity," he exclaimed.

"Is the cob's shoe secure now, dear?" enquired Sarah.

"Yes, indeed, Mamma, and he goes like a good'n to beat."

"The influence of Nelson, no doubt," remarked Sarah indulgently, "after Trafalgar."

"Your divination is correct, my dear Mater," replied Hughie. "The shoe is clenched, and the Learned Pig has been watered and fed. So give a man credit for punctuality with the vittles, as Sam Weller would say."

"You are a dear boy," said his mother.

They sat down in the shade of a tree on the slope leading to the backs of the Royal Naval College. Rugs were spread, the hamper opened. There were meat pies, flavoured with thyme and other herbs; sausage rolls and a veal-and-ham pie; sandwiches of egg and cress, tongue, ham, cheese, and cucumber and lettuce (Theodora would not eat meat) together with mince pies and a sultana and saffron cake. To drink, there was a flagon bottle of milk, another of lemonade, a third of lime juice and water.

"Yes dear, do you take the poor man a little something," said Sarah, when Hughie suggested they would enjoy their tuck the better if hungry eyes yonder were not first eating it in imagination. "But pray do not let him have a glass to drink out of, you never know what such men may have got."

"I brought him a bottle of beer," said Hughie.

"How thoughtful of you, dear, but I hope it will not be the means of leading him to the downward path."

"Allsopp's light ale is certainly not of sufficient gravity to lead him to the upward path, dear Mamma," replied Hughie.

Theodora smiled at his bit of wit. Hughie gave her a warm glance as he went away with a napkinful of pies and sandwiches.

When Richard had taken round the basket, Sarah said he must come and sit beside her.

"I hear you are taking your holiday now, Dickie."

"Yes, m'am," he replied. "I have fifteen whole days before me."

"And where shall you go, have you decided yet?"

"I am going on a bicycling tour," he said. "I thought of going down to the West Country."

"Ah yes, you were born there, were you not? Well, it is the best time of the year now. But penny-farthings are such dangerous things, I think, especially down the steep hills. You will dismount, will you not? Or have you the new safety bicycle?"

"Yes, I have a splendid Starley Rover, ma'm, with Dunlop pneumatic tyres."

"Ah, I am relieved that it is a safety machine, Dickie. There are such steep hills in the West, are there not?"

"Flints are likely to be my worst enemy down there, Mrs. Turney."

"Flints, Dickie?"

"Punctures in the inner tube, and cuts in the outer cover, Mrs. Turney."

"I am afraid it is a little beyond me, dear, all these modern inventions. But I shall pray for fine weather for you, if that is not too old-fashioned these days."

"I like the old-fashioned ways best, Mrs. Turney."

Hetty was taking frequent happy glances at them, she was delighted that they were getting on so well together. Oh, things would come all right in the end with Papa, she was sure they would.

When the hamper was being packed, Theodora said to her brother, "I suppose you know, Dickie, that Father is at home just now, arranging for some of the land to be sold? If you see him, boy, be kind to him. He is a much misunderstood man, you know."

Richard said nothing.

They went down to the waterfront, to watch the traffic on the river. A sailing ship with long sharp bow and raking masts was coming upriver, towed by a tug with creaming bows. On the decks below furled sails bearded men were roaring out a song. Men and women on the riverside were shouting and waving caps and arms.

"What are they singing, is it a shanty?" asked Sarah. The words were nearly indistinguishable; but Hughie, with head on one side caught a phrase. He looked at Richard and winked.

Richard, who also had caught the phrase, looked at Hughie and smiled a slight smile before turning his head away.

He felt that one should not take notice of such things, especially in the company of ladies.

"They are singing something about a sailor wanting some lodgings," said Sarah. "I expect many of them, poor fellows, have no homes to go to—but there are the Missions, thank goodness. Just hark at them!"

Richard was thinking that some of the later verses might be less indistinguishable, so—"I think we should go and see the Museum, ma'm." He offered his arm to Mrs. Turney. "It is one of the Australian wheat-clippers, ma'm. The most romantic run in the world, before the trade winds! I can smell that blue water and see the flying fish, Mrs. Turney."

"You should have been a sailor, Dickie. Did you never think of being one?"

"Yes, I suppose most small boys do, ma'm."

"How jolly they sound!" cried Hetty.

"Just think of it, that ship has come from half way round the world!"

"Yes," said Hughie. "Salt pork, biscuits crawling with weevils, water-barrels filled from the river. But give me that life before pen-pushing, eh Dick?"

"It is a man's life, Hugh, certainly."

They watched the clipper moving away up-river, now half concealed by smoke belching from its tug.

"Ichabod," remarked Hughie.

"Oh hush, Hughie, hush!"

"I wasn't swearing, Mamma; I was using a word from the Semitic tongue to convey my feelings on the imminent obsolescence of sail before steam."

"You have a ready reply for everything, Hughie," his fond mother replied.

"A condition of mind that I would not deny to the ladies, Mamma," said Hughie, raising his billycock with a little bow.

The glory seemed to have departed. Dingy colliers issuing drifting smoke, floating crates and boxes, reams of straw sodden in the turbid waters were of ordinary humdrum river-life; so they went inside the Royal Naval Palace, with its architectural splendour so redolent of history, Sarah remarked, recalling the enthusiasm of her husband, who had loved the place. If only she could remember what it was Tom had told her of the Kings and Queens who had built the various buildings, so that she could pass it on to the young folk; but there, it was the things themselves that mattered, not the names.

They went along the River Terrace, past the granite obelisks, and found their way to the Painted Hall, the walls of which were hung with pictures and portraits of naval victories and heroes. There were so many of them that Sarah went along happily disregarding them, her feelings directing her to the Museum, where, among model ships and their rigging, was something under glass that she had remembered always as being so pathetic. Others shared her mood; they stood there in silence before the relic of a faded blue tunic, the silk lining broken and stained by the blood of the gentle Nelson.

To Richard the place held a memory poignant to himself, for here a long while ago, far away in his boyhood fifteen years before, he had come to be examined for the Navy—and been rejected at the preliminary medical examination owing to his defective right eye. And had not his Father deliberately wrecked his chances, by writing to the Examiners to call particular attention to his eyesight?

While the others were looking at the model of the battle of Trafalgar, with its blue glassy sea and cotton-wool puffs from tiny cannon, Hetty moved away gradually with Dickie into another room, which was empty; and there they kissed each other, in a world of extraordinary wonder and beauty.

Hughie was beginning to feel the world altering, too, in the company of Theodora. He drove his mother and sister home to Cross Aulton that evening after a shrimp-tea with such consideration for other vehicles on the road that Sarah guessed what image possessed his mind.

It was only when they reached home that they remembered they had forgotten Aunt Marian—the fate of some spinster ladies. Hetty was sad, for Aunt Marian was such a dear. There was some consolation, nevertheless, for Aunt Marian had not known they were going to Greenwich that day.

Chapter 5

SURREY DAWN

VERY EARLY next morning, as the house-martins were beginning to twitter within their grey-mudded nests under the eaves above his open bedroom window, Richard got out of bed and started to dress without first taking his cold tub. He washed in the hand-basin, combed his hair and beard, put on his shirt, drew on his woollen stockings, buckled the ends of his knickerbockers, and with his special shoe-horn (discovered inside a drawer: how could it have got there?) he inserted his feet into his cycling shoes. His rüksak was already packed. A plate of sandwiches kept moist by another plate pressed on top was waiting on the table, beside a jug of water and a glass, his breakfast.

Richard had planned many weeks before to leave before dawn, without disturbing the household: a romantic start while yet the stars were shining. He was sitting down to the sandwiches by candlelight when there came a tap on the door; and opening it he saw a twin candlelight, and with it Mrs. Cummings standing, in her dressing-gown, her hair covered by a lace cap. In her hand was a cup of tea.

"I didn't fancy you starting off all that way without something warm inside you," she whispered. "Now don't let me fuss you. It's a lovely day, or going to be, and you'll have the sun behind you all the way through London and out of it. I'll leave you now, just you creep off as you want to, and send me a postcard, won't you, letting me know how you are getting on? Got your money all safe?"

Yes, he had four sovereigns and two half sovereigns in his sovereign-purse, and some silver loose in his pocket. "Now tata and good luck!" Mrs. Cummings closed the door softly. He munched the sandwiches more as a duty than a pleasure, for into his mind had come a shaking idea: he would go by way of Cross Aulton, and through the lanes of Surrey to Kingston, instead of directly to the Bath road through Brixton, Clapham and over the

Thames by Chelsea Bridge as he had planned, and see Hetty. There was a door in her garden wall, he had noticed, and dare he open it and go along the path, and perhaps stand under her bedroom window? His heart beat faster as he thought of such a terrifying thing.

Once the idea had started, the impulse, however disturbing, had to be followed. Time, too, was important; for it would be disastrous if he were to meet with Mr. Turney, who got up early and sometimes went for a walk before breakfast. Then he remembered with relief that it was a Sunday, when Mr. Turney might be expected to lie abed an extra hour, before going to church with his family. With slightly trembling hand holding the cup Richard sipped the hot tea, and there being no one present to see him do it, poured some into the saucer and blew upon it.

He took a big bite at a ham sandwich, while telling himself to chew twenty times before swallowing, lest he get indigestion. He did not feel hungry; and packing up his food, he crept down the stairs, carrying the plates and cup and saucer, meaning to take them to the kitchen; but Mrs. Cummings was there at the bottom of the stairs. She took the crockery from him, and told him in a whisper that she would close the door after him. He was relieved that she spoke in a whisper, for many times he had imagined himself creeping down the stairs—he had slept intermittently owing to so many mental rehearsals—and now it was happening almost as he had imagined.

The Starley Rover bicycle, cleaned, oiled, and all ready for the adventure, was lifted from its place by the cupboard, carried over the oil-cloth, and through the open door. "Good luck, Mr. Maddison! I'll expect you back Sunday evening after next. I'll be in all the evening, so don't hurry back, will you? Now mind you enjoy your trip!"

"Thank you, Mrs. Cummings. I hope I have not disturbed you unduly. Do not forward any letters, I shall be moving about. I shall send you a card when I arrive. Goodbye, and thank you indeed for the tea." He tip-toed down the tessellated path, past the little yew tree planted beside it, and mounting his low Starley Rover by the step extending from the rear axle, sat on the saddle and pedalled away down the dim road, in the direction of the station. He wanted to conceal the direction in which eventually he was going.

At the next turning to the left he quit the high road, returning along a street leading south with houses on either side, one row with their back gardens ending at the railway embankment. He followed the street across another and continuing down it, came eventually to the high road again. Now he was really started.

He was alone in a dim world, deserted but for stray dogs and cats. As he pressed harder on the pedals up the rise, having passed the Jack public house, he saw that the eastern sky over Shooter's Hill was flushing with a clear golden pink to the zenith, where small high clouds like flamingo feathers were scattered. It was exhilarating to be alone in the water-dim dawn, in the cold fresh air of morning silent except for the slur of his tyres on the dust of the road laid by dew, to see the northern face of the Crystal Palace, flanked by two towers beside its great breadth, its glassy scales beginning to gleam in the dawn from the east, and to know that already he was come to Sydenham. He alighted on the crest, and turning to the east, sighed with the cold beauty of the morning.

Now for the reward of uphill work: feet on fork-rests and pedals revolving faster than his feet could possibly stop them, should horse or dog or other obstacle suddenly come before his rattling, perilous descent. Oh lor', there at the bottom was a milk float, coming out of a side street without its driver, the horse drawing the low yellow cart by habit across the road. Hi! Hi!

No good putting on the brake, it would pitch him over the handlebars: no good trying to regain the pedals, they were going like the paddles of a steamer. Hi, look out!

But if the horse neither knew nor cared for modern speed awheel, the milkman did care for his horse, his float, and his cans of milk; and running across the road to seize the reins, he was just missed by the dangerous flying figure with accusing blue eyes whizzing by so near that he declared afterwards the bicyclist's beard brushed against the brim of his straw hat. A near shave! The milkman was a mild man, a steady and devout Wesleyan, and all he said at the time was, "You ought to know better'n not to look where you're a-goin' like that!" As for Richard, it had happened before he could think, and when the exhilarating rush through the otherwise empty street was over, and the roofs of Croydon to be seen in the distance, he sang a few snatches of his favourite song, *The Arab's Farewell to his Steed*, without connecting his words with the milkman's horse.

The sun was rising as a more cautious Richard cycled into Cross Aulton. The streets were deserted, swallows played over the pond which reflected the high cloudlets, now red and gold as the sun bent over the field and roof-tops of the east. He dismounted, and looked down into the water, seeking for trout; but his thoughts were not on fish, for now he was quivering within as he hesitated whether to turn up the familiar lane which led to the back of the garden, and then—what? Dare he open the door in the wall, and stealing through the apple trees, cross the lawn and throw a handful of gravel at her window? That is what one of his heroes of fiction, Sherlock Holmes, would have done.

He shrank from such an intrusion upon another's property, especially Mr. Turney's . . . and after the way he had been treated on that—that—that *terrible* occasion. The humiliation still had power to make him writhe inwardly when he thought of it. Oh, never, never could he enter the house again!

A breeze ruffled the mirror of the pond. Ephemeridae which had spent the night on wall and leaf were in flight with the rising of the sun, but to be slain by swallows and sandmartins which haunted the sheet of water enclosed within iron railings. A spent drake, relic of the vanished world of yesterday's rising and setting of the sun, fell aslant and helpless to the water, and as he watched a swift with whirling wings cut down with audible swoop and he heard the snap of its beak as the mayfly was taken. That was the reality of life.

Then he found himself wheeling his bicycle towards a watery lane, shaded by elms, from which arose on one side her garden wall, in which was the door he must open. But supposing he were taken for a burglar? Well, he would turn the handle; and if the door were bolted, he would go away! There could be no harm in that, surely? No harm? Whatever was he thinking of? He jumped the next moment: for startlingly near and clear came the sound of a clock striking the first quarter after the hour. A moment afterwards, two other clocks, more distant, chimed together.

He left his bicycle at the bottom of the lane, concealing it well down in the ditch lest it be stolen, and continued along the wall on tiptoe, relieved that his footfalls were inaudible in the sounds of running waters. A jay flew out of a tree, saw him, flew back and screamed harshly, making him stop in apprehension. At last he was outside the door: and thinking with agitation to himself that he might as well be hanged for a sheep as a lamb, he mounted the steps, turned the handle, and pushed. The door opened to reveal Hetty coming down the path towards him.

He could not believe that it was she, and not a trick of his mind; but it was Hetty, who came to him with a cry of "Dickie, Dickie, I knew you would come."

She overcame his hesitation and put her arms around him; and responding, he put his arms around her and bending down hid his face against her neck, as one seeking refuge there from the fears of life. There he remained awhile, at peace, feeling the warmth of her cheek upon his left temple.

"I knew you would come, I knew it!"

"I could not help myself, Hetty."

They sat down in the summerhouse, hardly daring to look at one another.

When their emotion was easier, there were so many reassurances needed.

"How did you know I was coming?"

"I felt it strongly, dearest, when I awakened at dawn. And ever since I have been expecting you. I went up to the attic window, and saw you standing by the pond."

"I came this way hoping to see you!"

"Oh how thoughtful of you, dearest. You are happy now, aren't you?"

He sighed. She could see that he was still in doubt. What could she say? Then he said:

"Are you sure you might not want to give me up?"

"Oh how could you say such a thing, Dickie!"

"Well, people cannot be sure of anything, can they, in this world?"

How could she reply? How *could* he be unsure of her?

"We will be different, dearest."

A thrush was singing in the orchard. A horse neighed in a paddock, seeing the sun, and they heard its cantering hoofs. "There's Bogey, Dickie, do you remember when we came to meet you and Dora at the station?"

"Bogey, is he? A fat Bogey, isn't he?"

"Yes," she laughed, happy again. "He nearly came yesterday, but Hughie hired the cob."

The clocks struck the half hour.

"I must be getting back, Dickie, Papa is an early riser. You have lovely weather to begin your holiday, dearest."

"I wish you were coming, too, Hetty."

"Yes, dearest, so do I. I will be, one day." She kissed his hand.

"Oh, Dickie, you never said yesterday if you wanted to join the Tree Frogs Club. You do, don't you? There's only Mamma, Dora, and me in the Club, dearest, no one else at all, dear. You will join, won't you?"

"First tell me if you and Mrs. Turney and Dora climb up trees, and honk to one another, will you? What do the neighbours say, may I ask?"

She laughed with delight at the picture. "Oh they are scandalised! But my reputation is already gone, I fear. Now Dickie, I think I ought to slip back into the house. Oh, I do hope you have a lovely holiday, really I do! You will take great care of yourself on your bicycle, won't you? Walk down the steep hills, promise me? And mind you don't go falling in love with some beauty or other down in the West Country!"

"H'm, what about yourself? How about that young fellow who plays the flute, has he been around lately?"

"Oh Dickie, it is so funny! While I was away in France, Hughie and Lancelot used to play together, and Hughie persuaded Lancelot Mallard to buy a second-hand bassoon. Hughie thought they could amuse people like that, only he didn't tell Lancelot, of course. Hughie thought it would be funny at Christmas parties, playing his violin, with things like *May I Come over the Wall* with a bassoon obbligato. Only, you see, Lancelot is serious about his music, although he cannot play very well, poor boy."

Richard thought that it was the sort of practical joke Hugh Turney would play on someone he looked down upon: but the sympathy shown by Hetty to the victim alarmed him.

"Have you played together since I was last here?" he asked.

"Once or twice, with Dora and Hughie, dearest, before I went abroad with Mamma. Not since then."

"But this—this Lancelot has been over, I suppose?"

"He came over once, Dickie, to practise the *Skaters' Waltz* with Hughie. I only heard it through the door, it was ever so funny. Lancelot Mallard really has no ear for music, I am afraid."

"Then he cannot really care for music. So why did he come in the first place, I wonder, if music was not the attraction?"

"He came to see Mamma in the first place, Dickie, she invited him over. His Papa is chairman of the Firm, you see."

"Oh I see," replied Richard, with mild irony. "Young Mr. Mallard comes over for the sake of establishing a better business relationship?"

"Now Dickie, pray do not worry yourself. I love you, dear, and only you, can't you see it?" She put her arms around him, and pressed her cheek against his jacket. She could feel him thinking, feel that he was still worried. How absurd it was! Lancelot Mallard!

"Well, I must be off. Goodbye, Hetty." He got to his feet.

"Honk!" cried Hetty softly. "Honk!" she cried again, as he stopped by the door. He wanted to say "Honk", too, but an inner restriction held him silent.

She went to him. "Don't be unkind to me," she whispered. "There now, I didn't mean it. Of course you could never be unkind. I understand you so well, I think."

"You are all I've got—or not got!" he cried. "You are a happy family—you have many friends—whereas I—I am a misfit, a sort of ne'er-do-well! I am not good enough for your people."

The clock sounded the half hour. From the distance two other clocks chimed musically.

"I ought to be going!"

She took his hand and held it to her heart.

"Please don't doubt me, dearest."

"Will you write to me, Hetty?"

"Yes, of course, dearest."

"Would you like me to write to you?"

"Oh, dearest, pray do!"

"I will write to Poste Restante, Cross Aulton, and do you write to me the same at Rookhurst. No, make it Colham, for I shall be moving about, and probably make that my headquarters. My Father is now at home, or what is left of it. He——" Richard checked himself.

"I've a good mind to come with you!" said Hetty, on an hysterical impulse. "I'll steal the gardener's penny-farthing, and disguise myself as a boy! As Rosalind! I could easily wear boy's clothes. Oh dear, what am I saying?" She went pink in the face.

Richard was stimulated by her animation. "You are somewhat small, I must admit," he said, suddenly cheerful. "A tiny little

Tree Frog with a fur hat and tippet, stolen from a seal. So very small a lady froggie!"

"I used to lie on the floor once upon a time, and try and stretch myself longer."

"I am glad you did not, for you are a shapely young woman as it is."

"But I would like to be, oh, so much like Theodora! She is so ladylike, she reminds me of a swan."

"Swans can be cruel. They drown ducks near their nests by holding them by the neck under water."

"Nature can be very cruel," said Hetty, reflectively. "But then," she added, brightly, "life is so very beautiful!"

He stroked her head. She put her arms around him once more, and laid her cheek against his coat. He thought her head was like a child's. The delicate ear and curve of cheek and chin, and above all the smell of her hair, roused his passion, and he made an excuse to turn away, his back to her, while pretending to blow his nose, a little ashamed of himself. Then feeling in his pocket, he took out the crown piece he always carried there with his key-bunch, and said, "I thought for a moment I had left this at home."

"What is it, dearest?"

"My lucky crown. I have kept it since my grandfather gave it to me on my tenth birthday. Would you like to keep it?"

"Oh, but I might lose it, then I would never forgive myself."

"Oh, it does not matter if you do. It is a William the Fourth crown piece. Keep it until we are married!"

"Yes dear, I will. I'll put it in my sandal-wood box, where it will be safe. It is worn so thin, oh, I do love it."

"I shall want some interest for the loan, you know!"

"Of course, dear."

"A kiss every day while you have it. How much will you have paid by the time we are married, I wonder?"

If it were two years, then it would be twice three hundred and sixty-five, thought Hetty; over seven hundred days. It seemed a terrible long time; and if she mentioned the number, might it not make him unhappy? A better idea came to her. "All the kisses you want, dearest," and then she blushed again, lest he think her forward.

"Well, how many will they total?"

"Oh dear, I can't say, Dickie! But it won't be very long, I promise you. Papa will come round, I am sure he will. He is very kind, really."

Through a gap in the fruit trees a casement window in the eastern wall of the house was opened, followed by noises of sniffing, the fastening of the hook, and the loud clearing of a man's throat.

"Oh dear, that is Papa, he has got out of bed!"

Richard showed unexpected calmness. "Back in the summer-house, Tree Frog, the heron is about!" he whispered. "That is better, we are concealed now. Tell me, does he ever come down on the lawn, I mean after getting up?"

"Sometimes he does, dearest. Papa likes to walk in the dew with his bare feet. Oh, I really think you should go!"

"Oh, but I have only just come to the land of Frogs!" Richard was enjoying the feeling of delay, the excitement. But Hetty's terror was real. "You have not kissed me goodbye yet, Tree Frog. Honk! Tree Frogs are persistent, you know. Why else do they climb all the way up trees? Why, to be able to find a Lady Frog, of course! Honk!" he kissed her. "When are you going to come away with me, eh?"

"It won't be long dearest, I promise you. Now Dickie——"

"One more kiss, Lady Frog."

"Dickie dearest, Papa might be coming down this moment! Oh, if he finds out about yesterday, he will be so angry with poor Mamma!"

"Well, I will go, but do not look so frightened, Frog. Goodbye, do not forget to write, now!"

"No, Dickie, of course not." Hetty was feeling sick with apprehension. Poor Dickie, would he feel she was trying to get rid of him? But Papa——

He kissed her again, then walked rapidly down the path to the door. "Honk!" he called softly, and the door was closed behind him.

Hetty was quivering. She could not, she dare not, leave the shelter of the summer-house for a few moments. The thrush was singing boldly in an apple tree. As she heard its notes again, it seemed to be saying to her, *Cheer up, Hetty! Cheer up, Hetty!* again and again. "I will, of course I will!" she answered. "I am ever so happy, really." Her breathing was still a little constricted. She undid the hook from the eye of her bodice neck. In relief she sighed deeply. Then closing her eyes, she prayed for Dickie's safety, and that all would come well for everybody, for Dickie, Mamma, Papa and Hughie. She must not forget Charlie so far away across the sea, and Dorrie, and little Joey.

Ah, that was better! She thought of Dickie pedalling away for dear life on his safety bicycle. It had a good brake for the steep hills, and he was a careful rider. Oh, all would come right, there was a good God looking over all.

The clocks struck the third quarter of the hour. How beautifully clear they sounded, clear as water.

To her relief, Papa did not come into the garden in his dressing gown as she went along the garden path, with hard-beating heart, and dry throat. Oh, what a relief to be in the kitchen again! She took a cup of tea with Cookie, and with Polly the maid, and never did tea taste so refreshing. As it warmed her she felt a wonderful joy coming to her, so wonderful that the tears came into her eyes once more as she thought of Dickie, so good, so true, so brave to have come into the garden for her.

Richard was pedalling into his own long wavering shadow cast in front of him by the rising sun, conscious of the great distance he had set himself to cover that day. He had planned to reach Colham by nightfall, which meant that he must be upon the eastern approaches of the Great Plain by the middle of the afternoon. He would pass by Stonehenge, and hoped to be able to rest there for half an hour or so; for once during a long summer day his father had driven the family there, and it was one of the bright memories of his childhood. Mother and Father, brother John and the sisters with Minnie their German nurse looking after little Hilary, and baby Dora.

Chapter 6

MUCH ADO

DUST WAS dust: glittering and gritty dust, covering knickerbockers, stockings, and flannel shirt: dust on the bare arms, mudguards, bicycle frame, and grinding in the chain and sprocket wheels despite the treatment in hot Russian tallow: dust on neck irritating skin rubbed by starched linen collar with wide Gladstonian wings. Who was there to recognize him, should he take off the beastly collar? He had already removed his Norfolk jacket, and strapped it to the handlebars. What would they say in the Shop, should anyone chance to see him bicycling, on Sunday too, without a collar? He had his red silk handkerchief in his pocket; but that, knotted round the neck, would hardly look better than any Irish navvy with bandanna around his throat. Who could possibly recognize him if he went without cap or collar?

Along a lonely stretch of rising road with woods on either side he stopped, and after making sure no one was about, removed collar and studs, and with shirt open at the neck went on again, feeling cool and daring, and exhilarated by this utter defiance of convention. The sun burned down upon his neck and arms, the great friendly sun, giver of all life and beauty. He and his faithful steed, the Starley Rover, alone under the great English sun!

Field upon field, hedged and posted, slowly receding; field upon field everlastingly in front, patiently to be passed. Being a Sunday he had the road to himself. The fields were empty, too, except for occasional shepherd's mates among the hogget and ewe flocks in the hurdled folds, deep in lucerne, sainfoin, and clover.

Alone in the waving fields of wheat and oats and barley stood the scarecrows, their arms out-held like men drowning among green seas in motion to the wind from the south-west. Alone in the sky burned the great sun, hour upon hour. Alone on the winding road he pedalled with his shadow slowly moving from west to north of west, to north, and then to north-east—and at last he dismounted in weariness, and lay upon his back, face to the sky, eyes closed, feeling at one with the radiant sun.

After a while he sat up, and reached for his rüksak. Therein was a bottle of lime-juice and water, and some sandwiches. How hungry he was after drinking, the moment he tasted food! How far away was London, and Hetty of that magic morning! This was the edge of the Great Plain; but he must hold himself back until he reached the high ground, and saw again the land of his longing.

As he was about to continue his journey, wheeling the Starley Rover out of a field, strange sounds appeared to come from the wheels. Thinking that a stick had caught in the spokes, he looked, but could see nothing; then he realized that a corncrake was calling quite near, hidden among the grasses. And listening, he heard another sound, which continued when the corncrake had ceased: the sound as of a distant scythe being whetted on a soft stone. He pursed his wetted lips and called to the bird, a liquid *phuit-phuit*, *phuit-phuit*: now indeed he felt he was returning home, to the downland country of the summer quails.

He toiled up the slope, pleased that he had had no punctures so far. The pneumatic tyres certainly gave an added speed. The sun was now mounted high upon the south-west, burning face and forearms as he pressed to the skyline.

And topping the crest he dismounted, to draw a deep breath as he beheld the grey spaces of the chalkland pastures beset with wild juniper and thorn, with beech hangers upon distant ridges, while remotely the blue shadowy woods of summer were dissolved in the haze of heat that lay upon the Plain. The wind had gone: bees burred to the thyme and bedstraw in the sward: the place was to the larks, stonechats, and wheatears: remotely the cries of unseen sheep quivered upon the heated air. Oh beautiful, beautiful England! While the sun was reigning in the sky over all life, how unimportant seemed the ways of men in cities, their feet deadened by asphalt and pavement, their thoughts enclosed in brick and stone of counting house. O, it was just the same England of his boyhood . . . Hetty, Hetty, your love has brought back all the loveliness to me again!

He sat down on the sward, and let his thoughts stray back in time, while his fingers touched the empty shell of a hill-snail among the yellow and red flowers of the bird's-foot-trefoil beside him. He began to feel terror rising within him. The Plain was beautiful, but wide and empty, invisibly filled with the lives of those who had gone for ever, the blue butterflies and the larks alike with the faces he had known in childhood. Gradually his habitual cast of thought, made by his experience, reasserted itself. Sitting on the dry, brittle grass he saw a grave deep in the shadow of Rookhurst's flint church, and while jackdaws called upon the tower above he stood with his brother and sisters, and Father with tears running down his cheeks, beside the grave-digger clad in long smock dusty white with chalk, chalk on face and eyebrows, on hands and boots and long-handled shovel, touching his whitened forelock as Father dropped a handful of chalk on the planed oak boards of the coffin in which Mother was lying in pallid immobility, alone and remote for evermore, Mother gradually shrinking and withering with open lipless mouth and lidless eye-sockets until the coffin collapsed in fragments brown as the bones and wisps of cloth . . . six feet down in the chalk but open to his seeing, so that the bird's-foot-trefoil in the sward beside him was insubstantial as the voiceless cry within. O God, what was the purpose of life, since it led only to pain and oblivion? Mother—Mamma, dear Mamma of Christmas so long ago, the carols outside and the lanterns, excitement and magic of Santa Claus on the Eve, Mamma and Papa standing by the lighted Christmas tree, and himself between them, holding in each hand one of their hands, and looking at their smiling faces so high above . . . it was gone quicker than thought, it would never be again, it was gone for ever and ever.

What was there at Rookhurst, now that all the mind and substance of that life was departed, broken, ended? Other memories rushed upon him, fragmentary and fleeting, vanished before they could form themselves into pictures, dismissed as by a silent cry from the back of the mind—from the darkness imminent upon all life, the mournfulness of Father angry with Mother, Father always complaining about the house, Father's terrible shouting heard from the schoolroom, the darkness and fear in the passages, Mother crying and holding him in her arms when Father had gone: and so, through aimless time to the darkness of the grave, to the final obliteration of the chalk upon the coffin. Let the parsons say what they might, that was the truth of life, a tragedy ending in oblivion.

It was a weary Richard who pedalled into his native village at twilight that evening, having coasted along the white winding road through the downs with the constellation of the Plough behind him. The lime-washed cottages with their low brows of thatch glimmered in the starlight and many windows were without light, their occupants having already gone up over to bed. Feeling himself a ghost, but serene with purpose achieved, he cycled down the main street, past the Norman church and the yews beyond the lych-gate, and with a salute of the hand to the thought of his Mother buried there he went on past the blacksmith's, the wheelwright's, and the village shop, making for the lane leading to the farm where lived a young yeoman named Temperley with whom he had been friendly in boyhood.

Frank Temperley and his wife greeted the traveller with surprise and delight, and on hearing how far he had cycled that day—"All the way from London, my, you must be beat, Dick!"—would not hear of him going on to Colham, but insisted that he stay the night with them. Which Richard was most pleased to do, for once he was seated in the comfortable yew-wood armchair in the parlour, he felt he would never be able to heave his limbs out of it again. A bowl of milk-sop, however, with sugar and cream added, soon restored his strength, and after some talk by the open hearth, on which a beechwood fire smouldered, since all cooking was done in or before it (the remembered turn-spit for roasting stood in the inglenook) he went upstairs to undress and to fall asleep in the soft deep goose-feather mattress of the four-poster bed.

At breakfast Frank Temperley asked Richard if he knew that his father had gone up to London last Friday. "I took him in the dog-cart to Colham. He's looking a lot older, I fancy. What is he, fifty two or three, Dick?"

"I really do not know."

"Have you seen him lately?"

"Not recently."

"He said he'd be away until Tuesday or Wednesday week. He's a real lonely man these days, Dick."

Relieved that Father was away, Richard walked into the village, to visit the grave of his mother. He approached it with feelings quite different from those he had imagined while in London. It was as though Mother were smiling at him in the air, smiling her gentle South German smile, the patient smile she had maintained, or tried to maintain, through all the storms and hurts of her life, and of the lives of those about her. In his mind the son said, I have come, Mother, you are telling me to be happy. Hetty is much like you, Mother. And feeling strangely free, Richard stood by the grave, light of heart, before bowing, with eyes shut, and turning away.

The Temperleys insisted that he spend as much of his holiday with them as he wanted to, and so the days went by, Richard taking sandwiches and a bottle of milk or cider in his rüksak after breakfast, and returning in the afternoon for meat tea, at half past six. He avoided the neighbourhood of his old home: if he should chance to meet with Father, well, he would meet him, and be easy about it. Trying to maintain himself with an equal mind, that his life was now entirely changed with the coming of Hetty, he walked far upon the downs, scenes of happy days with his brothers coming back to him with the scent of thyme upon the air, the hill flowers of crane's bill and ladies slipper, bedstraw, dog-violet, and the brown-yellow silky disk of the carline thistle. It was pure happiness to lie on his back among the passing butterflies, with no desire to pursue or capture them, but only that they should remain happy and free, he among them. He read again and again the letter Hetty had sent *poste restante* to Colham post-office, and thoughts of her were as the summer day. I am fortunate, I am happy at last, I shall never be unhappy again, he said to himself many times. There was only one thing now that could allay the sunshine.

"Your Father's back, Dick. Aren't you going to see him?" And seeing his face, Frank Temperley said, "Let bygones be bygones, old man. Your Father ain't so black as he's painted, not by a long chalk. There now, perhaps I shouldn't have said it, but I'm a plain man, Dick. I know what you went through in the past, but life ain't easy in the best of circumstances, you know, for any man these days."

Every time Richard made up his mind to visit his father, an almost equal reluctance held him indecisive. He could not think of it, his mind refused the mental picture. He was happy, he had found happiness with Hetty, her coming had entirely altered his life! Why should he have to go back into the past again? He had done with the old life, he belonged to the new generation.

And he would set out to walk farther across the downs, the dust settling thick on his boots with the hours, the sun burning face and hands and wrists—twenty five, thirty miles a day; but wherever he went in his long loping stride he could not outwalk his thoughts, or the feeling that he was not really where he was. He set forth in the early mornings and returned late in the evenings, tired out; to rest awhile, eat some supper, sit at the table afterwards and play the nightly game of picquet with Frank.

"They say there's a rich brewer from up country buying of land in the neighbourhood. Laycock o' Colham, the valuer, who acts for him, has been driving over to look at some o' your Father's land, Dick. Have you heard aught about it?"

Richard shook his head.

"It's a pity, you know. I don't like to see it. Land has dropped in value just now, too. It's not the right time to sell. Besides I don't care to see it passing out of the family, Dick, and that's a fact."

"Oh, I have long since given up worrying about what cannot be helped, Frank."

"That's the only way to look at trouble, I'll admit," said Frank. "They say the new fellow is a City man, as well as owns a brewery. I hear well of him—Tofield his name is, Sir Roger Tofield."

"Oh," said Richard, peering at his cards. He thought a moment. Was not Sir Roger Tofield one of the customers of Doggett's? Surely he was; he recalled writing the name, again and again, in the ledger. But Frank should get nothing out of him.

"These rich London gentlemen bring money to a district, helping trade, I'll say that for 'em," went on Frank Temperley. "Though sometimes 'tes all pheasants and partridges, and they let the land go as a preserve for the birds. I don't blame 'em, really; if they can't get tenants. Who wants to farm land now, in a depression? Cheap corn from 'Merica and Canada and Australia, all hard wheats, has knocked English arable farming into a cocked hat, I reckon. The money's all in industry these days, and only wealthy gentlemen like this Tofield can afford to start farming, as a hobby."

"It's Free Trade that has ruined the country, Frank."

"I'm inclined to agree, though I'm as good a Radical as Gladstone; but there's no doubt, Dick, as your Father says, Free Trade has spoiled farming, in this country at any rate. You know, where the old gentleman went wrong, and I say it with all due respect, was in not reckoning what it would cost to serve his land as it used to be served. He was too good. Everything with him, from the start, when your grandfather died, had to be perfect, so I've heard my old Dad tell. I'll give you an instance. All that deep plowing by steam cable, to break up the sour soil, was money wasted. It only turned up the chalk. And then the guano, trucks and trucks of it delivered to the Halt! Hundreds, maybe so much as a thousand pounds' worth, and all sold to the tenants at half market price! Most of it wasted, the rains washed it down among the flints. It grew good roots, I grant you, while it lasted; but the market for wool and mutton wasn't there, Dick, to get it back! This land, you know, won't grow more than six or seven sacks of wheat even with a ewe flock in the four-course shift; and mutton don't pay like it did thirty year ago. I reckon he lost a fortune on his land, all the cottages and farm-premises done up regardless, new fences, tree-planting—why, he got nothing back out of it for himself. And now, what? A rich man comes along and buys it all up when the market for land is the worst for half a century! There's such a thing as being too good, you know."

Richard said nothing.

"Still, he was a good landlord, I'll say that for him. He was the first to reduce rents in those bad seasons when we were small boys blowin' eggs with a pin. He is a generous man to a fault."

"Ah," said Richard, who remembered his Mother's never-ceasing anxiety about money for the younger children's boots and clothes, for the household food, even. And the money squandered on—he winced away from formulating in his mind the word *mistresses*.

"Is the house going to be let, d'you know?" asked Frank's wife. She asked the question a little timidly, since she did not want to appear to be what, naturally, she was—curious.

"I do not really know," replied Richard, shading his eyes from the oil-lamp with his hand. Frank Temperley gave his wife a warning glance. Then he changed the subject.

"Will you take a glass of special strong ale, Dick? I expect the long walk, and the rare wind on the ridges today, has tired you. It's as heartening as rum to a tired man. My old Dad brewed it, and then bottled it. It's been in the cellar these twenty years."

"Oh, I am not tired, Frank. But I would like a glass of water."

"How about tea?" suggested Mrs. Temperley. "I'll remember you like it weak."

"Yes, strong tea keeps me awake."

"Then I've got some nice cocoa. Frank often has cocoa at night, last thing."

"No, I will not risk it, thank you. A cup of hot water I find is best at night."

"Not hot milk?" suggested Mrs. Temperley. "That can't hurt anyone's stomach, surely?"

"Ah, I would like some hot milk, Mrs. Temperley."

"With some of my old Dad's rum in it, Dick," said Frank. "Does a man good on occasion."

"I will play you another game of picquet, Frank!"

Both men had come to look forward to the evening game. Richard had brought with him his set of pocket chessmen, with which he often played against himself; but Frank had at once shied away from what he called "such a brainy game".

They sat there until nearly midnight, animated by the rum and milk; which was followed by sloe gin, and finally, a large glass each of neat whiskey. Richard sang *The Arab's Farewell to his Steed*, and Frank sang *A Farmer's Boy*, followed by *Little Brown Jug* as a duet with Richard. It was a wonderful evening, ending with Richard asking the Temperleys, one arm around each of their shoulders, to join him in a new life in Australia, starting a fruit farm.

"But you'll want a little wife, Dicky boy! Mine belongs to me, d'ye hear, you'll want a woman o' your own, Dick!"

"Ah!" cried Dick. "How d'you know I have not got one, Frank?"

"Dark horse, eh, Dicky boy? Who is she?"

"Curiosity killed the cat, they say, Frank, old chap. But I will tell you this, in confidence mind, that if we go, we shall go as a quartet, that we will, and not a trio! This country's finished, Frank, let me tell you that!"

"Not on your life!" cried Frank.

"Well, the candles are," said Mrs. Temperley. "And there's the hay tomorrow to think of. To bed, you two tipplers."

"Well, I like that!" laughed Dick. "Who had two glasses of sloe gin, eh?"

If only Hetty could have been there with them!

The next day, as he was on his way back to the hayfield in the morning, he saw his father coming up the lane, a hundred yards away. Immediately he vaulted over a gate, and concealed himself behind a clump of brambles. The footfalls came nearer, and he crouched down while they passed away up the lane towards the farmhouse. Relieved, and yet disappointed that he had avoided the meeting, the son crept to the gate, and peering down the hedge, watched the figure that was the cause of contrary feeling in him turn the corner.

Instead of going down among the mowers, Richard went up on the downs, with their wide views over the plain of Colham; he watched the mowers in the field, advancing in line; and it was evening when he returned.

"Your Father called twice today, asking for you," said Frank. "Once in the morning, again in the afternoon. He asked me to tell you that he would be most pleased if you could spare the time to go and see him. Also, it's right, Dick, that four of the farms have been sold to Sir Roger Tofield. Your Father told me so himself. He said the mortgagees determined the sale, it was out of his hands."

The hay had been scythed. The hot sun wilted it the next day; on the following day it was turned. Richard helped to fork it into windrow, working throughout the long hot hours. The night was close; on the Friday morning an oppressive white light lay over the fields. There was thunder about; distant rumblings were heard; but towards evening the air cleared.

"Aren't you going to see your Father?" Mrs. Temperley asked, with reproach in her voice. She liked the old gentleman, he was so considerate to her, he treated her as though she were a fine lady. She thought Dick a bit perverse. She had come from another district to marry Frank a year before, and knew nothing except hearsay of the family trouble.

"Yes, I think I will, Mrs. Temperley." He never called her by her Christian name.

At the gate, standing at the entrance of the weedy drive, Richard met the woman who had been coming every day, she said, to clean up and cook for the squire.

"He left for Lunnon this afternoon, sir. I don't know when he may be returning, he didn't say, Mr. Richard." She did not like to ask if it was true that the house had been sold, as the tale went in the village.

Richard thanked her, and hastened back the way he had come, his mind now fixed on the necessity of seeing Hetty. He felt hopeless. He must see Hetty. He had written to her, confirming that he would be in the summer-house at six o'clock on the Sunday morning.

During that Friday night the wind blew from the south-west, driving in from the coast. He had intended to start the following morning, an hour before sunrise, and to spend the night not far from Cross Aulton, in order to arrive at the door in the garden wall at the prescribed hour; but the rain kept on all during the morning of Saturday, continuing throughout the afternoon and evening, while he hung about, trying not to appear impatient or uneasy during the dragging hours. At night the rain began to clear; the transformation was exciting, as though a new world had come; gone were the greyness and the cold; high summer brought hope and keenness of living once again. The night sky was liquid with stars above the magnetic blue line of the downs. He wanted to start in that wonderful midsummer glow and cycle through the short night into the dawn and the sunrise to keep tryst with Hetty, imagining her waiting for him in the garden, waiting for him to come, waiting while the stable clocks chimed the hours until the church bells of Cross Aulton scattered their peals across the water and dashed all hope away. Hetty! Hetty! he cried to her in his mind. He wanted to begin his journey at once under that steel-blue north-western sky; but the Temperleys, knowing nothing of his inner compulsion, declared that he must stay the night, and start on the morrow after a good breakfast. Not wanting to disappoint them—with some dismay he had seen the preparation for a real good supper going on during the afternoon—he yielded; but with inner mourning. He had, with his habitual reticence, told them nothing about Hetty.

On the Sunday, shortly after four o'clock, he started out, and set himself in steadiness to achieve the journey to the source of all hope, all happiness, of his being. He was helped by a following wind. Recklessly he rattled down the hills, his feet upon the rests, his imagination beginning to plague him with thoughts that would not be deterred, however much he tried to set them aside. Perhaps Mr. Turney had taken her away? What would she think when he did not keep the appointment? Should he take the plunge and leave Doggett's, and elope with her to Australia? He had nearly two hundred pounds saved up. One thing was certain, and that was he must never give Mr. Turney any opportunity to report him to the secretary of the bank. At the slightest hint of scandal, a man had to resign his position there. He would surely be reported by Mr. Turney if he ever found out about him and Hetty. Well then, why not marry her secretly? He might as well be hanged for a sheep as a lamb. But not yet. He must do nothing rash. And there was Hetty, and her regard for Mr. Turney, and for Mrs. Turney, too. Well he must never do anything to compromise Mrs. Turney, after the extremely kind way she had behaved towards himself. But supposing Hetty changed her mind, where was he? He must hurry on, and see her, and find out if she still cared for him.

With such mental impulsions, the journey became appallingly slow and tedious, an exercise in self-torture upon an unending road across a bleak Plain. Obsessed by his fearful desire to see her, he did not stop to eat, but forced his aching legs to thrust upon the rat-trap pedals, while the carefully packed luncheon of roast chicken, blue vinney cheese, soda cake, and wheaten scones with butter and honey remained untouched in the rüksak. Across the unending Plain the thin bearded figure pedalled desperately into its own shadow now beginning to slant to the left of the road.

Soon the shadow vanished; clouds came up on the wind; the landscape darkened; a chilly gust spun the chalky dust past the humming wheels; a cold drop of rain fell on the bended neck. Another, another, another; then like swanshot whipping into water the storm broke about him. The dust leaped and contorted and lay in mottled castings; lightning cracked the base of a livid cloud and *crash!* the sky descended upon him. He could not see; he was beaten to immobility; he dropped off the Starley Rover and crouched on the water-prickled verge of the road, his head bent to the storm. The attitude gave no shelter; he wore a jacket of cold water already. Cold and shivering when the storm had passed he got upright and flapped heavily at the pedals, moving eastward slowly in a bluish-red light pierced distantly by one ray from the muffled sun.

The weather looked to be clearing; and when the sun did burst out of the floating mist and colour returned to the earth and warmth to his body, he felt happier, and decided to stop and eat, in order to keep up his strength to continue.

It was a hasty meal. He was optimistic again afterwards, and he pedalled onwards, winding his way past puddles and water-filled ruts, and when he felt the sun burning with its old heat upon his back, so that soon his jacket and knickerbockers were steaming, he began to sing *The Arab's Farewell to his Steed*, animated by the idea of the Temperleys and himself, with Hetty, on a ship sailing for Australia. After all, brother Hilary had a fruit farm there! What fun it would be to work all day in the open air!

Calculating the distance to Cross Aulton, and the time it would take to get there, Richard reckoned that if he kept going people would have come out of evening service two hours before he was due to arrive; so he could afford to rest for half an hour, and spread shirt and jacket to dry in the sun.

Coming to a beech hanger on the left of the road he dismounted and went among the tall grey boles, and through to the other hedge, where two tumuli, burial mounds of ancient chieftains, arose side by side. Here he undressed unseen from the road, and after spreading his things out, lay down for the wonder of the sun upon his body, in the relief of relaxation feeling that the warmth and light were as the love of Hetty flowing upon him.

With renewed hope and optimism he prepared to continue his journey. The urge to find peace in the actual flesh drove him to put on his damp clothes and never did bicycling seem so weightily slow.

At last the Great Plain was behind him: his holiday was over! If only he had seen Father! *He's a real lonely man these days, Dick.* As he pedalled into Andover the afternoon was growing grey again with the sun behind clouds and more rain blowing up. Out of a leaden sky it fell, prickling the east-stretching chain of little lagoons where iron of shoe and wheel had worn away the metalling of the London road.

Dusk was descending as Richard passed by Virginia Water, on his way to the village of Staines. Suddenly he made a startling discovery. Soon it would be nightfall, it was a Sunday when all the shops were shut, and he had no lamp on the Starley Rover.

Some time later, in the misty darkness of that sodden mid-summer night, a pale globe of light moved slowly on the left of the road into Cross Aulton. The globe was about ten inches in diameter, and wider than it was deep: a fragile globe, made of paper stretched upon a frame of thinly split bamboo, and lighted within by a candle. The paper was pale yellow, with a dragon roughly stencilled in red around its wider circumference. It was a Chinese lantern swinging from the handlebars of the Rover. Richard had been fortunate in finding a bicyclist in the village of Chertsey, who was about to enter his cottage with a Chinese lantern on his handlebars; and he had purchased both lantern and two fresh candles for sixpence—more than they were worth, he thought, but beggars cannot be choosers.

Arriving at the pond, he alighted stiffly, blew out the candle, and proceeded wearily on foot, his mind on the tryst in the summer-house at the bottom of Hetty's garden. He was wet through to ribs and loins; his worsted stockings were heavy in his shoes. He had set his mind upon one thing, upon one question, upon one answer, with its alternative the thought of which seemed to clench mind and body together with the darkness of the night. He would enter Maybury Lodge; demand to see Hetty; ask her to marry him in the near future; and were the answer in the negative (as he said to himself) he would never again darken Mr. Turney's door. But first, he must see Hetty.

Leaving his bicycle in the lane he tip-toed to the door in the wall below the splashing runnel. A clock struck the four quarters of the hour; others chimed in. It was ten o'clock. He had been fifteen hours on the road.

He lifted the latch of the door, and pushed. It was unbolted. So Hetty expected him. With hands held out before him, and eyes half-shut, he moved gradually down the path to the summer-house. A candle light showed in one of the upper windows. He waited, listening. He could hear only the drips from branches of trees. Should he risk making the cry of a wood owl, by blowing on his hollowed hands? After anguished hesitation he tried to do so; the sound was but a hiss, his hands would not clasp themselves together. He managed to pick up, laboriously, some specks of gravel from the path and to toss them up to the lighted window. A shadow showed there, and then disappeared. Was it Hetty? Could it be Polly the maid? If so, would she tell Mr. Turney? Would he be summoned for trespass? That certainly would lead at once to the loss of his post in Doggett's. He retreated into the summer-house and waited. Steps came down the path.

They stopped.

"Honk!" came the plaintive cry through the darkness.

The steps came nearer, hesitant and slow.

He resisted a desire to answer: he would go away without showing himself when she had gone back. He clenched his hands in desperate indecision.

"Is that you, Dickie?"

He cleared his throat, and managed to say, "Yes."

She hastened forward. Eagerly, compassionately. All her thought for him, she spoke of food, a hot drink, a change of clothes—Hughie would help her—Was he ill? Oh, he had caught a chill, he was shivering.

Richard's teeth suddenly started to chatter. Hetty wondered what to do. Richard's body was rigid.

What had happened? He could not speak; he was shuddering. He had half-pretended to himself, and now really he was unable to speak.

She took his hand. "Oh, it is icy cold. Dearest——" She recovered herself; spoke quietly, surely. "I'll get some brandy. Wait here, won't you? I know where it is kept." She led him into the summer-house.

"N–n–not Mr. T—T—Turney's, I w–w–will n–n–not——"

"No, dear, not Papa's. I will get the cooking brandy. Oh dear, what a state you are in, never mind—I will be back in a moment."

"Hetty!"

"Yes, dearest?"

"Do you—do you—do you——"

"Oh you poor dear! Of course I do, surely you should know by now without asking? Don't ever worry, dear." She kissed him on the brow. "I'll be gone for only a little while."

Cook in the kitchen was heating some milk for Mrs. Turney's bedside cup of arrowroot, and being in the secret, readily poured it out for Hetty, with a generous addition from the cooking brandy bottle, which since she was a staunch Wesleyan, was kept unlocked in the kitchen cupboard, together with the cooking sherry. She said she would cut some mutton sandwiches with some good sweet pickles, and told Miss Hetty to take out the hot drink to her young man at once.

After the warming drink, and the food, Richard was in better heart. His previous determination to force a decision now seemed to him to be somewhat shameful, and he was glad he had not said a word of it to Hetty. It was like a bad dream when it had passed. Food and drink had put the inner man right, he declared; and scorning the idea of changing into a suit of Hughie's—"Thank you, Hetty dear, but I fear that once on, I should never be able to get a suit of Hugh's off again. And anyway, you know, the cold tubs I take of a morning harden a fellow"—he left after half an hour, the Chinese lantern glowing beside the pond like a playful moon as it swung on the handlebars of the Starley Rover, fully complying with the requirements of the law. Richard had not forgotten the constable's warning about Greenwich Police Court.

Chapter 7

YOUNG MAN'S AUTUMN

THE CONICAL thatched house in the garden of Maybury Lodge became, for the rest of the summer, but only after darkness, the clandestine meeting place of Dickie and Hetty. He went there as a moth to the light, driven by his inner need. He was not a passionate man, and certainly not a sensual man. He needed Hetty; and as one who grieved in mind and feeling, without realizing it—a state or condition accepted as a part of life—grievousness with him sometimes became grievance.

"Hetty, how long are we to continue like this? I cannot endure for ever to creep about like a thief in the night. I am in my twenty-eighth year, yet I feel myself like a boy at school again, under constant threat of detection and punishment."

Richard had bicycled to Cross Aulton, directly from London. It was a moonlit September night. Already Orion had risen from under the horizon of the south-east as warning of frost soon to replace flower, of the northern hemisphere turning to the winter solstice. Leaves were drifting down audibly in the garden weighted with mist; drops struck the roof of the summer-house; an apple thudded on the lawn. Periodically the chimes of clocks came through the night. The lantern stood on the table between them, a shaded beacon and giver of warmth.

"Yes, Dickie, I know how very worrying it is for you, I know how you feel, but it won't always be like this, Dickie." She did not like to tell him that Papa and Hughie had been disagreeing, after it had come out about the expulsion from the University, and that she and Mamma were waiting for a favourable opportunity to broach the subject, when Papa should be in a good mood.

"It is the hole-and-corner aspect of the whole thing that goes against the grain, Hetty."

"Yes, dear, of course, naturally. But try and be patient a little while longer, Dickie. Now I am going in to fetch a tray I have prepared, you'll feel better after a nice hot drink."

"You speak as though it were the material things of life which alone count, Hetty. I do appreciate the creature comforts like anyone else, of course, but a man's pride means something to him, you know."

"Yes, dearest, of course. But we must be patient. Have you been practising any more on your 'cello?"

"No, I have given up all idea of it."

"Oh Dickie! It is entirely my fault."

"No, you must not think like that."

"We shall be able to play in a quartet in the future, dear, and enjoy ourselves more than ever before."

"Why not a quintet, including a bassoon?"

"Oh no, Dickie. Why, Lancelot's bassoon is only a practical joke of Hughie's. Nobody hearing those two together could possibly take *The Skater's Waltz* seriously."

"Well, I shall never play the 'cello again."

Poor Dickie, feeling himself left out in the cold! He could play so tenderly, he loved music so deeply, and now no one to whom he could play his 'cello. Could he not bring it to the summer-house? And play to her with the mute on? At once the ridiculousness of the idea struck her. Dickie and Lancelot playing bassoon and 'cello together in the summer-house, both scared of Papa! It was terribly funny. O, what a fool she was, for laughing at such a moment.

"Well, the plight of one in my position may be amusing," he said, "but for myself I feel that the time has come to state a policy."

Hetty's heart missed a beat. What did he mean? Was he going to speak to Papa again? It was an awful thought; for Papa would fly into one of his rages, and if so, she was sure that Dickie would go away never to return. And this haunting dread remained with her for the rest of the evening.

"What policy, dear?"

"I think I will consider it more fully, and let you know next time I come."

When Richard had cycled away into the night, shortly after eight o'clock that evening, Hetty returned into the warm familiar house and found, as always, in her mother a companionship and reassurance that helped to sustain her thoughts. Sarah was making lace at her pillow; it was mid-week, and Thomas Turney was away in the Eastern Counties. Sarah had more than once suggested to Hetty that she should invite Richard into the house; she had no scruples about Tom's veto in the matter, since she considered it to be unjust, and not according to the Word; but Richard would not go farther than the summer-house.

Sarah had her mother's lace-stool beside her. On it was a candle, and a narrow globe of glass filled with water, on a stick. The globe magnified the flame of the candle upon that part of the pillow on which she was working. Sarah preferred a candle to gas. It was more homely.

"Well, dear, how did you find Dickie?" she enquired. "Was he a little happier this time?"

"I think so, Mamma, now that he is considering a policy."

"A policy, dear? Do you mean he has insured his life? Well, that is a step in the right direction."

"Not that kind of policy, Mamma, but one that concerns our future together." Hetty spoke faster than usual, owing to nervousness.

"Well, dear, I hope this policy will turn out well for you both." The lace bobbins clicked. "Dickie, I feel sure, will do nothing precipitate." Sarah was a little apprehensive, but she waited for Hetty to tell her more.

As Hetty did not speak, her mother went on for awhile.

"Of course Dickie is worried by it all, dear, but he is the worrying kind, I fancy, and plans made on worry are seldom the right ones. All things come to him who waits. That's what I tell your Father, too. He worries that Hughie should be a credit to him, and learn the business of the Firm, so that, as time goes on, Hughie can take more and more off his mind and shoulders. Nobody gets younger, you know, and it won't be long now before he will have to think of doing less, of taking things a little easier. He has worked very hard, and it is largely due to his energy that the Firm has expanded as it has done during the past fifteen years. Mr. Carter, and Mr. Mallard the chairman, are both rather stick-in-the-mud, but both have their sons in the Firm, and now Charley has gone, there is only Hughie to take Papa's place in course of time."

"Yes, Mamma, I am so sorry that Papa is worried about Hughie. If only he would not expect too much at once; for Hughie feels, I think, that Papa is watching him all the while, instead of letting him find his own feet."

"Yes, that is part of the trouble, Hetty, for Papa has not yet realized that his children are growing up. He is so anxious, after all his care and thought for them, that they shall do well for themselves. Ah well, I must not work any more by candlelight, my eyes are not what they were. Now you ought to go to bed, dear, and try not to worry about Dickie. Things will turn out all right, we must trust in the One Above. I will come up and tuck you in and kiss you goodnight, when I come to bed presently. I suppose Hughie will be late again tonight, I do hope he comes to no harm, London is not a very safe place for one so young."

"Well, Mamma dear, I think I shall go to bed, I have a headache."

"Yes, dear, an early night will do you good."

When her daughter had gone to bed, Sarah put aside the lace pillow with a sigh and closed her eyes for a quiet moment, to smooth herself out, as she put it to herself. She would not wait up for Hughie, he was a man now, and for good or ill had his life in his own hands; and she did not want him to think that what he did was subject to too much concern on her part. He was a good boy, and her part must be confined to prayer that he would always do what was right.

Sarah was afraid of London, the London of the Strand and Regent Street where Hughie met some of his old Cambridge friends, the London of the Empire promenade and the cigar and billiard rooms, of the music-halls where the poor dear boy might so easily fall in with bad companions. Sarah was ever afraid that Hughie, who had wanted so much to follow a musical career, but who after a scene with Tom had been put into the Firm—would come to some harm. Once he had arrived home late at night very nearly tipsy; and on another never-to-be-forgotten occasion, he had not come home at all.

She sighed.

Sarah still hoped that Theodora, whom Hughie had met at Cambridge the year before with Hetty, during the inter-college boat-races of May Week, would prove a steady influence in Hughie's life. Once, after the Picnic in Greenwich Park, it had seemed to be turning that way; but so far Theodora had not responded to poor Hughie's almost feverish obsession for her. Sarah admired Theodora: she admired her for her clear, soft voice, her long and delicate fingers, her fine golden hair piled in Greek style on her head, for her calm and candid blue eyes. What a beautiful mother she would make! And Hughie, too, she would guide him along the path of his true nature.

Sarah sighed again.

It was strange how the affections of the heart worked. Hughie and Hetty were so alike; and on the other extreme were Dora and Dickie, also alike, but in a different way. Dickie and Dora had the same beautiful hands and the same eyes, though Dickie's were clouded with inward thoughts while Dora's were bright. That was because she had been brought up by a nanny, who had given her the affection that all young things needed if they were not to become cross-grained in later life. Poor Mrs. Maddison, she had been an invalid then. But maybe Dickie had been born a worrying sort? Would Hetty be happy with him? She could not see that the two young people had very much in common; but you could not always tell.

It was a difficult time, of course, for them both. Even so, life was like that, difficulties were sent to try us. *Could* Hetty be happy with Dickie? They were not at all alike. But that would not matter very much if they truly loved each other. Dickie seemed deeply attached to Hetty, and the dear child was devoted to him. If the woman loved the man, and made his home comfortable, perhaps that was all that really mattered; questions of taste and differences of opinion were after all not the real things of life. A woman's place was to give way to her husband's wishes in all such matters. Ah well, the Lord had us all in the hollow of His hand.

Roland Tofield came before her mind. Now there was a really jolly young man, and perceptive, too, like Hetty. The two had got on very well together. If only Hetty had met him first; perhaps by now she would be happy as the day was long, her old merry self; for Tom could not possibly have raised any objections to such a match. Though Tom was no fool: he attached no undue importance to rank or fashion for their own sake. Country people like themselves were different from the townsfolk who always seemed to be wanting to be above themselves. Mrs. Mallard, for example. She was not really happy.

Resting by the fire, her eyes closed, Sarah recalled the incident near Hyères, and how her darling had entreated her never to mention the proposal she had received from young Roland

Tofield—as though her own mother would think of such a thing!—lest it upset Richard as he sat in his bed-sitting room at night, arranging his moths and butterflies. Mr. Tofield was quite the poet: in a poem which Hetty had shown her, he had spoken of the nightingales "which sing away the perfume of the night", quite a pretty way to describe that wonderful coast of flowers and sun and blue sea, to one who knew it.

It was strange how things happened. Dickie, on his holiday, had heard of the Tofields, so Hetty had told her, or rather of Roland's papa, who had bought some of his own father's land. Well, if Tofield senior were like the son, he would be a good landlord. Oh, Hetty surely would be happy with her Dickie: how happy she had looked, after she had read to her darling one of Dickie's letters: how her eyes had brightened, and her gay spirit returned! No wonder Roland Tofield had wanted her for himself!

And living momentarily in happy memories by the fire, Sarah smiled again to herself. Then as when the mistral blows across from the Parthenopian shore and the acquescent blue of the Mediterranean is discoloured by the wind coming from the ruin of the ancient Roman cornfields, her smiling picture broke unhappily; and she found herself yet once again netted within the dreaded trammel of ordinary life. One was caught in a net of circumstance beyond one's control. One morning she and Hetty had been rowed in a boat upon the blue water, and near the rocks, corks were lying and a net hung down below them. Peering over the side they saw, in the clear depths as flaws in glass, many fish twisting in the trammel, which was of two nets, one with a wide mesh to entangle them while the smaller mesh held them by the gills. There they would remain until the fishermen returned. It had seemed so cruel, and they had never eaten fish again without thinking of the poor things twisting and turning in the trammel, unable to escape.

Ah well, it was no good dozing by the fire, what was to be, would be. All was in the hand of God. With a final prolonged sigh Sarah got out of the chair, put the fire-guard before the hearth, shook out the pillows on the chairs and sofa, and opened the door to let in the light of the hall gas before blowing out the candle. Then she went down into the kitchen for her cup of arrowroot, and a glass of milk for Hetty, saying goodnight to Cook before going upstairs softly to Hetty's bedroom, the door of which was open. The curtains had not been drawn across the window, and peering round the door, unseen and unheard, Sarah saw her child lying in bed with pallid face and dark eyes staring at the moon in the sky.

In the same distracting moonlight Richard was cycling uphill, the lantern secured by cord to his handlebars, the oil of the wick burning but providing no illuminant in the beam projected through the glass lens. The street was almost as light as day, but the more real with its dark shadows. He felt himself to be fully alive, without body. In the quietness of the night, and under the moon, life's reality became sharply apparent. A man could think clearly then.

Now how could he formulate a policy, based not on the heart, but on the head? First, let there be a recapitulation of the situation since he had returned from his holiday, three months ago. What had happened? A dozen times he had cycled to see Hetty, once a week regularly; and a dozen times nothing tangible had come of the journeys. It had always been the same thing on each visit. Nothing had resulted except irresolution. It was all *sub rosa*, even underhand. A dozen times he had made up his mind to bring the situation to a climax, but each time he had been brought to the same dead-end. Hetty's fears had rendered him impotent.

At this point Richard's thoughts took a direction opposed to his previous line: for if Hetty were to agree to stand by him openly, what would happen? It would be a worse situation! For Mr. Turney had the power to report him to the Secretary should he and Hetty defy his authority, and get married. Then he would lose his billet in Doggett's, and be little better than a pauper.

That was a terrible and chilling thought. Oh, what could he do?

Well, a man must on no account allow his feelings to overcome his head. Now then, let the matter be considered with the white logic of the moon:—What were the prospects, should he continue to temporise, in default of any positive policy? He was earning a salary of one hundred and ten pounds per year, with an increment of ten pounds due the following Lady Day. That would be one hundred and twenty pounds per annum. He had eighteen months to go before he would be in a position to earn the minimum salary of one hundred and forty pounds per annum. A year and a half of skulking, eighteen months in which Hetty might change her mind, or be prevailed upon by Mr. Turney to change her mind!

Now he must look at the situation from that standpoint as it behoved one in the banking profession: *for what security had he that a woman would not exercise her well-known prerogative and change her mind?*

Richard's doubts had some basis other than the sense of insecurity which had been with him since his early boyhood, when dread of Father had replaced the former childish delight and admiration, when Father had been the best and most wonderful man in the whole world. Hetty had recently lent Richard a book to read, *Sesame and Lilies*, by Ruskin; and within the leaves of the book, written on a piece of writing paper with an armorial crest embossed upon it in blue, was a poem—a love poem dedicated to Miss Henrietta Turney, and signed Roland Tofield. The poem was entitled *A Vision of Hyères*, dated the third of May, 1893, and one of the lines in the poem was identical with a phrase used in a letter from Mrs. Turney to himself during the past spring, when she had written to him from the south of France. It was in reply to a letter of his, when he had described the nightingales singing in the cemetery below the Hill; and Mrs. Turney had, in her reply, written these words.

> Hetty, dear child, was greatly moved by your beautiful description of the nightingales, and says that I am not to forget to say that whenever she hears one singing away the perfume of the night, it is to you only that her thoughts take wing.

Richard had sought in a book of reference in the Shop and found out that Roland Tofield was the son and heir of the selfsame Sir Roger Tofield, second baronet, member of several West End clubs, a landed proprietor in Surrey, and a director of a number of City companies, who, according to Frank Temperley, had purchased from his Father four of the family farms. The two facts, placed together in Richard's mind, had been a great shock to him.

Thinking of them now, Richard dismounted from the Starley Rover, and leaned upon the saddle, the more squarely to face the situation, as he put it to himself. He sighed deeply. Logic had forsaken him, black fear taken its place. He was standing in the diffused shadow of the western end of the Crystal Palace, an appalling cold mass of glass towering above him, something which in the moonlit night looked like the slough or pellicle of a gigantic and scaled inter-planetary monster, which by way of a story by Jules Verne, had alighted there and found petrifaction in rows of bricks and mortar inhabited by unnaturally living objects, *of which he was one*. It was like a momentary glimpse of the end of the world. For a moment he felt, with a kind of terror, to be entirely unreal, somebody else's ghost lit by a spark of thought: his life was baseless and unreal. He held the frame of the bicycle for support; and then the fancy, passing through his mind in the lunar night, was gone; and in its place returned the fear of losing Hetty.

His unhappy mood was abruptly dispelled by a multiple screaming in the sky. At the same time the pallid shell of the Crystal Palace was scored by rising streaks of golden light; and other coloured lines broke through its glitter and greyness. There were pops and explosions, a raining fire of green and silver. Plumes and cascades of colour filled the sky: there were tigers and bells of light, balls of soft blue descending, flowers opening in darkness with yellow streaks curving up—up—up—far above the glassy towers, and pop—pop—pop—softly the blooms broke and spilled their luminous seeds. Cries of admiration and wonder came from the street, where at open window and from garden gate many faces were looking up. All south London seemed to be watching. More whistling rockets swept up: fountains of fiery rain spilled under the moon; golden trees grew in the sky, making canopy of the night.

Crackling and spluttering, the set-piece revealed behind drifting pale smoke the Lord Mayor's coach and horses, the postillions breaking into controlled outline of flame. In the street a carter cursed as he hung to the heads of his Percheron horses, whose hoofs struck sparks from the cobbled way; a child screamed in terror, its cries muffled in little sister's skirt.

It was the Crystal Palace's final firework display of the season. Often Richard had watched it from the Hill, amidst the long-drawn *Oh's* of wonder from the poorer children seated in groups on the warm summer southern slopes there.

The harvest moon declined; and its ghost rising from out the east of an early morning hung wasted upon the day-sky over the City of London. The darkness of the nights deepened with black death upon the lunar face; and no visits to the garden door. The new moon brought new hope, and a visit to the summerhouse, with the return of *Sesame and Lilies*, its covers carefully enwrapped with an old copy of *The Morning Post*. No word about the poem within.

Then as the hunter's moon rode across the night with its silver spectres and phantoms of the mind Richard began to feel like a man with a spear through his vitals: and when Hetty's birthday came, it passed for her without a letter, or a visit, or any message whatsoever from the one she loved.

Richard spent the early part of the evening of the following day in wild tramping upon the sodden pastures of the Hill, a man divided against himself, longing the more for Hetty's comfort as he felt himself the more unable to creep, a suppliant self-destroying, through the dark door to the summerhouse in the garden of sighs.

Chapter 8

THE SEVEN FIELDS

His upset had been due to a misinterpretation of a sentence in a letter Hetty had sent to him, several days before her birthday. The letter had told him of the party she would have to attend on her birthday night. Several people had been invited, but among the names she gave there was no mention of Theodora.

When he read the list of names, Richard at once wondered why Theodora, whom Hetty had always spoken of as her greatest friend, had been omitted. It was not long before he began to think that this, perhaps, was her way of telling him of her wish to end it all.

This idea he had not believed when it entered his head; but he played with it until it became resident; and the more he considered the figment, the more likely it became. A dozen other conjectures supported it. Had she not written that he was on no account to come if it were wet? But if he did come, would he wait in the summerhouse until she came out to see him? On no account must he throw gravel at her bedroom window, as her room might be used by someone else that night. The post-script seemed to confirm his fears.

> Perhaps after all, dearest, it would be better for us both if you did not come over, as my movements are bound to be uncertain, indeed I might not be able to see you at all.

Yes, she was beginning to cease to care for him. This was the thin edge of the wedge! Try as he might to put the idea of who that someone else was out of his head, and to think rationally (as he urged to himself) the figment gradually became for him a reality. For three nights he slept fitfully, always awakening with a dull, deadly feeling within. The treadmill of the heart, he called it to himself. And out of the dull grinding feeling always the same figment arose, of Hetty smiling by the piano at Roland Tofield.

Indifferent to what happened to him, indeed hoping that he might get pneumonia and so be found, a wasted figure, by Hetty remorseful for her perfidy, he walked many miles around and upon the Hill, down to Pit Vale, up to the Heath, and down by the riverside village of Deptford: to arrive back at his lodgings just after three o'clock in the morning, wet to the small of the back. There was no letter beside his plate at breakfast, a jaded meal of porridge and kipper; and by the time he was seated in the train to London Bridge he was unable to look at the announcements of forthcoming marriages in *The Morning Post*, for he was by then obsessed by the fear that on the previous night Roland Tofield, the honoured guest in Mr. Turney's house for the birthday party, had proposed to her, and been accepted. A score of times Richard had, in imagination, seen himself tossing up a light handful of gravel, from which he had picked the larger pebbles, at the familiar bedroom window: it had opened: the debonair face of Mr. Tofield appeared in silhouette for a moment: the curtains were then pulled across the blind. Ah—ah!

By the time he arrived back at his lodgings, Richard felt that it was only a question of time before he went down with brain fever, his reason gone. He was a doomed man! Eating none of his supper, to Mrs. Cummings's consternation, he left the table with but half a cup of tea inside him, and went out of the house without cap or coat.

"My goodness," said Mrs. Birkitt to Mrs. Cummings later in the evening, "if you ask my opinion, Mrs. C., the Old Man is active again. What a plague some fathers are to their children, to be sure. Aye, and to their poor wives too, the animals. Where has your young man got to this time, back to Surrey? Or running amok on the Hill again?"

"I don't think it can be Surrey, Mrs. B., for he did not take the Starley Rover. On the Hill, I should not be surprised. I do hope he don't do anything desperate. You know what young men are, when crossed in love."

"Oh, that Hill! And after the way those roughs set about him last summer. Well, if you ask my opinion, he's asking for trouble if he goes up there again."

"He can give it, too, if called upon, Mrs. B. Those Indian clubs don't whizz around my second floor back every morning for nothing, you know."

"Ah, I can see your young man is quite the hero to you, Mrs. C."

Which was a fact: for Mrs. Cummings thought the world of her reserved young gentleman.

The hero, walking rapidly and slipping about on the wet grass of the forsaken Hill, noticed in a break in the clouds a jewelled and shining belt trailing from the darkened sky above. Orion's Belt! The rain had ceased; the sky was clearing, a wind from the south revealed other stars. There was Sirius, trembling in colours low above the horizon. The sight had an effect on him as of the sky being cleared of its clouds as he looked at the dog-star seen so often galloping along the sky when he and his brothers and sisters had skated on the Longpond at home. What did he care about Hetty! Let her go, if that was what she was! And in sudden relief from his figment the impulse came to him that he must see Hetty. Perhaps after all he had imagined the worst needlessly!

He hurried back to his lodgings, meeting Mrs. Cummings on the stairs.

"The weather is better, Mrs. Cummings," he said. "Now I think I shall go for a spin on the Rover."

"But you'll change your wet things, surely, first?"

"Oh, I am used to cold water, Mrs. Cummings, it never did me any harm yet."

"But look at your City trousers! Take them off, and let me sponge and press them for you, then they'll be nice and dry by the morning. We can't have you running about and catching your death, you know."

"I think I shall put on my cycling suit, Mrs. Cummings. But I am rather short of time."

"Well, don't let me keep you, Mr. Maddison. Don't forget your hat. Put on that Sherlock Holmes cap of yours, it will keep your ears dry if it rains again. Once you've had earache, you won't want it again, believe me."

Having changed his clothes, he went downstairs to find Mrs. Cummings waiting for him with a cup of cocoa and a slice of his favourite brown bread and butter, with honey spread thick on it. Though impelled to leave without a moment's delay, he sat down in her kitchen and finished the food and drink, while listening with polite attention to her lecture on how he wanted someone to take care of him, as he did not know how to look after himself.

"You will have to find a wife, Mr. Maddison," she said, meaningly.

"Oh well, Mrs. Cummings," he replied, "I do not think that anyone of the opposite sex would give me a moment's thought."

"You want to think more of yourself, Mr. Maddison. There's as good fish in the sea as ever came out, you know."

He did not respond to this lead; and smiling as he got up, thanked her for restoring the inner man, as he put it, and then having affixed his lantern to the forks of the Starley Rover, he started to pedal with all his strength in the direction of Cross Aulton. He felt optimistic again, and even thought of himself as having exchanged a treadmill for a safety bicycle. He would carry Hetty off, like the arab on his faithful steed, before he had said farewell to it, of course. Wildly he rattled down the slope beyond the Crystal Palace.

His mood of exaltation had gone by the time he crept through the garden door, to put his dark lantern on the summer-house table, and then proceeding, with the utmost caution, to pick up gravel, remove any pebbles likely to crack a pane of glass, and toss up an ounce or so in a delicate rattle upon her window.

The reconciliation was as optimistic as the previous mood had been pessimistic; but it did not alter the situation. Stability could only be obtained by taking the fish out of the sea. Hetty gave her promise.

"Mamma and I have been talking things over, dearest, and she is coming over more and more to our side. So do not worry, Dickie."

"Worry? How can I help worrying? Do you not realize that if I marry you now, I shall be in danger of losing my billet at the bank?"

"Yes, dear, I realize that, of course, naturally."

Hetty did not know what else to say: and soon he said he must be getting back.

Sarah wrote a letter to Richard. She wrote in her slanting, spidery hand, not easy to read at the best of times, as Richard said to himself; but in addition she had the old-fashioned habit, dating from the time of the need to make a postal packet as light as possible, in order to save postage, of crossing her lines of writing with later lines. This lack of clarity did not add to Richard's reassurance, for about a third of Mrs. Turney's letter was indecipherable. She would not stand in the way of her dear child's happiness: she asked him to burn her letter as soon as read—"H'm, that may take years, my dear Mrs. Turney," he muttered to himself, locked in the lavatory in the vault, for the sake of privacy—he was not to reply in writing: then there was something about Camberwell.

He would have to go over that very night, and find out what she meant. Why did she use one of the modern thin steel pens? And what was she, a potting-shed spider, making an inky web to trap a fly? No, no, he must not think like that, it was unchivalrous to the old lady who had always shown him such consideration. *Honneur aux dames.* And he returned upstairs to his desk.

Once again the Starley Rover lay hidden in the watery ditch outside the postern door of the garden. It was an easy meeting. The idea was becoming familiar, not so alarming, even rather exciting, especially as he wore his deerstalker cap. Sherlock Holmes would have approved the conspiracy to defeat a selfish and somewhat revolting old man entirely lacking in the instincts of a gentleman.

A week later, with great trepidation spiced with excitement, Sarah and Hetty went up to London by train, ostensibly to shop.

"Oh, I do feel I am a wicked girl, Mamma!"

"You are not wicked in the eyes of God, dear, for God is love."

"But Papa——"

"Man proposes, God disposes, Hetty. Papa is not just to Dickie, that is *his* fault, not yours, dear child."

Hetty's heart beat so loudly in her ears as they entered the dark Register Office in Camberwell that she felt sure the man asking the questions would know she was doing wrong. The worst moment was in giving the name, address, and occupation of Dickie; but to her relief, it was not necessary to mention Doggett's. So it might be any bank clerk, and not Dickie at all. How wonderful when it was all over! She could hardly restrain herself from skipping down the street. They went into a coffee shop which Sarah had known years before, and had a halfpenny bun each, and some cocoa, for there was no coffee now. It was so much altered, Sarah said, with a reminiscent tear in her eye. So many of the good old things were passing away, in the change that had come upon the world. But they found the little sweet shop, where she had bought the sugar mice and toffee-apples years before, and went in, to find the same woman there, a wonderful meeting.

Sarah purchased one dozen pink and one dozen white sugar mice, for the sake of old times.

From Camberwell Green they went by horse-tram to Vauxhall, crossing over the river; and from there they took a cab to Oxford Street, to call in Peter Robinson's shop, to take a look at the latest fashions. Sarah usually dealt with Dickins and Jones, having gone there in the first place as she had felt sure the name of Dickins, her favourite story-teller, was a hall-mark of honesty. That was over twenty years ago now; and she was faithful to that house alone, where haberdashery was concerned. So to "Dee-and-jays" they went, feeling more at home than in Peter Robinson's, and wandered about, with an eye to Hetty's trousseau. Suddenly Hetty said, in an urgent whisper, "But Mamma, whatever are we thinking of? For of course I shall have to continue living at home, after the, you-know, for Dickie's sake. There is his billet at the bank to consider!"

They decided to put off the idea of a trousseau for the moment, and to come up to London another time. Sarah's fear returned. The notice of the intending marriage would have to be displayed at the Register Office, by law, a short while before it could take place; and so there was a risk of someone seeing it and communicating with Tom, whose name and address as the father of Hetty, together with similar details of Dickie's father, were now for all to see!

Sarah reassured herself by thinking that, if Tom *did* find out beforehand, he could not stop it, as Hetty was of age; he could of course turn her out of his house, but Sarah hoped that it would never be necessary, as she put it.

So the marriage was fixed for a Saturday afternoon in early December, when Thomas Turney was away in Algiers with Alfred Carter, one of his partners, for a holiday in the sun, after recovering from bronchitis.

Richard meanwhile had cycled one evening to a place he knew of a few miles south of his lodgings, and arranged to stay with his wife at a gamekeeper's cottage in a lane beside the Seven Fields of Shrofften. It was one of his favourite places of pilgrimage. They would spend the rest of Saturday there, and all Sunday, walking about, and he would show Hetty the pond in a belt of woodland where he had put some roach a year or two previously, where they had thriven, together with some German carp. They would walk in the woods, hear the woodpeckers and the nut-hatches, and the owls by night. Hetty was looking forward greatly to sharing this lovely-sounding place with him. And on the Sunday night she would return to Cross Aulton, and continue living at home until, in her mother's words, "a favourable opportunity to tell Papa should present itself."

The disturbing night before the marriage arrived at last. Richard cycled over to say that all was well: he had the ring, Theodora was coming, and the rooms in the keeper's cottage were engaged. When he had gone, Sarah spoke to Hetty about the duties of a wife to her husband.

"Men's natures are different from those of women, dear," she said, gently, "but there is nothing to be afraid of, especially as Dickie is a gentle man, in both senses of the word. I think it must be love which makes a man tender towards his wife, as are all creatures in nature, I am sure. So do not be afraid, it is after all God's way for the fathering of little children. All the same, dearest, you must both use some discretion in the matter of a family arriving not too soon. But your husband, Hetty, will see to that."

Hetty sat quietly while Mamma gave her the kind little homily, while thinking that it was not really necessary, as Dickie had already given her a book, *What a Young Wife Should Know*, which told you everything, while Dorrie had assured her that there was nothing to worry about.

"Yes, dear," went on Sarah, "we all have to suffer our dear husbands at times, but it is a duty we owe to them, and the first thought of a wife should be the creature comforts of the master of the house, her dear husband." And Sarah laid her hand tenderly upon the back of her daughter's hand.

The momentous day dawned, after a sleepless night for Hetty, Richard and Sarah. In the early afternoon of Saturday five people set out to arrive by devious ways at the meeting place at Camberwell Green. Sarah with her two daughters drove in a four-wheeler from London Bridge Station, and met Richard and Theodora under the trees. It was a fine afternoon. All were determined to behave as though nothing untoward was in the air. After the greetings were over, Richard stepped to the side of Mrs. Turney, and offered his arm; and with the three young women following, they set out for the Register Office. Several times Richard, coming down from Ludgate Hill by the Metropolitan extension of the Chatham and Dover Railway, had felt in his waistcoat pocket to reassure himself that the ring was safe, and as he shortened his step to fit in with Mrs. Turney's, a dreadful thought came to him that, not having been content to let well alone, he might indeed have caused it to roll out of his pocket. Trying to feel it under his coat, with the fingers of his gloved hand, to his sudden dismay he could not feel its hardness against his ribs. But he contained his inner agitation, and spoke of the weather.

Hetty had wanted to wear her butterfly dress, as Richard called it. He had imagined meeting her in it; for when away from her he had pictured her as the Camberwell Beauty, as the prize, as he put it to himself, of his collection. Hetty had divined this; but having little confidence in her own feelings, had accepted what sister Dorrie had said about the etiquette of being married in a new stylish tailor-made costume. The result was a dark blue serge skirt, and a neat short jacket with a rolled-back collar faced with white cloth and fastened with a silver buckle. Hetty wore it with what was called a tailored blouse and a straw boater, the crown of which was encircled by a blue and white ribbon tied in a bow at the left side—one of the very latest styles, purchased from Mrs. Heath's at Hyde Park Corner. It was held on by two long blue-steel hatpins, which transfixed cloth, straw, and hair. Her French silk gloves had the fashionable six buttons, from Pemberthy in Oxford Street; while as for her new underwear, oh dear, she did not fancy it one little bit. Pray that Richard would not see it!

Dorrie had persuaded her that the "Deeandjay" style of combinations were the very thing for the occasion. They had lace at the top of the neck, and again near what Hughie called the pedal extremities, with pink bows of satin in addition, tied below the knees, for both warmth and security. When she had seen herself in the long mirror in Mamma's bedroom Hetty had exclaimed, "Oh dear, I feel like a walking ham," and all had laughed so much that the tears had come into her eyes. Seeing the tears Sarah had motioned Dorrie to hush, lest her darling be upset; for she could see that Hetty was nearly to the point of being overwrought. She was such a good child, and the thought of doing anything without her Papa's sanction was wearing.

As he walked through the streets beside Mrs. Turney, Richard was thinking, If only Hetty and I could have gone straight away, without all the tedious aftermath, to the Seven Fields! And why had she not come simply dressed? He had imagined her in the butterfly gown; now she was like any other young woman of villadom. Mrs. Turney, he supposed, had a right to decide such things, as she had a right to be present at the marriage; but how much easier it would have been if he and Hetty could have been by themselves; though Dora's presence was a help, always.

The next half an hour passed in a kind of unreality. The Registrar, having warned them of the solemnity of the occasion, instructed him to place the ring on Hetty's finger, and thereafter pronounced them man and wife. The certificate was signed. At last they were in the street again, breathing more freely, Hetty walking with her hand on her husband's arm, as they retraced their steps to the Green, to take a cab from the rank there. They all squeezed into the four-wheeler, and were driven over the Thames in the twilight of the calm winter afternoon, seeing the light burning in the Clock Tower of the New Palace of Westminster, indicating that the House of Commons was sitting. Two cormorants flew over as they were crossing Westminster Bridge, and the sight provided an ease of the tension, as Richard explained that the birds might have followed a school of bass coming up with the tide. In a release of feeling Hetty dared to seek his hand, and her warmth comforted him; but in the presence of others he did not like what he considered to be demonstrativeness. If only they could have been alone!

The growler took them up Whitehall. They were just in time to see the tall Life Guards, in scarlet and buckskin, booted and helmeted, leaving their post of duty as sentinels before the office of the Commander-in-Chief of the Army.

Round Trafalgar Square, with its memories for Richard of Bloody Sunday of November 1887, when as a constable specially enrolled, he had been on duty with others in a vedette just off the Strand in Northumberland Avenue. Richard stared out of the cab window, imagining the scene over again. He heard the cries, saw the swaying, bawling mob embattled with the regular police, felt again the emotions of chilling fear and exultation as he watched the fighting, alternately dreading it would not spread to where he was, and then that it would. And the thrilling moment of swelling pride, the involuntary cheering, as the Guards advanced from Whitehall and with bayonets held aslant, pressed through the ragtag-and-bobtails! An evil agitator, John Burns the socialist, and a traitor to his class named Robert Cunninghame-Graham, had been sent to prison for their parts in what might easily have become an insurrection, but for the determination of all good men and true. A red-bearded Irish ruffian named George Bernard Shaw, after making an incendiary speech, had escaped. Ah well, those days of youthful adventure were over, and now he was a sober married man, he supposed. However, he still had his truncheon and white-and-blue cuff band in his lodgings, hanging on the wall, as mementoes of that romantic occasion far away in the past, when he had been but a beardless boy starting his career at Doggetts'.

The cab moved on, and turned into the Haymarket.

Sarah's destination was a Vienna pastrycook's shop in Regent Street, the famous Petrzywalski. There in a few moments they were sitting, and soon Richard began to enjoy the scene. Amidst soft lights, and a string band playing, they sat under chandeliers hanging from the ceiling, watching the elegant and fashionable throng about them. To Hetty it was fairyland; the patisserie and ices and creamy coffee reminded her of Brussels. With a wistful smile she recalled those days of long ago, when she had been with Dorrie, Papa and Mamma. Oh, Papa! Poor Papa! What would he think of her now? What had she done! She was a wicked and ungrateful daughter. She sighed, as she had sighed many times before, whenever the face of Papa had come to mind. Ah well, she must make the best of it. Her duty was now to Dickie. Oh, poor Papa.

Hetty sighed again, with little feelings of terror, when the time came to say goodbye to Mamma and to Dorrie, on the pavement of lighted, fashionable Regent Street. Goodbye, goodbye! Mamma's face smiling, and yet a little sad. The inward cry—Oh, Mamma, Dorrie, Dora, if only we could all go to the Seven Fields together! Then she and Dickie were driving away in a hansom and though she wanted to wave to the others on the pavement, through the little window at the back, she must sit still beside her husband and behave like a wife.

Richard, too, had his own feelings on the matter, judging by the way he sat upright on the seat, almost anxiously, beside her.

He was expecting any moment to be seen by Mr. Turney or perhaps Hugh. Hetty wondered if he was disappointed in her. It was all so strange, so different from what she had imagined. Was she really married? Ah, she would soon be seeing Mamma again! She was not *really* going away for ever! She would see Mamma again the very next night. She felt suddenly happy. But poor Dickie, *his* mother was dead. She must try and make up for it, now she was his wife!

They drove into Charing Cross Station. Richard bought two third class tickets. There was a penny change from a shilling. A bare-footed boy wheedled it from his palm, while thrusting a green evening newspaper by his waistcoat.

With his wife, and a copy of *The Westminster Gazette*, Richard went through the barrier to the train, the safety valve of its engine screeching underneath a great geyser of steam. They got into an empty carriage. A dim blue gas-jet wobbled inside the dirty glass dome in the roof. The carriage stank of stale beer and shag tobacco.

"Well, Hetty, here we are at last."

"Yes, Dickie." She smiled at him from her corner opposite. He had seated her face to the engine, as she was liable to suffer from train-sickness.

"I hope it will keep fine."

"Oh, I am sure that it will, Dickie."

Five minutes later the whistle screamed, the guard waved his green lantern, the train clanked and jerked forward.

"Well, we are off!"

"Yes, Dickie."

Hetty snuggled into her corner, and looked out of the window with expectation. How the Thames gleamed below, and the lights of London made the sky like a bonfire behind the houses!

They stopped at London Bridge. Would anyone get into their carriage? The platform was deserted. Again the whistle, the dancing green light, the jerk forward. Suddenly Hetty found her self pitched on to Richard's knees. He held her steady, and sat her back safely.

The train ran on faster. The tannery smells of Bermondsey, the hops of breweries, came into the carriage. Street lights everywhere were winking under the night.

The train stopped every few minutes; ran on again. The lights outside became fewer, more remote. Then dark fields.

"We are nearly there," said Richard.

The keeper's cottage was some distance from the railway station where they alighted, the only passengers to walk past the ticket collector. They had to go along a footpath under starlight and cross a brook before they came to the beginning of the lane.

When they reached the brook he went first over a plank, and asked her to give him her hand.

"Now come over steadily. Take your time. Mind the obstruction at this end. Step high over it."

She crossed the plank safely, but her skirt caught in the obstruction, and there was a tearing noise.

He was all anxiety. "Now what have you done to yourself? I begged you to go carefully!"

"Yes, dear, but it doesn't matter. I can sew it up when we get in."

"But you cannot arrive 'all taggled and torn', like a gipsy." He put down the two bags he was carrying.

"We should have got married by ourselves, as I wanted to, then we could have arrived by daylight, in more suitable garb. These clothes are quite unsuitable for the country, you know."

"Yes, dear, I thought so, but the others liked them." As though in reply a sudden harsh chattering came from the ground near her feet. She moved in fear beside him.

"What is it, Dickie?"

"A stoat caught in the gin."

"Oh, Dickie, a trap?"

"Yes, that is why I asked you to step high over it. There is a tunnel trap at the end of the plank."

There was a rattling of chain on iron, more chattering. "The poor creature! Who put the trap there?"

"The keeper. Stoats and weasels go down a drain if they come to one, after rats and mice, and the keeper knows it. There is half an old pail nailed to the plank, a gin inside. I expect he gets all the stoats that come this way, as they usually cross a stream dry, if they can."

"Oh, what shall we do, Dickie?"

"I know what we must not do, and that is to interfere with another's affairs." He picked up his hat, and smoothed it with the arm of his frock-coat.

"But the poor thing must be in agony, to cry out like that," she said, clasping her hands tightly.

"Well, try and release it, if you want a bitten finger, and a septic wound."

She made herself say as easily as she could, "Yes, dear, I understand. But cannot we put it out of its misery, perhaps?"

The chattering became more staccato, accompanied by rattling of chain and iron.

"Have you ever tried to kill a stoat? It's a ferocious little beast, hardy as anything alive. We had better come on."

They continued their walk across the field in silence, and went down a quick-set hedge. The glow of London's night-sky could be seen away to the north. They turned south, seeing a light in a cottage in the distance. It was the keeper's cottage, set back from the lane. A dog barked, a voice reproved it.

"Well, here we are. We must clean the mud off our boots."

When this had been done, Richard went down the path, followed by Hetty, and rapped on the door. Hetty, holding the torn end of her skirt in her hand behind her, waited with some apprehension.

The door was opened.

"Good evening," said Richard affably, to the woman. "Here we are at last, Mrs. Kendon. I hope we have not kept you waiting. Mrs. Maddison and I were delayed."

"That's quite all right, sir. Will you please come into the parlour?"

Supper was laid in the small room where sometimes Richard had had tea during his cycling expeditions. A fire burned in the grate, two candles were alight on the chimneypiece. Stuffed birds in glass cases gleamed on the walls. The keeper's wife, who had been in service before her marriage, was quiet and deferential. She brought them boiled eggs and toast, with a pot of tea. There was a cottage loaf, with honey and greengage jam, and a soda-cake on the table. With a smile she asked madam to ring if anything was wanted, and left them alone. Hetty had not spoken to her, as Richard had not made any introductions.

At the beginning of the meal she felt like crying; it was all so strange, so different from what she had imagined. Praying that her feelings would not overcome her, she poured out a cup of tea for him.

He waited for her to fill her own cup, then sipped his own. He spluttered. "Dash it, I have burnt my lips! May I have some more milk?"

"Oh dear, I am so sorry. I quite forgot you liked a lot of milk. Your poor mouth!"

"Oh, it is nothing, my own carelessness."

She saw him biting his lip, and was overcome with shame. No wonder he had not wanted to kiss her, ever since the marriage. And now—she bent her head, and wept.

"Oh come! Please! You are overwrought. Drink your tea, there's a good girl. Well, it is a nice comfortable little room, what do you think?"

"Yes, it's very homely, dear," she replied, in a little voice, and trying to smile. Oh, Mamma, Mamma, are you happy? she cried within herself.

"Feeling a bit lost, eh? You should have come with me cycling, then you would be familiar with the place. It is an oasis, away from the crowd."

"Yes, dear, I wish I could have come with you."

"Well, here we are now, at any rate. They are quite a decent couple, from what I have seen of them. I hope they do not find out that we are just married. Keep your marriage certificate locked in your bag."

Hetty stared at him. "Dickie! I must have left it behind!"

"Oh Lord, now the cat may be out of the bag! Supposing the registrar posts it to Mr. Turney!"

"Oh no, I'm sure he wouldn't!" cried Hetty. "I expect Mamma has it. O, how wickedly careless of me. I must have left it on the table! Pray don't worry."

"How can a fellow help worrying? It comes of all this hole and corner business." He sighed, and turned away from his half-eaten egg. "If they find out at Doggetts', I am a goner."

Hetty went on eating, or trying to eat. She did not know what else to do, or say. But she must say something. "What a dear little room this is, how clever of you to have found it. How did you find it, dear?"

"Oh, I happened to call in one day for a bottle of pop, and stayed talking with the keeper, then I had an excellent tea of boiled eggs for which they charged but fourpence, so I came again. You wait until you see it by daylight. Now what is the matter?"

for he had seen a tear roll down her cheek. "Come, tell me. I shall not eat you."

At the kindly tone Hetty looked at him and said, "Oh Dickie, what have I done! If you lose your post, I will never forgive myself!"

A wooden cuckoo suddenly clicked out of a door in a clock on the wall, called *cuckoo* rapidly seven times, and with a click vanished.

"There you are, he is answering you!" said Richard. "You cuckoo!"

"I feel *sure* that Mamma took the certificate, Dickie."

There came a tap on the door. The keeper's wife entered, and a cat.

"Why, here is my old friend Tibby," said Richard. The grey cat purred round his legs.

"She's no business in here, but she always comes to see Mr. Maddison, ma'm. Is the tea strong enough, sir?"

"Why, yes, Mrs. Kendon, it is so refreshing after the walk across the fields."

Hetty bent over to call the cat, to hide her eyes. "Puss, Puss, I mean, Tibby, Tibby."

"I expect you'll find it very quiet after London, Mrs. Maddison. We are used to it, of course. Are the eggs boiled to your liking? Mr. Maddison likes his soft boiled."

"Yes, my husband does," said Hetty, brightly. "I think I shall want a little more hot water, if I may, please."

"Certainly, ma'm. I'll fetch a jug."

Hetty felt happier. She had not made Dickie to look foolish. The cat was purring on his lap. "Now Tibby," he said gently, "you must get down, like a good cat, for you have been eating a rat, for all I know."

The meal proceeded more easily, the cat purring by the fire, kneading with its paws on the mat made of odd bits of coloured rags. When they had eaten the toast and eggs, both felt better. The table was cleared, and they sat by the fire, watching the flames. The cuckoo popped out again, calling eight times. "Oh, I love him, he is so friendly!" cried Hetty.

"I brought my chessmen," said Richard, presently. "Shall we have a game?" He had tried to teach her chess on the summer-house table, in the lantern-light; but Hetty had not been an apt pupil. She could never get used to the moves, and always tried to save the little pawns from being taken; so was easily checkmated.

"Yes of course dear, I will play if you would like a game."

"You must try and win, this time."

"I will do my best, dear." She yawned, but quickly concealed it behind her hand. She had hardly slept for forty-eight hours.

A minute or two later, as he put the board on the table, Richard said, "Perhaps we should not stay up too late, these people go to bed fairly early, I expect."

"Yes, dear, shall I ask?"

"Mrs. Kendon will be in again before long. Come on, let us have a game, it is not so late, really."

He looked happier as he opened the box of chessmen and drew out the carved ebony and ivory pieces. Carefully he set them out.

"Now, no favours given or taken, mind!" with a warning wag of his finger. "Your move."

It was soon over.

"One more, and mind you beat me this time."

The cat jumped off Richard's lap, and hopped on to Hetty's, after sniffing like a dog at her boots. "Ah, Tibby smells that stoat." With twitching tail, the cat sat on the rug and washed its face.

"What a shame, to turn you down like that! Shall I kiss you in compensation? Or would you prefer Tibby?"

The cat purred by the fire, after settling on its paws.

"I suppose a husband is allowed to kiss his wife, eh?"

"If you like, dear."

"You do not want me to kiss you, perhaps?"

"Yes, of course, dear, naturally," and Hetty blushed.

Once again the black and white chessmen faced one another, pawns and knights, bishops and castles, kings and queens, in formal array. "My move this time."

It was over before long.

The cuckoo bobbed and called again. There was a knock on the door.

"Shall I take up your hot water, sir? And what time do you usually have your early morning tea, ma'm?" She looked at Hetty.

Hetty looked at Richard. "What time do we, Dickie?"

Richard looked at the cat's ears, which were raised to catch all sounds from within and without the room. "Oh, the usual time, you know." He could not think of anything else.

Mrs. Kendon looked from one to the other. "It's Sunday to-morrow, sir, so would eight o'clock suit you?"

"Yes, thank you. This air makes one sleepy."

"Well, I'll leave you to blow out the candles, sir. There will be one in a glass chimney outside, lighted, for you to take up with you. Goodnight, sir, goodnight, madam."

When she had gone Hetty, who had been sitting uneasily on a stool, said, "Oh, Dickie, do you know the whereabouts of the—the convenience?" She blushed.

"It's outside, down the path, at the bottom of the garden. Now if only I had my lantern here with me—— There is a large bed of nettles on one side of the shed, so pray take care."

The keeper in the kitchen had a lighted lanthorn, and all was well.

"Dickie," said Hetty, "I would like to thank you, dear, for lending me this." She gave him the crown piece he had entrusted to her in the summer.

"Oh yes, well, thank you very much."

He put it in his pocket. "My mascot!" He was glad to have it back again.

When Hetty had gone upstairs to undress, Richard sat by the fire, with mixed feelings. Allowing her a quarter of an hour by his watch, he arose to follow her. With almost painful consciousness he put the chessmen carefully back in their box, folded the board, put it back in his bag again, removed his boots, left them to dry well back from the hearth, put on his carpet slippers, opened the top of the window, blew out the candles, closed the door, and with bag in one hand and glass candle-lamp in the other, crept upstairs. He paused before the bedroom door, put down the bag, and tapped on the panel. Hearing her answer, he turned the handle. His mouth had gone dry, why, he did not know, for he felt but the least excitement. Indeed, if anything, he felt a strange reluctance. It was the first time he had entered a woman's bedroom.

Hetty had folded and hidden all her clothes, except her boots, under the bed; and having washed and said her prayers somewhat hurriedly, was lying in the soft depths of a feather mattress, the patchwork quilt drawn up to her chin.

Richard came near to her, and pleased by the face in the candle-light, exclaimed jocularly, "I cannot vouch for the couch!" almost before he realized that he had made a joke.

For a moment Hetty thought he meant the couch downstairs, until he said, "You are looking pretty as a peach, is not that what your brother-in-law calls you?"

"Sidney did once," replied Hetty. "He is ever so nice. I hope you will meet and be friends, soon."

"Oh, I do not make friends, I am afraid. Sidney certainly looks to be a pleasant enough fellow. Now you will not be afraid if I blow out the candle in a moment or two, will you?"

"No, Dickie, of course not."

She wondered what he was going to do. From the comparative security of the bed she watched him through half-closed lids. He unfastened his gladstone bag and took out a canvas roll containing his toothbrush and box of precipitated chalk, a sponge, a nail-brush, a comb; and having set these on the wash-stand, he drew out a long white nightshirt, which he unfolded carefully, and put on a chair.

Having washed, and brushed his teeth, he took the candle and put it on the floor. Then he went down on his hands and knees and looked under the bed. He found what he was looking for, and saw beyond it what appeared to be a bundle of Hetty's clothes. What a strange place to put clothes, he thought, but perhaps there was a reason for it.

He stood up again, and Hetty thought that perhaps it would be proper for her to appear to be going to sleep. She opened her eyes again when he said, "Now the candle is going out, Hetty. Do not be frightened, will you?"

"No, Dickie."

Having looked round the room to fix in his mind the position of the bed and other furniture, with his night attire, Richard snuffed the candle and put the glass cylinder on the chest of drawers. He removed his coat, waistcoat, tie, collar, and shirt; and having folded them he put them on a chair. Then pulling his nightshirt over his head, to conserve warmth, he drew off his woollen combinations, added them to the pile; and folding back his half of the bedclothes, he sat on the edge of the mattress, wrapped the skirt of the long garment around his ankles and feet as was his custom, and got in beside his bride.

Hetty moved over. She had been warming his side of the bed for him.

He settled beside her, released a long sigh, and lay silent. She was aware of his head near her own in the darkness, and then of a distinct smell of Keating's Powder, and with it, a desire to laugh. But pray that she did not laugh! He might think she was laughing at him. But Keating's Powder!

Hetty put her hand over her mouth, and tried to think of anything, *anything* rather than of the ridiculous picture the smell had brought to her. Sunday morning in church, a long sermon, Sidney, Dorrie's husband, beside her, drawing something in the fly-leaf of his prayer book. The sermon had the text, *The wicked flee when no man pursueth*, and Sidney had drawn a flea sitting at a table, knife and fork in hand, a plate of food before him and a pot of beer beside it. She had tried to prevent her giggling from breaking into laughter: but it had happened, to her shame: she could hear the sound of bonnets and silk rustling even now. She held her breath, pressed hard against herself to stop herself from laughing. Oh, oh! *Dickie in the bed when no Papa pursueth!*

"Well," said Richard. "You seem very quiet."

She made an odd little sound, which he took to be fear; he recalled her behaviour over the trapped stoat, and a feeling of incipient scorn passed over him. He moved to put his arm over her breasts, to draw her to himself.

Hetty uttered a gust of laughter. He could hear that it was strained laughter; his slight lust was abated; and he said, "Well, will you not share the joke?"

"Oh, it was nothing in particular, Dickie. I was just thinking how nice it was to be alone together." Why did she now want to cry?

"Both of us alone together at the same time, so that is how it seems, does it?" he said, removing his arm.

"No, dear, of course not. I really was not thinking properly of what I was saying, that is all. O—o—oh!" She opened her mouth, gaped, quivered, and released a sneeze.

"Bless you!" said Richard. "I am afraid it is a little precaution I took last night, Hetty. I sprinkled some powder on my night-shirt when I packed, and perhaps put on too much, thinking it would do for both of us. O—o—oh!" and he sneezed.

"Bless you!" she cried, with relief, for now they were alike. And how very kind of him to think of her like that!

"Well, it is better than running a risk of a disturbed night, Hetty."

"Yes, Dickie, of course."

"Once I stayed in a cottage on Sedgemoor during a bicycling tour, and would you believe it, I spent almost the entire night between looking for fleas in the bed and banging roaches on the floor and walls with the heel of one of my shoes. So you see, once bit, twice shy!"

The ease in his voice made Hetty happy. He was the Dickie who had come to the house with Dora, at the beginning of their romance. But she must be practical, like him.

"I looked very carefully at the sheets, dear, before you came up, as Mamma advised me to do. There were no signs of anything at all, the sheets were fresh. I put a sachet of lavender in while I undressed, it is now under your pillow."

"Well, how considerate of you that was. Whereas I have been more severely practical!" he laughed.

They lay silent side by side. He sighed. She heard him swallowing.

"Now I would like to ask you a question, Hetty."

"Yes, dear?"

"I should have asked you before, I suppose."

She waited.

"Well, here it is. Do you like anyone else?"

"Anyone else, dear? Do you mean any other man?"

"Well—in a way, yes. A poetical young man, shall we say?"

At once she thought of Roland Tofield.

"Why, of course not, dear! I love only you."

He felt her hand beside him, and took it impulsively. Her thigh was warm against his leg. How wonderfully soft she was. He lay still awhile, and then turned to her and felt her cheek with his nose, nuzzling it and nipping the skin with his lips. Thereupon Hetty turned to him, and both lavender and flea-powder were forgotten. She felt that he was her child, for whom she would live, her little boy to whom she would give all of herself, for ever and for ever.

He was restless in her arms. After a while he said, "I feel rather strange, Hetty. I had no sleep last night at all. I am sorry if I seem so dull."

"Oh dearest——"

"I—I—cannot quite realize things yet."

"Dearest Dickie, pray do not worry yourself any more. Just go to sleep, Dickie. Poor Dickie, you've had an anxious time, I know."

He lay still in her arms. He was not happy, she knew. She could feel him thinking. Her lips touched his brow. He was her child, at last.

The next day was fine, and taking sandwiches, they wandered over the Seven Fields of Shrofften beyond the belt of woodland; and descending from those pleasant green slopes intersected with hedges they crossed the turnpike road and came across other fields to the Randisbourne brook.

It was an adventure to follow the stream to its source at Caesar's Well on Reynard's Common, four miles distant. By the deep ponds they sat and ate their sandwiches, drinking spring-water that bubbled out of the gravel, in the shade of ferns and water-cress not yet slain by frosts. Hand in hand they wandered into the woods adjoining the common, and there, lying on a bed of dry skeleton leaves he scooped together under a hazel brake, Richard made love to his wife.

The occasion was memorable in that, as he was kissing her, a woodcock flapped through the bare branches of the nut trees and pitched beside them. They saw its deep-brown liquid eyes, its open beak as it palpitated: then with whirr of mottled dead-leaf wings it was gone, and Richard thought that her eyes were like those of the bird. Their innocent look roused him to overcome her; while to Hetty's instinct, this was the truth; and she clasped him as her babe.

December was a damp month, with the Thames often in flood. In mist and fog the London year drew to its close. Christmas came with Dickie and Hetty still separated, but in the frosty night of the New Year he bicycled to Cross Aulton, to a rendezvous in the summerhouse. He returned to his lodgings as the bells of all the towers and steeples were ringing their multitudinous changes of Grandsire Doubles and Grandsire Trebles, Stedman Caters and Triple Bob; and on the crest of the hill by the Crystal Palace he dismounted to listen to the bells of the City mingling with those of the country—London Surprise Minor, Cambridge Surprise

Maximus, Kent Treble Bob Major—names that came to him from boyhood's memory, of himself a colt among the ringers in the tower of Rookhurst Church.

Thus the year of 1894 began for Richard Maddison. So far the secret of his marriage had been preserved. There was to be another visit to the keeper's cottage when Richard took his annual holiday, in the middle of a week of July while Mr. Turney was away on the road, travelling for the Firm. It was during that time that Hetty conceived of a child; and as the autumn of the year advanced, and it became evident that she was pregnant, Sarah her mother realized that the marriage could no longer be kept from Tom.

The time chosen to tell him was the occasion of the twenty-fifth anniversary of Hetty's birthday; and as the day drew near, there was much concealed emotion in Maybury Lodge: for Hetty was still living under her father's roof.

Part Two

HETTY'S BIRTHDAY PARTY

Chapter 9

A WALK THROUGH THE CITY

THE EIGHT passengers, closely-seated in one of the third-class carriages half way down the train, had already ceased their desultory conversation as the Norwich express of the Great Eastern Railway began to slow up through Bethnal Green, awaiting the signal to enter Liverpool Street Station. It was towards three o'clock of an October afternoon of the year 1894. The weather was fine, the air warm. The windows of the carriage were closed, and the heavy copper foot-warmers of two of the corner passengers had long since been pushed under the seats, unwanted.

The passengers had already taken their bags and packages from the over-head racks; and prepared to resume another phase of their travelling, were waiting for the train to move on. One of them, sitting in a corner seat with his back to the rear of the train, pulled a watch from his waistcoat pocket by means of a heavy gold chain, and pressing a spring that caused the lid over the glass face to slip open, studied it a moment before closing the lid with a snap and dropping the gold hunter into its pocket again. Clearing his throat he said across the carriage to the young man, "We're nine minutes late, Hugh."

Seated with one leg cocked over a knee, the young man addressed continued to look out of the window. He appeared not to have heard. He had taken no part in the talk in the carriage since entering it with his father from Diss station between Norwich and Ipswich.

Thomas Turney had a black leather gladstone bag by his feet, and a rush bag containing a fat Michaelmas goose, already plucked and dressed, on his lap. On his head was a hard black felt hat, with braided brim and crown tapering slightly to the top. He wore a frock-coat of heavy broadcloth, the skirts of which covered his knees. His trousers were of the same material. It was his usual uniform of business when on the road.

By contrast, Hughie, sitting across the carriage (as far away from the Old Man as possible) was dressed in a light grey suit, the jacket being without tails in the modern fashion. Upon his head was a small grey bowler hat, close fitting to the skull, with a smart upcurving brim. He wore a pair of lavender gloves, and held in one hand a walking stick of malacca-cane with a gold band near the handle on which an heraldic crest and the letters H.F.Le T.T. had recently been engraved.

His father leaned in his direction, and said again that the train was nine minutes late. "Did ye hear me, Hugh?"

Hughie thereupon turned his head away from the window, and said gravely, "I beg your pardon, sir, were you addressing me?"

"I said we were nine minutes late—ten by now. The Great Eastern is the worst-run line in the country. Don't buy any shares in it."

The other passengers continued to look down, as though withdrawn into themselves. They were, judging by their dress and demeanour, working-class people, used to doing what they were told, and accepting all circumstances in their living as inevitable. They had, after an initial regard of the two corner passengers, recognized them as belonging to a world and life completely removed from their own. The gold watches and chains, the clothes and manner of the two, showed that.

The train seemed to be waiting an intolerable time for the younger man. After a while he uncrossed his legs, looked across the carriage, and said, "Do you mind if I open the window, sir?"

"I shouldn't do that if I were you, Hugh, we're nearly in now. It's not healthy round here, the air is tainted."

Hughie's face turned paler; his eyes looked very dark in his thin face. He turned away, muttering to himself about the airless carriage. His father apparently had keen hearing, for he said:

"Can't you wait awhile, my boy?"

As no reply was forthcoming, Thomas Turney turned to his immediate neighbour. "When I was a young man, they had cholera in this district. These rookeries of the East End are a hotbed of disease. What's the matter, Hugh, feeling sick? Per'aps it was those oysters at Colchester the night before last." He spoke to his neighbour again. "You can't tell the younger generation anything these days. My son ate six dozen natives at dinner in Colchester—nothing else. Too much of a good thing, by far."

"Go on," murmured the neighbour, simulated incredulity on his face.

Abruptly Hughie got up and wrenching at the broad leather strap, jerked the window out of its slot, pushed it down, and leaned out of the window in an attitude so obvious that the other seven passengers waited for him to be sick.

They waited for half a minute; for a minute. There was no sudden lowering of the grey-hatted head; no sudden hunch of the narrow shoulders; no muffled cry followed by splattering noises below. Instead a mixture of smells entered the carriage from the factories, streets, and human tenements beside the railway tracks. There was no wind eddying among the buildings which stood, grim and grimy with acid-rotting brick and tile, in irregular rows and clusters almost entirely devoid of design and colour. Coal smoke from a thousand chimney pots of all shapes and sizes, many leaning at the tops of cracked stacks, rose straight into the misty air. Some of the broken windows of the houses were stuffed with bits of sacking and paper; others were partly filled-in with wooden boards. The rays of the sun setting unseen beyond the sooted edifice of the railway station and refracted through particles of coal smoke and dust of metal and cloth and paper had a purple pallor, for the human scene had power to vitiate its authentic solar beams.

"'E'll feel better when e's shot 'is bundle," remarked the man to whom the details of the oysters had been imparted. "Meself, I don't trust to no shell-fish." He spat sympathetically on the floor. Thomas Turney thereupon took a cigar from a leather case carried in an inside pocket, clipped one end with a gold clipper, put it in his mouth, and lit it from a lucifer match which he struck on the heel of his boot.

Hughie leaning out of the window felt the scene before him to be at one with his own desperate fears. He did not feel physically sick. He had opened the window to escape not so much from the intolerable propinquity of the Old Man, as from his own thoughts, which had made his stomach feel as though drawn into a hard knot, while his throat had gone dry, the palms of his hands became clammy and cold. His eyes shut, he tried to control his thoughts.

The train moved on.

Taking the cigar from his mouth, which he had lit in order to fumigate the air against possible infection, Thomas Turney called out to his son still leaning out of the window that he ought to sit down, lest he hit his head on an obstruction; but the advice was unheeded. Only when he was poked in the back by the point of a rolled umbrella did Hughie withdraw from the open window and stand with his back to his travelling companions.

The carriage became dark. The noise of steam increased as slowly the train moved beside platforms, whereon bewhiskered porters waited to take bags, some springing on the running-boards and thrusting their heads in the carriages, crying, "Porter, sir? Porter?" in the hope of collecting twopenny tips. The station was gloomy; soot had almost entirely obscured the glass roof overhead.

"There'll be a fog tonight," said Thomas Turney, grasping the rush bag the firmer in his hand.

Rows of horse-drawn cabs waited on the sett-stoned way beside the flag-stones of the platform. Beyond stood the 'buses with their distinctive colours—green to Bayswater, brown of the London Road Car Company to West Kensington, the yellow and chocolate of the Old Ford 'bus, the green Paragon 'bus to London Bridge. Mingling with sulphurous whiffs of smoke were the odours of horse-dung and urine. Flocks of sparrows squabbled on the girders overhead, and among the feet of the horses. Almost as numerous as the sparrows seeking food among the horse-droppings in the street, and nearly as active, were the ragged boys of all sizes who sought pennies from the travellers for carrying their bags. The boys were generally thin and pale, with close-cropped heads, and without boots, shoes, or stockings. All of them wore clothes that did not fit them, for the reason that the coats, jackets, and trousers carried on their white and bony frames had been discarded as worn out by their elders. The normal adult lengths of sleeves and trousers were no obstacle to movement on shorter limbs, for as they had been worn by many children in descending order of size so the extremities had rotted off.

"We'll walk," said Thomas Turney, to Hughie beside him. "And get the benefit of the fine weather while it lasts. Carry the rush bag, will ye, Hugh? Walking will do you good."

Hughie made no reply. He followed his father through the barrier, raising his hand carrying the malacca cane to acknowledge the salute of the porter taking the tickets. The figure of Thomas Turney was well-known along the Great Eastern Line.

"It's a fine afternoon, Hughie, so what say to walking to London Bridge?" repeated Thomas Turney, as the two went up a slope to the street outside the station.

Hughie still made no reply, but continued to walk near the curb, the rush bag in his left hand, while swinging the cane with the other. Father and son reached the street before the station.

As they stood on the curb, waiting for a break in the traffic of cabs, drays, and omnibuses in order to cross the street, a ragged unshaven man with broken boots from which his toes protruded seemed to flutter from out of a wall as drab as himself and in a hoarse voice pleaded to be allowed to carry their bags. Thomas Turney ignored him, beyond a brusque shake of the head.

"Come on, guv'nor," wheedled the fellow, in a hoarse voice. "Gi' us yer bag, sir! I got a sick wife and starvin' kids at 'ome, they 'aven't 'ad a bit o' grub for two days, s'elp me bob." Receiving no response he continued more hoarsely, "Gi' us a chanst, guv'nor! I'll carry yer bags s'arv'r river if yer like, and won't arst yer nothin'. Just gi' me what yer fancies, guv'nor! I aint arstin' nothin', I'll take just what yer gives me, straight I will. I can't get no work, guv'nor, and me little 'ns are cryin' wiv' 'unger."

Brewers' drays and other wagons drawn by heavy-draught horses of chestnut, grey, and bay colours were moving past among the four-wheelers and hansom cabs. A continuous clattering of iron shoes on granite sett-stones filled the air. Behind nearly every cab a boy or boys were running, in the hope of a copper or two when at the vehicles' destinations they would open doors and if lucky be allowed to help with baggage. Here and there a policeman in tall blue helmet and cape concealing the truncheon hanging from black leather belt round waist kept an eye on men and vehicles. Young women with shapeless hats which had seen better days on less unfortunate heads were standing in the gutters, offering posies of flowers. Their faces were a dirty white, their eyes generally blank, they looked many years older owing to semi-starvation, prostitution, and other circumstances of being alive.

As father and son waited to cross, the ragged fellow continued desperately his plea to be allowed to carry the bags.

"Gi' us a chanst, guv'nor! I'm no beggar, I'd work if I could get it, guv'nor. I'll take what you gimme, guv'nor!"

"All right," said Thomas Turney, puffing his cigar. An amused expression had come over his face. "That's a bargain, mind!"

"Gor bless you, sir!" and the dirty hand seized the gladstone bag, while a sigh escaped from between rotten teeth.

"Give 'im your bag, Hugh." To the fellow, "You walk in front, and don't go too fast. D'ye know London Bridge Station?"

"Yus, guv'nor! Trust me, guv'nor!"

They crossed to Old Broad Street, walking under buildings which became taller as they proceeded towards the south-west, following the fellow flapping along on his boots worn to the uppers. He turned now and again like a happy dog to see if his master were following.

"I thought we'd go into Pimms in the Poultry and get a glass of brandy for you, Hugh. But we'll have to keep an eye on the bags, these fellows are all thieves if you give 'em half a chance. So we'll take 'em in with us, and he can wait outside. A noggin of good cognac will settle your stomach, my boy."

"I don't take spirits any more, sir."

"A sensible decision, my boy. However, taken medicinally, brandy is an excellent purifier of the stomach. It will settle any contamination in those natives you ate the other night at Colchester. A glass o' brandy is the very thing to put you right."

To this advice Hughie did not respond. Gripping his cane the more tightly, he walked as near the curb as possible, seemingly indifferent to the cab wheels which at times appeared almost to touch him as he stepped out suddenly to avoid someone coming towards him on the paved side-walk. Every standard of a gas-lamp he passed he touched with the cane. Behind him but keeping to the middle of the side-walk came his father, thinking to himself that Hugh had inherited his mother's weak stomach; and her lack of business instinct. He had seen all during the week that Hugh had not made a good impression on the customers he had introduced him to in the Eastern Counties. The boy would have to alter considerably if he was to do any good as a traveller. He had the wrong ideas; violin playing and musical taste was all very well in its place, like literature it was a good walking stick, but a bad crutch. Perhaps it was a mistake to have sent him to Cambridge University: it had given him the ideas of a *dilettante*, of no use whatsoever to a business career. He himself had had to work hard ever since thirteen years of age, learning the only way, by trial and error; and it had made him what he was, partner in Mallard, Carter and Turney, Limited, law-stationers, printers, and lithographers, of 20-24 Sparhawk Street, off High Holborn.

The walk past the Royal Exchange to London Bridge was one of Thomas Turney's favourite walks. He loved London, equally with the countryside where he had been born and bred, fifty miles or so north of the City. He enjoyed walking for exercise, as well as for the interesting things he saw. Entirely without introspection, which he dismissed in others as a defect of character, confusing it with rumination, he accepted the world as it was. To him, black was black and white was white; work was work and idleness was idleness. The test was money, in the sense that money was the token of value, of production, of something achieved. Gambling, no—whether on 'change, horse-racing, or cards. That was not the proper use to put money. And as for value for money—only the best was good enough. That had made England's name and fame abroad; that had made the strength of Great Britain, under the greatest Queen in history, God bless her. And pushing his hard felt hat more firmly on his head, Thomas Turney walked on, puffing at his cigar and looking about him with satisfaction.

The three men were now approaching the Royal Exchange where the power of the London Thomas Turney loved was made visible in the broadening of the street with its hundreds upon hundreds of vehicles of all sorts and sizes, its wide paved side-walks trodden by thousands of men like himself all intent on business which was the stability of the work which made the nation's greatness. Here were silk hats and frock-coats of bankers and brokers, the uniforms of messengers and porters, here were the solid forms and red faces of the successful, the assured, the solid middle class which bore the burdens of the majority. Over the way was the dark and extensive building of the Bank of England, built like a fortress and looking like one—in its vaults the stored gold bars which was the life-blood of commerce. Threadneedle Street and its Old Lady: Buckingham Palace and the Old Queen—they were one and the same institution. Lombard Street, Poultry, Fenchurch Street, Gracechurch Street, Mincing Lane and its tea and sugar, Mark Lane and its corn—what romance were in those names and markets! Why had no poet since Shakespeare ever understood or written of the reality of the life lived by those who understood those places, those trades and crafts? The poet of the age was—Tennyson, fellow of drawing room and deer park, a mere maker of pretty rhymes and romantic nonsense!

Thomas Turney's thoughts inevitably passed from Tennyson

to his younger daughter, for whose birthday supper that evening the goose had been bought in Diss market that morning. For Hetty's favourite author was Tennyson; and despite his own disregard for the cadaverous fellow, Thomas Turney had been keeping for her, packed up at home, a morocco-bound collected edition of his works, bought through the trade wholesale, of course. Hardly the stuff to put on the shelf beside his own duodecimo set of Shakespeare's plays and poems, but no doubt she would in time come to that poet who alone expressed the comprehensive and diverse spirit of England. Shakespeare's characters were real people, and no modern nonsense about all being equal—Pistol being born equal with Henry the Fifth!—that fellow in front, the type of Pistol, equal with Bessemer, Rhodes, Barney Barnato, or anyone else who had got on entirely by his own efforts! Well, he would read him a lesson! Pistol's word and Harry of England's word were of an equal bond—well, let it wait to be seen at London Bridge!—all men being equal, according to that flibbertigibbet son of his, looking about him, or *not* looking about him, as though he were a lost soul. What was the matter with Hugh? He had been self-withdrawn, almost taciturn, during the entire week. A glass of brandy would put him right. They must cross to Pimm's in the Poultry.

"Have I ever pointed out to you the Mansion House, where the Lord Mayor resides during his year of office, my boy?"

"Not that I can recall to mind, sir," said Hughie, groaning to himself with impatience when the Old Man went on:

"If the Bank of England can be said to be the muscle of the country, and working men the bone, the Mansion House is the real mind, or policy."

"Quite an anatomical locality, sir," said Hughie, and made as though to raise his hat to an audience of unseen undergraduate friends. To himself he muttered, "And I'm the skeleton at the feast."

"Hey, what say? Now you know this place, don't you? The Royal Exchange. The motto up there expresses it all in a nutshell —'The earth is the Lord's and the fulness thereof'. I'd like to take you to see over it inside, but time is short, and that fellow might clear off with the bags. Take a glance at the group up there, above those Corinthian columns. That's Commerce, in the centre, holding the charter in her hand; on the right are the Lord Mayor and Aldermen, and the other figures are Greek, Turk, Arab, Chinese, Persian, Negro, et cetera, all the inhabitants of the countries we trade with. You should make yourself acquainted with all that appertains to the City, m'boy, since you are to inherit, one day, most of my debenture shares in Em, Cee, and Tee."

"Have we ever traded with Negroes, sir?" asked Hughie. "When? Before Wilberforce? When was this extraordinary erection built? Who erected it, sir? And why?"

"One question at a time, my boy. This was built just fifty years ago, in eighteen forty-four. Before my time, he-he."

"At that time Negroes were surely articles of trade, rather than traders, sir?"

"What say? There's too much noise going on. Speak up, my boy. There's a fine gilded grasshopper on the campanile inside—Gresham the founder's crest. He was an Elizabethan, the golden age, when men said what they meant, and did what they said."

"But I thought you said the edifice was erected in 'forty-four, sir?"

"So I did, Hugh. But the founder was Gresham, in Elizabeth's reign. It was rebuilt, I said, in 'forty-four."

"Who rebuilt it, sir, in 'forty-four?"

"Someone called Tite."

"Tight, was he?" exclaimed Hughie. "Well, that explains it all, of course." He pulled out his watch, and seeing the time, exclaimed "Good God!" Then to his father, "I'll see you later, sir!"

"Wait a moment, Hugh, don't interrupt me! I was going to say that we must make a call at Birch's in Cornhill, for a box of confectionery for your sister's party tonight. It's the oldest shop in London, and your great-grandfather married—Hi! Hughie! My boy!" for Hughie was about to jump into a hansom he had hailed before the Royal Exchange.

The ragged fellow carrying the bags stopped and stared at the unexpected sight of the old toff running, with rolled umbrella raised, towards the cab. He wondered if he ought to nab the youngster, who might be clearing out of it with some of the old toff's rhino. But chronic lack of food had exposed his nerves to chronic fear and hesitation, and to sudden flaring rages and verbal violence which was but the substitute of the will to action. Crying, "Drive on! Drive on!" Hughie got away in the black and clattering stream of cabs and growlers going westward, through the agitated pool of traffic, leaving his father staring after him beside the ragged fellow.

"Blime!" remarked that individual hoarsely. "Done a bunk, 'as Ooie."

"The young fool," remarked Thomas Turney to himself. Obviously it was a woman. Why didn't he say so? Boys would be boys; but if only boys had the sense to trust to the advice of their elders, instead of thinking that they had never been young like themselves, with the same situations and feelings to deal with, they would save themselves a deal of trouble. And with such tolerant thoughts, he prepared to cross the wide asphalt-laid space before the Royal Exchange, with its clattering wheeled streams flowing to and from the streets called Cheapside and Wallbrook, Lombard and King William, Princes, Cornhill, Victoria and St. Stephens.

One of the streets was a canyon of fire. Hughie's cab, entering the canyon, remained dark a few moments before dwindling as though its flashing wheels, its roof and driver sitting behind and above were melting, were being consumed in the radiant rusty fume that dissolved all movement together with the faces of the buildings rising above it. Shielding his eyes with his hand, Thomas Turney watched it disappear, then he glanced beyond to where the cross set upon the great leaden dome of St. Paul's was a burnished gold in the low rays of the setting sun.

As he waited for an interval in the traffic to cross Cornhill on his way to King William Street and London Bridge, Thomas Turney saw a splendid carriage approaching, driven by a coachman wearing a tall beaver hat and fawn coaching coat of west of England cloth reaching to his ankles. Beside him on the box seat sat a groom with silk cockaded hat and folded arms; while behind sat two footmen, also in livery, looking straight in front of them. As the carriage came into the wide pool before the Royal Exchange, he saw that a mounted policeman was holding up some of the east-moving traffic, for the carriage to pass unchecked. Horses were being reined back everywhere. People on the sidewalks were peering to see inside the carriage; there was a lady sitting there, but she kept herself well back. Thinking that he recognized a face associated with the Prince of Wales, Thomas Turney on an impulse of grim humour removed the cigar from his mouth, and moving forward in the space of the cleared traffic, raised his hat and bowed slightly. The lady saw him, started perceptibly, and recovering, inclined her head.

The carriage rolled away on its rubber tyres; and with the ragged fellow beside him, glancing with interest at his face, Thomas Turney crossed the road in the curious press of pedestrians beside him and continued his way with an expression of amusement on his face. It was not the first time that he had used his facial resemblance to the Prince of Wales in order to create a momentary speculation in the eys of idlers and passersby.

Some years previously, crossing the Channel from Calais with his wife Sarah and younger daughter Hetty, it had so happened that the packet had arrived about the same time as a ship of the Royal Navy carrying the Royal Personage, travelling *incognito* as the Duke of Cornwall with his suite, among them his well-remarked *belle amie*. At Dover bunting was displayed about the quay, and Thomas Turney, hurrying off the packet ahead of his wife and daughter left with the luggage, to secure corner seats in the train, one particularly with its back to the engine for Hetty (who had suffered badly from *mal-de-mer*) had walked alone, wearing brown bowler and fawn coat and carrying a heavy yellow walking stick of lemon-wood, between the lines of spectators, who had buzzed and quizzed and finally broken out into half-hearted, uncertain cheering. Whereupon Thomas Turney had raised his hat, still smoking his long cigar, and with hat repeatedly lifted to left and to right, had gravely acknowledged those cheers. His children knew the tale by heart, oft-repeated as it had been, with many chuckles as he sat at table with them. His son Hugh, home for the holidays from his boarding school, had had the idea, secret to himself, that there might be royal blood in his father's veins, by one of the various mistresses of a previous Duke of York, well-known for his favours to the ladies. Later, as a joke, he had confided this idea to his mother. Hush, Hughie, hush! Sarah had pretended to be shocked.

The ragged fellow with the bags, from what he had seen of the lady inside the coach and the upheld hat of the toff, had conceived an idea that he was carrying the bags of somebody real classy, a proper toff who wanted to walk about disguised for a hobby. There was class in the young gent who had hopped it with the ansom keb. Blime, the old gent might be good for 'alf a jimmy o' goblin, or at least a crown!

Thomas Turney's imagination did not extend to knowing what the ragged fellow felt or thought. He had neither believed nor disbelieved what he had said about a wife and children; he disregarded such familiar utterances from what he thought of, always briefly, as the lowest of the low—a term of accepted and settled condemnation of those in the unskilled labour market.

His cigar by now half-smoked, Thomas Turney passed the Monument on his left hand, and glanced up the stone column to the ball of brassy flames at the top, marking the site of the outbreak of the great Fire of London. The Monument recalled the fish market, and one of his favourite dishes, smoked eels from Holland; but it was too late to go down Fish Street now. Then he thought of Hughie and his silly action, and was troubled momentarily lest his son should not arrive home in time for the birthday party. But Hughie and Hetty were devoted to one another, and so the boy was sure to be home by eight o'clock.

The two men, separated by less than half a dozen paces, were now walking among scores of thousands of other drab-coated city workers upon the paving stones of London Bridge, all walking southwards across the Thames to the railway stations on the other bank. The great majority were men, most of them wearing tall silk hats which rippled away into the purpurate distance like so many smoke-blacked chimney pots carried on a tide. Indeed, it was a tide, with movements almost as rhythmic as those of the estuarial ebbings and flowings of London river rushing and wimpling between the piers at the bases of the arches bearing the bridge. The human tide of business men flowed northward in the morning beginning between the hours of seven and eight o'clock and swelling to the flood shortly after half past eight. It began to lessen a few minutes before nine o'clock; and was slack long before the hour of ten.

Then between five and six in the afternoon and early evening the scores of thousands would return again, weary after the pressure of the day's routine which occluded most of the natural daylight in office and counting-house lit by gas-jet and candle except in the months before and after the summer solstice. The flagstones were worn by the passing of leather iron-tipped at toe and heel; the pillars supporting the arches of massive masonry vibrated upon the oak piles and tods of wool driven and pressed deep into the clay and shingle of the ulterior river-bed. But if the human traffic flowed and ebbed as a tide, the wheeled traffic upon the centre of the bridge seldom ceased in volume, although it changed by day and again at night. Simultaneously with the human pressure upon paving stones the coloured omnibuses clattered and shook over the uneven setts of granite, while the better sprung and lighter rubber-tyred cabs in the traffic-lane of the middle of the road swung by on their elliptical springs; and as these diminished with the morning flow and evening ebb of business men, the heavier drays and warehouse wagons rolled by on their massive wheels, drawn by draught horses each weighing to within a hundredweight or two of a ton. Late at night and very early in the darkness before dawn market wagons predominated, bringing vegetables to Covent Garden from the fields beyond the rows of shops and houses surrounding the misty length of the Old Kent Road.

Many a time during the darkness of early spring and summer and autumn Thomas Turney had crossed the Bridge, after working late at his office in Sparhawk Street. He loved the sight of the river, which he had first seen as a boy of thirteen apprenticed to a firm of Law Stationers with warehouses in Lower Thames Street across the Bridge. After forty years the scene still held a romantic aspect; he rejoiced in the movement and weight of trade that passed in and out of London by its oldest bridge, whose history went back beyond Roman times. He felt himself to be part of an historic flux which had built, and was ever maintaining, the greatest city and port in the world. The sight of shipping in the Pool eastwards of the Bridge, the masts and rigging of sailing ships and the funnels of tugs and small steam-craft always exhilarated him. Usually he walked that way when returning home on Friday evening and sometimes on a Saturday in the early afternoon, after his week's work of visiting customers in what he called his territory. Every return home was keenly anticipated; as every departure early on Monday morning was an adventure directed towards the creation of new business and the pleasure of seeing again, after a month's interval or so, the faces of his customers and those of the proprietors and waiters in the commercial hotels and coffee houses of the country towns where he rested after the day's business, dining among other travellers like himself whose faces he knew well, if not their names, and who invariably addressed one another as Sir.

The river was lapsing with the ebb-tide; red and green and white lights shone on the darkening shipping moored and moving below; the wharves were garish with oil-flare and gas-jet. The halves of the Tower Bridge were raised for a Dutch steamer to pass away on the tide. A distended livid moon was rising beyond Gravesend and the estuary widening to the Nore and the German Ocean. A steam police-pinnace went swiftly with the tide, passing two Greenwich barges whose brown sails were filled with the breeze which had sprung up with the turn of the tide. The sun had gone down, and westwards the river gleamed with streaks of yellow and amber light. Hoots and whistles from river-craft resounded over the water.

The homeward press of unspeaking men and boys bobbing down Duke Street beyond the bridge was in the main making for the higher and lower levels of the two railway stations, wherefrom local trains stopped at suburban platforms which had stood until a few years back among green fields and wooded hills, and now were enclosed in row upon row of houses extending, as the expansive years followed one another, into the counties of Kent and Surrey.

Under the clock on the wall of London Bridge Station Thomas Turney, taking a final puff at the stub of his cigar, faced the ragged fellow who, after putting down the bags of rush and leather, snatched off a filthy cap and fixed his eyes expectantly on the toff's face.

"'ere y'are guv'nor, all safe an' sound." He wiped his hands down the seams of his trousers, for the incidents on the walk from Liverpool Street Station had given him a slight feeling of self-respect.

Thomas Turney took the stub of the cigar from his mouth, and held it out to be taken by the ragged fellow, whose eyes, permanently hard and seemingly the darker for a fixity of thought, stared blankly at his face.

The prosperous man took the black and bitter glance fully upon himself for a moment, and misinterpreting it as something hostile began to feel his anger rising. In the features before him he saw brutality and callousness, evil and negation: he saw a rotted mind that if not held in check would steal, commit rape and even murder. A Botany Bay fellow! He saw a threat to his own security in that look, parasitism of the worst sort, a whining, treacherous ill-condition that would ruin all that honest endeavour could build up by hard work in a competitive world. A rick-burning fellow! Charity merely made such a condition chronic. What was a bargain to Pistol? His word was worthless—he hadn't a word. Well, now he would have to learn to respect a bargain sought and made by himself.

"What's the gaime, guv'nor?" the hoarse voice demanded.

"You said you'd take whatever I liked to give you, didn't you? Well, I am giving you the end o' my cigar!"

The destitute man's mouth dropped open. He sniffed loudly, drawing a finger across his nose and wiping it on his trousers. Thomas Turney faced him with a grim smile. He was deliberating whether or no to give the fellow a sixpenny piece, after the lesson had gone home. But the next act of the fellow stopped any such thought and intention. A cold fury of oaths and obscenity was directed upon Thomas Turney. A man of quick and violent temper on occasion, the insults brought an angry red to his neck and face.

"Get you gone, you ruffian, or I'll give you in charge! You'll get no more from me now! And let this teach you not to pester people in future, but to seek honest work! D'ye hear what I say, eh?"

Several people had hesitated in their hurrying to the platform barriers, and were lingering out of curiosity. Among them was a tall bearded young man of anxious demeanour, wearing a frock coat and black silk hat—but recognizing the face of Mr. Turney, he turned away abruptly, and made as though to be leaving the station. He carried a bunch of roses in one hand. A rolled umbrella hung on the crook of his arm.

Richard Maddison checked his pace as he entered a concealing archway, in time to see the ragged fellow hurl the cigar-stub at Mr. Turney's feet before turning round at the approach of the railway constable and flapping through the arch. He passed Richard peering round the coign of the wall, watching Mr. Turney.

That individual breathing the faster through widened nostrils, picked up his bags, and went to the barrier, which he passed through to the respectful nod of the ticket-collector, who regularly received from Mr. Turney at Christmas a little leather-bound diary, with the Firm's compliments and name printed on the cover in gilt letters.

Chapter 10

AT MAYBURY LODGE

HEARING FROM the basement kitchen the beat of hooves on the gravel sweep, Polly the maid left the sink where she was peeling potatoes, snatched a drying-up cloth and rapidly wiped over her coarse red hands, then springing up the stairs to the ground floor she gave a rap on the sitting-room door, opened it and called out, "Master's come, ma'm!" and went to stand by the hall door, ready to open it the moment the bell-pull set the bell jangling in the basement below.

Polly was a country girl of sixteen years, but she looked as though she might have been any age up to thirty, with her red hands and shiny red face, her thick ankles and limbs and mass of dark hair done up in a nondescript bundle behind her sturdy neck. Two years before she had come to live with the Turneys to better herself; her father, a labourer, had worked all his life on one of the farms occupied by the many Turney brothers and cousins. So she knew the family well, was happy in her work, and received fourteen pounds a year. She liked her mistress, and adored Miss Hetty, the younger daughter of Mr. Turney. Who didn't, indeed?

Hearing the carriage in the drive, Hetty ran out of the sitting-room and stood beside Polly. "Oh Polly," she whispered, while the gas-jet in the white opaque globe on the ornate lacquered brass bracket flickered yellow-blue by the pitch-pine post at the bottom of the stairs.

"Be easy with yourself, Miss Hetty! It's going to be a lovely party for your very own birthday, Miss Hetty!"

Hetty had been sitting beside her mother learning the art of lace-making on the pillow set with pins and hung with bobbins in the sitting-room for the past hour, waiting for Papa and Hughie to come home. All the morning and afternoon they had been getting the rooms ready for the guests. When about two o'clock upon the front door had sounded an imperative double knock, followed immediately afterwards by two more knocks resounding throughout the two-storied house, Hetty and her mother had clasped each other by the linen cupboard on the second landing where they were in the act of taking out sheets and pillow slips, kept there among little bags of lavender, for the second spare bedroom; and running to the front of the house, Hetty had peered down from an upper window and seen the blue and red peaked cap of a telegraph boy below on the hearth-stoned steps, and his new safety bicycle leaning against the chestnut tree by the gate. A telegram, Mamma! Oh Hetty dear, whatever can have happened? No, Dickie would not send a telegram here, do not worry, dear child. Perhaps Joey at school had got pneumonia after his cold, or something had happened to Charley's ship as he was crossing the ocean to South Africa—the dear boy should never have gone so far away—or Dorothy and Sidney were not coming, after all, not daring to trust their two babies to anyone since their servant-girl had left with such threats—perhaps Hughie——

"Yes Mamma, open it, dear Mamma, pray open it quickly, Mamma!"

Soon mother and daughter were laughing together for having done all that worrying for nothing; for the telegram had said ARRIVING 5.54 TONIGHT WITH GOOSE AND HUGH HAVE OVEN HOT HAPPY RETURNS HETTY LOVE TOM. They read the message many times, before setting it up by one of the ebony elephants on the mantelpiece flanking the ormolu clock. Then Hetty had gone down to the kitchen, to tell Cookie the news that Papa was bringing a goose from Norfolk. Cook replied that if the company ate half of what was being prepared, they wouldn't want no more food until Christmas. For beside the usual Friday night saddle of South Down mutton, Papa's favourite joint, there was a Porterhouse steak, a Bradenham ham to be studded with cloves and baked with a coating of Demerara sugar, two cold roast pheasants, pigeons to be stewed with pears (another special dish of Papa's, first appreciated in Brussels), a large Melton Mowbray veal-and-ham pie, and of course Papa's favourite scallops baked in their shells after the soup and before the broiled turbot. Then there were the subsidiary dishes of devilled kidneys, fried oysters (Papa had first eaten these in Canada, where he had taken Hetty two years previously, to visit Charley who had been working on a prairie farm) and fried mushrooms, with ortolans taken in horse-hair springes on the downs above Brighton.

Now Cookie was resting in her room at the top of the house, next to Polly's dark cubicle which she shared, judging by the noise, with several families of sparrows just over the coving ceiling. And Jim the gardener had brought back Papa and Hughie from the station, there was Jim's voice speaking to Bogey, who was fresh from lack of exercise, and Papa's footfalls on the five steps leading to the front door. Wait, Polly, let him ring the bell first!

Hetty had trepidant memories of the time when brother Charley had pulled the door open just as Papa was rattling the letter-box with his fingers, to save wear-and-tear on the bell-pull since he had heard voices of children behind the door. Alas, Charley on that occasion had pulled the door open so enthusiastically that Papa had been pulled with it, and how he had stormed and blamed poor Mamma for not managing her staff properly, that the children had to open the front door when anyone came! Oh, pray that Papa was in a good mood for tonight!

The wire on its complicated system of metal arcs fixed on pivots by the door-post and rising thence to the ceiling and round various corners to the kitchen in the basement, was alive. So were half a dozen metal semi-circles on the pivots. Far down in the basement the largest bell of a dozen each hanging on its strap-spring side-by-side and diminishing in size, began to agitate in the glow of the kitchen range and then to tumble out its message. It had seemed to Hetty when a child to be saying, Hurry! Hurry! to the kitchen clock on the wall swinging its brass pendulum, green with verdigris from the vapours of cooking; while the crickets in their hot crannies beside the range fiddled dryly as before.

Upstairs in the hall the gas-jet within the globe at the bottom of the stairs flickered as the heavy front door opened and at the same time from the sitting-room Hetty hurried out, followed by her mother in black bombazine dress and a lace cap on her greying masses of hair.

"Here's master come, ma'm," announced Polly, happily, as though nothing had gone on in the hall a moment before.

"Well, Sarah, how are ye? And my little girl is twenty-four today!" Thomas Turney gave his hat to Polly. "Jim's got the goose," he said to the maid. "Tell Cook not to forget plenty of basting, eh?" He laughed, he was glad to be home. "Well,

Hetty my dear, how do ye feel, eh? Many happy returns of the day. Going to give Papa a kiss?" He opened his arms slightly, a sturdy figure looking considerably shorter without his hat. He was going bald on the crown of his head. His daughter dutifully kissed him lightly on the brow, her arms with hands half closed held before her bosom as a precaution against being held too tightly. Thomas Turney put his arms around her shoulders, and pressed his hairy cheek, with its familiar smell of cigars, against his daughter's cheek, while holding the back of her head with his left hand. Her forearms and wrists held against his coat, Hetty kept him at a distance.

Then he kissed his wife lightly on the cheek, and she helped him out of his overcoat, which Hetty took to the coat-rack made of stag's-horn standing down the passage.

"Now you'd like your toddy, I expect, dear," said Sarah in her gentle voice. "The kettle is steaming on the hob. Is Hughie outside? How did the orders go, Tom?"

"Oh, Hughie's bolted," he said, standing still and laughing first at daughter, then at wife. "Yes, he bolted from me, just like his Spotted Dog, he–he–he."

Hughie's Spotted Dog was a joke in the family. He had often talked of owning a carriage dog, a black and white Dalmatian, to run behind his smart brown and yellow turnout on Sunday mornings. There had been much talk about the coming of this dog, and when at last it had appeared, just before dinner one Sunday at two o'clock in the afternoon, beside Hughie in the cart, its tail between its legs, its collar tied by string to the side-rail, it had on being released sprung from its new owner's arms, and with backward glance of fearful eyes had fled down the drive, through the gate, down the road, round the corner, and so out of sight, pursued by Hughie's vain whistling and cries of, *Come here, Sir! Come to me at once, Sir!*

"I expect the dear boy will be back in time for supper," said Mrs. Turney gently, while fear stirred within her. "Perhaps he went after an order."

"H'm," said Thomas Turney. "I've not heard it called that before."

He went into the sitting-room, followed by mother and daughter, who exchanged glances.

The polished copper kettle with its neck and spout like a swan with open bill was simmering on the hob. The key to the master's wine and spirit cellarette was on the master's key ring, attached by a silver chain to one of his trouser-buttons. Hetty waited to take the key, burnished by much jingling in the pocket against coins, and went into the dining room where Papa kept those bottles he had brought out of the cellar under the stairs. Here was a piece of furniture consisting of a cabinet about a yard in width and a couple of feet in depth standing about five feet off the floor, with a bookshelf on top of it. It was, like most of the furniture in the room, of mahogany, and made by the most careful craftsmanship. The lock was of brass; it turned noiselessly; the panelled door opened equally silently but with a perceptible resistance, owing to its perfect fitting. Inside were several shallow grooved shelves one above the other; each could be withdrawn so that the cigars laid in the grooves could be examined from time to time. Their condition, like that of wine, improved and matured if kept dry and at the right temperature.

Below the cigar-trays was a fitted bin, to hold a couple of dozen bottles; while above them were a pair of drawers, with countersunk handles. Above these drawers was a space in which stood the master of the house's bottles of gin, schnapps, Irish whisky, rum, and brandy.

Friday night was toddy-night; the slices of lemon, the brown Demerara sugar, the tumbler on the silver tray were ready on the little circular disk of mahogany standing on its stalk held by three feet beside the armchair by the blazing coal fire. Laid against the heavy brass rail of the fireguard were the master's carpet slippers.

Hetty gave the bottle of Irish whisky to her mother, and then knelt to take off her Papa's boots, while he gave them an account of his doings during the past week. When the slippers were on his feet, and one leg cocked over the other and he was settled back comfortably into the chair, Hetty handed him his tumbler of toddy, which was one part whisky to two of water, and two slices of lemon floating on top, while grains of brown sugar whirled at the bottom of the tumbler, stirred by the glass rod with the blob on the end.

"Thank 'ee," he said, putting his index finger into the liquid; and finding it of the right temperature, he put it to his lips, blew once or twice and then sipped. With a sigh, he relaxed. Whereupon Hetty, receiving a slight nod from her mother, left the room, closing the door behind her.

When the glass was about half empty, Sarah, who had been sitting quietly with her hands folded on her lap, ventured to ask again how business had gone that week. Hardly had she spoken, when she regretted it; for she did not want Tom to think about Hughie, and so get upset. She had hoped against hope that Hughie would have been a great success, then it would have made it easier for her to tell Tom, whose temper at times she dreaded so much, what she felt could not be kept from him any longer. Indeed, mother and daughter had been discussing it with increasing dread and anxiety all that day. What time would be the best to tell Papa? If too early, it might spoil the party: but then, if later on, when Papa had drunk some wine, well—— If the next morning, might he not have a liver? And then, would it be best if Hetty went away and Mamma told him? But might that not make him the more angry? Hetty, though not a Catholic, had prayed on her knees to the Virgin Mary, praying that Papa would not be angry, and so make her mother cry, for it was of her darling Mamma that Hetty was thinking nearly all of the time, if Papa were to get one of his terrible rages.

Sarah had tried many times to reassure herself that the best way to start to tell Tom was first to explain that as Hetty was now twenty-four, and being, as Tom well knew, a girl of the most beautiful and steadfast spirit, as the Mother Superior had told him when they had gone to fetch Hetty away, as he would remember—that Hetty would never do anything wrong, she always thought of others before herself——

But at this point, invariably, Sarah's rehearsal of an imaginary plea to Tom broke down. The trouble-scene just before Charlie had left home came back to her. For Tom had struck her in the face, a thing which she had not minded for herself but for what had followed—the terrible fight between Tom and Charlie, that she could not bear to think about. It was Tom's Irish blood.

Thomas Turney's head was leaning forward; his eyes were closing; the tumbler in his right hand was tilted. He was tired after his journey, and more worried than he would admit to himself over his disappointment with Hugh. For Thomas Turney wanted to feel that his sons would follow him into the Firm and help to increase its business until, from being a private company with limited liability, it would become a public company whose shares would be quoted in the House. First Charley; now Hughie——

Thomas Turney sighed, and settled for a cat-nap.

Sarah had risen from her chair and taken the tumbler from Tom's hand, when the loose white china handle of the door made its slight noise on being turned. As she moved across the carpet the door opened a little way and a voice from outside uttered a soft and musical *Honk!* Opening the door Sarah saw Theodora standing there, a smile upon her wide mouth. Sarah held up a finger to her lips, whereupon the other leaned her head forward and gave Sarah a light and silent kiss upon her finger, then another kiss on her forehead, before stepping back and opening the door wider for her to pass out. Then she closed the door, holding the handle a moment to subdue the noise of its looseness; and safe in the hall whispered, "I came in through the garden door."

"Oh dear, Dora, I hope you closed it securely?" said Sarah, in a subdued voice.

"Yes, dear Mrs. Turney."

"If it blows, and the door is unlatched, it may bang, and then Mr. Turney——"

"How is Tree Frog Number One?" whispered Theodora.

"She is upstairs, resting, the dear child. Do you go up now and see her."

She exchanged a significant look with Theodora. "I do hope Tom won't be too upset when he is told," she went on, faintly. "Have you seen Dickie?"

"He said he was coming down, Mrs. Turney. We will not be afraid, will we? Now, dear Mrs. Turney, pray do not worry. 'Only the Truth can make ye whole.' Honk!"

Sarah felt easier. Her corsets were always so tight, she really must get a new pair. Restricted by her thoughts as much as by whalebone and steel, she stood by the pitch-pine post of the banisters, her hand placed under her heart. Dora was such a dear girl, her presence was always so reassuring. Smiling, and saying she was a foolish women to meet trouble half-way, she recovered herself.

"Let me take your coat, dear. What a pretty little muff and hat you are wearing. And gloves to match! Hetty has a sealskin set just like that, with a jacket, she brought them back from Canada."

"They *are* Tree Frog Number One's!" said Dora, smiling widely. "She lent them to me."

"How nice to share things with a friend," murmured Sarah, a little anxious that Dora should take them off in case Tom should wake up from his nap and coming out of the sitting-room, recognize his gift to his favourite child.

Theodora knew what Sarah was thinking, and immediately asked if she might go upstairs to Hetty and return them. Sarah nodded, and saying she must see how Cook was getting on, she went down into the basement as Dora pulled herself up the stairs two at a time on the wide and elaborately fashioned hand-rail which was broad enough to slide down on a cushion—but only when Hetty's papa was out of the house.

As she went upstairs Theodora met Hetty's Aunt Marian, who had come from Greenwich on a visit to her brother Tom. Impulsively she kissed Miss Turney, whom she admired. That lady, delighted, fluttered a moment and then returned a sound, firm kiss on the young woman's forehead. "There! That's what you asked for, one good turn deserves another!" Aunt Marian went downstairs to the stillroom, to do some sewing for Sarah, and Theodora went to join Hetty.

Chapter 11

CANDLELIGHT AND MAHOGANY

ALL THE dishes had to be brought up from the kitchen to the dining-room and Polly the parlour maid (who was also house and kitchen maid) had had a busy evening. In between the laying of the table, under the eye of her mistress, Polly had had to answer the front door bell, and let in the guests as they arrived. She knew them all, for she had been in service at Maybury Lodge for nearly four years.

First to arrive were Mr. and Mrs. Cakebread. Polly liked him, and her too. Mrs. Cakebread was the elder married daughter of Mrs. Turney. Mother and daughter went upstairs happily together. Left alone with Mr. Cakebread, Polly felt a little abashed: he was such a fine gentleman, with his tall upright figure and brown moustaches, his shiny hair and lovely soft black cape and his clouded cane with a big gold top to the handle. Polly knew by the cane alone that Mr. Cakebread was a very high-up person. Hardly had she taken his hat lined with white silk, his cape lined with dark blue silk, and his lavender gloves, and announced him into the drawing room when she was hurrying back to open the hall door to Mr. and Mrs. Mallard, and their son Lancelot.

Polly, having seen them before on several occasions, greeted them with a smile. The old gentleman (who was fifty-five) and his son both bade her a good evening, but the lady did not speak to her, nor appear to see her. Polly waited to take the gentlemen's hats and coats, while they adjusted their ties and cuffs, and the lady patted the pads in her hair to make sure they had not slipped, or the attached tails come loose behind, as Polly pretended not to notice. She did not like Mrs. Mallard—a stuck-up old thing.

Master Lancelot had his case with the "grunter" in it, as Polly and Cook called the bassoon. She noticed that he hid it at once in the corner.

Polly opened the door, to announce the guests.

Mr. Turney was sitting on the sofa between the two young ladies Miss Hetty and Miss Theodora, telling them a story which made him laugh, while Mr. Cakebread stood looking attentively at him, as he stood before the fire, warming his behind. "I was just telling Hetty and Dora, Sidney, about a fellow who persisted in taking m'bags out of m'hands outside Liverpool Street Station——" when Polly called out, "Mr. and Mrs. Mallard, and Master Mallard," whereupon the story was interrupted for the second time that evening.

Polly closed the door behind her, to see Mrs. Turney coming down the stairs. "It's Mr. and Mrs. and Master Mallard, mum," said Polly. "I took 'em all into the drawing-room, I hope I did right, m'arm. Mrs. Mallard didn't want to go up over."

"Of course you did right, Polly, like the good girl you always are," replied Mrs. Turney. "Now do you go down and give Cook a hand, and when all is ready, just come and give me a slight nod in the drawing-room, and I'll come out and take a last look around the table, just as we always do together, you'll recollect."

"Yes, m'arm," said grateful Polly, and hastened down the stairs to the kitchen.

"Lawks a-mussy me, where've you bin?" grumbled Cook, her red face busy among a flotilla of pots and pans of tin-lined copper upon the kitchen range. "Leavin' me to do all the work! You Jim over there, you ought to slip on a house-parlourman's blue striped coat when we have company, and stand, ready to open the door to 'em. That's what the coachman 'ad to do in my last place, but that was Epsom, where there's real class."

"Mr. and Mrs. Mallard come from Epsom, they come in an orniary cab—they ain't got a carriage like us has," said loyal Polly.

"Aye, they hire from Tompkin's Livery," remarked the gardener-coachman, sitting on a chair in the corner.

"Still, Mr. Mallard's Chairman of the Firm, and you don't find a Chairman growing on any old goosegog bush," replied Cook.

At half-past eight supper was ready, upon the table and on the sideboard of the dining-room. Polly in her best apron with its starched shoulder straps and streamers and white starched cap had given her face a final sluicing in cold water to make it less red. The vigorous rubbing on cheeks and brow by a coarse turkish towel, however, served only to give a polish to those healthy cheeks. Polly's cheeks were her secret dismay—if only she could get them pale and lady-like, like Miss Hetty and Miss Dora! Blowing out the candle beside the tarnished mirror Polly ran downstairs; paused outside the drawing-room door to give a last wiping of her mouth on the back of hand, a quick rub of her palms upon her black thread stockings, then turned the rockety handle, and entering, gave the pre-arranged nod—which turned out to be several double winks accompanied by a wrinkling of the nose in the direction of Mrs. Turney.

"Has Mr. Hugh arrived yet, Polly?" enquired Mr. Turney, half turning on the sofa.

"I hain't seen 'im, sir."

"Oh," said Mr. Turney. "Perhaps the boy's working late at the office." He looked at his sister Marian sitting stiffly upright on a straight-backed horsehair chair against the wall, "Perhaps I'm the Shah of Persia," with a laugh.

"You might be one day, dear Tom," replied Marian, who, being the eldest of a family of twelve children had helped her mother to look after them all in turn.

One of Tom's little customs was to get himself dressed up in the costumes of the countries he visited, for the purpose of being photographed. On the mantelpiece was his latest—he and his partner Mr. Carter dressed up in Algerian garb, holding spears in their hands: Tom grinning, and Alfred Carter looking what he was—a nonconformist Father of his local Chapel.

"H'm," said Tom, and went on with his humorous story, which had just passed to the point where, Hughie having bolted like his Spotted Dog, a certain famous lady had passed in her carriage and recognized the Prince of Wales "incognito" in front of the Royal Exchange.

While the story continued Sarah slipped out of the room with Polly to make a final inspection of the table, which had been unwound that morning for the insertion of two extra leaves, each a heavy slab of mahogany brought down from the boxroom by Polly and the gardener, to accommodate eleven places for the party.

The candles had already been lit upon both sideboard and table. Sarah stood back, to give a final scrutiny of the work which had kept the household in a state of earnest preparation since the afternoon of the previous day.

In the centre of the sideboard stood the cold dishes. Chief of these was the dark Bradenham ham, cured in black treacle and spices, and baked with cloves stuck into the massive haunch thickly coated with sugar. It rested on a big pink and white dish, a pink frill of paper covering its knuckle. Flanking it were the cold roast pheasants, garnished with sprigs of thyme.

The sideboard, of gleaming, massive mahogany, was an affair of silently fitting cupboards, topped by a row of drawers which opened and closed as smoothly under a surface nearly nine feet in length whereon the victuals were placed. Lambent flames of wood alcohol licked Sheffield plate dishes holding under their covers the saddles of mutton, the steak lying in its own brown gravy and fat-bubbled lacing of blood, the goose under the biggest cover of all, and the dish holding the turbot. Beside them were the tureens, part of a Willow Pattern set, holding the vegetables. Sarah lifted each lid to inspect in turn roast potatoes, mashed potatoes, and potatoes baked in their jackets; brussels sprouts, carrots, braised onions, cauliflowers with sauce, buttered parsnips and haricot beans. Tom sometimes liked haricot beans with his hot mutton, so a dish had been specially made for him.

Sarah's eye, having satisfied itself upon the vegetables, moved over the cheeses—a Stilton under a blue and white Wedgwood cover, Norwegian goats' cheese made of cream simmered brown, Italian gorgonzola, and Tom's favourite Gruyère, which he always ate with fresh mustard. Had she forgotten anything? Once again Sarah gazed upon the dishes on the sideboard; but though she was counting on her fingers as she looked, she was not checking the dishes. Sarah was suddenly tired, for dread of the ordeal awaiting them all after the party should be over. Come come, this will never do, she told herself, compelling a return to the matter in hand. Red currant jelly—yes, it was there; the gravy; the onion sauce—yes, she could safely say nothing had been forgotten.

But perhaps she ought to make quite sure about the table. The tureen holding the turtle soup was placed by the master's elbow, together with the plates—Sarah counted them, making eleven. She had already inspected the laying of the table: knives, forks, spoons, glasses, and little plates. The wines had been left to Sidney, dear helpful Sidney, who always arranged things so satisfactorily, with the least apparent effort. Eleven places—there should have been twelve—Dickie should have, by rights, been coming to the party.

Was the silver clean? It had been polished by Hetty and herself that morning, but Polly had a habit of leaving what Tom, who missed seeing very little, called broad beans and broader beans upon it—Polly's greasy finger and thumb marks. It was beautiful silver, and Sarah was proud of it. The crest engraved on each handle made all the pieces seem to be of one family, a little family inhabiting the brass-bound oak-box fitted with green baize-lined drawers and pockets and crannies all made to fit the coffee-pot, the tea-pot, the milk and cream jugs, the salt cellars and pepper castors, the sugar dishes, the toast rack, fish-slicers—everything, including forks, spoons, and the ivory-handled knives bearing the engraved device of dead and gone knights-at-arms.

Hughie had been responsible for the armorial crest. During his second year at the university he had examined books on heraldry in the college library in order to prove to himself that his fine sensibility was due to noble or at least to armigerous blood. His study of the matter, quite brief, had brought the conclusion—he had had to jump to that conclusion across an abyss of time—that the Turneys were a branch of the baronial family of Le Tournet which had come over with William the Conqueror, and settled, before ceasing to exist as landed proprietors in the sixteenth century or so, in the same county where he had been born.

Thomas Turney, who had long thought of acquiring some plate, had taken to the boy's idea, so with Sarah beside him he had purchased the square oak box, bound with brass and fitted with a strong lock, at Mappin Bros.' shop in Cheapside. He wasn't particular about the crest, and before deciding had enquired the extra cost. With or without motto? had enquired the frock-coated shop-assistant, with a deference the greater owing to a face pimpled with barber's-rash only partly concealed by Veloutine powder. Thomas Turney was familiar with crests and mottoes; every month the Firm engraved scores of copper-plates for the blue and grey writing paper and envelopes of the nobility, gentry, and successful merchants coming to swell their ranks. Some bore crests only, others required crests together with enscrolled mottoes. The manager assured him that the crest only was *de rigueur* on silver. Anyway, what was the motto, he asked humorously of his wife, suggesting *I turn the spit*, in reference to the alleged knightly Tournets having descended to the Turney farmhouse kitchen. So for five guineas, which became pounds after discount, the work was done. And very proper it looked, on every spoon, for soup, mustard, salt, tea, tea-caddy, dessert, table, and four sizes of tureen ladles; on every ivory knife handle, long and short, thick and slender, pointed and rounded; on fish-slicer and four-pronged broad fork, swan-necked cheese scoop with stubby ivory handle, on grape-clippers and candle-snuffers, asparagus tongs and fish-slicers, crab-claw crackers, nut-crackers, and egg-decapitator. On silver and ivory a mailed fist upstanding held a dagger.

Everything was in order, so far as Sarah could see.

"Shall I announce supper, m'am, or call it dinner tonight?"

"Supper, Polly, Mr. Turney likes the old words best."

"Yes, m'am, and 'tis the same food arter all."

"Give me a minute, will you Polly, before coming in to tell Mr. Turney that supper is served. And light the gas, do. Be careful to put the lucifer in the fire."

"Yes, m'am."

Sarah went back to her guests. Tom was chuckling over a story of Mrs. Mallard's about the house of Stanley being the only one which had stood out against the name of a certain famous lady being added by the Prince of Wales to the list of guests to be invited to Knowsley submitted for H.R.H.'s approval. "The Countess of Derby drew her pen through the name, although it was written in the hand of the Heir Apparent himself, so I am informed on the best authority," concluded Mrs. Mallard.

"And most proper, I am happy to add," remarked Mr. Mallard, twiddling the albert seal hanging from his fob. "I know it is true, for I heard the same story myself from a City Alderman. How did you come to hear of it, Maude, may I be permitted to enquire?" and he twirled his moustache.

"A little bird, told me, too," remarked Thomas Turney, "a little bird interested in a fat worm that can be found on the Thames-side at *low water*." He exchanged a wink with Mr. Mallard over this play on the name of a rival firm. To supply Royalty with writing paper, and to receive permission to display the Royal Arms on the vans, letter heading, and office windows of Mallard, Carter, and Turney, was one of the chairman's ambitions.

Mr. Mallard, not quite liking the tone of familiarity from his junior parner—decidedly impertinent, to refer to himself, Chairman of the Firm, as a little bird after a fat worm!—assumed an expression of amiable nonchalance. In addition he was a trifle disconcerted because his pretence of enquiring the source of the story had been exposed. He must be more careful about his memory in future.

The slight hiatus in the conversation was filled by Polly announcing supper.

Sarah rose to her feet, the others followed.

Mr. Mallard advanced and, pulling at his lapels, bowed to his hostess, offering an arm. "The animals went into the Ark, two by two," exclaimed Thomas Turney to Mrs. Mallard, with a mock bow as, imagining himself in the character of the cat in the pantomime wearing a hairy skin, he offered his arm to—a gnu.

Lancelot Mallard, concealing his mortification that at the last moment he had not the courage to advance towards Hetty, took in Mrs. Cakebread, leaving Sidney to escort Aunt Marian and the two younger women. Which Sidney Cakebread did with his usual kindliness, treating his Aunt by marriage with an attention equal to that given to Hetty and Theodora. "I am the lucky man tonight, with three charmers all to myself!" Nor was he pretending; for he appreciated each woman for her own quality.

Twin-gas jets fluttered twistingly inside their opaque globes beside the mantelpiece, mock butterflies; tallow candles fixed with paper collars into sticks of Sheffield plate imitating Ionic columns burned in the centre of the table, winking at others set upon the sideboard. Polly stood by the master, taking the plates of turtle soup which he ladled from the tureen at the head of the table.

After the soup had been swallowed, the plates collected and borne away with the tureen, the master pushed back his chair padded with dark green morocco leather, and went to the sideboard, to do business, not with a Tournet dagger, but with the various knives laid in order upon their rests beside the steel.

Thomas Turney was particular about the correct sharpening of knives, having once been shown by the white-hatted chef in the London Tavern in Fenchurch Street the art and mystery of removing flesh from the bones of various joints. There was one knife for the ham, another for the saddle of mutton, a third for the birds. Each implement of Sheffield steel had to receive its ritual stroking at the correct angle towards the point, the opposite stroke of a mower flicking an edge upon his scythe. With swift dexterous movements of elbows and wrists the master of the house flicked, as it were, a precise cutting edge on his tools, which shone with much rubbing upon the brown-powdered board in the scullery adjoining the kitchen beneath the dining-room. While Sarah served the turbot, and the plates were taken round by Hetty, Thomas Turney wiped knife and tapered steel together so lightly and swiftly that Theodora, watching and enjoying the sight, saw in fancy specks of steel whirling upon the air to form themselves into stars planeted by dust and falling in Time even as meteorites in space.

Theodora, who read Euripides and Aeschylus in the original Greek, had decided that she was an agent, by means of poetry, for a new way of living, or rather by a return of the worship of God through handicraft as taught by William Morris. Theodora under her calm exterior was a whirling nebula of emotion: she lived almost wholly in the imagination and sought continually to lift her heart above the material things of a so-called civilization which she believed had doomed itself because it denied the true things of the spirit. She wrote poems and little essays in the secrecy of her room, and only Hetty had been told of her writing, after promising never to tell anyone. *Honk!* she cried inwardly to her muse or inspiration, as she ate only a little of her turbot. She preferred vegetables. Marian's eye across the table, peering through a gap in the flowers, caught hers, and sent a special little smile of amity.

Thomas Turney, who had forgone the fish in duty to the roast, was at the sideboard carving the mutton. In fancy a white crumpled hat was on the side of his head. He felt himself to be in Falstaffian mood. Nothing like mutton, Banstead Down mutton, flavoured with thyme, well-basted and browned, saddle-brown skin holding soft-grained slices that melted in the mouth with red currant jelly, the onion sauce being reserved for his second helping. Thomas Turney had a secret: there were two saddles of mutton, one held in reserve for the carver, who had to work while others champed their chops. Let them have the steak, fine steak it was, too, Smithfield's best from the pastures of Leicestershire, three-year grass-fed shorthorn beef, with the most delicious white fat from nut-cake eaten out of cast-iron bowls, one each to a beast, filled night and morning by the stockman. Masticating quickly, his palate cleansed by short gulps of Burgundy warmed to the right temperature since the morning by Sarah, Thomas Turney expatiated on the value of good British beef, while he saw to it that most of the reserved saddle of mutton went on his own plate, and down his gullet into his round and solid yeoman's middle. He patted his stomach, and went on with his story, he-he-he, of the beggar who wouldn't take no for an answer, an evil-looking cut-throat who so scared poor Hughie, he-he-he-he, that Hughie took fright and bolted like his own Spotted Dog in front of the Royal Exchange, ha-ha-ha.

"Well, to continue the story," he said, his eyes roving to the faces around the table, "I'd got so far as London Bridge station, and on giving him the butt o' m' cigar, he said to me, he said, 'What's the game, guv'nor', as I gave 'm me cigar-butt. He-he-he! No idea of keeping his word! You can't be too careful with men of that kidney," he concluded, raising a forkful of juicy mutton. "They ought to send 'em to the Colonies!"

Mr. Mallard thought so, too: but qualitatively, for he was a Liberal, and a faithful follower of Gladstone. "Such fellows are a menace, I admit, Turney, but if they were compelled to emigrate, as some declare, to people the wide-open spaces of Empire crying out for bold pioneering to help trade, what would happen to the necessary surplus of the home labour market, by which wages are kept at a natural level?"

"'The poor ye have always with you,'" Mrs. Mallard ventured to quote, in support of Mr. Mallard.

At this point Theodora, who had been dreamily masticating carrots and cauliflower in silence, stared fixedly at the massed yellow and brown chrysanthemums in the bowl in the centre of the table and said in her clear and musical voice:

"But we are also told, on the same Authority, are we not, to give all we have to the poor."

In the silence that followed this remark her glance dropped, until she appeared to be regarding Hugh's empty place beside her, as though for reassurance.

"H'm," said Thomas Turney, pausing in his rapid chewing to swallow a draught of Burgundy. He had seen that Sidney had given Hetty only a quarter glass of wine, and had diluted it himself with water. A look at Theodora's place revealed a glass of water, and some wine untouched in another glass. Theodora had accepted the wine with which to drink Hetty's health when her father should propose it.

Aunt Marian gave Theodora a bird-like glance through the

chrysanthemums as she nodded vigorously. "We should give of our utmost service to our fellows, how I agree with you, dear Theodora."

Mrs. Mallard, having cleared her throat with a disapproving cough, turned to her host and remarked, "Do you find that the use of bear's grease, for the hair, saves the antimacassars, Mr. Turney? I can remember the time when Macassar oil stained even the horse-hair backs. All the young men use bear's grease now, do they not? Lancelot does, but I hope he will not take to that queer Hongroise pomade for the end of the moustaches, should he ever decide to grow a moustache."

Thomas Turney chuckled. "Masherdom and chappiness," he replied. "They'll be putting cart-grease on their heads next, and you ladies will all be wearing little cartwheels, if the Princess of Wales should do so first." He beamed round the table, chuckling at his humour. Sarah, Dorrie, and Hetty laughed too, in relief. Slightly emboldened, Lancelot Mallard, sitting between Hetty and Aunt Marian, remarked with a stutter:

"That's g-g-good enough for *P-Punch*, sir."

Sarah smiled at Theodora. That young person smiled back, and put a slight frown on her forehead as she tapped the back of one hand with the forefinger of her other hand, to convey to Sarah that she, Theodora, needed whipping.

For Theodora was the sort of young woman whom Thomas Turney, while admitting that she had brains, did not approve of. She was a busybody, in his opinion. Theodora was associated with the East End settlements run by both men and women from the universities among the poor of London, together with such institutions as the Dorcas Society for the making of clothes, the Destitute Children's Dinner Society which in the past year had provided nearly half a million dinners at a charge of a halfpenny each, and the Children's Happy Evenings Association. Then there was the Metropolitan Society for Befriending Young Servants between the ages of thirteen and twenty.

Thomas Turney could not make up his mind about Theodora, whether she was an influence for good or for bad with Hetty. He suspected that she was the cause of Hughie's unsettled condition. There was only one right place for a woman, and that was in the home, with children. Women out of place were the devil. This Theodora person, who looked as though butter would not melt in her mouth, had, until recently at any rate, got Hughie to accompany her sometimes to her Missions in the East End. She it was who had taken his thought, if not his time, from his work in the Firm. If he really wanted her, he ought to work harder, so that he could offer her a home for children. That was natural, and far more useful, as it created employment—instead of encouraging the working classes to think above their station. But there, it was Hetty's birthday party, and young things were young things!

"Mrs. Mallard, let me give you some Norfolk goose? I bought it myself in Diss market this morning. Come come, don't be shy—I won't take no for an answer—that's right, bring the plate, Polly." He carved, Polly took the plate back. "Sarah? Why, bless my soul, what's come over you? Bring Mrs. Turney's plate, Polly."

"Only a very little, Tom, really, thank you."

He carved. "Dorrie? 'Only a very little?'" he mimicked. "What's come over you ladies tonight? Hetty, my dear, help out Papa! There's a good girl." He stood by the goose, holding the long thin handle of the short and pointed knife which was a pleasure to use. Nothing like the right tool for the job: British craftsmanship! "That's a good girl, I got this goose specially for you, you know. At home we always had a Michaelmas goose, remember Marian? Why I was quite forgetting you, Marian! Bring me Miss Marian's plate, Polly, there's a good girl. There we are! Mallard? He-he, the men can always be relied on for trencher play! When I was a boy we had Michaelmas goose at the harvest supper, and what fun it was, dancing in the Corn Barn by lanthorn light afterwards. Eh, Marian? Why, that occasion when——"

"Now, Tom," said Sarah, mildly. She knew the story of Marian being found in the Hay Barn with the under-teamsman, and the belting she had got from her father then and there. Tom had been a small boy at the time; he had not witnessed it; and Time had made it a funny occasion. The under-teamsman had left the farm that very night, and later had emigrated to one of the colonies. There had been much violent talk among the grown-up sons, following their father's lead.

"Yes, the harvest suppers were quite an occasion in the lives of us children old enough to be allowed up," chuckled Thomas Turney. "People weren't so squeamish in those days. They thought nothing of gorging plates of mutton and then going outside to the yards to tickle their throats with straws, to come back and fill up again with ham—— The dogs had the time of their lives, ha-ha-ha."

Mrs. Mallard allowed her gaze to wander to the ceiling. Really now! Such conversation would not be possible in Epsom.

"So did the Romans, but their Empire fell all the same, Mr. Turney," remarked Theodora, quietly.

"Yes and Nero fiddled too, didn't he, eh?" This was a pointed reference to the absent Hugh.

"Did Lancelot remember to bring his flute, Mrs. Mallard?" enquired Sarah from the other end of the table. She wanted to turn the talk away from Hugh.

"By that time," went on Theodora, "the patricians had neglected their responsibilities and duties, assuming instead that they were the heirs of privilege, with the result we know."

"Now in my humble opinion——" began Mr. Mallard, impatiently; but his attention was diverted by his wife's voice saying, "Mrs. Turney is enquiring if you brought your flute, Lancelot."

"Er—well, as a matter of fact, I have not had much time for practising lately, Mrs. Turney."

"Why not say straight out that you brought your bassoon, my boy? Yes, Mrs. Turney, he brought his buffoon's bassoon, isn't that correct, Lancelot? Then shame the devil!" Mr. Mallard emptied his glass of Burgundy. "You have provided us with an excellent goose, if I may be so bold as to say so, ma'm!" He allowed young Cakebread to fill up his glass. Go hang to indigestion for once! "Yes, as I was about to remark," he went on, swelling his chest to relieve his belly, "in my humble opinion, Miss Maddison is far too charming a young person to become a blue-stocking!" and with a smirk he raised his glass to Theodora's curve of neck and golden coils of hair.

Lancelot Mallard, sitting on his hands, appeared to find interest in the flowers before him.

"I think all wind instruments possess such a kindly tone, Mrs. Mallard," said Sarah.

"I agree, Mrs. Turney, but there are wind instruments and wind instruments, surely?" Mrs. Mallard looked at her husband, who happened to be trying to relieve the pressure on his stomach while pretending to a polite cough.

"I suppose each one has its own place in the world of music, Mrs. Mallard."

"Of course, naturally; but I must say that I infinitely prefer a flute for social occasions."

Mr. Mallard coughed loudly; but the tail-end of his cough was unmistakably a belch. Hetty tried not to giggle.

Here Aunt Marian, who was feeling sorry for the young man who had brought only a bassoon, suddenly made up her mind to speak. She laid down her knife and fork. With deep seriousness accentuating the lines upon her face, much given to meditation, she exclaimed, "The bassoon? Has someone brought a bassoon?" She looked around at the faces earnestly. "The bassoon is a most impressive instrument!"

"Especially when it plays the toon the bull frog died of, eh Hetty?" chuckled Thomas Turney, aside to his daughter.

"As a practical joke, it may have its place, I do not doubt for one moment, Mr. Turney. However, I shall continue to believe that the place for a bassoon is hardly a drawing room." Mrs. Mallard looked down her nose. She did not approve of Hugh Turney, who had egged-on Lancelot to buy the silly thing, no doubt to make him appear foolish in the eyes of others. Mrs. Mallard was convinced that Hugh Turney was a bad companion who, given half a chance, would lead her son astray.

At this point Sidney Cakebread, who had been listening with grave amusement to the conversation as he went round the table with the Burgundy, put the half-empty bottle on the sideboard, and returned to his place. Spreading his tails, he sat down, drew up his chair, and leaned forward with the manner of one about to impart a confidence.

"I am told that the bassoon is one of the hardest of all known wind instruments to play," he began, in a voice of some gravity, "and that only musicians of serious determination and love of their art would persist in their endeavours to master its technical intricacies. Moreover——" he went on, his tone becoming more confidential, "only men with the best heart and lungs can stand the physical strain, according to what I am told by one of our customers—I am not at liberty to give you his name, of course, but he is an internationally noted figure in cosmopolitan artistic circles. And this particular Grand Duke knows what he is talking about, too: he is one of the backers of the opera in Paris, in Milan, in Monte Carlo, in Madrid, and of course our own Covent Garden."

Sidney Cakebread kept a straight face during his improvisation. He had a sense of humour that usually he kept to himself. Young Hughie and his sister Hetty were his occasional sharers in the family circle: at times devastatingly so. There was that never-to-be-forgotten occasion in church, when in the fly-leaf of his prayer-book Sidney had drawn, complete with bowler hat, *The wicked flea when no man pursueth.*

Sarah glanced at Sidney, and smiled. What a dear boy he was, so dependable for every occasion! He seemed to know exactly what to do and what to say, no matter what turn affairs might take. He would have made his fortune equally as diplomat or hotelier. Of course he had had great advantages, coming from a family so well-connected, his father having been on the Viceroy's staff in India, before becoming Prime Minister to one of the Maharajas. Sidney came of a family of soldiers, sailors, and prelates; it was bred in him, his ease and charm on all occasions.

Sidney Cakebread had gone round with a light sherry with the soup, a Chablis with the turbot, Burgundy with the meats, Claret with the goose and cold game; and a sparkling Moselle for the ladies—recommended to be sipped with the ham, and much superior, in his humble opinion, to Champagne, that wine popularized by the Marlborough House set. This last verbal tit-bit specially for Mrs. Mallard, without the least trace of irony, concealed or overt.

Sidney Cakebread made a habit of trying to understand people with whom he was not naturally in direct sympathy. He found he had made many friends that way. His father, whom he loved, had by example revealed to his sons that the only way to live was by considering other people's feelings as more important than one's own; and Sidney, as the youngest son, had had a continuously happy childhood.

"Of course we are to hear some music tonight?" suddenly asked Aunt Marian, of Hetty. "I remember how Hughie used to love his violin. I do hope the dear boy comes before long. I so enjoy his playing. Do you still sing Gounod's 'O, that we two were Maying', together?"

"Oh yes, Aunt Marian, and you played the piano, when we were children!"

"Well, Hetty, my girl, it's a pleasure to see you your old self again," pronounced Thomas Turney. He patted her shoulder. "Are you enjoying your birthday, eh?"

"Oh yes, Papa, thank you. I am so enjoying it all!"

"That's right, my dear. Why bless my soul, of course you're wondering where my present is! Be patient a little while longer," he spoke intimately. "Wait till afterwards. Now, let me give you some ham? Just one slice? Come on, 'twill do you good!"

"No, thank you, dear Papa, really, thank you indeed. I couldn't eat another thing."

"You were always so excitable as a child," he said, "you and Hughie, up one minute, and down the next. Where can the boy have got to, I wonder," he muttered, as he put an edge on the knife with half a dozen delicate strokes of the steel.

The ladies having been served with a little ham each, to be but toyed with, of course, for the sake of Lord John Manners, the turn of the men came; and like men, each would try the Bradenham ham. Polly was waiting beside the master with Mr. Lancelot's plate when there came a pealing of the front-door bell followed by a bang on the knocker and a succession of four or five lesser percussions which terminated in a final extra loud thump.

"I rather fancy that might be Hughie," said Sarah. "Perhaps it is very foggy outside," she added vaguely.

"Shall I go to the door, mum," asked Polly, uncertainly.

"Let him wait," replied Thomas Turney. "He's kept others waiting long enough, so it won't hurt him to stand there awhile."

"His chest isn't very strong, Tom," pleaded Sarah.

"Nor's his head," replied Tom, carving meticulously. "Have you got any of your pickled pears to go with this ham, Sarah?"

"Oh dear, I forgot to bring up a jar," cried Hetty, suddenly animated. "With your permission I will go and fetch one from the cupboard, Papa."

"Polly can go in a moment, there's no particular hurry." At these words a look of strain came upon his daughter's face. He did not notice it, being busy with the dark and aromatic meat.

"That's what you're here for, isn't it, Polly my girl?"

"Yes, sir," said Polly with a nervous simper.

"Good girl. I'll ask Mrs. Turney to give you an extra half day next week, for the way you've worked tonight!"

Polly blushed, and gave a glance at Mrs. Turney.

The door knocker beat out another tattoo. Thomas Turney went on carving the ham.

Lancelot Mallard took a peep at Hetty, on his left. He had been stealing glances, with what he believed to be deceptive carelessness, ever since he had come into the house. The young man thought that she looked so sad, her eyes were like a gazelle's eyes. He had never been to the Zoo but he had read the novels of Marie Corelli and (secretly) those of Madame Sarah Grand. Recently he had been absorbed in the fiction of Rider Haggard; and longings, at times agonisingly nebulous, obsessed him as he imagined an Ayesha come mysteriously to his side, her eyes luminous, her hair falling upon her white shoulders as she held his head against a warm, soft, virgin breast, brooding over him with red lips and a profile of purity and innocence. Lancelot Mallard's days were passed in the counting-house of the Firm; in the evenings he longed to be a masher, to go to the Alhambra and the Empire Promenade and be a regular chappie; while at night his erotic longings were expended upon himself, and sometimes in the mornings, too, with their consequent guilty feelings and shyness in the presence of feminine beauty.

Across the table his father, Albert Mallard, was half-meditatively, half-furtively using a quill toothpick concealed in his left hand, the hand farthest from Mrs. Turney, as behoved a gentleman. Mr. Mallard obtained supplies of these useful little objects from his favourite coffee-room of Ye Mecca Company in the City. The waistcoat pockets of his coats bristled with them, and often pricked the fingers of Mrs. Mallard valeting her husband's clothes.

Sidney Cakebread, opposite the older man, was a traveller in wines and spirits for a celebrated West End firm of wine merchants, which supplied the Royal Household. But Sarah was only half-listening to his pleasant account of the great wine-cellars in the Adelphi arches, for her heart was beating irregularly, due to nervous agitation of her thoughts, to her rib-compressing corsets, and to indigestion adding its gaseous pressure against her heart. Her thoughts just then were sad, as she pictured in her mind the face of Charley, her eldest son: dear, impulsive little Charley, the rolling stone, as Tom called him, before ordering him to leave the house. And from Charley in tenderness she thought of good, steady little Joe at boarding school (the poor boy could not learn his lessons, and was often being beaten, her dear little Joe who had taken so long to come into the world, and then been dropped on his head by the wet-nurse when he was eight months old) and of—the bearded face she had seen at the window, the long thin anxious face peering in the gap between the curtains a moment before, visible in the candlelight, hollow-eyed. Poor Dickie! *Oh, the wrongness of it all.* And now Hughie—Oh, why was life, which should be so happy, always so sad? But then this life was but a preparation for the next, when all tears would be wiped away. And to her dismay and shame Sarah felt a tear beginning to slip down her cheek.

Sidney Cakebread saw the tear, and exclaiming, "By Jove, sir, it's somewhat hot in here, d'you mind if I open a window?" he pushed back his chair, got on his feet, and bent down a moment to kiss Sarah on the brow. "Pretty as a peach!" he exclaimed next, to Hetty, whose upward glance moved him to affection. "May I sir?" as he went to the window.

"Yes yes, my boy," exclaimed Thomas Turney. "Just a little bit at the top, Sidney. Cold air can be dangerous at this time of year. You can't be too careful. Now Polly, you may open the front door and let the late bird in!"

Polly almost ran to the front door. She positively ran back, with round eyes, saying, "There be no one there, sir!"

"Bless me soul!" exclaimed the master, indulgently. "Has he taken to his heels again, like the Spotted Dog, eh?" And he laughed, looking round the table at the amused faces.

Lancelot Mallard, emboldened by the sudden ease, had an idea. "I suppose, sir," he said, while squirming slightly on his hands, on which he was sitting, "it was not someone else knocking at your front door? A decoy, perhaps?"

"A decoy?" asked the host. "Anyway, whoever it was, he has done a guy."

"A d-d-dec-dec-decoy, sir. To focus attention on one part of the house, sir."

"Whatever are you talking about, my boy?" demanded Mr. Mallard, staring at him across the bowl of flowers with stern and pale yellow eyes.

Lancelot squirmed on his wrists, and began to stammer that any thieves who might wish to rob a place swiftly, would perhaps create a diversion; but the pale minatory eyes across the table held him to silence. "All those stories he reads of Dick Donovan—" Mr. Mallard turned to Mrs. Turney. "All the sordid happenings of the underworld should go unrecorded, as fiction or otherwise."

The unaccustomed wine had turned the varied contents of Mr. Mallard's stomach to acid. Usually he drank but a glass of hot water before and after, but never during, his evening meal.

"Oh dear, the pickled pears!" Hetty jumped up and almost running round the table, pulled open the door, called back over her shoulder, "I'll get them in an instant, Papa!" and was down the stairs into the basement before Thomas Turney could protest.

In the kitchen Hugh was sitting by the fire, his hat on the back of his head, his malacca cane between his knees. Hetty was shocked by the look he gave her. His face was drawn, his eyes fixed in a blank stare. A bowl of untasted soup stood on the iron top of the range before him, beside the black-leaded bricks.

"Hughie, what is the matter?" cried Hetty. "Hughie dear, shall I call Mamma?"

"No, for God's sake don't let anyone know I'm here," said her brother. He stared at the fire and said dully, "Many happy returns of the day. I'm sorry, I forgot about a present, Hetty, I—I—oh, I'm—I'm not very well. Leave me alone."

"Master Hugh's got a cold, that's my opinion, Miss Hetty, and should be in bed, his chest well rubbed with embercation," remarked Jim, who was sitting in his usual cane-bottomed chair in the corner, waiting for another instalment of his supper.

"Try and drink your soup, 'twill do you good," urged Cook.

Hetty stood irresolute. It was five and twenty minutes past nine o'clock, and the strain of sitting still at the table upstairs, every moment of it, had increased the weight of dread upon her. At last, unable to bear her thoughts any longer, she had risen from the table on the pretext of fetching the pickled pears. Now she stood irresolute before Hughie, unable to speak; and then, overcome by her interior anguish, she went to the basement door, opened it, and hurried up the short steps to the gravelled drive above.

She was familiar with the way through the darkness, but even so she moved with her arms held out in front of her, her eyes nearly closed and tremulous, while she tried to control her fear of something imminent that would move silently upon her from behind and then she would scream. Fighting these fears, which had their origin partly in fear of her father, and consequent greater devotion to her mother, partly from the repressions of the body withheld by circumstances from a natural active life, Hetty hastened down the path beside the lawn, with its croquet hoops not yet taken up for the winter, and to the summerhouse where she hoped to find Dickie.

Sitting between Mr. and Mrs. Mallard with Hugh's empty place beside her, Theodora wondered whether Dickie had gone away, after waiting so long in the summerhouse. What a tragedy people made of life, their own lives and those of others, because they lacked the imagination to know what others were really feeling! That poor brother of hers waiting in the cold outside, while for two hours Hetty was forced by circumstances to dissemble, to smile, to say anything but what was oppressing her; and Mrs. Turney was suffering in like manner, and Hughie, too, because he wanted more than she, Theodora, could give him. And Mr. Turney at heart was a not unkindly man. Was then modern life to be no different than that old life revealed by the Greek poets? Surely not, with such progress of the mind being made! With a start she heard Mr. Turney saying:

"Where's our little Hetty got to?"

"No doubt she will be back soon, dear," replied Sarah quietly; and Thomas understood what he was meant to understand.

Bearing a load of plates Polly went out of the room and down the stairs to the kitchen. On the long deal table below stood two objects which were to end the meal, except for the cheese and celery, the dessert, and the gentlemen's wine. The first was a plum pudding on a plate nearly two feet across. The second was a large cake covered with almond paste two inches thick under its icing of white sugar set with crystallized rose-petals and the word H E T T Y picked out in little silver balls. Upon the icing were impaled twenty-four little bees-wax candles which had yet to be lit. The pudding was ready to be set aflame, and Cook was about to pour brandy over it when Polly came into the kitchen.

"Let me do it!" cried Hugh, suddenly. He sprang up from the chair where he had been reclining and felt in a waistcoat pocket for the silver box of cross-threaded lucifers he carried there. "No, wait a moment, the lights in the dining-room must be put out first." He crossed the room to the speaking-tube which connected with the room above. Taking out the stopper, he blew into the mouth-piece. A faint sound, as of a bo's'n's pipe, came from upstairs. Sidney's voice said, "Is that you, Hugh?"

"Yes, good evening, old chap. Now listen. Put out those ghastly gas-jets. And all but one candle. Douse that as I come through the doorway with the pudding. My God, I'm glad you're there. I was detained, tell the pater, will you, blast his eyes. Au revoir."

Taking the bottle, Hughie poured brandy recklessly over the pudding. Then he took one of the lucifers from his box, struck it on the serrated under-edge and touched the spirit with the yellow light. Immediately pale flames ran up the dark and glistening sides of the pudding and spread until the entire dish was writhing with blue breath. "Now Polly my gal, light the candles on Miss Hetty's cake, and follow me."

"Go carefully, don't you go and set yourself alight, Master Hughie, for goodness gracious sake! You don't want to kill yourself."

"I do," replied Hughie, putting the brandy bottle in a pocket.

He went out of the kitchen, preceded by lambent fire.

At the top of the stairs he put down the tray, and taking the bottle from his pocket splashed the spirit over one cuff of his jacket, then over the other. He put the empty bottle to one side of the stairs, and taking the dish again went forward to the dining-room door.

Within that room with its heavy plush curtains drawn across the windows a genteel conversation in the light of the single candle had been started by Mrs. Mallard and was being carried on by that lady who now held herself upright and gracious as befitted one conscious of her own superiority. During the meal she had felt herself restricted by the thought that her tail of hair had come loose: but when the light diminished, a quick pat and fingering had assured her that all was well. So feeling more sure of herself, Mrs. Mallard introduced her favourite subject: modes of the contemporary scene in Town, as she called London, imitating the society-writer in *The Queen*. She was saying, "I hear on good authority, Mrs. Turney, that sidewhiskers in gentlemen and ringlets in ladies are coming back," when through the door came a corona of pallid flame and a livid countenance with dark eyes behind it, and a sepulchral voice said:

"God forbid!"

"Ha Mephistopheles," Sidney Cakebread exclaimed jovially, as though he were selling the mood of Hughie's entrance to the Old Man. "Good God, Hughic old chap, you're on fire!"

"Purely anticipatory of the physical end in due course of all males of the Turney family," said the sepulchral voice. Hugh held out the dish, while from his arms pale flames arose.

"Be careful, I say!" cried Thomas Turney. "Beat them out, Sidney, I say, before they burn the cloth!"

"Your hands, Hughie!" cried his mother. Those delicate slender fingers—Hughie had the best hands of all the children. Sidney Cakebread took the dish and put it on the table; then turning to Hugh, he enclosed first one sleeve and then the other in the thick and voluminous folds of a table-napkin, and Hughie was declared to be none the worse for his prank.

Before the Old Man could ask any questions Hugh turned to his mother and, the polite 'varsityman, made his apologies for appearing so late at the dinner table; then to his father he said gravely, "You will I know forgive me for my most abrupt departure this afternoon sir, but I remembered an urgent matter, and as a student of the Immortal Bard you will no doubt remember Hamlet's direction to suit the action to the word."

"So you bolted like a Spotted Dog," exclaimed Thomas Turney; and at Sidney's immediate laughter he too laughed. Sarah sighed to herself with relief.

A tap at the open door, and Polly appeared bearing the birthday cake on which the flames of the lighted tapers were wagging about.

"Lor' bless me soul!" exclaimed Thomas Turney. "First a pudden to tighten us up, now a cake. Piling Ossian on Pelion, eh Hughie? You were at school last, so tell us what it means, my boy."

"I can venture to give only my own explanation of such a phrase, sir," said Hughie, seating himself carefully between Theodora and Mrs. Mallard. "Ossian was an old huntsman of centaurs on Mount Ida, feeding them on lemons, and Ossian's piles of peel were notorious in the mythology of Brummagem. At least, sir, that is the only explanation that your phrase evokes in my mind."

"Dear me," exclaimed Thomas Turney. "Have you been to Toole's theatre lately?"

Theodora smiled at Hughie. His eyes brightened. Mrs. Mallard was impressed with Hugh Turney's ease of speech, and wished that Lancelot had been to the university; but Mr. Mallard had been dead against it, as a waste of time and money.

"Now where's your sister Hetty, my boy?" asked Thomas Turney. "We must wait for her to blow out the candles."

"I expect she will be here in a moment, Tom," said Sarah. "Mrs. Mallard, a little plum pudding? Or will you wait for some birthday cake? We kept the cake until the men were home, so the two together may appear a little unusual."

"An old country custom, Mrs. Turney, which I hear the Queen keeps up at both York Cottage and Balmoral."

"What, pudding and cake together?" enquired Mr. Mallard.

"No, only a cake, to round off a meal, so I hear on good authority. Taken with a little light wine, medicinally of course, such as a glass of marsala or even sarsaparilla. On informal occasions, needless to add. What a wonderful reign it has been, to be sure. The greatest queen in all our island story."

"And yet you know, none of the credit for the improvements in woman's status during the reign so far can be placed to the Queen's personal account, Mrs. Mallard." Theodora spoke in a slow meditative voice, as she stared at the tapers on the cake. "An age is truly great and advancing when its men and women of genius are appreciated, and their talents are used, by the sovereign. Elizabeth was a truly great queen, using the natural leaders of her age, not frustrating them by inertia. The frustration of Florence Nightingale is typical. As everyone knows now, she dared to suggest that wounded men in hospital should be cared for by women, the natural nurses and guardians of the young and the hurt. The spirit of the times almost broke her, before, during, and after putting her humanitarian idea into action. The spirit of the times has endured to this day."

"Hear, hear," said Hughie.

"I could not agree with you more," remarked Aunt Marian, with sudden intensity as she peered through the chrysanthemums.

"May I offer you some pudding, Dora?" asked Sarah.

"May I wait to have some of Hetty's cake, Mrs. Turney?"

"Certainly dear. Now Lancelot, may I call you Lancelot, you will have some, won't you? Take it to Mr. Lancelot, Polly, with the brandy-sauce on the sideboard. Mr. Mallard, you will have just a little?"

Mr. Mallard said he would take just a trifle, really the veriest trifle, thanking Mrs. Turney.

Mrs. Mallard felt impatience with what the younger woman had just said, but determined to be always correctly genteel, she remarked that a woman's proper place was surely in the home, and not in the outside world which was the natural sphere of men. "Though I am not saying that Miss Nightingale was not right in her contention during the Crimean War, Miss Maddison, I can say with conviction that I most sincerely hope that she will never allow herself to be associated with the present deplorable trends for the equalisation of the sexes."

Thomas Turney chuckled. He enjoyed what to himself he called hearing the hens cackling among themselves.

"I haven't the pleasure of Miss Nightingale's acquaintance, nor do I think I would derive any benefit from propinquity with her, despite the fame of her youth," went on Mrs. Mallard. "But I am convinced that only trouble to a few deluded women can follow in the matter of the present feminist agitation. The suffrage is outside woman's proper sphere. I cannot say I am at all impressed by any young woman bothering herself with the idea of such ridiculous nonsense."

"My dear," said Mr. Mallard, chewing a spoonful of pudding. "I have never heard you speak so eloquently."

"Do you know," Theodora's voice went on, almost dreamily, "during the past fifty years the Indian Government alone has engaged in nearly one hundred wars and what are called punitive expeditions. Our country's so-called success is based on force, by which we take from the rest of the world what we require for—not the nation, but for the basis of the vast fortunes of the few."

"You talk like a Socialist, Miss Maddison."

Mrs. Mallard was upright with disapprobation.

"Oh no, I am sure she is nothing like that," protested Aunt Marian anxiously through the flowers.

"I have no politics," went on Theodora, serenely. "I care only for human beings as human beings. And forgive me saying it, but one feels that the present trends can only end in one way, as the true virtues of countrymen, who are the basis of our healthy stock, are simply disregarded in what is virtually worship of mammon. Young men die, in the high beliefs of their patriotism, when they are but—but——" Theodora's voice quivered, faltered, ceased. Silently the tears ran down her cheeks. She tried to smile them away.

Hugh Turney, who had been silent during Theodora's words, his eyes staring at the bright blown points ringing the birthday cake, began to speak in the awkward silence.

"With the company's permission, and yours, father, I would like you to hear what the poet wrote in this connection.

"'*In vain the laughing girl will lean*
To greet her love with love-lit eyes.
Down in some treacherous black ravine,
Clutching his flag, the dead boy lies . . .'

Then the poet says, in another verse, I must apologize for not recalling it properly:

"'*For some are by the Delhi walls,*
And many in the Afghan land
And many where the Ganges falls
Through seven mouths of shifting sand.

And some in Russian waters lie
And others in the seas which are
The portals of the East . . .'

I can't remember further, but the poet has expressed the truth which is the mission of the artist——" his voice became harder with satire, "Alma-Tadema, Lord Leighton, and all the other fashionable propagators of sentimental nonsense notwithstanding, as the lawyers phrase it."

Mrs. Mallard was equal to this modern wrong-headedness. Turning to Hugh on her right hand and glancing past his forward-staring profile to Theodora beyond she said firmly, "Does it not occur to you young people that we are but the agents of a Power Above, and that by bringing a Christian civilization to so many savage and backward tribes and races we are but acting with the Will of Providence?"

We give a Bible with one hand, and receive a bag of gold in the other, sneered Hughie to himself. Even Hughie would not have dared to utter such dangerous thoughts aloud.

"Who wrote those poems, may I ask, not Tennyson I should say?" enquired Mrs. Mallard.

"A modern-minded man called Oscar Wilde, Mrs. Mallard."

"I cannot pretend that I have ever heard of him," said Mrs. Mallard, with an air of triumphant finality.

"I hope not, indeed," said Mr. Mallard, in a quiet aside to Thomas Turney. "Hardly a savoury topic for a family gathering, eh?"

"Surely Oscar Wilde wrote 'The Silver King'?" Aunt Marian made hazard. "I saw it on Brighton beach once, in a booth of acting folk, next to the man who ate broken glass for a living. It was most affecting, where the poor little boy died."

"What, did he eat the boy as well as the glass, he–he–he?" chuckled Thomas Turney.

"Perhaps he needed a lesson, that little boy," said Sidney Cakebread trying to maintain a light note.

"The 'Silver King', I fancy, was by the author of 'The Murder in the Red House Barn'," remarked Hughie. "The well-known friend of Dickens, Mr. Mellow D. Rama."

"Of course, Hughie's right!" declared Aunt Marian, fluttering her eyelids at the dear boy.

"Now then, Hugh, leave philosophy and such matters to those who know more about them than you do!" Thomas Turney winked at his son. "Stick to your last, or rather to your resin, ha–ha–ha. What d'ye say, Sidney, you're a level-headed fellow?"

"Literature is a subject a little beyond my scope, sir," replied Sidney Cakebread. "But if I may say so, I find all points of view most interesting."

The pudding was removed to the sideboard, the plates were taken away, and dishes of apples, nuts, grapes, tangerines, fruit preserved in *sucre-glace*—figs, cherries, apricots, bullaces, plums, medlars—were placed on the table with various kinds of confectionery and sweetmeat, including pink and white sugar-mice, which Sarah had included for old times' sake, remembering the early days when Tom and she had started their married life together in a little wooden cottage, with a pantile roof, in the village of Camberwell. For a penny, four sugar-mice could be bought in those days; such delight for the little ones, Charley, Dorrie, Hughie, and Hetty! She smiled as she recalled the excitement of the children, eagerly opening their Christmas stockings in the first light of dawn.

Taking the opportunity to forestall any enquiries from Tom about the absent Hetty, Sarah prepared to get up from her chair as soon as she saw they had finished. Mrs. Mallard, Aunt Marian, Dora and Dorrie took their cue from her, and saying, "Let us leave the gentlemen over their wine," Sarah led them through the door held open by Hughie.

Chapter 12

HETTY HEARS BAD NEWS

RICHARD MADDISON had remained silent when first Hetty had called softly in the darkness, "Honk!" and again, "Honk!" She waited, uncertainly; then he coughed, and after an interval, his voice said from the darkness, "Do not catch cold, please, on my account. You had better go back to your party."

"Oh Dickie, I am so glad you are here!" She went to him, and feeling the lapels of his coat, laid her cheek against his chest. He stood unmoving.

She took his hand, which was cold, and pressed it against her bodice. "Dearest, why haven't you lit the lantern, to warm your hands by?"

He made no reply to her question, but said, "Are you enjoying the party?"

"Oh Dickie, you know that I cannot possibly enjoy the party under the circumstances. Please try and understand, I could not leave before, really I couldn't."

Richard had waited by the summer-house for almost two hours, in suspense, and in a desperate state of mind, owing to what had taken place that afternoon in the office of the secretary of Doggetts' Bank. His marriage had been discovered; he had lost his billet.

For two hours he had been in the summer-house, sometimes advancing upon the path towards the house; returning to rest on the seat; getting up again; starting to leave, a man distracted. Once he had gone to the dining-room window and peered through a gap in the curtains, preparatory to entering and demanding an interview with Mr. Turney, whom he imagined to be the cause of all his misery. And, final blow, his dark lantern had been removed from its usual place in the summer-house.

As he had grown colder, his feet especially so, his dejection had increased to the point of hopelessness. The old familiar wild impulse had come to him, to hurt himself beyond recovery; to end his life by going to London, entering the river by the steps on the newly-built Embankment near Cleopatra's Needle, a lonely place where little traffic passed, and being carried on the ebb-tide to oblivion. He would hold his face underwater, and without struggle, seek the darkness into which Mother had gone. He had fought against the feeling that Mother was awaiting him, remote and sad, in the shades beyond the torment of life. Oh, why could she not leave him alone?

"I've got some sandwiches for you, Dickie. You must be terribly hungry. I came out, before Mr. and Mrs. Mallard and Sidney and Dorrie came, but you weren't here. At last I made the excuse of getting a jar of pickled pears, which Polly had forgotten. Please eat, dear, you need food at the right times, you know, more than most people."

"I am afraid that there are more important things than food to be considered just now."

"Dickie, I couldn't help it, truly I couldn't! Papa gave me no chance to leave the table before. Oh, I wish it wasn't my birthday without you, really I do. Please eat, *do*, dearest. I left the lantern all ready to be lit, in its usual place in the corner behind the sparrow-net, and filled it with colza-oil. I would have lit the wick, but it might have burnt up, and set fire to the summer-house, as you said it might, so I didn't." She was near to tears.

Richard had eaten nothing since midday, when he had had his usual glass of milk and bathbun in the Golden Grain Company's tea-shop in the Strand. For a year now he had been what he called economising, in order to save for the time when he would be able to set up a home of his own with Hetty.

Hetty's tears at first made Richard the more bleak; but as she broke down and sobbed, his own unhappiness began to dissolve, a black icicle, within him. "Oh, please do not cry, and so make matters worse."

"No dear, I'll try not to."

He sat down, and allowed her to put her arms round his shoulders and to kiss him; gradually he responded to the warmth he so desired. He put his arms round her, and held his bearded cheek against her cheek, while she hugged him and stroked his hair, and feeling a tear falling on her wrist, she gave a low cry, and rose beside him to comfort him the more.

"Why haven't you lit the lantern, dearest?"

"I could not find it."

"But I put it behind the sparrow-net. Are you sure it isn't there?"

"I felt for it, when first I arrived, and not finding it in its usual place, I concluded that you had forgotten all about me—and did not want to see me."

"Oh how could you think such a thing! Oh, poor, poor Dickie! Do forgive me, dearest. I will find it this very moment."

"No, the floor is dusty. I will look again."

Richard felt behind the sparrow-net, which belonged to the gardener who took the birds sometimes in the ivy after roosting-time, selling them for a halfpenny each to the local Sparrow Club. He could not find the lantern.

"I am positive I put it there, Dickie."

To herself she said, I must pray to Saint Anthony, and having done so, she remembered suddenly that *she had left the lantern in the kitchen.* Hardly had a feeling of relief arisen in her when she became afraid again, lest Dickie be cross with her for doing such a careless thing. Supposing Papa had seen it! Desperately she tried to summon up courage to tell Dickie. He was patting the floor now, on his hands and knees, methodically patting every square inch. Swallowing and then taking a deep breath, Hetty made a clucking noise with her mouth, and said in a loud whisper, "There now, I do believe I must have left it by the kitchen door. How very very stupid of me, I'll never forgive myself!"

Her hand went to her mouth, and she began to bite the nail of her index finger, an action which gave relief to her thoughts until realizing what she was doing she pulled away the hand and held it clenched by her side, thankful for the darkness, for Dickie hated to see her biting her nails.

For many years Hetty had been struggling within herself to give up the bad habit. Thomas Turney had offered her a gold Waltham watch, the twin of her silver one, as soon as she could show him two sets of fingernails "grown to within reasonable distance of the fingertips." Sarah had bought from the chemist a little blue bottle of bitter aloes to put on her nails to remind her, as well as a pair of cotton gloves to be worn at night; but without result. Once her father had become angry, and told her that she had a guilty conscience over something, and ever since Hetty's sense of guilt had deepened. She knew herself to be a wicked, deceitful person, and she prayed frequently on her knees to the Virgin Mary, asking humbly for help to be a better girl, in the privacy of her bedroom and also during her visits to church at morning and evening services on Sundays. But the habit had persisted.

Hetty fetched the lantern from the kitchen, where she had left it. Hurrying back, she gave it to Richard, and with a sigh of relief watched him lighting the wick. He trimmed it, closed the front, and then placing it on the table sat down. Hetty sat beside him, and opened the tin box she had hidden in the summer-house that afternoon. The lantern began to give out its comforting smell of hot Japanned metal, and he swung back the front to look at the flame, which was inclined to rise quickly when the dark slide was shutting off the beam. Then closing it again, they watched the chinks of light emanating from the angular metal cap.

He turned the metal screen, and a warm glow illumined her face and throat. "There, it will dry your tears." Smilingly she took out of the tin box a table napkin, which she spread on the table before setting out the supper.

"This is my real birthday supper, Dickie, the other doesn't really count. Please eat everything up, dearest. I hope the sandwiches aren't dry."

"They are excellent," replied Richard, eating ravenously.

"I'll go and get you your coffee."

Hetty went away, after reassuring him several times that she would return. She came back with a jug of café-au-lait which Cook, who was partly in her confidence (but not about the marriage) had ready. With the hot milky liquid inside his stomach, Richard's mood lightened, and remembering the gifts he had brought, he leant over the table, picked up the bunch of roses tied in a spray of maidenhair fern, and gave them to her, together with a book tied up in brown paper.

She took the roses and smelled them, delighted with them; knowing with what care, and after what thought, he had bought them; and then opening the packet with hurried movements, she took out a leather-bound volume and held it in the light. It was *The Ingoldsby Legends*.

"Thank you ever so much, it is just what I wanted," she cried, and kissed him on the top of his head. "What a wonderful book it is, to be sure. I've always wanted to read the stories. Oh, what a pity you cannot come into the house, and be with the others.

But it won't be long now, dearest, before we are together. Mamma is going to tell Papa everything, when the guests have gone, tonight."

She felt him stiffen.

"I am ready to leave home, and come with you—if you still want me."

She heard him take a deep breath.

"I have got something I must tell you, Hetty," he said. "I have given up my billet in the bank."

"Dickie!"

"Yes," he said, "the fact of our marriage has come out at last. And you may as well hear the worst. It may mean emigrating to Australia."

Hetty was now unable to speak. Again the thought of leaving Mamma, Dorrie, Hughie, Joey, Papa—leaving her home, friends—everything of her life—for a blankness half way round the earth, appalled her. Then she realized that even to think of herself at that moment was disloyal to Dickie. Of course her place was by his side.

"I have enough money saved for the passage," went on Richard, and again Hetty's feelings sank. "It is a new world, and there are many chances for anyone prepared to work hard. As you know, my younger brother went there some four or five years ago, and he has already fallen on his feet. He has a farm in the fertile coastal country, and writes to say that he is starting a ewe-flock, and the growing of corn as well as fruit. What is the alternative for me? A life such as I have lived for some years now—if I can secure a post in a commercial house, which is doubtful, as I shall have no references as to character. Also, the competition is severe."

"But Doggetts', Dickie—how did they find out?"

Richard was silent awhile; then he said quietly, "Well, perhaps I had better confine myself to saying only what I know. The Secretary called me in this morning and said that my presence was required before the Partners at three o'clock. He told me that I would be given an opportunity of answering a charge that I had broken a rule of the Bank. I knew what was coming, of course. He said it was a matter of punctilio, as I had undertaken to observe the rules as a condition of entering upon my service. So I had no alternative but then and there to write out my resignation."

"Dickie!"

"With it, I tendered my apology, and asked the Partners' consideration in the matter of not allowing it to go further, for the sake of my wife."

"Oh, Dickie—Dickie——"

"Well, it is no good crying over spilt milk. The Secretary took me before the Partners. The Baroness was there. I said I had come to express my regret to her Ladyship in person, and to ask them to accept my word for it that there were extenuating circumstances. The Secretary spoke a word for me, saying that in all the years I had been there I had been punctual, and meticulous in my duties."

Hetty was surprised at his calmness. She felt confidence coming back to herself. She sought and found his hand. "Were they, the Partners, severe with you, dearest?"

"No, on the contrary, they listened with every consideration, including the Baroness, though she did not speak. The Senior Partner said that the rule had been made as much for the protection of the young men in the Shop as for the good name of Doggetts' itself. He said that in some circumstances a young husband might be tempted to behave otherwise than scrupulously, perhaps in monetary difficulties due to a wife's sickness. He said also that it was his duty to uphold the prestige and traditions of Doggett and Co., and therefore had no alternative, much as he regretted it, but to advise the Secretary to accept my resignation. So there we are."

"Oh, Dickie, and it is all my fault!"

"No, you must not think that, Hetty."

"Oh, Dickie, whatever shall you do?"

"Become a cab-runner, or go to the wall." He added bleakly, "You must remain at your home here, for the time-being, Hetty. I am afraid there is nothing else for it. Unless, of course, we make up our minds to emigrate. But I do not wish to influence you in any way," he added bitterly, "I have seen too much of parental interference in the lives of others, to wish to obtrude in any way on your judgment."

Hetty sat silent, the small concealed glow beside her. She made an effort to fight against the dreadful feelings that had come upon her. "Oh, I love your little lantern, Dickie. What should we do without it?" Her words made him feel less alone. He asked a question that he had thought to keep to himself. Almost without knowing what he was saying, he cried, "Do you think that Mr. Turney has found out about us, Hetty?"

"Oh dear no, I am sure of that, Dickie! No, certainly not. Oh, I see what you are thinking! No, I am sure Papa would not do such a thing as to tell anyone, in any event." She moved to him, and kissed him. Poor Dickie!

He allowed himself to be comforted. "Well, I hardly know what to think."

"Oh, I am sure it was not through Papa, dearest."

Richard remembered the incident of the cigar stub at London Bridge Station earlier that evening.

"Well, what shall we do now? Are you determined to tell Mr. Turney tonight, as we had arranged?"

"I think it is the best thing, Dickie. Mamma is going to tell him. I shall be with her, of course."

"Do you think I should come, as well? I do not much care for the thought of skulking in the background. But at the same time, I do not want to be more fuel for the flames."

"Oh, no Dickie, pray do not think of affronting Papa! Mamma will break the news to him gently. Now won't you eat the cake, Dickie?" she said faintly, for her heart was thudding in her ears. It had been her determination to tell him that very evening that she was with child; but how could she tell him now? Her hand strayed to her mouth; he saw her; she pulled it away. Perhaps after all it would be for the best to write and tell him. Or would it cause him to misunderstand, and to go walking all night in the rain? Oh, she must acquire more courage, through prayer, to face Papa and to tell him the truth, and not wait to let him find out for himself. Perhaps if she threw herself on his mercy, Papa might relent, and even help Dickie. But the image of Papa's face turning red, and his angry voice, arose before her . . her fingers went to her mouth again.

"There is no need for you to bite your nails," said Richard, unhappily. "I do not bite mine."

"I am sorry, dearest. I forgot for a moment."

"I must not keep you any longer," he said. "Well, do not worry too much over what I have told you," he added, without conviction. "A pretty poor birthday you have had so far as I am concerned, I am afraid. Ah well, perhaps after all Australia is the solution. This country is very nearly played out. Free Trade has ruined it."

"Oh something will turn up, I am sure it will!" cried Hetty. "Meanwhile, do please try and not worry. I have a strong feeling that things will come all right in the end. I have faith in divine Providence, dearest. If you could, too, it would help you, I am sure."

"Oh well, I have seen too much in my time, to prove the contrary, I am afraid. Now I must be getting back, it is nearly ten o'clock."

Hetty sighed. "Yes, I suppose I must go into the house, too. Ah well, this separation won't be for much longer, dearest. Oh, I nearly forgot to tell you, Dorrie is going to have another little one. That will make four. She is so pleased, she wants a daughter, she has three boys already."

"You'll be telling me next that you are on the way to becoming a mother yourself," he replied, with a suggestion of irony.

Now was her chance. What could she say? Dare she tell him, after his bad news? If only she could speak. Oh dear, it was a lost chance; for he said, "Well, it is rather a long walk back to my diggings, but the exercise will do me good. Now you will keep me posted about Mr. Turney's attitude? And if the worst should happen, do not hesitate to call on me, will you? After all, Mr. Turney has no legal jurisdiction over you, since you are of age, as well as a legal wife."

"Yes dear, of course, naturally!" She gave a little laugh of relief, and kissed him.

Having blown out the flame in the lantern, and hidden it under the seat, Richard went to the door in the wall; and uttering a subdued "Honk" in reply to Hetty's would-be cheerful "Honk", he went carefully down the watery lane, as the clocks of Cross Aulton began to chime the hour. Hearing them, Hetty closed and bolted the gate and hurried back into the house.

Chapter 13

A MUSICAL EVENING

THE FURNISHINGS of the drawing-room of Maybury Lodge, whither the ladies had retired, had started as a mixture of Sarah's country style and what she and Tom had purchased from London shops after they had moved away from Camberwell when it was yet partly rural in spite of the railway and the rows of brick houses springing up to the south. In their early days tame geese still walked on the green, with cows and dingy-fleeced sheep. Coming in middle age to the Surrey village, they had entered a new society, commensurate with their larger income. Neither Tom nor Sarah had any social ambitions, for themselves or their children. Born on neighbouring farms, they came of people who touched their hats or curtsied to the gentry as a matter of tradition rather than of subservience, while feeling themselves as established upon their own acres as the premier ducal family of the county whose park was enclosed by a wall twelve miles in length, and whose land outside the park extended to many thousands of acres. Sarah's forebears had been tenants for more than four centuries of the Duke bearing a name famous in the history of England; while Thomas Turney's forebears had held the copyhold of their land since the seventeenth century.

The hatstand in the hall at Maybury Lodge had been made of the head of a fallow deer given to Thomas Turney's father, Nathaniel, by the Head Forester of the Duke. A haunch of venison had arrived every Christmas within living memory from the Great House.

When setting out to select furniture for Maybury Lodge, which had been taken on a long lease, Tom and Sarah had meant to buy for use rather than for ornament. But the shops in Tottenham Court Road had for sale only the kind of stuff, as Tom called it, that was modern, otherwise the latest thing, as the tall white-faced shop-walker described the various suites and pieces. Tom chose himself a heavy roll-top desk, or *escritoire* as the animated dummy in the frockcoat called it, and then went away to his office, leaving the rest of the choosing to Sarah, who had been given a hundred and fifty pounds to spend.

As Sarah could not make up her mind, Tom had returned with her in the afternoon, and selected for her. He bought for value; he bought for solidity and endurance.

During the years since, the drawing-room had come to express the new prosperity, and one by one the old simple pieces of oak furniture brought by them from Camberwell had found their way into the servants' rooms, the box-room and the garret under the roof. The Turneys had conformed to the style of villadom. In the dining-room the heavy mahogany table, capable of being extended thrice its smallest length, was surrounded by chairs of similar wood, upholstered in horsehair covered with green Moroccan leather. A mirror on the chimneypiece, now called mantelpiece, was likewise framed in mahogany, holding about twenty square feet of glass nearly a quarter of an inch thick. In the drawing-room a smaller chimney glass stood behind a framework of many shelves, on which stood various knick-knacks and mementoes of holiday travel. Below the overmantel stood a dark green marble clock; on either side of the clock were tall vases holding bullrushes, a couple of fragile glass domes keeping dust off waxen flowers; a bronze statuette of St. George killing the dragon; and at each end of the mantelpiece, flanking it, was a red glass column from which depended crystal drops matching the glass chandelier hanging from the centre of the ceiling. These shimmered pleasantly when in movement. The ceiling itself was overloaded, ornate with bas-relief and pattern of fruit, birds, and mixed-up architectural decoration made of plaster-of-paris in moulds and then stuck upon it. Hughie had once called the drawing-room a repository of the irrespectable for the irreparable.

There was indeed something of a furniture repository in the room. One had to be careful not to bump into or knock over some of the more fragile objects standing within it. There were seven stools and two firescreens worked in embroidered patchwork; several cabinets and what-nots; shelves of china vases; above the cornices of the walls were rows of plates and dishes, many of beautiful design; below them hung framed steel-engravings of Landseer's stags and Leighton's classic reproductions, partly covering a thick wallpaper of dark red, on which were golden clusters of unnatural birds and cornucopia of alleged flowers and fruit. There were several chairs, settees, sofas, and couches of varying comfort; pillars of china holding bowls from which ferns drooped; a grand piano in one corner, a harp (one of Hugh's discarded ambitions) in another; a tall open corner cupboard loaded with "chiney", otherwise china cups, saucers, and bowls, in a third. A carpet covered the floor, and various rugs lay on the carpet.

Sarah was relieved that Hetty had returned while the men were still in the dining-room, talking over their port wine, nuts, and cigars. She knew at once by her face that she had been seeing Richard. Hetty entered almost blithely, and went to sit beside her older sister and talk about her three nephews, Bertie, Ralph, and Gerry. Dorrie was knitting a baby's sock, for her baby expected in April. For a moment Hetty felt an identical satisfaction, for her own little one would be coming about that time. They would be able to play together as they grew up! Dorrie knew that Hetty was married, but she had not yet been told of the pregnancy. The secret marriage had been kept from everyone else, as Sarah had not wanted Tom to feel the more hurt when eventually he found out.

"Shall we have a little music?" suggested Sarah. "How is your migraine, Hetty, has it passed, dear?"

"Oh, have you the migraine?" asked Mrs. Mallard. "Do make use of my vinaigrette, it belonged to my grandmamma, who was given it for a wedding present by the sister of a man who knew the mother of the wife of Charles Dickens."

She held out a little gold and enamel box containing smelling salts. "A long sniff is an excellent restorative, I find." Turning to Theodora, "I don't suppose you ever suffer from migraine, Miss Maddison?"

"Well, do you know," replied Theodora, "I have never experienced any kind of headache since I gave up eating meat and wearing constrictive clothing. But then," she smiled, "I am supposed to be what is called a crank, and believe that half our ills come from the artificialities of the age."

Often Theodora did not wear the sort of clothes that normal young women wore; she made her own, wearing a sort of loose gown, based on the flowing robes of the women of ancient Greece.

People stared at Theodora in streets and omnibuses, and children sometimes called after her.

Out of politeness Hetty took the box from Mrs. Mallard, and after admiring its workmanship, she took a discreet sniff and then announcing that she felt ever so much better, returned it to Mrs. Mallard.

"Are we going to have the pleasure of hearing you at the piano, Hetty?"

"I am very much out of practice, Mrs. Mallard."

"Oh come, you know several test pieces, Hetty," her mother reminded her, gently.

"*Several* test pieces!" remarked Mrs. Mallard. "What an accomplished daughter you have, Mrs. Turney."

"Dora is the real musician," said Hetty. "And of course, Hugh."

"Lancelot as you know is so very fond of music," went on Mrs. Mallard. "Really, he has a delicate touch with the flute, but likes to hide his light under a bushel, if I may so describe that dismal object he now affects to play. The buffoon, Mr. Mallard calls it. No wonder he has taken to playing only in a room by himself."

"He did bring the bassoon, did he not?" enquired Hetty.

"Yes; but I should warn you that Lancelot declares he will never play a solo before company until he has achieved complete mastery over his instrument."

"Of course I would not dream of asking him, Mrs. Mallard. In any case it would spoil the effect of the duet in the Skaters' Waltz. The two together are really very good indeed. I wish they would dress up for it, perhaps in gipsy costume, it is ever so funny, as well as being musically interesting."

"Well, I suppose hearing is believing, like seeing, they say; but I shall have to be fully convinced first. Now do tell me, has the idea of the quartet been given up altogether?"

"Well, for the time being, Mrs. Mallard."

Mrs. Mallard turned to Theodora. "I understand that your brother used to play the 'cello. Does he not play any longer?"

"I think he feels he needs more practice, Mrs. Mallard."

"Well, in that he is matched by Lancelot, who spends much of his leisure time in a room at the top of the house, out of the way of Mr. Mallard, who has little or no ear for serious music, although of course like most men he likes to sing. I expect he will sing tonight, should anyone care to ask him for a song. He has brought his latest song—The Bandolero."

"I will certainly insist that he sings," said Hetty. "But Dora must play the piano. You *must* hear her play Chopin! Do play one of the *Etudes* to Mrs. Mallard, will you, Dora dear?"

"It would give me the greatest pleasure to hear Miss Maddison play, after such a testimonial," said Mrs. Mallard, smiling graciously.

Hetty lifted up the lid of the music stool and took out her sheets. She found her favourite Chopin *Etude*, and putting it on the music-stand, smiled to Dora to come to the piano.

Theodora in her white flouncey dress strode to the Bechstein grand, and seated herself on the stool. Hetty stood beside her, to turn over the sheets, her eyes bright with expectation. For within Dora's quiet and gentle aspect was a spirit that could, and did, astonish many people when she played the piano. Mrs. Mallard was so affected the moment Theodora's hands moved over the keyboard, suddenly to bring a startling crash of chords and trills upon the air, and then a flowing sadness which seemed to Mrs. Mallard to be pleading for something beyond life, and then to be arising in triumph and beauty. She forgot herself entirely, and with closed eyes leaned back against the sofa. The visit to the Turneys, which she had dreaded, as many people in a room together usually gave her a headache, was all of a moment something infinitely wonderful. She had not known that the piano could be such a beautiful thing, almost alive.

In her mind Mrs. Mallard was walking through a meadow, amidst flowers and the singing of birds, infinitely fair, accompanied by a man whose movements beside her were light as air, a man who was wise, and strong, and gentle as he was noble in bearing. But sadly, ah sadly, he was dedicated to a mission beyond mortal following, and she had to walk in the sunlit meadow alone; and though darkness came, and night with only the stars for guidance, she knew his spirit was watching over her, asking her to be happy, and to know that he was always with her, as she followed along the path of life alone.

The music ended, and Mrs. Mallard touched her nose with a lace handkerchief, coughing discreetly as she dabbed her eyes. Theodora sat smiling before her.

"How it all comes from those fragile fingers, I do not know," said Dorrie, who had been affected in the same way as Mrs. Mallard.

"Thank you, thank you indeed! That is your true bent, dear young lady," cried Mrs. Mallard. "Now tell me, where does it all come from?"

"It comes from the soil," said Dora, softly, so that only Hetty should hear. Aloud she said, "Chopin had learned to be true to himself."

Later when the two friends had a moment together, Theodora explained. "You see, Hetty, Chopin always carried a pot of his native Polish soil when he went from capital to capital in Europe, playing before kings, princes, and audiences of rank and fashion. The soil reminded him of his true life, his thoughts and feelings which had come from the land which had borne him. He knew that if the artificiality of the world of privilege came between his true self, otherwise the spirit of his native soil, and his art, he would cease to be the medium of genius. I am afraid that it sounds a bit obscure, Hetty dear, but I cannot express myself very well. It is hard to describe a feeling, or an emotion."

"I think you do it wonderfully well, Dora dear. Oh, why do you not write a book, you are rather like the Brontë sister who wrote *Wuthering Heights*, I sometimes think."

"I am not so intense as Emily Brontë, she was truly efflorescent within herself. Besides, I think my metier is action, rather than words. Lots of people can write better than I can ever hope to do—I have no real talent."

"You are too modest, Dora dear. Your playing is so beautiful."

"Ah, you should hear Paderewski playing Chopin. He is the sun, I am but a candle." Her voice lowered. "Hetty, did you notice that Hugh is looking far from well? I have been thinking that perhaps I ought not to come here any more. If only he were content to be friends! He has such depths in him, and I feel I am the cause of his distraction."

"Oh no, Dora, he is not in his element in the Firm, that is all. Mamma is quite worried for him. Hush now, they are coming in."

The door opened and Mr. Mallard strolled through, the lumps of his fists showing in his trouser pockets, a smile of contentment on his face; for Mr. Mallard, after three glasses of port, had overcome an earlier acidity and thereby reached a plane where for the moment he felt well-disposed to everyone, and therefore everyone to be well-disposed towards himself. He felt young again, he wanted to sing, to stand at the piano and to feel that the deep resonance of his baritone voice was lifting all before him out of a humdrum everyday life into the romantic regions of *The Bandolero* among the mountains and the picturesque scarves and headgear of barefooted *banditti*. Mr. Mallard had brought his music with him into the drawing room when Polly had announced him, and laid it on the piano himself. He had instructed Mrs. Mallard to be sure not to forget to ask Mrs. Turney to invite him to sing.

Behind Mr. Mallard came his son, nervously pressing the wings of his starched linen collar. Lancelot also sang songs at home, his mother playing the piano, but never when his father was there; for Mr. Mallard had a critical ear for his son's tones and method of voice-production, and was ever on the alert to advise him and give him the benefit of his superior experience. In practice, this meant so many interruptions that Lancelot lost all desire to sing the various ballads which expressed his yearning for a wider life, wherein he saw himself leaving for ever the counting-house of Mallard, Carter and Turney, Ltd., and sailing away on the moonlit tide, singing a shanty as he worked the capstan, and standing on the bowsprit with the trade-wind spray on his brow and the peaks of the Andes rising among clouds in the distance.

Politely Lancelot Mallard held the door open for Sidney Cakebread and Hughie, while Tom Turney remained in the dining-room, putting corks into unfinished bottles, taking the cigar box under an arm, and snuffing the candles. Afterwards he turned one gas-jet out, the other low, and went to the drawing-room, a place he did not care much about, as it could never be homely like the sitting-room.

It was now getting on for a quarter past ten o'clock; the Mallards' carriage would be coming for them in three quarters of an hour. However, the time would pass pleasantly enough, despite Mallard's howling, as he had described it to his children at breakfast some years before, after an evening visit with their mother to the senior partner's home at Epsom. "The fellow howled like a dog, then blared like a bull-calf," had been his description, as he chuckled with head hunched into his shoulders, looking from face to face around the breakfast table.

This joke, or description, had been often repeated, until it was an established event in the Turney household. Hughie had given Mr. Mallard's latest song another title—"The Bandy-Legged 'Ero." And now that, at last, it was about to occur in actuality, Hetty felt it to be in the nature of an ordeal. Oh, pray that she did not laugh at Mr. Mallard singing! When therefore Sarah dutifully said as she laid down her crocheting, "Mr. Mallard, you will delight us all with your latest song, I hope," her agony began —the struggle not to burst out laughing. Hetty had to make herself very still, to compel herself, with something like a prayer, on no account to catch Hughie's sardonic eye across the room.

"I fear I am not in very good voice tonight, ma'm," replied Mr. Mallard, bowing, and glancing to see if his songs were on the piano top. Reassured, he added, "Got a bit of a cold in the larynx, the dry dusty City weather." He coughed, and cleared his throat.

"I trust you are going to give us 'The Bandy—er, lero', sir," said Hughie, with some gravity; and Hetty feared for a moment that she would scream; then came an alarming, quavering impulse to cry. Theodora, observing her, laid her hand upon Hetty's, and pressed it firmly.

"I trust you are going to sing with an obbligato by the bassoon, sir?" went on Hughie. "I am sure that the bassoon is the only instrument in the known history of Cacophony to be able to do justice to the more tender passages of Leslie Stuart's latest."

"Oh no, Hugh, no, do not suggest such a thing!" exclaimed Mrs. Mallard in a loud whisper, flipping away the idea with a hand.

"Mrs. Mallard, would you accompany your husband?" suggested Sarah.

"Really, ma'm, somebody else might care to perform first? Does not someone play the pianoforte?" Mr. Mallard gallantly looked around the room. "Miss Hetty, won't you oblige?"

Then as he saw hesitation in Hetty's attitude Mr. Mallard declared that, if they insisted, he would sing—*The Bandolero!* His genial eye sought the eye of his son, then Hughie's, then Mrs. Turney's, as though to find in them the same pleasant anticipation that he felt himself.

Thomas Turney, seated in a chair, one sturdy leg crossed over another, gave a pull to his nose and stared at the ceiling, thinking about an Italian stone, used in lithography, that had been offered to the Firm.

Mrs. Mallard, who as a girl had gone through the approved motions and exercises of learning to play the piano under the eye of a hopelessly depressed spinster with a stick in her hand to indicate tempo and also to award an occasional rap for wrong notes, stared anxiously at the music spread before her, and her fingers pushed at the appropriate keys, while Mr. Mallard beside her, after a swift wipe and twirl of his moustaches, took a deep breath and informed a far corner of the room that he was the Bandolero, the ga-ha-hallant Bandolero, a King with sward for pillow, who roamed the mountains, and claimed as contraband what came his way-ee-ee, he was the ga-ha-hallant Bandolero, he was an outlaw, but with a kingdom be-ne-he-heath—his sway.

All this in a voice that alternated between the mournfully nasal and the throatily blaring; but the second verse, or the sentiment of it, caused a change both of tone and production. The singer sang this with what to himself he imagined to be a wealth of great courtesy, of true chivalry, of aristocratic *noblesse oblige.* He saw himself in the part: clad in gay silks, earrings of gold, white flashing teeth, smile irresistible to the ladies, knee-breeches (also silk) and silver buckles on his shoes—one of the leading Epsom Thespian Amateurs of thirty years before. His throat very nearly closed with his delicacy of expression, so that all sound appeared to be stifled in the cavity at the back of his nose, Mr. Mallard proceeded *sotto voce*, which Hughie had once translated as 'the voice of a sot'.

> "*Senora, no danger from me need you fear*
> *For my heart beats for a maid fair as you to me dear.*
> *She prays for the pardon I soon may obtain*
> *That I shall be free to be with her again.*"

The Bandolero then referred with the most oleaginous punctilio to the jewellery he had stolen, and the new concord of ethics struck up after the robbery.

> "*I thank thee for these gracious gifts*
> *These trinkets will my men delight*
> *Now on your way, no more molested,*
> *I now salute you—Friends!*
> *Goodnight!*"

Hughie, who had been grimacing at Sidney Cakebread during the ordeal, and bending down to hide his laughter, hand over mouth, disappeared hurriedly through the door as the song was ending, his red silk handkerchief stuffed into his mouth. Sidney followed after the song was ended and found him sitting on the stairs; but Hughie was not laughing any more. His face was haggard.

"What's the matter, old man?" asked Sidney. He was alarmed.

"Sid," said Hughie, "I would like to speak to you, if I may, in confidence."

"What have you been up to, young Hughie? Got entangled with some married woman, who wants to marry you after her husband's divorced her, eh?"

"For God's sake don't joke, m'dear fellow. Come upstairs to my room, d'you mind?"

Sidney followed his young brother-in-law, for whom he had a warm affection, up to the first landing and down a passage to a room at the end. On the door was a painted shield in wood, the arms of his college. Inside the room, when he had lit the gas, Hughie turned to Sidney and looked at him with tragic eyes.

"Well, Hughie, what is it? You can trust me."

"Oh my God," groaned Hughie, and gripped the brass bedrail. Sidney was perplexed; he knew that Hughie was capable of playing the ass, as well as of crying wolf; but if he were acting now, it was a damned good performance. The boy's face was dead white, and there were deep lines beside his mouth, running down from his nose.

He put his arm round Hughie. For a moment he thought that Hughie was going to hide his face on his shoulder—Sidney was a tall man, the top of Hughie's head came well below his chin—and he was surprised by the tenderness that arose in him, a pure tenderness that he had never felt for Dorrie, much as he considered that he loved her, or for his two small sons. But Hughie did not yield to the impulse. Instead he bent his head so violently that he struck the rail of the bed, causing the loose knob at the end to rattle. Half-unconscious, Hughie hung there upon his hands, until Sidney, realizing that he had hurt himself, led him to the bed.

"What is it, Hughie? Have you hurt yourself, boy? Let's have a look—turn round——" he felt his forehead—"You've given yourself a wallop, old man, there's a bump nearly as big as a pigeon's egg on your forehead. You mustn't do such things, you know, you'll hurt yourself one day. Now sit down, and tell me all about it."

Hughie said wearily, averting his head, "You'll loathe me, Sidney. I'm not worth your kindness, old man."

Sidney waited for him to speak; but Hughie continued to sit with head turned away. He took a deep breath; he looked at Sidney; a wry smile turning to a suggestion of a sneer passed over his lips.

"Very well, I'll tell you. I've got syphilis."

"Good God!" ejaculated Sidney, and stared at Hughie. Then recovering from the shock he said in friendly tones, "Are you sure? Is it painful?"

"It's hell at times."

"Then it probably isn't the pox, but clap. How long have you had it?"

"I noticed it first about a week ago."

"Then it's clap. It hurts like the devil at first. You've got a yellow discharge, haven't you?"

Hugh shook his head. "No, it's syphilis all right. I saw a doctor this afternoon, in Villiers Street. He cauterized it, that's what hurts like the flames of Hades. It's a hard chancre, and I've got to go to him once a week and have it cauterized."

Sidney did not know what to say. Thank God, he thought, I've never had it; pure luck, of course.

"Where did you get it, old man? Not that it matters."

"Like a fool, I was half tight one evening with some chaps, friends of mine at the 'varsity, and I went home with a tart."

"Well, it's a good thing you've taken it in time. Are you going to tell the Old Man?"

"Good God, no, don't you tell him!"

"Of course not. Only it might be a good thing to tell him. What sort of a doctor is it you've got? Not a quack, is he?"

"I don't think so, he was recommended by a friend of mine, whom he cured of clap. But he's dashed expensive."

"How much has he charged you?"

"Three guineas the first visit, and he says it will be two for each subsequent visit."

"That's the devil of a lot to have to pay, old man, if you don't mind me saying so."

"I know, but what else can I do? Go to a pox hospital, and stand in a row with the sort of fellows who go there? Well, it's all up with my hopes with Dora. God, I was a damned fool. I can never marry anyone now."

"You wait and see, Hughie m'boy. There's many a man had what you've got, and no one ever been any the wiser. I should tell the Old Man if I were you. He'll help you, he's a man of the world. He's a bit of a dog himself, you know. One hears things on the road."

"At his age! It's positively immoral. He's a swine."

"Now, now, Hughie, hold your horses. A man doesn't change his nature just because he's the father of a family, you know. What does Shakespeare say in *Hamlet*—'Every man hath business and desire'. It's true today as it was then. Take my advice and tell the Old Man, Hughie."

"He'll pitch me out into the street."

"Of course he won't. If he does, you can come and live with your sister and me."

As he spoke, Sidney regretted what he had said. He remembered his young children. Hughie ought to tell the Old Man, and get proper treatment, mercury was the thing, and so catch it in the early stages.

"Look here, Hughie, let me tell the Old Man, when I get him at a quiet moment, and——"

"I told you in confidence——" Hughie cried; but Sidney went on, "Of course I won't say a word without your consent; but do think it over. There's no need to feel it a disgrace—lots of men get it, it's quite common; and you need proper treatment, modern treatment. That cauterizing business is out of date, I'm convinced. No, you needn't think I've had it, I haven't, I've missed it in my younger days, and more by luck than judgment. Let me tell the Old Man, Hughie. Don't decide now. Let's go down and join the others. Bring your fiddle, and give us a tune. And keep your pecker up, Hughie. I'll see you through." He patted his brother-in-law on the shoulder.

"I feel that I'll never be able to play the fiddle again!"

"Nonsense. Of course you will. And when you're cured, as you will be in the proper hands, you'll laugh at this evening. Now come down with me—it's your sister's birthday, after all. Poor kid, she doesn't have much of a life, does she? Feeling better?"

"The burning pains have gone, for the moment." Hughie got up from the bed. "Well, thanks, Sid, you're a friend in need. God, I nearly threw myself in the river tonight. I fainted when the doctor told me what I'd got, though I'd suspected it."

"We'll soon have you right again, in no time. Actually, though, I believe it takes six months or so, to cure. I have heard that it came originally into England from the Holy Land, brought back by the Crusaders. Perhaps one of your ancestors introduced it, young fellow."

Hughie's cheeks had more colour. He was cheerful again. They went downstairs to the drawing-room, where they remained with the others until the Mallards' cab came just before eleven o'clock.

"Very well, you tell the Old Man," whispered Hughie to Sidney, when the guests had gone, and good-nights spoken. "I'm going to bed. Come up and tell me what happens, will you? But for God's sake don't bring him up. Be tactful, won't you?"

"Leave it to me, Hughie."

But Sidney Cakebread did not tell Thomas Turney about his son's plight that evening. Nor was the father to know about it until several months had passed. That night at Maybury Lodge was to be remembered long by all who were in the house, as a night which changed the course of several lives; at least, that was the illusion.

At about ten minutes after the hour of eleven, while the Mallards were bowling away in the rubber-tyred cab towards their home; and Richard Maddison was striding through the streets echoing with the wheels of waggons taking vegetables to Covent Garden market; and Dorrie, upstairs in her bedroom with Sidney, whom she had led away from the drawing-room at a whisper from her mother, was waiting while the bow-knot of her corsets was being undone by Sidney's fingers; and Hugh was lying in his nightshirt in bed, sleepless and heavy hearted; and the embryo within Hetty, sitting still on the sofa, was giving its first tremulous flutterings within the water-jacket of her womb; and Theodora was brushing her hair in the bedroom she was sharing for the night with Hetty; and Marian Turney was on her knees by her bedside, praying with the simplicity of a child taught by a loved mother; and Cook and Polly had gone each to their rooms, with the smallest windows facing north, at the top of the house:—then Sarah, swallowing the saliva in her mouth and feeling a weakness in both chest and legs, turned to her husband reclining in a chair by the fire for a few moments' relaxation before going to bed, and said:

"Tom, I have something to tell you, but first will you give me your promise to try and keep calm?"

"Hey?" he exclaimed. "Something to tell me. Well, what is it?"

Hetty, beside her Mamma on the sofa, closed her eyes.

"It concerns our dear daughter Hetty, Tom. But I beg of you to keep calm, for her sake, dear. She is far from well."

"What are you trying to say, woman? What are you keeping me in suspense for? Is she ill? Has she seen the doctor? Why haven't I been told? For God's sake speak out, why can't you!"

"Tom, pray keep calm. The girl must not be upset in any way."

"Who's upset her? I'm sitting here, aren't I? Come, out with it? What's the matter with Hetty? Are her lungs weak? Speak woman, speak!" he shouted.

"Tom," said Sarah, "pray be a little quieter, for Hetty's sake."

Sarah's voice was weak; and her agitation, imperfectly concealed, had the effect on her husband of disturbing him the more. His overloaded stomach went sick.

Sarah hardly knew how to continue. She dared not say what she had to say; she dared not keep silent. God, come to my help, she thought wildly within her mind.

"What is the matter with your mother?" He sat up in the chair, and turned to Hetty. "Why is she tormenting a man like this? Come, you have a tongue in your head, unlike this—this—this fool of a woman sitting here. Speak, my girl, speak!"

"Papa!" cried Hetty, seeing the tears running down her mother's face. "Oh Mamma, oh Papa, I beg you, dearest Papa, not to continue so, please Papa!"

Thomas Turney drew a deep breath. His neck and face were flushed. His hands gripped the handles of the chair in which he sat so hard that the knuckles were yellow. He watched his wife's face with stony contempt. He breathed deeply again, and the grip of his fingers on the chair lessened.

"Very well," he said. "You have something to tell me. I will wait until you find your tongue."

He waited, in a silence disturbed only by the noise of Sarah, held by Hetty, trying to subdue her weeping.

"Tom," said Sarah, trying to smile, "forgive me for being so silly, I am a silly creature, indeed. Tom, when you and I were young, we—we—loved each other dearly—Tom—did we not?"

"What has that got to do with what you have to say? Speak up, woman!"

"Everything, Tom. Hetty, our daughter Hetty, has loved long and truly, and she is no longer a child. She's a woman, Tom, with a woman's feelings."

Now Thomas Turney was rising to a proper rage. After all he had done for them both, for all the family, to be treated like this!

"I think I know what you are prevaricating over! Well, let me tell you once and for all, that I shall never give my consent to Hetty marrying that niminipiminy fellow—what's 'is name—Richard Maddison!"

"Then Hetty will have to go her own way, Tom, without that consent."

"What d'ye say, woman! You! You speak like that—*to*—*me*!" He got on his feet. "How dare you tell me, in my own house, about my own daughter! She shall never be thrown away on the son of that filthy blackguard! Never, never, never! D'y' hear me? Not while I have breath in my body will I consent, or permit, my own daughter to throw herself away on that fellow! So let this be final! D'y' hear? I am master in my own house!"

"You cannot stop it, Tom, I tell you you cannot——"

"What?" he roared, flinging his arms about as he stood over her. "Have you taken leave of your senses? I think you have! I think a doctor should examine your head! You dare to defy me, do you? Eh?" He turned on his daughter. "Answer me, Hetty, have you been seeing that fellow?"

Hetty nodded, unable to speak.

At this moment Thomas Turney espied the volumes of Tennyson, which he had put behind a screen against the wall. Picking up the parcel, he tore it open, and let the leather-bound books drop on the floor. He kicked one across the room.

"This is what I foolishly procured for you, this rubbish!" He picked up another volume, and hurled it into the fire, watched by the tearful women. Then turning to Hetty he cried, deeply red of face and brow and neck,

"You—you—you ungrateful girl—you cheap—you—you——" He wheeled round as though to leave the room; spun round again and shouted, "Give me your promise—you shall not leave this room until I have your promise!—your solemn oath and promise!—never to see him again! Else, before God, I shall turn you out on the streets! D'y' hear me? What you want is a good thrashing, to bring you to your senses!"

Upstairs Sidney Cakebread heard the loud and angry voice of the Old Man. He was not yet undressed; with a word to Dorrie, he opened the door and listened. He heard Hetty crying in distress:

"Papa, please, Papa! Papa, I beg of you! I love him, Papa! Please don't be angry, Papa! Papa!" she shrieked, as he strode to her.

Closing the bedroom door behind him Sidney Cakebread ran down the stairs, feeling himself taut all over, but telling himself to keep calm, and on no account must he raise his voice.

Hetty cowered before her father's rage. Sarah cried out, "Don't touch her, Tom, don't touch her! She is pregnant, Tom—Tom!—Sidney!" she screamed. As her son-in-law entered the room her husband dashed his fist upon Hetty's head, and the girl fell on the carpet, to lie there twitching and foaming at the mouth, her eyes staring fixedly.

Sidney Cakebread went for the doctor, returning with him on foot a quarter of an hour later. Hetty, lying on the sofa, had not recovered consciousness. Thomas Turney, subdued and looking to be a man much older than his years, waited in the dining-room with Sidney while Sarah and the doctor, with Dorrie, were in the drawing-room.

Hetty recovered consciousness soon after midnight, and cried out for her mother. On being helped upstairs to bed, immediately she fell into the appearance of deep sleep.

In the morning Sarah asked Sidney Cakebread to go and see Richard at Doggetts' in the Strand, to acquaint him with the situation.

Richard obtained leave for the afternoon, and having first called at his lodgings to arrange with Mrs. Cummings for Hetty to join him there later in the day, made the journey to Cross Aulton.

When he got to Maybury Lodge, Thomas Turney had already left the house. He was deeply upset by what had happened. Sarah had deceived him, she had betrayed his trust in her; Hetty, poor girl, had been misled by her mother; and as for that humourless stick, Richard Maddison, it was all that could be expected of the son of a dissolute blackguard! It was entirely due to Sarah's deceit and treachery that what had happened, had happened.

Blow blow, thou winter wind Thomas Turney muttered to himself, as he walked over London Bridge, holding on to his hat, while a tear rolled down his cheek.

Part Three

NEW HOME

Chapter 14

TWO IN A HANSOM

WHILE RICHARD was waiting to leave with Hetty, her mother made a pot of tea; and Cook having brought up from the kitchen a plate of hot buttered muffins, Sarah invited him to sit by the fire, and to eat and drink. He had been standing by the window, feeling as desolate as the wintry day outside. The sight of Hetty's face had shocked him. One eye, and half the cheek below it, was bruised heavily; the skin above the cheekbone was broken, where Thomas Turney's wedding ring had struck the bone. All the morning a slab of beef-steak had been tied in a cloth against the contusion, to draw out the bruise.

Richard was thinking that, if only the whole matter had not been taken out of his hands from the start, this would never have happened. Hetty had been unconscious, Sidney Cakebread had told him, for nearly three hours. Why had not Hetty told him, her husband, that she was pregnant? Why this conspiracy of silence and subterfuge, from the start? And on top of it all, he was practically one of London's great army of the workless.

Sarah had invited him to take tea with her; he had politely refused. He would accept nothing whatsoever from Mr. Turney, now or in the future.

"Won't you change your mind, Dickie? I have put a spoon for you into the pot. Oh dear, what a pity it all is, to be sure." Sarah touched away a tear with a lace handkerchief, and then she smiled. "Pray forgive me, there now, I feel better already."

Richard, not to appear ungracious, but against his main feeling, sat down on the sofa. Sarah smiled at him. "Ah, there's a good young man! Now I'm going to pour you out a good strong cup of tea."

"Not too strong, Mamma, Dickie likes it weak," put in Hetty quickly.

"Of course, dear, every man to his taste. Now do try the muffins, won't you, they are such nice ones today. We mustn't neglect the inner man, whatever else we do. Now you two eat them all up—they were got specially for you." She saw that Richard was really hungry. "At my age, I cannot eat them, I'm sorry to say." She sipped her tea, blowing on it gently. "Ah, that's better. Tom won't be back until late tonight, he has gone up to the City on business. So do not hurry. Things will come all right, I feel sure of it. We shall all look back on this time and laugh at it one day, I'll warrant we shall." Her lips were quivering. "Now if you will excuse me, I have to see Cook about something."

She left the room, to find out if the provisions she had asked Cook to put up were ready. Among other things the hamper contained half a dozen bottles of Raggett's stout, to keep up her daughter's strength. Downstairs in the kitchen she called the gardener's boy, telling him to fetch a cab from the station rank. Then upstairs, to get two shepherd's plaid rugs for the journey to Dickie's lodgings, which were distant by an hour's trotting.

"Well," she said, some time later, as the cab came round the gravel sweep, and stopped below the stone steps of the front door, "now you will be wanting to be off." She took a copper hot-water bottle, shaped like a small shoulder-of-mutton, from the hearth, and filled it from the kettle. "Don't forget to keep your feet warm, Hetty dear, it is most important. I have put the flannel covering for the warmer at the bottom of the hamper. You will find in it something all ready to eat when you get to your home. Have a nice little supper party all by yourselves, my dears."

Sarah was trying not to cry, and touching her eyes with her handkerchief she said cheerfully, "I do declare, my eyes are not what they were. I must see Brayley about some spectacles. Well now——" She looked at Hetty, trying to control her voice, trying not to say how she would miss her; but it was the pathetic sight of her daughter's face that caused her to break down.

Mother and daughter clung to each other, weeping. Richard moved away and looked out of the window, as though to find interest in the sparrows in the chestnut tree regarding the motionless figure of the cab-horse below them. He would have left the room, had he thought where he might go. Mr. Turney's home! Sarah moved to him and said, "You will take care of her, won't you? You will be all she has, now."

"Oh come, Mamma!" cried Hetty, smiling with forced gaiety. "Why, I have you, and Dorrie, and Hughie! And there's Charley still, and Joey! And—and—Papa. Life will be such fun, now that I am free of worry. And after all, I shall not be very far away, shall I? So pray don't fret yourself, Mamma! I intend to write to Papa, and tell him how sorry I am that I deceived him, and then everything will come all right, I am sure it will!"

With a glance at Richard, Sarah said, "Yes, I am sure that in a little while Tom will come round. I am positive about it, for blood is thicker than water. He loves you, you know, and has a lot on his mind, poor man, so we must all try and forgive him for his little hasty ways. We are all sinners in the eyes of God, I know I am!" she smiled. "Now Dickie,"—giving him a light touch with her lips on his cheek dutifully held down for it—"take your little wife, and may God bless you."

Richard bowed, and shook her by the hand. "Please accept my thanks for all you have done for me," he said. "And for your kind services in ordering the carriage."

"You have a long drive before you, but it is a mild afternoon, and both the carriage and these rugs are a little present to you both." To Hetty, "Don't let the moth get into them, dear, keep them well brushed and aired. They should last a lifetime, then. Well, I hope you will find them useful when the weather gets colder." Sarah was speaking like that to distract Richard's attention, while she slipped a purse into her daughter's hand. As he went down the steps carrying the rugs she whispered, "It may come in useful, dear, but do as you will with it. I have been saving up for your bottom drawer for some time now. Hush, here's Cook and Polly come to say goodbye."

At last the tearful farewells were over, and the hansom cab was bearing them away to a new life together. The sun declining upon the downs in front of them hazed the horse's head and filled the cab with warm light. Hetty turned to Dickie, but his bearing subdued her. He was staring straight ahead, not looking at the view at all. The trees and hedgerows were glorious in their autumn colourings, what a pity to miss them! But of course he was worried, poor Dickie.

Hetty sought and held his hand under the rug, squeezing it between her own to warm it. He sighed, and turning to her said, "Well, here you are, and I suppose you must make the best of a bad bargain, eh?"

The cab moved past a field wherefrom smoke arose in several places. A poignant sweet scent of lavender hung upon the air.

"Oh," said Hetty, trying to make him think not of what had happened. "It's Rootes burning old stocks in his nursery. I have smelt it every year for ever so long. Isn't it a beautiful smell?"

"Are you sure it is not Stocks burning old roots?" he asked, and she laughed with relief.

"No, really, Dickie, he is called Rootes, that's his proper name." Squeezing his arm, "Just as my proper name is Maddison. Oh, I am proud of it, Dickie! Mr. and Mrs. Richard Maddison! How lovely it sounds."

"Humph. Look at those swallows over there. They will be flying away very soon. It is after Michaelmas Day."

"Yes," said Hetty. "I do not like to see them go." She sighed. "But they will come back in the spring, won't they? Do you remember the nest in the summer-house, the birds flying in and out, calling phil-lip, phil-lip, at first, and then getting used to us?"

Richard remembered the swallows; and when the young had flown from the nest on the wall-plate of the summer-house, he had felt a loneliness for which her presence had not compensated. And now that he would not see the summer-house again, he felt strangely sad. He dared not look at her face.

"Now do you mind telling me what is in that basket."

"Some eatables Mamma gave us. There's some ham, a cold pheasant, mince-pies, oh, and yes, some Raggett's stout for me to drink—you must drink it, I don't think I could, it is black as black, ugh!"

"Stout? What, have you taken to tippling, then?"

"Mamma says it is good for expectant mothers, Dickie. The Queen drank it when she had her babies."

"That's where the Prince of Wales got his taste for liquor, no doubt."

Hetty sought his hand again and held it between her own. Papa had said that Dickie was entirely devoid of a sense of humour, but it was not true. He had his own sense of fun. That was the difference.

They passed through fields being ploughed, and others upon which farmyard muck was being carted and set out, as on a chess-board. Then the cab went under a railway bridge, and turned left-handed into a village. Here was something most interesting, for behind a huntsman mounted on a grey horse fox-hounds were trotting, while whippers-in also in red coats, yellow waistcoats and blue caps following on weary horses, rode beside the pack. Their white buckskin breeches were stained with sweat and saddle-soap. They were returning to kennels after a by-day before the opening meet of the season. The cab-horse lifted up its ears.

"Ah, I know where he came from!" said Richard, adding, "I will never do that again. Now what are you laughing at?"

Hetty had an absurd vision of Dickie's ears going up and lifting his tall hat with them, until it was perched upon two upright brown ears.

She leaned upon him, dressed in her seal-skin cap and cape, happiness welling up in her in her feeling of relief. Fields and copses passed slowly by, the sun was now on the right, very red as it sank upon the rim of the sky. Hetty began to feel uneasy. Did the driver know where he was going? But of course someone must have told him.

They entered the outskirts of a large village, or town. It seemed vaguely familiar. Richard said, "Have you any idea why we have come to Epsom?"

"No, Dickie, I thought you knew where we were going."

"Well, it is not my cab, I really know nothing about it."

They stopped the driver. He opened the trap above their heads. Then to Hetty's dismay, she saw Mrs. Mallard, tall and thin, coming across the street to them.

Mrs. Mallard was wearing a hat on which several pairs of green and blue wings, amidst open beaks, were clustered. The hat was perched upon a high coiffure of tight little curls with a fringe. Mrs. Mallard's manner was more animated than that of the previous evening, as of one who was more in her element.

Hetty held her gloved hand over her face.

"My dear, fancy seeing you in Epsom! How enjoyable was our evening with you last night! It was so jolly, was it not, and so advanced in some ways, but all the same, your young friend Theodora Whatsername was a wee bit naughty, don't you think." Richard had removed his hat. "Do introduce your escort to me. Charmed to meet you! Oh, you must be the brother of our advanced young friend! Hetty dear, how becoming is your little seal-skin hat and cape. Why, what is the matter, dear?"

"I have a bad toothache, Mrs. Mallard. A gumboil, I think."

"Oh dear, I am sorry! Now let me tell you something to cheer you up." Mrs. Mallard went closer to Hetty, and lowering her voice, said in a sudden intimate tone, "It has quite a bearing on something that was said last night. You see, I lost recently one of my servants whom more than one of my neighbours had been tampering with—one actually offered her, and in my own front hall, too, another five pounds a year!"

Hetty wondered what to say to this, but she tried to look interested.

"Now the best of the joke is that, after I had bundled the ungrateful creature out, bag and baggage, the lady who had offered her the bribe wouldn't have her at any price—for a Nemesis was at hand!"

Hetty tried to accommodate the expression of her eyes to one of puzzled anticipation.

Mrs. Mallard, fearing that perhaps it might be an error of breeding to tell such a story to a young girl, concluded rather lamely, with a self-righteous expression. "You see, my dear, the girl had been keeping low company! Well, I must be on my way, I have just been leaving cards on Lady Catt, the wife of a recent lord mayor of Birmingham, who has come to grace our little community. Rather a vulgarian to be given a title, entre nous, but then it takes all sorts to make a world, don't you agree? You will come over and visit us one day, won't you. Dear Lancelot so admires your playing of the piano. Au revoir! I have *so* enjoyed our conversation. Goodbye, Mr. Maddison!" and Mrs. Mallard trotted away.

"One of your friends of villadom?" asked Richard.

"She is the wife of the chairman of Papa's firm, Mrs. Mallard. You remember Lancelot? He is her son."

"Oh."

Richard had a married sister living on the outskirts of the town, but he did not mention it to Hetty.

"Well, we seem to have come some distance out of our way, Hetty. The light is beginning to fail, and we have some way to go yet. Now can you tell me, is the cab hired by the hour, or for the journey?"

"I don't know, Dickie, but it will go on Mamma's account."

"Well, I must say that I do not like the idea of it. Of course I shall pay."

"Oh no, dearest, Mamma would be hurt."

"But if Mr. Turney should see the item on the account—no, I shall pay the fare myself." After all, he thought bitterly, I can afford such luxuries, now that I am out of a billet.

Alas, things were not made any better by the driver, an individual with a face of terra-cotta crowned by a bowler hat tarred against penetration by rain, clambering down in order to enter a public house across the way. Richard sat still and upright beside Hetty. After a couple of minutes the cabby returned, sucking first one end of his moustache then the other, having just put the entire lower portion of his face into a double-handled quart pot of porter. He seemed more cheerful.

"'Ome again?" he enquired. "Sin enough?"

"Where are you supposed to be driving?" asked Richard.

"Anywhere you like, sir. Always ready to oblige a gent, especially with a lady. Like to see the race-course? Or 'ave you sin it already?"

"I think there is some mistake," said Richard. "Can you take us to the Crystal Palace?"

"Anywhere you like, sir. Let it be the Crystalled Palace, by all means. Come up, *zuk-zuk*, you!" to the horse. The loose glass in the window at the back rattled once more.

"We are miles out of our way."

"I'm so sorry, dearest. At least it is a warm evening. Would you like something to eat?"

"No, thank you."

They returned the way they had come, passing through Cross Aulton again, and along the familiar road to the east, seeing dark woods across the fields and sometimes among the trees roofs and windows of large houses. As the sun went down it became colder. Hetty tucked the rugs around their knees, and lay back against the padding of the seat.

When they came to the outskirts of the town, with its low red roofs, the lamplighter was walking by with his long pole, at the top of which was a little canister which wavered with a spirit-flame. Coming to a post, he opened the glass of the lamp by a hook on the top of the pole, beside the flaming canister, and lit the gas-jet. Then closing the glass frame of the lamp, he walked on to the next post. Evening had come to Croydon.

The cab turned into the main road through the town, illumined by a row of gas-jets. The driver turned into another street garish with colza-oil flares of costermongers' stalls which lined the pavements on either side. Raucous voices shouted and cried their wares of fruit, fish, meat, clothes old and new. Hetty saw a stall on a barrow built up of cages, each a six-inch cube of wire and wood, containing wild linnets, larks, and finches recently netted, selling for threepence each, with the cage. Then with a gleam of polished copper horns and thundering of wheels and hooves a four-in-hand passed them, coming from the south. Rowdy singing inside, the flourish of a bottle, the sudden protrusion through the window of a jovial and battered face familiar to the cabbie made that individual croak exuberantly and flick his horse and he uttered a hoarse cheer as a multi-feathered head of yellow curls was shoved out of the window beside the other face, for the coach contained a celebrated prize-fighter who with his companions had been having a week out at the Old Ship Inn at Brighton.

Stimulated by the lively sight the cabbie whipped up his animal to follow the coach, but after a quarter of a mile his exuberance took another turn. Pulling into the kerb, he tied the reins to the nickel guides; and breathing stertorously, opened the trap in the roof and called down that he would have to light up. Laboriously in apron and padded tarpaulin jacket he got down from the seat, and set about putting a flame upon the wicks of the spring-loaded tallow candles in the lamps. By coincidence or otherwise he had pulled up outside a public house; and with the candlelight reflecting upon the cruppered hind-quarters of the horse he muttered hoarsely about relieving Nature, and disappeared within the swing doors of The Swan.

A couple of minutes later he reappeared, wiping his blue lips with the back of his hand, while reflecting on the increasing cost of liquor since his young days—porter now being three ha'pence a pot, and a quartern of gin with it, fourpence extra.

Thus fortified, the cab proceeded at a regular pace upon its journey, passing slower drays, horse-drawn tramcars, omnibuses, and the local fire-engine out for exercise, supporting its uniformed team wearing polished brass helmets and big moustaches and drawn by a fine pair of greys. An ordinary sight: but to Hetty, together with all the other things seen on the journey, wonderful. If only Dickie, so worried about having a wife to support just when he had lost his post in the bank, were able to enjoy the romance of the scene! She must try and look after him properly from now onwards.

Up the stone-paved way to the heights of the Crystal Palace the cab went at a walking pace, towards a tawny haze hanging in the sky above the dark roofs and chimney stacks of the houses.

When they reached the crest and passed the darkly glittering glass scales of the great building looming among the stars, then the lights of London were spread before them, and Richard sat up, staring at the variegated pattern and perspective which drew from him an exclamation of surprise. "By Jove, isn't it a fine sight! I've never cared for London until now!" and Hetty sat very still beside him, lest the tears in her eyes spill down her cheeks.

As gossamers upon the loaded fields of night the street lamps flickered away into the distance, radiating as a broken or dispatterned web, becoming smaller and browner until they diminished and were lost in the haze of smoke from factories and dwelling houses built upon nearly a hundred square miles of marshland beside the Thames. Towards this area the cab descended, pulling up at last before the lodging where Richard Maddison, having paid off the cab, took his wife, to begin their new life together.

Chapter 15

THE HORSELESS CARRIAGE

Mrs. Cummings was expecting them. She made no reference to Hetty's bruised cheek and eye. She wore her best bodice above a full-bustled skirt, and her hair depended in the ringlets fashionable a quarter of a century before. She welcomed Mrs. Maddison to her parlour, with a manner of gracious dignity which was soon relaxed into warm friendliness. Supper was laid for two. The kettle was steaming on the hob. There was ox-tail soup, to be followed by grilled herrings and apple-dumplings, she told them.

Hetty took an immediate fancy to Mrs. Cummings, and as is usual with instinctive likings, Mrs. Cummings had approved of Hetty within the first moments of their meeting. She had known of the marriage for some months past, through a friend who lived in Peckham having a sister living in Camberwell whose son worked in the Register Office of Births, Deaths and Marriages; but as her young gentleman had not seen fit to confide in her, Mrs. Cummings had maintained an aloofness in the matter proper to her pride. She knew, too, more than the fact of the marriage; for one morning she had found a copy of a book left under Richard's pillow, *What a Young Mother Should Know*, was its title. A dark horse, was Richard! The bruise on the cheek told her the rest of the story, duly recounted to Mrs. Birkett.

"Ah," remarked Mrs. Birkett later that evening, "If your Richard had not been so reserved, it would be him what would be wearing the black eye, Mrs. C!"

Mrs. Cummings' late husband, the merchant skipper, had left her the brick-built house which, one of a row, had been erected along the main road soon after the coming of the railway to that district of north-west Kent. The house was on a lease of nine and ninety years, nearly half of which remained. With the house was the furniture and a couple of hundred pounds, which represented the dead sailor's savings. For nearly twenty years Mrs. Cummings had taken in as lodgers young City gentlemen, as she called them. If all of them, she confided to Hetty the next morning over an extra pot of tea after doing the rooms, had been as quiet and reserved as Mr. Maddison, who had never given her the slightest trouble, then her lot in life would indeed have been easier. But there, she mustn't complain, it took all sorts to make a world, though she couldn't abide young fellows coming home tipsy, though she was thankful to say, none of her present young gentlemen were that way inclined.

Hetty wondered if this were a hint after Mrs. Cummings had noticed the bottles of Raggett's stout standing in a row inside the bedroom cupboard. To dispel any doubts that Mrs. Cummings might have about herself in that direction, Hetty remarked that she thought public houses should be closed for part of the day and night, as some reformers were urging. Then feeling alarmed at her own boldness, she added,

"Mamma gave me some stout to drink medicinally, but I cannot take to it."

"Pardon my curiosity, dear, but you are expecting, are you not?"

Hetty blushed at the question, and replied, "Oh yes—I am indeed! It will be in April, if all goes well," and she gave a little laugh.

"Well then, you'll need Raggett's in April, it will keep at the bottom of the cupboard. Or will you have a wet-nurse, like some ladies do?"

"Oh no, Mrs. Cummings! I shall nurse my baby myself! No, I am not like one of those fashionable ladies in high society, who do that sort of thing, for the sake of frivolity and self-indulgence."

"They can't always help themselves, poor things," said Mrs. Cummings. "Their way of living is so different, you see, from country-bred folk. Why," she went on, irrelevantly, "my poor mother was up and about four days after having me, and hoeing in the fields, while I was laid in the shade of the hedge, and little harm it did to me, or her either, God rest her dear soul. She's been gone thirty year, now, she died from a fall from a damson tree, picking fruit she was, and stung by a hornet. In the midst of life we are in death, as the preacher says. Then I lost Mr. Cummings, Captain Cummings of the "Benvenue", to give him his proper style and title—there's the picture of his barque over there on the wall. She settled on the Goodwins, during the great March gale of eighteen seventy one it was, over twenty years ago, and all hands lost. She was sucked down into the quicksands within a fortnight of foundering. It was God's will. Now I must go and do some shopping for my young gentlemen's suppers. Do you fancy anything special, dear? I never had a child o' my own, and you appealed to me as if you were my own daughter the moment I saw you." She finished her cup of tea, and tied on her bonnet. By the door she said, "Now you will tell me if you fancy anything special, won't you, Mrs. Maddison? Right, dear, don't forget to say. If you like I'll go on as I have been, and charge just for the extra plate. There'll be a little more wear and tear of the room with the two of you, but I won't charge no extra, just five shillings and sixpence a week as before, and four and six each for two good meals a day, but a coal fire will be fourpence a day, if that is satisfactory to you? Well, wait and ask Mr. Maddison, dear, and then let me know. I'll serve the ham you brought and the cold roast bird for tonight, and some of the mincepies, and allow for them off the account, shall I? The food should last you three suppers, with a light luncheon for yourself at midday. I'll make you some soup, that's nourishing, I'm a great believer in Scots broth, as I expect Mr. Maddison has told you."

"He says it is the finest he's ever tasted, Mrs. Cummings."

"My father was Scots, you see, dear, and it's in the blood. Well, I'll be trotting out now, and leave you to your knitting. And don't be afraid left alone, will you, this house is on the main road, and burglars keep away as a rule. Though there have been some rough characters about lately, due to not enough work to go round. After all, a man with starving children will sometimes get desperate for food to feed them, won't he, if he has a spark of decent instinct left in him? Oh dear, I can see I have alarmed you, well, don't you be. There now, I'm always letting my tongue run away with me, when I ought to be shopping. I think I'll get some nice tripe and onions for my other gentlemen, it's nourishing if cooked properly, the secret of which is slow simmering in milk and a tight lid on the pot to keep the goodness in."

Richard was hungry by the time he arrived home at a quarter past seven in the evening. He had decided to economise on his luncheon in the middle of the day, and to obtain extra clerical work, to be done at night. He had spent his midday break from the bank in a visit to a stockbroker's clerk in a basement office of a firm attached to "the House", otherwise the Stock Exchange. The work consisted of addressing envelopes from lists, to be paid for at the rate of eighteenpence the thousand. Speculative business in mining shares was increasing with the opening of the South African goldfields and diamond mines, and firms of kerbside jobbers were sending out scores of thousands of investment lists and prospectuses to small potential investors among the increasing middle classes.

Hetty knew that Richard had been worrying; but she did not know the depth of his anxiety. Her world had been one of warm houses and happy faces, and while she had always had her own secret fears and dreads, they had never been linked with the fear of living without a room to return to and food to eat. During the past year Richard had made a mid-day chess acquaintance, with whom he sometimes shared a table at an Aërated Bread Company's shop; an elderly clerk from whom he had heard how it had been necessary for him to dye his hair when he had approached the age of forty, in order not to go to the wall; for London was growing, he said, and many young fellows were coming up from the country in order to better themselves.

One day he had seen his acquaintance sitting at the table with a white face. He had told Richard that he had a wife and three children, and had been given a week's notice. He was forty-two years of age. "Old man, I'm done for. I'm too old to emigrate to the colonies or to the United States of America." Richard often wondered what had become of him, for he had not seen him again. And now—it had happened to himself!

Seeing the bag of envelopes and lists of names and addresses, Hetty was much relieved. Dickie had secured other employment, she thought. Night after night he worked at a little three-legged table, two hours after she had gone to bed, sitting with his overcoat on for warmth, and by the light of the lantern. She began to wonder if he were not doing too much. She looked forward to Sunday for him; he would take the day off, he had said, for the body must not be neglected, otherwise it would go stale.

"First I want to show you the Hill, where I saw the Camberwell Beauty," he said, "then shall we go for a walk to the Heath?"

"Yes, dear, I would like nothing better."

They walked up to the crest of the Hill. It was a fine clear day, with yellow leaves still upon the elms, and sheep grazing on the pastures. He pointed out to her the Thames, marked by the varnished masts and spars, and red and white funnels rising above the distant dark brown buildings. Then, turning in the opposite direction, he watched her face delighting in the autumnal prospect of tree-topped ridges and fields of plough and grass lying before them.

"When you have your bicycle, we will go far out and explore, Hetty."

"Oh yes! I think it is a lovely place."

They walked over the Hill and down into Pit Vale, where of olden time bricks had been made, and from there up the steep hill leading to the Heath.

"Why, this is where I came with Mamma that never-to-be-forgotten day," she exclaimed, recognizing the bow-windowed houses of the terrace above the road. "Hughie walked the cob up the hill here when we were coming to see you, dearest!"

Beyond the open Heath lay Greenwich Park of happy memory, behind its great wall of brick in which the iron gates of its entrance were set. Before going there, Richard suggested that they should walk down into the village, or that part of it called Tranquil Vale, for the purpose of looking at houses, particularly seeking out any of an old-fashioned appearance, timber framing covered by painted weather-board being his fancy.

"This is a neighbourhood of prosperous people, Hetty, but there can be no harm in pretending we are looking for one."

"Yes, dear, it will be lovely to pretend."

"You never know what you can do until you try. We might find a cottage to rent for the five shillings and sixpence I pay to Mrs. Cummings weekly."

"And we should have the common stretching in front of us, Dickie."

"And I would have a shed for my Rover, with space for a carpenter's bench and my tools. And a room to be set aside for a study, where I could have my butterflies, and the books my grandfather gave me, now in a chest at Mrs. Cummings'".

"And there would be a garden! I would grow flowers, and we might have a summerhouse, and some fruit trees, and shall we have a cat, or would you prefer a dog, Dickie?"

"A cat perhaps, but a dog, no! They are not clean animals like cats. I think dogs should be kept in kennels, and used for their proper purposes, which are not domestic." Oh lor, he thought, here am I talking like this, when I am soon to be out-of-work, and there is the baby to be considered.

They looked around Tranquil Vale, and then continued their

walk past the Prince of Wales pond—"Oh, Dickie, this is where I first heard your voice, and knew you were so sad!"—and so across the Heath to the gates of the Park. They visited the places where they had walked and sat eighteen months before, but did not go down to the river, as it was time to think of returning for tea.

During the following week, in the course of conversation, Mrs. Cummings told Hetty of a house not far away that was to be let. Hetty went to see it with some trepidation, as Mrs. Cummings had said that it was in a rather low part of the neighbourhood. It was at the end of a road, beside the railway embankment. It looked a dear little house. She did not tell Dickie about it that evening, owing to the effect Mrs. Cummings' description had had upon her; but the next Sunday morning when they were walking on the Heath again, and once more the idea of having their own home came up, she told him of it, and what Mrs. Cummings had said.

"Well, the entire district could scarcely be described as a fashionable neighbourhood at its best, could it?" he replied, gently. "Where is the low little house, pray?"

"At the very end of the road opposite the cemetery, Dickie."

"Oh lor!"

"It's not the cemetery end, Dickie, it's at the top just before the railway cutting. I went to look at it, from the outside only, of course. It's quite nice, really, with a little garden in front, and white pillars beside the front door."

"Is there any other garden?"

"I am almost sure there is one at the back. The house stands by itself."

"That is something. Shall we go and see it?"

"Yes dear, of course, if you would like to. Only you won't expect too much, will you?"

"Now do not be so anxious," he replied, good humouredly, as they turned back to descend the hill again, Hetty taking three steps to every two of tall Richard.

Beyond the bottom of the hill and the railway arch they came to the high street, which was a continuation of the Old Kent Road. On fine Sunday mornings this route was much in use by jaunting couples and parties in all sorts of vehicles driving into the country. There were spanking light carts painted and varnished in bold colours and driven by horsey individuals wearing brown and grey bowler hats, stock-ties, and fawn-coloured overcoats with velvet collars; there were brakes and four-wheeler cabs; tradesmen's carts and floats; and an occasional fast-trotting tandem racing past all vehicles. Tramcars with clanging bells, hauled by weary nags whose feet had long since ceased to ache on the sett-stones between the rails, proceeded in two directions in the centre of the high street.

As Hetty and Dickie came into the main road they saw an extraordinary sight at which all on the side-walks were stopping to stare—one of the things they had heard about but never yet seen—a panting horseless carriage preceded by a youth on a bicycle carrying a red flag, and followed by a little crowd of the curious. Several ragged youths were jeering at it.

The driver of the auto-carriage seemed not to be enjoying himself, while his companions seated behind on the noisy, shaking contraption sat there as though oblivious of the stir their passage was causing. As Hetty and Dickie watched, two ragamuffins followed by a smaller boy darted into the road, and stooping to gather brown wet pellets of horse-dung, ran up behind the vehicle and flung their missiles at the occupants, shouting, "That'll larn yer!"

The ragamuffins could scarcely miss at so close a range; and picking up more dung, they measured with arms drawn back, threw rapidly, and turning about, ran away.

"You young blackguards!" cried Richard, as they passed, disappearing into the traffic.

"Filthy little ruffians," he remarked, seeing that some of the missiles had found a mark.

"Lowest of the low!" This utterance came from Hetty, an expression she had sometimes heard on the lips of her father. "What a horrid thing to do! Vulgar without being funny! They must have a depraved appetite, to do such a thing." More of Thomas Turney's phrases.

A crowd was collecting in curiosity around the strange vehicle. Some voices were jeering at the occupants. "Sarve yer right!"

"Let us get away from this sink, to the cleaner air of the Hill. There is a short cut beside the river, which goes under the bridge over there. Are you feeling tired? We can take the ha'penny tram to Pit Vale if you like."

"No dearest, it is so kind of you, but I am not in the least tired."

They came to the bridge. "Look at the rags and bottles and tins down there. I wonder that any trout are left alive in the water. And to think that this was once crystal-pure water, coming from the ponds of Reynard's Common."

They crossed over the bridge, and turned into the lane, and went under a railway arch, coming to a row of small houses on their right. Richard paused to look at them. They were scarcely bigger than boxes, of yellow brick almost black with smoke, with slated roofs. What a place to live in!

His scrutiny, brief as it had been, brought to one of the doors several white-faced children without boots or stockings. The boys had close-cropped heads, the girls wore frocks of old material held about them by string. Behind them a woman with uncombed hair falling over her shoulders regarded the strangers truculently. Taking Hetty's arm, Richard walked on, past a small pot-house called The Maid of the Mill, but locally known as the Rat Trap, for terrier-dog matches were held in its yard.

"Do you think it is safe to come here?" asked Hetty, apprehensively, as the lane narrowed beside a tall mill-house, its lower windows barred with iron, and stuffed with sacking where stones had broken the dusty glass.

A few loungers by the brick wall above the mill-race stared with near-hostility at the two strangers walking past. A thin and dingy white terrier-dog, long tail between legs, showed its teeth and growled.

"Take no notice," whispered Richard.

Worst of all, they were being followed by the three ragamuffins, the dung-flingers of five minutes previously. The youths began to catcall when they had got beyond the mill. Richard and Hetty were walking on a footpath between untended gardens leading to the river on one hand, and a row of brick houses on the other. Men and women stared at them. Fortunately no horses had walked that way recently; but when Richard glanced back he observed one of the boys in the act of picking up a stone from the black dirt of the uneven path.

"Walk a bit faster, Hetty," he said. "But do not be alarmed. I hope it will not be necessary to read the young hooligans a lesson."

At that moment a stone whizzed past his cap, which he wore with his cycling jacket, knickerbockers, and worsted stockings—country garb which evidently was resented by the ragamuffins, judging by their jeers.

"Walk a bit faster, Hetty." Another hundred yards and they would be clear of the houses.

A second stone passed between them, nearly striking Hetty. Richard turned round, brandishing his stick. With a shock, Hetty heard one of them jeering.

"I knows oo you are, Je's Christ on tin wheels! Yah-boo! Mob 'im, boys! Come on, pelt the —— out of 'im!"

"Oh, Dickie, please don't pay any attention to them, please!" as Richard started to move after the boys. It was what they wanted, the thrill of being chased.

"Yah-boo! On to 'im, boys!"

More stones were flung. One struck Richard below the knee, causing him to wince with pain. Then there was a crash of glass —a half-brick, missing him, had struck one of the windows obliquely. The casement was flung open, and an angry head looked out. "You little bleeders!" roared a voice. "I'll break yer —— necks when I cotch yer!"

"Blime, ol' buck navvy, 'op it, boys!"

The boys took to their heels, much to Hetty's relief. "Are you much hurt, dear?" she enquired.

"It was not a flint, fortunately, only a pebble."

At the end of the row they had to climb over a style, and then they were in a wider street between larger houses extending up a slope to the distant thorn-crowned Hill.

Half way up the slope, beside a lamp-post, stood a police constable in helmet and short cape. Richard approached him with serious face, for he was shaken, and informed the constable of what had occurred.

"You want to keep away from that little lot, sir," said the constable. "They're a rough lot down there in Botany Bay."

"I might have lost my eyesight, had that stone struck my eye, officer! Are you going to take any action in the matter?"

"I'll report it to the sergeant, sir, but unless the culprits were appre'nded in the act of assault and battery, or identified at a line-up at the school, I don't think we could do anything, lacking evidence."

"Well there is the evidence of the broken window down there, officer."

"Very good, I'll go down and make an inspection. Would you give me your name and address, sir?"

Richard was now feeling slightly ashamed of himself; his manner, he thought, had been far too strained when first he had approached the constable. He thought of the Indian clubs and iron dumb-bells in his lodging, unused for some months now. He was stale. Unless he were careful, he would become set in his ways, like the middle-aged fellows in the Bank, almost completely enclosed in their little sedentary world. A year ago he would have sprinted after the little beasts and laid his stick across their bottoms, and that would have settled the matter.

The policeman was taking out his notebook; and once out, it did not go back again until the name, address, occupation, and age of the informer had been inscribed laboriously within it. At last, bidding the officer good-day, they continued to walk up the road to the distant summit of the Hill—tall Richard taking long slow steps while shorter Hetty, muff hanging before her and gloved hands swinging, walked obediently by his side.

Meanwhile the boys, who had left school at the age of twelve in order to start work for their living, were in a state of pleasurable excitation. They had run down Mill Lane to the high street, and turning up Pit Vale had made a circuit. In due course they arrived at the top end of Mill Lane, panting and gasping, but maintained by the thought of further sport with Tin-wheels. The bearded apparition had provided them with the best sport for months. They chattered excitedly among themselves.

"Cor, bleedin' fine sport, boys!"

"Look, there 'e is, goin' onto th' Hillies!"

"Come on, Billee, you ain't got no stitch!"

"I 'ave!"

And tucking their elbows into their jacket-sides, the three laboured on under the railway bridge. They had gone through it and were some way up the road when behind them sounded the face-blanching *frann-nn-n* of a police whistle. Glancing back fearfully they saw a copper following, and behind him, the ol' man in shirtsleeves who had mobbed them out of the broken window. In an instant feelings of pleasurable excitement were changed to genital-gripping fear by which their legs became heavy and their lungs as though solidifying. The biggest boy drew away from his companions, while Billee the smallest one, lagging behind, wasted scanty breath in cries of "Wait for us," intertwined with sobs and cries of despair. All three since early childhood had been knocked about by their fathers, one of whom had been in prison several times for drunkenness and wife-beating. Nobody had a good word for the two elder boys; they had been flogged frequently during their days in the tenebrous Board School.

Richard and Hetty reached the top of the road, beyond which was an open space of uneven grassy pits where during past time gravel had been dug. Flocks of fieldfares and redwings were gathered on the wildling white-thorns which grew there, leafless and sooted-red with haws. The birds chattered and made their clicking noises, rather like the fragmentary rattling of wooden police-rattles, which Richard remembered from his boyhood. He was thinking of those days, and trying to believe that the landscape before him was part of the same English country he loved so much; in fancy he was hearing again the old police-rattle used by crowstarvers in the fields after October wheat-sowing. Then his thoughts moved to scenes of the riots in Trafalgar Square on Bloody Sunday; and strangely he became aware that what he had fancied himself to be hearing in memory was actually upon the present air; and a moment later Hetty clutched his arm and pointed the way they had come, at the figures of three boys struggling across the waste land with a constable following a couple of hundred yards behind. As they stared, the constable stopped and blew long blasts on his whistle.

"It's the same boys!"

"Oh dear—oh Dickie——"

"Now do not you get sentimental like Dora!"

"Oh, that poor little fellow behind, constantly looking back over his shoulder——"

"They deserve to be taught a sharp lesson! Why, if unchecked, that sort of thing leads to anarchy!"

A moment or two later the fugitives changed course, frantically trying to run the faster, as another and nearer *frann-nn-nn* pierced the dull afternoon. Hetty stood in anguish as the two leading boys came nearer, their feet dragging, their gasping audible, their white faces piteous. Her hand went to her heart as the constable gained upon them. Richard, too, was breathing faster.

"Don't—don't stop them," she said faintly, and her mouth remained open to aid her breathing.

Richard stood still, gripping his walking stick. His lips were in a thin line.

"Dickie—Dickie—they have mothers."

"They should have thought of that before. But I do not intend to interfere, though it is my duty."

The two boys struggled up to them, their eyes beseeching, their breath coming with groans near to retching. Their trousers were torn, revealing thin legs filthy as their feet. The eldest, whose face was disfigured by copper-coloured sores, flung himself on his knees before Richard, wringing his hands, and gasped out that he was sorry, sir, he didn't mean no harm, sir, he would never do it agen, sir, straight 'e wouldn't, sir, 'e would kill isself if they sent 'im to prison, sir. The second boy hung doubled-up beside the first, his white face and open mouth revealing decayed teeth as he pressed his clenched fist into his side against a cramp. The smallest boy, called Billee, lay face down in the grasses.

The constable lugged him to his feet, and brought him along to where Richard stood in an unhappy state of mind.

Among his thoughts were how the case, were it to be reported in the papers, would affect his chances of new employment. Having laid information against the wretched urchins, the case would have to be proceeded with. Perhaps he might venture to say that they had been punished sufficiently already?

"Well, sir, these are the boys, I take it?" enquired the constable. "Do you identify them?"

"Yes, they are the boys, officer. They have been well frightened, I think. What will the glass panes cost to be replaced? We do not want to be too hard on them."

"I shall have to report the matter, sir, and take them in charge."

At these words the boys, who had been looking with desperate hope from one adult face to another, collapsed into abandoned sobbing. The smallest fell on his knees and held his hands together. "Pray don't! Pray don't!" he cried.

"My handcuffs will be too large for their wrists," said the constable. "I'll have to take these two to the station. You!" to the smallest waif, with sudden harsh voice, "You be off now! And if I catch you agen, I'll run you, mind!"

"Yes, sir, I'm sorry sir," and the boy got up and fled.

"It was Billee done it," whined the biggest boy. "I seed 'im do it."

When the two had been marched off, each gripped by the back of the coat collar with knuckles hurting the base of the skull, Richard and Hetty walked on in silence as blank as the landscape, with its heaps of garbage tipped into the disused gravel pits. An old harvest wain, its broken felloes and spokes collapsed about decayed hubs, was half-sunken into the matted grasses where brown spires of docks arose with black thistle stems.

"Well," said Richard at last. "It will teach them a lesson."

"They are more sinned against than sinning," murmured Hetty.

It was then that the baby moved inside her, giving two convulsive kicks. The blood rushed to her cheeks. Then her baby was not dead after all, as she had feared, ever since Papa had been so angry! Mamma had told her that a baby began to move between the fourth and fifth month, so everything was all right!

"Oh Dickie, I am so terribly, terribly happy!"

He looked at her. "Well, I must say, I do not exactly share your happiness over what has just happened!"

"Oh, I was not thinking of that, dearest, I was——"

"Well, I was, I must say. For it means an appearance at Greenwich Police Court, and a report in the newspapers."

"Oh yes, those poor boys——"

At the thought of them sadness overcame her. Richard walked on, a little apart from her, proceeding with his long slow stride alone. How characteristic of women that they could never see an action clearly, but must always cloy and distort it with sentiment. He felt lonely.

Hetty wanted to tell him that the baby was alive after all, but his mood subdued her. They came to the crest of the Hill, where a gentle wind was moving from the autumnal wooded distances. They passed the sheep-fold, wherein ewes were enclosed with rams on swede turnips.

"Now you see what London smoke does to the colour of the wool, Hetty. I have read it in the *Morning Post* that, when the wind is not blowing, quite an appreciable number of tons of soot, several hundred indeed, fall every day upon London. Just think of the thousands of tons that must fall every year!" He looked north towards the City, dissolved in grey air. "Well, I suppose it is one of the things we have to put up with, in the name of progress. Have you ever seen such wretched little turnips? Scarcely so big as golf and cricket balls! I'll warrant that the farmer has been taking what he can get out of the soil for some years now, knowing that sooner or later it will be swallowed up by the London County Council."

Hetty looked at the turnips, but her thoughts were of the boys.

Chapter 16

NEIGHBOURS

COMFORT ROAD, opposite the gates of the cemetery, appeared to be deserted. They walked in silence through the smells of cabbage water poured down drains outside. Evidently the occupants were at Sunday dinner. The houses, heavily curtained, with glimpses of aspidistra ferns in the lower windows, had pillars by the front doors, and dummy balconies over them. Trees planted out at regular intervals gave some relief to the drabness of the street.

Near the end another road crossed at right angles. This was the road Richard had cycled down at dawn in the summer of the previous year, when he had not wanted Mrs. Cummings to know that he had changed his mind about going on his holiday by way of Cross Aulton. Mrs. Cummings had once described it as "a back street with an unsavoury reputation." The smell of cabbage-water was certainly not exactly savoury, he thought.

Beyond the back-street, between two rows of houses only slightly smaller than those in the high road, was what was known as a dead-end to some, a cul-de-sac to others. The stub of Comfort Road, its dead end, terminated at railway property. Richard saw it as a little oasis, detached from the uniform row of houses. In the oasis were but three houses, two on one side, a single one on the other. A row of spiked iron railings protected the railway embankment, and through the railings were to be seen plots of vegetables and a few damson trees, with overgrown bushes of lavender and currant. Forlornly facing the west, a donkey stood on one of the mounds of soil raised high upon the embankment.

The empty house was the one that stood alone. It was on the north side of the cul-de-sac, so that its front faced south. It looked to have been at some time a small lodge. The style of building was pleasing. There was a side-gate to the garden, at the end of the brick wall dividing the house from the embankment.

While they were gazing at the top window of the main bed-room, which, together with that of the room beneath projected with a three-sided bay, and wondering what it was like inside, a woman appeared from the house on the corner, and with a cheerful smile enquired if they had come to see Comfort House? She had the key, she said, she was taking care of it for the landlord, who came there only on Saturdays to collect the rents.

"I'm Mrs. Feeney, sir, I work every morning for Mrs. Cummings. I know you better than you know me, for your bicycle is quite an old friend of my pail and scrubbing brush."

"Yes, of course, Mrs. Feeney. This is my wife."

"I've met your lady already, Mr. Maddison. How d'you do, m'am."

Over her shoulder appeared an elderly, blue-shaven face with a long upper lip and two hurt-looking eyes under shaggy brows and grey wiry hair. "Sure, and is it house-hunting you are, and all? 'Tis a nice little house, well-built, and tight as a cup, and so clane inside you could eat your dinner off the floor, and it's Michael Feeney declarin' it to ye. Sure, and here's the kay, m'am," and he came to the iron gate and gave it to Hetty. "Now mind you carry her over the threshold, sorr, in the manner that's proper to the occasion, for 'tis myself and no other who knows who you are, and what's in your mind, I'm thinking."

"Don't heed what Feeney says, sir, he's been to the Jack today."

Richard heard the fellow's address with misgiving, dreading a garrulous neighbour, and one of whom he had heard vaguely from Mrs. Cummings as being work-shy. He took the key, saying that he would return it when they had made their inspection.

Hetty felt already that the house would make a dear little home, and was overjoyed that Mrs. Feeney, whom Mrs. Cummings had declared to be completely honest and an excellent worker, lived next door.

A semi-circular glass window over the front door let light into the hall-passage within. Upon opening the door of the downstairs front room it was seen at once to be dry and clean, although the wall-paper had marks upon it which washing had not removed. Richard took out his penknife, and opening the large blade, stuck it into first one floor-board then another. He went round the room doing this, finally remarking, "The wood seems firm, with no sign of dry-rot." There was a small cast-iron grate, shaped like one half of a cockle shell, in the wall.

"Not bad," he said. "Now let us see upstairs. What is the matter. Are you nervous? There is not likely to be a burglar in here yet awhile."

Hetty smiled wanly. She had been thinking about the ragged boys. They might have been Charley, Hughie, and Joey, in different circumstances.

Richard's feet carefully clumped up the wooden stairs. The window on the landing looked out upon a strip of garden about the width of the house, and possibly fifteen yards in length, enclosed by a wooden fence many of the boards of which were askew. The remains of a partly burned bonfire lay in the middle. They went into the larger of the two front bedrooms, and looked through the pane westward of the three-sided bay window. There was a view over the uneven embankment to cabbage fields beyond the railway cutting.

"Well, what do you think? It gets the morning sun. Quite roomy, considering." He trod upon the planks of the floor. "Appears to be sound. If we take it, it ought to be fumigated with sulphur candles. What are the other bedrooms like, I wonder?" They went into one, their footfalls hollow in the enclosed space. "Small, but sufficient. I suppose you are thinking of this one for a night-nursery, eh? Well, what do you think?"

Hetty was already planning where the bed, the chest of drawers, and the wash-hand-stand should go; but knowing how cautious he was, she said, "Perhaps we'd better see the downstairs first, before venturing an opinion. Mrs. Cummings said she thought the rent was six shillings a week."

"Well, that is an extra expense of sixpence a week to be considered. Then there are the rates. And gas will be extra, of course, though we can save on candles sometimes. It will be nearer seven and six, I expect, when all is considered. A poky little back bedroom this one, but it might do for a study."

They went downstairs to the kitchen. There was a range with an iron hot-water container standing on it. The brass tap was polished. A single tap over a sink in the scullery brought water into the place. Outside the back door was a water-closet under a porch. The unpainted square wooden seat over the blue-flowered pan was scrubbed clean, the walls were white-washed.

"There is some work to be done here," said Richard, peering into the garden. "It is probably sour soil, needing lime. Deep trenching and frost, too—if I shall have any time to do it, with the extra work of addressing envelopes at home."

The thought of earning only eighteen pence a day filled him with fear. Half a guinea a week, of which seven and sixpence would be rent and rates! Three shillings for food, fuel, light, clothing and a baby on the way.

"I think we would be very happy here, dearest. It has such a nice atmosphere about it."

"Ah, you should have married somebody like young Tofield, then you would have had a nice comfortable villa a dozen miles from town, with whist in the evenings, and music, and pleasant friends about you."

"I have got what I want, dearest," murmured Hetty, laying her head against his shoulder, and longing for him to hold her.

Richard recalled to mind that he had a little over two hundred and thirty pounds saved up; but that was for real contingencies, such as illness. Two hundred and thirty pounds between him and the wolf at the door.

"Oh lor', there's the furniture to think of—I was forgetting that."

"I have some money of my own, dear," said Hetty. "I have saved up ten pounds." This was the sum her mother had given her in the purse.

"I would very much like to help, dear."

"You keep it in the bank, you may want it one day."

"Well, I shall buy the curtains, and the linen. After all, I was given the money for a wedding present, by Mamma."

"Of course, it is yours to do with as you like. I shall give you some money, as is right and proper, to buy the necessities. Well, shall we take the place, on a weekly tenancy?"

"Oh, I would be so happy! A house of our very own!"

He stood in the middle of the room, with furrowed brow. Was he not acting precipitantly? Contagious disease? Drains? Sulphur candles for the former—try the plug for the drains. He went outside again, and pulled the chain. The thing made a noise like an iron hen, no water came. "There, I thought so. A catch in it!" He turned the tap in the sink. A few drops dribbled. "But perhaps it is turned off at the main."

Mrs. Feeney confirmed this when, having locked the front door, he went to return the key. The water was all right, and the drains, too, she said. Thanking her, they walked back to Mrs. Cummings, after another gaze at the front of the house.

Richard felt more cheerful after his Sunday dinner, when he lay in the horse-hair armchair beside the fire, his feet on the fender. Afterwards he addressed envelopes for three hours, while Hetty knitted.

The walk had made them both sleepy, and they went to bed early. Richard got up half an hour earlier than usual, at six o'clock, and having washed and dressed, swung Indian clubs and exercised with dumb-bells, he addressed one hundred envelopes before breakfast. At seven minutes after eight o'clock as usual, he closed the iron gate behind him carefully, and clad in frock-coat and dark trousers, wearing his silk hat and carrying his umbrella with the spokes held together by a rubber band around the whangee-cane handle, he set off with his long loping stride towards the railway station, arriving at that superstructure of wooden posts and boarded platforms at sixteen minutes after the hour. As he had done on innumerable occasions before, he waited on the Up platform among hundreds of other drab-clothed men and an occasional pale-faced young woman for a couple of minutes while the train approaching from the Crystal Palace caused the wooden superstructure preceptibly to tremble. Punctually at 8.19 a.m. the engine whistled and drew the carriages forward to the thuds of its piston-strokes, while Richard, unlucky with a seat that morning, stood with others in a carriage filled with tobacco smoke from the pipes of the seated occupants trying to read *The Daily News*, *The Daily Chronicle*, *The Daily Telegraph*, and in one case *The Kentish Mercury*. No window was permitted to be opened; no one dared to ask for it; the fug was acrid to the eyes of the standing men and youths. So it remained until the train pulled up at London Bridge Station, where there was a hurried exit of passengers, most of whom strove to get through the ticket-collector's barrier in advance of others, though this was of small advantage except as an athletic ambition, for by now from both high and low level stations thousands of similar figures were pouring, to join the black bobbling of clerical humanity upon the nine-foot eastern pavement of the oldest bridge across the Thames. Most of them wore watch-chains of silver across their waistcoats, some with albert seals attached; a few wore similar chains of gold, but they were in the minority at that hour: the more affluent

City men arrived by later trains, or by carriage direct to their offices.

The western pavement of London Bridge was not so crowded; and hereon Richard strode by custom, as he had strode three thousand times before.

Over the bridge he caught the Cannon Street 'bus, which took him down to Ludgate Circus, and up Fleet Street and so to the Strand and the premises of Doggett and Co., with its sign of three swans hanging over the door. Outside stood the porter, wearing a uniform of black and gold, with the badge of the swans embossed on his gilt buttons and a gold band bound his top hat with a black cockade at the side. The porter raised a finger in salute, but did not pull open the door for him as he said, "*Good morning, Mr. Maddison*". Seldom at that hour, before nine o'clock, did customers of Doggett & Co. arrive by carriage or on foot for their business within; for them alone was reserved the full salute, the address of *Sir*, *Milord*, *Your Grace*, or *Your Royal Highness*, as the door was pulled open for their entry into what immemorially had been known as "the Shop".

Chapter 17

A VISIT FROM THEODORA

FEELING THE need for security of tenure, Richard agreed to take the house for a minimum of six months, at a weekly rental of six shillings. At once he made plans for decorating the interior. He bought a pair of wooden step-ladders, a pail and paste-brush, some paint, and a dozen rolls of wall-paper with vertical stripes on which were superimposed little caskets of flowers and birds at regular intervals. For the sitting-room the stripes were red and silver alternating; for the bedroom, blue and silver alternating, with identical bird-flower patterns.

On the first Saturday afternoon of his new tenancy he intended to start the job of re-papering the walls. He had been looking forward to it with happy expectation, and had planned and rehearsed in his mind exactly how it should be done. Upon this project he had spent a great deal of thought; for it would be easy to spoil the paper, which was costly. He had had no experience of such work, and therefore his preconceived plans for it were the more elaborate and meticulous, like those of most amateurs.

With his usual care he set about mixing flour and water in the pail to the correct viscosity, and then in measuring and cutting two lengths of paper. Thereafter arose unforeseen difficulties, and with them, repeated instructions, and even exhortations, to Hetty. It was Hetty's first job to hold down a section of paper unrolled upon the floor, while he covered it with paste. This done, they exchanged ends: she held the rolled-up paper, while he carried the unrolled end towards the wooden steps by the wall. "Now be very careful, Hetty, the next stage is rather ticklish." He began to ascend the steps with his wide and wet flimsy section of paper held in his two hands, while feeling his way up the ladder with his feet. It was not easy to balance like that, and his part was made more difficult because the paper began to curl and twist, to show a desire to attach itself to his person. Perched precariously up the ladder, the amateur paperhanger gave instructions to his mate below.

"No, no, Hetty, hold it stretched tighter—one hand there, the other over there—I cannot look round to direct, you must use your commonsense—hold it level—no, not that way—look, in the direction my nose is pointing—Oh, there you go again, letting it touch my trousers! Look out, you are tearing it! Hold it looser! Don't let it sag too much! It is curling up again! Hold it higher off the floor—come nearer this way—not too much—Oh! deuce take it, you have let it touch my cheek, ugh! Lower it, lower it! No, no, not on the floor! It will pick up dust! Look out, you are treading on it!"

He descended from the steps and decided to try again, this time mounting backwards so that the sticky length could be borne up without twisting or tearing.

This way, however, had its difficulties. He had to change hands as he turned round to face the wall, while Hetty had to wheel in line with the angle of change. She was not tall enough to hold the paper against the wall and exactly parallel to the line of the corner as he demanded; and the wet roll, once it touched the wall, clung there, being dislodged and unfurled again only with difficulty.

"Really, Hetty, I do not want to be too critical, but you do seem to lack the most elementary idea of what I am trying to do! And yet you think that women should have the franchise."

"I'm sorry, dear."

Trying to control his exasperation, he got down from the steps and stood on the sugar-box which had been her perch beside the ladder. "Now you go up the ladder, and see what you can do. Take care to lay it parallel with the cornice. Perhaps I should not have pasted so much. It might be better next time to paste the wall first, and then unroll the paper down the wall. Anyhow, try it this way first. I will lay it parallel with the corner. Now then, here goes. Oh, confound it," for the cold paste had dabbed his cheek again. Hetty tried her best not to laugh, it was so funny.

When the two sheets had been spoiled, the paper-hanging was given up. Richard sat dejectedly on the box.

"Never mind, dear, Rome wasn't built in a day," said Hetty.

"Oh pouff!" replied Richard. "Whoever said it was? Well, let us try again. I fancy I was wrong to cut the paper into lengths first, and then, to paste it while on the floor. There is another way, I am sure."

Mrs. Feeney was the means of bringing help. She ventured to knock on the open front door with the offer of a cup of tea; and bringing the tray upstairs, she mentioned that Feeney had been a paper-hanger in his young days, and would give help were it required. Having set his mind on doing it with Hetty—having imagined all during the week the work being done together happily on the first Saturday afternoon together in their new home—Richard was the more unprepared that his mind-picture be changed; and while Mrs. Feeney was talking to Hetty, he went into the other room and leaned his head against the wall in fear of his future after Christmas, when he would be out of work. Why could not Hetty help him? How could he afford to pay a man?

Fighting his fears, he returned to the room and sipped the tea; and when later Feeney came to help him, the two men got on well together, Feeney having shown how the job should be done.

They finished the bedroom together, and there being some light left, the question of white-washing the ceiling arose. Richard thereupon realized that this should have been done before the papering, to avoid splashes. Mrs. Feeney brought some clean lengths of cotton rag, and while her husband rubbed the old smoky ceiling reasonably free of flakes and fly-frecks, Richard stood on the sugar-box and followed his work with careful dabbings and brushings. Before it was completed, his neck and arms and back ached; but there was satisfaction in sitting down on the box, when he was alone again in the room, and viewing the work in the last of the sunset.

"Oh, it looks ever so nice!" exclaimed Hetty, coming into the room to tell him it was time to return to Mrs. Cummings.

"It is certainly a bit better than it was," he replied, regarding the work. "Now you can help me in the next move, only you must get a good apron first, to protect your clothes. The paint needs scrubbing to remove any grease, so we shall need some hot water and soda. The old paintwork, after being thoroughly washed, should be wiped with a clean rag dippped in water and wrung out, and so to remove all traces of soda. Then when it is dry, the painting can begin. I think I shall work tomorrow, but as it is Sunday, I do not ask you to help me. You must decide of your own free will."

"Yes, dear. The coalman is outside in the street, would you like me to tell him to bring in a sack?"

"The coalman, did you say? I do not want to see him, if he is the fellow I think he is. Will you see that he brings in a hundred-weight? Stipulate no dust."

"Yes, dear."

The coal was brought in and tipped in the cellar under the stairs, and Hetty returned to the bedroom. Richard had lit the lantern, and was sitting on the box. She was relieved that he seemed happier; he had trusted her to see that the coal was brought in to the right place, under the stairs. Then with a sudden movement he cried, "Oh confound it, I have entirely forgotten the sulphur candles—the fumes will take the pattern out of the paper."

He sat on the box while thoughts of so much to be done, and the weather getting colder and foggier, the days shorter and darker, seemed to be as lead upon his stomach. Hetty stood near him, wanting to comfort him, but not wanting to disturb him, as he seemed to be thinking. The flame of the open lantern above the fireplace cast loose shadows on the walls and ceiling. Then from below came a clear familiar whistle, and a soft voice called out, "May I come up?" Oh joy, it was Dora.

"Honk!"

"Honk!"

"Humph!"

"I have discovered you at last," said Theodora. "How are you, dear brother and sister? So this is your new home, the name carved on the stone above the door, too, what swells you are, to be sure! 'Comfort House'—a jolly name. Your good Mrs. Cummings told me where to find you. Hetty dear, you look positively blooming, does she not, Dickie?" Theodora lightly kissed Hetty on both cheeks, and then a longer kiss on her forehead before turning to her brother to bestow on him the same warm but impersonal salutation on the brow. "I do approve your blue and silver wallpaper, Dickie. Who chose it?"

"Hetty," sad Richard, who had brightened as soon as he had heard the whistle taught to the family by their father.

"It was Dickie, really," said Hetty.

"You both chose it, of course," said Theodora. "So you are leaving Mrs. Cummings?"

"In a week or so, when this place is ready."

"She will miss you, I expect. How many bedrooms have you?"

"Three—one for you whenever you care to stay," said Hetty. "The spare room is at the back, and ever so tiny. Come, let me show you."

It was becoming too dark to work any longer. Richard turned down the wick of the lantern so that hot oil fumes should not arise and spoil his work, which might happen if he blew out the flame while it was hot. He put the brushes and pail in a corner of the room, and placed the soap-box against the wall, lest Hetty coming in during the darkness fall against it. The two girls were talking in the next room in low voices, and to rest himself until they were ready to leave with him, he sat on the box, and with a deep sigh, closed his eyes. The family whistle brought a picture of what to him was the ultimate happiness: lying on the downs above Rookhurst in boyhood's summer everlasting, the fire of the sun pouring into his head through vermilion eyelids, his arms spread, and all around him the gentle wind sighing, sighing in the grasses where harebells waved on slender stalks and sky-blue butterflies of the chalk country fluttered on slender wings. To lie there as the grass, as the wind, as the sky—to feel one with the earth beneath and the sun above—that was peace; and life in London was the antithesis.

Richard had hoped that he would find this peace with Hetty; but it was not so. He sighed.

The two young women returned to the room.

"Well," said Richard, rising, as though he had just seen her, "I am very glad to see you, Dora. How nice of you to come all this way to see us. You must come and have some tea."

"Yes, do!" Hetty exclaimed. "I have some fresh Yarmouth kippers."

They went down the stairs, Richard first with the lantern to light the way. At the door he blew it out. The key, which he had rubbed bright with emery paper, locked the door behind him, and then went into his pocket beside the worn William IV crown piece. The iron gate no longer squeaked, since he had oiled the hinges.

Walking down the road between the two women, on impulse he took each an arm, and felt comfort in the warmth and gaiety of their companionship.

Hetty tried to conform to the longer striding of brother and sister. Theodora noticed this, and imperceptibly shortened her stride, murmuring that she was feeling a little tired. "You try to do too much, playing the charitable lady in the East End," remarked Richard; but Hetty had understood the true reason of Dora's remark.

They passed a row of shops, including the pawnbroker's with the three gilt balls, and walked on down the curve of the high-road, with its spaced elm-trees, and so towards the fourth lamp-post which marked where Mrs. Cummings' house stood well back from the side-walk. A police constable was walking about fifty yards in front of them, looking at the numbers of the houses which were displayed in figures on the glass pane above each front door. Filled with slight misgiving, Richard walked on with the girls, as the constable paused by the lamp-post, comparing the number of the house with the paper in his hand before opening the gate and walking up the white, black and red tesselated path to the door. He pulled the bell-wire as the three followed up the path.

Not wishing to interfere in any way, Richard waited behind the figure in tunic, helmet, and bell-bottom trousers until Mrs. Cummings opened the door, and in reply to a question, said that Mr. Maddison was there standing behind him, in person.

"Take Dora upstairs, will you, Hetty?" said Richard. It must be in connection with the little ruffians who had been taken into custody. The constable waited until they were gone, and then he asked if he were Richard Edward Maddison; and this being acknowledged he handed him a subpœna notice to attend at the Greenwich Police Court to give evidence on the following Friday.

In agitation Richard took the blue form, while thinking yet again that his name in the newspapers might prejudice entirely any chance of a clerical post. So far he had answered, without reply, seventeen advertisements.

"Is it essential that I appear, officer?"

"Can't say, sir. My orders are to deliver this subpœna to you at this address. Good day to you, sir."

Those wretched boys, why could they not play among themselves, instead of behaving to the distress of dẹcent law-abiding citizens?

Upstairs in the room, while the two girls were away for a moment, he said to Mrs. Cummings, his face strained and his voice with an edge of querulousness, "Why did this have to happen just now? I am already fagged out by working to past midnight every night."

Mrs. Cummings, who was drawing the curtains, replied, "Well, Mr. Maddison, if I were you, I'd have a bit of a rest. Why not let Feeney finish the decorations of the house for you? He is a tradesman and will work for eighteen pence a day, and be glad of the money. It's those little beasts, window-smashing, I suppose? But there, these things are sent to try us, there's no getting away from that. Now when Captain Cummings was alive, he used to say that life was like the weather, you never knew what was going to blow up next from any quarter. It's the same thing on land or water, and in the skies too, I expect, though man not having been given wings we shall never know about that. Well, we must all look on the bright side, and count our blessings. You've got a rare soul in your sister to console you, and as for your little wife, bless her sweet face, you've got a perfect treasure. Everyone likes her. As I was saying, Feeney's a tradesman, he painted this house you know, the only trouble is he likes a little drop at the Jack, so it's best to pay him when the work is finished, then all's satisfied, and what goes in the Jack after is nobody's business. It's that old wound in his leg that causes him to go off now and then, especially when the weather is bad and gives him twinges, which find their way, he says, without any help from him to the Jack. Otherwise he means no harm, and it must be dull for a man always to be sitting at home keeping the fire warm and the kettle singing for when Mrs. Feeney comes back. He got an assegai-wound at Rorke's Drift, you know, I expect? He was one of eighty men of the 24th Foot, behind ramparts of mealie bags and biscuit tins, who fought off all them horrid niggers."

"From what he has told me, he got his wound in the Crimea, Mrs. Cummings."

"Rorke's Drift or Crimea, what does it matter, it's the Jack where he does his fighting nowadays. Now I'll get on with the kippers. I want to see Marie Lloyd at the Empire tonight with Mrs. Birkett if I can."

It was advisable to make no mention of the game leg to Feeney, Richard had discovered, for at the slightest mention of it Feeney was liable to drop paper-roll or paste brush and sit on the box and start, "Sure now that you mention it, sorr——" and mere politeness demanded that one should listen to the old soldier's story, considering that he was giving his services. But at eighteenpence a day, the stories would have to be curtailed.

Richard had enjoyed working with the "dacent "Irishman; and while the circular mahogany table in the front upstairs room was being covered with the table-cloth for the laying of three places, and from down in the kitchen the smell of kippers was beginning to arise, he sat before the fire in the straight-backed armchair, one elbow on the pad of the mahogany arm, his hand covering his moustaches, while he tried to make order of his thoughts. For a day's work Feeney would charge eighteenpence: the price of a thousand addressed envelopes, done at the rate of one hundred the hour. Perhaps it would be economical to let Feeney, a tradesman, do the work, while he addressed the envelopes, wretched pay that it was. Nevertheless he enjoyed painting, and working with his hands; ah! the time-limit was the key to the situation! Rent was being paid all the time for an empty house, double rent was mounting up every day until they could move. So the house should be got ready as soon as possible. Feeney should do it.

Could Hetty be trusted to find some furniture, perhaps—but as soon as the thought arose, he winced away from it. He did not feel that she was capable; might she not buy the first thing that took her fancy? She was inclined to extravagance, too; had she not bought some expensive truffles from a shop in the West End as a present to him, almost the first time she went to London after he had brought her home? And all because he had told her once that his grandfather had had a Spaniel dog that marked truffles among the roots of beech trees, by scent, to enable them to be dug out with a spade. It had been her money, certainly; but what was the difference? She was no longer in a well-to-do home, but the wife of a poor man. Heavens, no, he mustn't give Hetty *carte blanche* to buy any furniture. He would have to do it himself, find time for it, that was about it.

The two young women returned to the room, carrying hot plates and a tureen of kippers, which were put down in the hearth until the bread and butter had been cut and the tea made. On the sideboard was a dish of cheese, some celery in a glass vase, and a pot of Richard's favourite bitter marmalade, one of a dozen sent by order of brother John for his twenty-seventh birthday the previous September, from Cooper of Oxford. The girls were hungry, but Richard continued to sit staring into the fire before him. Hetty had told Theodora about the poor boys, and they had agreed not to mention the subject.

"Eat your fish, boy," said Theodora, gently.

"I am not very hungry," he replied.

"You will be when you taste it, they are delicious. All of us Maddisons have nervous stomachs," she remarked conversationally to Hetty, "and need the right foods, and at the right time. Come, eat your tea, brother, and do not let anything put you out. Hetty, I do declare that these kippers are the nicest I have tasted in a long while."

"Oh, pipe down, little girl," said Richard, glancing sideways at his sister, a suggestion of smiling in his eyes. "You always were trying to arrange everyone's life for them. You are free to come and go, free as air, no responsibilities, and so of course you can take things easily."

"You are right, Dickie. The kipper is before me, it shall be munch, munch, munch henceforward!" Theodora champed her jaws. "I am an otter!"

Richard began to dissect his fish meticulously. He detached the tastiest piece, delicious with oil and oak-smoke, from the back-bone and put it in his mouth, with a piece of brown bread and butter. Immediately he felt hungrily cheerful.

"Humanity is like one enormous fly, with eyes of a million facets, each lens recording a different aspect of any one object," said Theodora, her otter-character discarded. "All human acts are relative, for a poor man does not think like a rich man, nor a sick man like a healthy man. And as acts are relative to the beholder, so they are all related to one another. Sometimes I think that nothing really happens outside ourselves, that the physical world is an illusion, and our thoughts the reality."

"My thoughts of another kipper are real to me, and come from inside myself," exclaimed Richard. "And after tea I shall challenge you to a game of chess!"

Dora's final words to her brother later that evening, after beating him twice at chess, while Hetty sat happily knitting, so glad that he had someone good to play with, were, "Now brother, do forgive me always appearing to offer advice: but if I may make a suggestion, dear boy, it is this: put in a good word for those unhappy children in the Police Court, it will never be lost." At the door she said, "It was Saint Paul who said, 'We are all members one of another'. Bless you, dear brother, and you too, dear sister. You have both made me feel so happy," and giving each a kiss, Theodora ran down the path, past the little yew tree planted beside it, her long skirts swirling the last of the leaves of the Virginian creeper which had fallen in the chill of the autumn evening from the front wall of the house upon the coloured tiles of the path.

Chapter 18

MOTHER AND DAUGHTER

THEODORA HAD come to tell Hetty that her mother wanted to see her as soon as she could manage to get over, about some pieces of furniture and other things which she might find of use for the new house. Hetty was in a flurry of eagerness to speak to her mother about it, as well as to see her old home again.

Richard did not sleep well during the night. He awakened in the small hours, and after turning restlessly for some time, occasionally uttering sharp cries of self-condemnation for humiliating episodes in the past which had come upon his mind, he woke her up, wanting to tell her about them. But his reserve had come back with full consciousness, and he had lain silently beside her. She took him into her arms, feeling him to be a poor little boy who needed his mother, but it did not suffice for long. She thought her bigness was between them in two senses, for his desire for her seemed to be gone. Richard turned away from her; he could not speak his thoughts to her, indeed he could not properly formulate them. He rearranged his pillow; dropped it on the floor; leaned over to recover it a minute later; tried to settle down with his knees drawn up almost to his chest, one arm round his own neck, the other round his ribs; turned over once more and thrust his head under her protecting arm.

"I believe it was that third kipper," he said. "And cheese late at night is bad. I ought not to have eaten that apple, either. My grandfather always told me, "Fruit in the morning is golden, fruit in the afternoon is silver, fruit at night is lead." I think I will light my lantern and get on with the envelopes."

"I should try and rest, dear, if I were you. You have a long day before you tomorrow."

"But I cannot rest if I cannot, can I, eh?"

"Yes, dear," replied Hetty. "I mean, no, dear. Oh dear, I think really I must mean yes, dear!"

"You can't even say what you mean," he grumbled. "Just like a woman, with no more stability than a restless flea."

Hetty began to laugh. She saw in her mind Sidney's Wicked Flea. It was awful, she knew, to think of the funny side of Dickie, but she could not help it. *He* was the restless one, if he only knew it.

At Thildonck no one had chided Hetty for her laughter; Mère Ambroisine, as well as Sister Anastasia, had stroked her head, and spoken so gently that the tears of sublime happiness had come into Hetty's eyes, as one to another had murmured, *Cette jeune fille, une vraie sensitive*. "The trouble with you is that you have never grown up," grumbled Richard, ameliorating.

"Yes, Dickie," said the child who had not grown up. "I am afraid I am a bad, unsympathetic wife. But I do *try* to understand, really I do."

"Oh, I know I'm a curmudgeon, but there is such an awful lot to think about just now."

"You are *not* a curmudgeon!" said Hetty. "I only wish I could help you more than I do. Can't I do some of the envelopes for you?"

She had offered to help before, but always he had replied that there must not be the risk of even one error, for there were many others who would be only too glad of the work.

Richard settled down soon after their talk, feeling that Hetty sometimes understood the reality of things. And it was during the blessed period before sinking to sleep warm beside him that the idea came to her to go to Cross Aulton the very first thing on Monday morning about the furniture. She determined not to tell him, then it would be all the more a happy surprise.

On the Monday morning Hetty went to Cross Aulton. Leaving the familiar station, she hurried home, but as she came near the pond her pace slowed; for perhaps after all Papa was there. Something might have occurred to prevent him going to business. How could she find out? By good fortune the muffin man, carrying his tray covered with green baize on his head, and ringing his bell, was passing by. She asked him to go to the kitchen door, and find out from Cook. He arranged with her to give a double shake of his hand-bell if the coast were clear.

She waited until he came out of the tradesmen's gate, and to her relief and joy he rattled his bell twice with every other footstep. She wished she had given him sixpence for himself, but she would ask Mamma to do this for her when next he called. She entered the house by the kitchen basement door, and after greeting Cookie, and being assured that her mother was upstairs, she decided to wait until Polly came down, and then to ring the front door bell, lest Mamma be taken by surprise and the shock made her feel faint.

But all was well; Sarah had seen her from an upper window, and hurried downstairs to save her darling from walking up to see her. So Hetty saw Mamma at the top of the stairs, smiling at her as she came down with her hand on the banisters.

"My dearest, dearest Hetty!" the gentle voice called down, and the hand paused on the banisters, for Sarah was a little overcome. She fumbled for her bottle of smelling salts, which cleared the fluffy feeling in her bosom. "I'll come down, dear; pray don't come up, you must go carefully, you know."

"Oh Mamma, I cannot wait!" Hetty went up the stairs, and hugged her mother. Then she must visit her old bedroom, to look at the familiar things which were part of her life. She nearly wept, the little room seemed so forlorn without her. She opened drawers and cupboards, to greet with touch of hands all her friends. It seemed years and years since she had last been in her room.

When many questions had been asked and answered by the fire in the sitting-room, Polly came in and asked if she should make Miss Hetty a cup of beef-tea, for the mid-morning cup of tea had already been taken by the others. Sarah suggested that beef-tea with some dry toast would be more sustaining and beneficial. "You have two to feed now, Hetty," she smiled. "Have you arranged with a midwife yet? And a doctor, is there a reliable man near at hand to you?"

Hetty said that as soon as they were in the new house she was going to see about it, and Sarah was much relieved. Hetty enquired about Dorrie. All was well, Mamma told her; and Sidney had been given new territory in the West End by his firm, as he had such a gentlemanly and considerate manner. How was Hughie? Sarah had been dreading that question. Trying not to allow her voice to quaver she said that Hughie and Papa had had some words, and Hughie had left home, and had taken a room in Bloomsbury. "Poor boy, he has not been near the office for nearly three weeks now. I do not think he was very happy in the Firm, and Papa as you know is inclined to be exacting."

"Oh, Mamma, dear Mamma, do not cry, dearest. Things will come all right, I am sure they will! Hughie was a square peg in a round hole, and will find his own feet. He is so clever, you know, and his heart is wrapped up in his music. Perhaps he will find something nearer his bent, than he would have by remaining in the Firm."

But Sarah shook her head. "He has had no real training for music, and is so sensitive, poor boy, I fear for him, a prey perhaps to bad companions."

"How will he live, Mamma? He cannot last for long on his savings."

"I know I can trust you, Hetty, and you must never tell anyone, will you, not even your husband, though Dickie is an honourable man, I know. But Papa must never get to hear that I am managing to send Hughie a little every week out of the housekeeping as a standby, until he can establish himself. Sidney, dear boy, is helping him too, though he has not much to spare, with his little family coming along."

"Perhaps Hughie may go for a schoolmaster, Mamma. To all intents and purposes, he has a degree. He would have got it, being so clever, if he had not been sent down."

"Well, we must hope for the best, that is all, Hetty. It is a sad thing that children have to grow up, though it is natural that they should leave the old nest. How time flies, to be sure. Why, it seems only a very little while ago that you were all little tots crawling on the floor, or pulling yourselves upright on the chairs, then riding your hobby-horses, then bowling your hoops. And all of a moment you are grown up, though to your Papa and Mamma you will always be the little ones! That is what your Papa, I sometimes think, though not critically of course, fails to understand, for he is so anxious that his children shall come to no harm, and to him they are still his dear children. So you must never think too hardly of him, for any little hastiness, will you, Hetty dear?"

"No, Mamma, indeed I do not. Why, I have only to think how I feel concern for Dickie sometimes, and then how easy it is to sympathise with poor Papa, with all his business worries and added to them his concern for Hughie, and Charley, and as for me—I have not at all been a dutiful daughter to him, have I?"

"Indeed you have, Hetty dear. You must never think otherwise. I do indeed blame myself for what has occurred; I am sure I did wrong in not letting Tom know first, how your heart was once and for all given to Dickie. Now let us talk of other things. Tell me all about your new house, and when you will be moving in. It is not damp, I hope, and the drains are in proper order?"

Thereupon Hetty told her mother of her scheme for furnishing Comfort House; and when the beef-tea had been finished, they went upstairs to see what could be spared. The boxroom contained two marble wash-hand-stands, which had come from their first home; and there was an old round three-legged oak table which had been Sarah's as a child in her father's farmhouse.

"It has a date carved underneath it, about the time of Cromwell, with the same initials as my great-great-great-grandfather, so it was probably made by him. You take it, dear. Then that old cupboard, with the brass drops—I have the key somewhere—that is somewhat old-fashioned, but it is well-made, and in walnut. People all want modern mahogany, but plain English walnut is nearly so sound, though out of fashion, save for gun-stocks. I will get Polly to bees-wax it. And there are a pair of little oak chests-of-drawers, the wood has gone dark, you see, and I fear will never come right again, but perhaps they can be painted white, to conceal it. The walnut cupboard, too, though it would be a pity to cover the beautiful shading of the wood."

"Dickie is so skilful at painting, Mamma, you should see his work. He says he enjoys the doing of it, ever so much more than being in an office."

"Yes, I have noticed that men are much happier when working with their hands. The Reverend Mr. Campbell, the wonderful new preacher at the City Temple, says that we worship God with our handiwork, and that it was not for nothing that Our Lord's earthly father was a carpenter."

"Dickie has bought a fork and spade, and is going to till the new garden, Mamma, and I am going to help him."

"Ah, then he is a wise young man," said Sarah, with a happy smile. "I can tell you, of all the men who worked for my father, those who kept the best gardens were invariably the most contented, and as my father always said, a contented man is like a contented beast, and does better than the restless ones with the staring coats and eyes."

"Do my eyes sometimes stare, Mamma?"

"No, Hetty, wherever did you get that idea? They gaze sometimes, to be sure, but Mère Ambroisine used to say that you were listening to the beating of the wings."

Hetty's eyes filled with tears. She smiled into space; Sarah took her hand and held it.

"You are like my mother, Hetty, she was the seventh child of a seventh child. But we must not talk about such things. Let us go and see that double bed in the second spare bedroom, which is too large for it," went on Sarah, equably. "I am thinking of putting one of Hampton's single beds in there, with the new spring mattresses. Sidney says he can get me one from a commission agent friend of his, at a discount. So will you take the double bed? It has good brass rails, and they are lacquered, and need no polishing. The hair mattress is nearly new, and I will give it a thorough airing in front of the kitchen range before it leaves, then it will be all ready for you. Now let us come and see it."

Hetty had often jumped upon the bed with Hughie when they were children together, but now she saw it with new eyes. It was an imposing affair, with its four round brass knobs on the posts, and heavy brass tubular railings at each end. The hair mattress, now rolled up on it, rested on a hessian coverlet, under which blued steel strips were interwoven—"Oh I remember!" cried Hetty, "how they used to jangle when Hughie and I tried to see who could jump the highest. How lovely, I could jump on it now!"

Sarah smiled at her younger daughter, thinking that she was but a child still, with her gay little laugh, sudden as the song of a jenny wren; a child soon to bear a child, what a sweet little mother she would be.

There was no doubt but that Sarah, though she dearly loved all her children, had an especial tenderness for Hetty, who from her earliest years had always been so sympathetic, so easily moved to laughter or tears.

"And now, dear," said Sarah, "I have kept the little cot for you, in which you and Hughie and all the other dear children used to lie. I have kept it for you, and may you lift your little one to your breast from it, as I did, with thanks to the dear Lord for his bounty. Each little one, as the French say, brings its own loaf under its arm."

Later on, when the removal of the pieces of furniture had been discussed, Sarah suggested that as the day was fine, why should she not drive Hetty back to her home? She would very much like to see it, with its pillars by the door, and the name carved in the lintel stone. Tom was away in Dorset, going on to Plymouth and Exeter, then to Taunton and Bristol, and would not be back until Friday evening at the earliest. At the mention of Friday, Hetty cried, "Oh!" and put her hand over her mouth, her eyes open wide.

"Oh dear me, I had forgotten! On Friday Dickie is to appear at Greenwich Police Court, to give evidence against two boys!" She told her mother of the incident; and Sarah said, even as Hetty had said, "Oh, the poor children. To think what their mothers must be feeling! Cannot something be done? They will be sure to be sent to a reformatory, which, as Dora so rightly says, often does more harm than good. So it all began with that horseless carriage appearing on the scene, did it? Those horrid things are the cause of a lot of trouble—they ought not to be allowed. There is one here in the neighbourhood, a positive danger to all and sundry, making the horses to prance, the dogs to bark, and even the hens scatter in terror from it. Those little street arabs fall into mischief as they have only the streets as their playground, where they are left to their own devices, poor little fellows. Still," she sighed, "we cannot help these things, they are part of the cross we all have to bear. There now, dear Hetty, you are quite upset. Then why not lie down and put your feet up, and have a rest? Jim shall drive you back this afternoon. Cook shall give us an early luncheon. I thought you might like to take back some of your things, and Polly shall help you pack. Now lie down and have a little sleep."

After luncheon the bay horse was brought round from the paddock where it was kept, fat through lack of work, and put into the shafts of the carriage. Jim the gardener then went to put on his long melton coat and beaver hat, thus changing into Jim the coachman; and well wrapped up in rugs, the ladies drove off along the way the hired cab had taken six weeks previously. Hetty held her mother's hand some of the time; Sarah understood, and seldom spoke. To Hetty's relief they did not meet anyone they knew, and reached Croydon without incident.

There Sarah asked Jim to stop outside the shop of a draper

where she had bought things before, and taking Hetty with her she selected some lengths of Nottingham lace curtains, which would keep out flies in summer, she said. Hetty chose a pattern. A little way along the street was an upholsterer's, and they visited this next, to see some carpets. As Hetty did not know the dimensions of the larger upstairs and downstairs rooms, they decided to choose the patterns now, and when she got back she would send the particulars. The frock-coated shop-assistant said that they could deliver within a radius of six miles by express van.

"Dickie must have a good armchair to rest in and read his newspaper," declared Sarah. "That is most important for all men after the day's work. So help me choose one, Hetty dear. Here is a nice one, in dark green leather. Do you think that would meet with his approval?"

"But it must be terribly expensive, Mamma! You are far too kind." She added doubtfully, "I wonder what Dickie will say to it all."

"This is an excellent chair, madam," put in the shop-assistant, quickly. "Many gentlemen have admired it, the latest design from a firm which also supplies Harrod's in Oxford Street, I dare say you have heard of Harrod's Stores, madam, patronised by people of rank and fashion? Since we are county furnishers, we stock the same line of the new easy chairs; this one is particularly popular with the gentlemen, it is called 'The Sportsman', madam. Only five guineas, it is guaranteed to last a life-time. Real Russian leather, imported by a leading firm of Bermondsey importers, madam. It is quite the best, and cannot possibly be bettered."

Sarah was impressed. She sat herself in it. It certainly was comfortable. Perhaps she had done enough for Hetty with the carpets, should she buy this one for Hughie? It was indeed a gentleman's chair, and Hughie inviting his college friends to his room would not feel in any way that it was beneath him. Five guineas, it was surely a good investment.

"Do you try it, Hetty. It is certainly most comfortable."

Hetty sat in it. "Oh, it is so cosy." She thought of Dickie in it, after digging the garden, taking his ease. Surely he would not be cross that she had bought him such a lovely chair!

"It is the only one we have at present," interposed the shop-assistant. "Christmas is near, and we may not be able to repeat the line before the New Year, madam."

That decided the matter. "I am sure Dickie would appreciate it, Mamma dear. Oh, you are so kind."

"Very well, I will take this chair," said Sarah, giving him her card.

Bowing and rubbing his hands, the pale assistant went to his superior, who with even a more polished manner made out the bill, and wrote down the address for delivery by express van on Christmas Eve. Yes, it would be well wrapped up.

The ladies entered the carriage again, and drove off towards the Crystal Palace glittering in the winter sun above the houses on the high ground, and so down to Comfort House. Sarah thought it was a dear little place, and though the railway was near, one would soon get used to the noise of passing trains. They measured up the floors for carpets, and having discussed every room, went to Mrs. Cummings' for a welcome cup of tea.

Part Four

WINTER OF 1894-95

Chapter 19

THE CHAINED DOOR

ALONG COMFORT ROAD a man wearing a shapeless cloth cap, whipcord jacket and bell-bottom trousers above a pair of broken button boots was pushing a barrow, in which, amidst a heap of nondescript articles, stood two flowerpots, each containing an aspidistra fern. Every few shuffling steps forward he uttered a cry which travelled the length of the street, as he glanced from left to right in the hope of seeing a door opening.

ENGASBOLL SAWBONES!

The hoarse and mournful cry, the rattling of the barrow, the shuffling of sodden boots might have been progressing along a street of the dead, for all the response he got. Nevertheless he journeyed on, sometimes varying his cry with additional information.

YBYENAGSBOLL SAWBONES!

The whipcord jacket, buttoned as it was to the high lapels of a past mode, revealed that he wore no shirt, as the bare shins above the boots, and his protruding toes, showed that he wore neither socks, nor their substitute of strips of rags wound round the feet. He called out his words opposite each pair of front doors, with quick glances at the closed upper and lower windows he was passing.

Each pair of front doors shared three pillars supporting a joint dummy balcony above. The lower windows on both sides of the doors were partly obscured by side curtains of heavy drab material to prevent passersby from seeing what was within; but this negative action was countered by a positive desire for decoration, or that conformity called respectability, and the desire was made manifest in a single pot placed on the window ledge inside the room: a pot standing exactly in the middle of the parted curtains, the home of an aspidistra.

IBYENAGSBOLL SAWBONES!

Again the raucous cry uttered from behind the trundling barrow. The crier muttered to himself as he pushed that he had done

Comfort Road brown, and that he would have to come next time on a Saturday when the kids were not at school, then he'd get 'em to bring their mas to the door wiv paper win'mills on sticks.

JEMJARS!

At the end of the road, as he was about to turn round before the railway embankment, his quick eye noticed a window without a potted fern, and unusual curtains of white lace. The door was fresh painted, too. And catching a glimpse of a young face between the hanging curtains of the window, he cried again his hoarse desire to buy any rags, bottles, or bones.

Hetty, behind the partial safety of the parlour curtains, saw with alarm that the ragged man had stopped his barrow, and had raised a hand to her! He had seen her! Oh dear, and he was coming to the door! She waited trepidantly, withdrawn into the semi-darkness of the passage, hoping he would go away if she did not answer the door. But after a few moments there came the bang of the knocker.

Almost desperately she realized that the chain was not fastened across the door. Dickie had told her never to open the door unless the chain were up, and so always to be on the safe side. He had told her that she was the very kind of person whom cheats and tricksters would be on the look-out for. Several times he had prophesied that once the door was opened to such people, a foot would be put in to prevent the door being closed, and then anything might happen, and she would have only herself to blame. No, she must never open the door to strangers unless the chain was fastened.

One of the first things Richard had done after moving in was to screw a heavy brass chain to the jamb of the door, and the slot to the door itself. The end of the chain was cast in the shape of a dog's head; the head fitted into the slot, thus holding the door from being opened more than a few inches. He had also fitted a strong bolt to the back-door, and having oiled it, had given instructions that she must see to it that it was always secured after the door had been closed.

That afternoon about three o'clock Hetty in her best gown had gone to the hall door and removed the end of the chain, for she was expecting a carriage to drive up the road, and stop outside. It was unlikely that the vicar's wife would come on foot to return her call, though she might decide to walk, to increase the circulation of the blood on that bitterly cold day. And it would not look well if, when she arrived, and had given the knock and tattoo on the door that was the sign of gentility, she was met by the jangle of the chain being taken off, before she could be bidden to enter.

So having swept and cleaned and polished all the morning, and set out her japanese lacquered tray with her best silver teapot and tortoiseshell tea-caddy, her silver kettle on its stand with the spirit-lamp under, beside the silver jugs of cream and milk, sugar bowls with tongs, her tea-cups and plates of Dresden china, Hetty had lit the fire in the front room or parlour, and sat there knitting the baby's jacket of Shetland wool, while rehearsing in her mind what she should talk about when her visitor was sipping her cup of tea. The weather? It was always a safe subject, though perhaps a little depressing. The coming Jubilee of their gracious Queen? No, that was too far off. Ah, the Hill! To buy it as a public park subscriptions were being canvassed, and a Sale of Work in the Church Hall of St. Simon was being arranged, to collect money for the project! Hetty was giving two knitted antimacassars, which were too big for her own chairs; and also Dickie used bear's grease for his scalp.

The proposed public park extended to about forty acres of grazing on and around the Hill, and the price asked by the owners was said to be so much as nearly fifty thousand pounds. Dickie had said that most of the money was being contributed by several local boroughs from their funds, and also by the London County Council, which was waiting to absorb those boroughs. Ah, that was it! She could talk about the cartoon in *Punch*, which Mamma had sent her, in which the County Council was a boa-constrictor waiting to crush the turtle of the borough. What was the word Dickie had mentioned, when he had read it out of *The Morning Post*, saying that soon they would all be Cockneys? A sticky word, like glue—oh yes, of course, how silly of her to forget, the word was *conglutination*. She pronounced it several times, to memorise it.

Perhaps, however, it would be best not to mention Dickie's opinions about being Cockneys, in case Mrs. Mundy had other views. Mamma had told her never to discuss religion or politics with anyone, then she would always be on safe ground.

It would be quite in order to say that the proposed public park on the Hill would enable many poor people to enjoy the airs there, together with the beautiful views over the City, and also the villages and fields of Kent and Surrey. And of course she could mention the wonderful Crystal Palace, and her visit there with Dickie recently, when the huge organ had played *The Lost Chord* so loudly that Dickie had taken her outside, fearing that the vibration—but no, she must not mention that. How considerate of dear Dickie, to have thought of possible harm to her baby within!

Hetty poked the coal fire so that the smoky flames of the best Derby Nuts would be burnt away, leaving the little blue and lilac flames that looked so pretty, by the time her caller should arrive about half past three. Perhaps Mrs. Mundy would only leave cards this time? Hetty was a little puzzled; for though the vicar's wife had called soon after she and Dickie had moved into the house, Mrs. Mundy had not left any cards. Hetty thought that, being so very busy, perhaps she had forgotten her card-case. Mrs. Mundy spoke like a busy woman; she had been most kind, enquiring after her health, and how long she had been married, and if she went to church, whether she was high or low church, and what her husband did for a living. How did they like the district? As she went out of the front door Mrs. Mundy had said that she hoped Hetty would be comfortable in her new home, and that she would find time to attend the Sewing Classes held in the Church Hall every second Monday evening in the month between the hours of seven o'clock and half past nine, with refreshments provided at a moderate charge.

So saying, Mrs. Mundy had left; and on the Thursday of the following week Hetty, dressed in her best silks, the skirt of which she had let out three inches at the waist, high button boots, sealskin cape, hat, and muff, had walked to the vicarage, one of the big houses in Twistleton Road, where lime-trees formed an avenue nearly as tall as St. Simon's Church, and left her cards with the maid who, in pink and white uniform, had reminded her of Polly. The houses had hearth-stoned steps leading up to heavy-panelled front doors, some with coach-houses on one side of the house.

Hetty left three cards, as Mamma used to leave when making a first call on a newcomer: two, engraved in copper-plate *Mr. Richard Maddison*, one for the Vicar, and the other for Mrs. Mundy; a larger one for the Vicar and Mrs. Mundy, engraved *Mr. and Mrs. Maddison*, on the pasteboard of which a smaller card was fastened in the corner, with the words *First Thursday* in small letters. There was no address on the cards, which Mrs. Turney had sent to her daughter, having had them done by the Firm.

Hetty had turned down the top right-hand corner of her card, as she had heard from Mrs. Feeney that Mrs. Mundy had an unmarried daughter at home; and she had also turned down the bottom right-hand corner, to show that the cards had been left by her personally, and not by a coachman.

The maid had taken the cards on a silver tray, bobbed to Hetty, who had smiled at her, and then the door had closed. Hetty returned the way she had come, upon the side-walk, or pavement as she had heard it called, of large square flag-stones under the tall lime trees, thinking what a nice wide road it was; and at the end of the avenue, where it joined the High Road, she gave a penny, taken from the purse concealed within her muff, to the poor old man with a wooden leg who had brushed a clean path on which people might cross the muddy road. Waggons and carts were moving on the wet grey surface, and men were scraping the mud of the main road into heaps in line between the lamp-posts.

It was four o'clock, and already the lamplighter was walking along with his long pole, to the top of which, as he approached a lamp-post, he affixed a wax-vesta, scraped it on the top of the iron post, and in a moment a blue-and-yellow butterfly, like the swallowtails seen in the South of France, was fluttering inside the glass. Hetty slowed her pace, so that she might walk behind him, for she loved to imagine the gas-jets as butterflies; and the presence of the lamplighter was reassuring, for she had been frightened of the people in the end houses of Comfort Road ever since the two boys at Greenwich Police Court had been sentenced to be birched and sent to a reformatory. One family, in the first house but one on the left at the beginning of the road, had somehow found out that Dickie had given evidence at the Court, where after leaving he had been booed, and someone horrid had shouted in a jeering voice, *There he goes, Jesus Christ on Tin Wheels!* as he rode past on his bicycle. And on the following Sunday, when she and Dickie had been returning from a walk on the Hill, screams and shouts had come from the house, the front door of which had been open, and the thuds of a brass-buckled belt on a woman's body. The woman had run out, her hair all tangled, the man after her, kicking and punching her, while their little children, pale and ragged, had wept, their hands over their eyes. Dickie had interfered, fortunately being the bigger of the two. The man had sworn at him. *We know oo you are, bleedun Judas, that's all yer are!* And as they went away he had shouted, *You wait! We'll get you, one dark night!* It had been horrible and frightening, and since then some of the end-of-street boys had taken up the taunt of *Tin Wills!* whenever they had seen Dickie.

A thing even more terrible had happened. Hetty felt ill whenever she recalled the occasion of a police-whistle shrilling down the street with its alarming note. She had returned from shopping only a few moments before; thank goodness she had remembered to put the chain up. A minute afterwards a man ran past the house, followed by a policeman. There was a chase over the hillocks and level vegetable patches of the railway embankment, and later the body of the man, handcuffed and unconscious, was carried by two constables to the beginning of the road. For nearly half an hour he lay on the grass there, surrounded by staring children and women, as a perturbed Hetty had seen from behind the curtains. At last the constable on guard, together with Mr. Feeney and the very old man who lived opposite, were joined by the second constable who had gone to fetch the police handcart. Horrified, Hetty had watched from the window as the body, with hanging head, was lifted up and strapped to the stretcher, before being covered by a brown canvas, from which only the boots protruded as it was wheeled away to the station.

When a few minutes later there had come a knock on the front door Hetty's heart had beat so fast that she felt she was going to faint; and Mrs. Feeney's voice calling through the letter-box had never been so welcome. Mrs. Feeney told her that the man had interfered with a girl of six years in the cemetery among the tombstones, and during the chase he had fallen down in a fit. A fit! Perhaps the man had been ill-treated in childhood. Hetty had felt quite ill afterwards, and even had wept when she thought of the life within her which might be affected badly by all the things she was feeling. Perhaps—but she dared not even allow herself to think of that terrible night on her birthday. Overcome, Hetty had prayed for the safety of the mind of the baby within her. Surely her prayer had been answered, for soon afterwards, when she had made herself a cup of tea, she felt suddenly happy.

And when the next day Dora had turned up unexpectedly, it was as though she had come in answer to her prayer, for Dora said that she felt Hetty to be in trouble, and so had come across London to see her. Hetty told Dora all that had occurred, and Dora explained that the social structure was at fault, being unbalanced; that wrong and excessive foods among the upper classes produced one kind of evil thinking, while insufficient nourishment among the masses, together with the unnatural confinement of the human body within office and factory, produced another kind of evil, which showed itself in acts arising from ill-health and the general miseries of childhood.

"It is a beastly age really," said Theodora, cheerfully. "Money success is almost the only ideal and this has cramped and warped the natures of rich men without them being aware of it, while fear or a sense of insecurity, has corroded the poor from within." She went on to explain that violence was a distortion of strength by fear; that true strength could come only from the spirit, which in turn could arise only from a balance of the senses of the body. "In the modern world nearly every human value, judged from what life should be, and could be, is wrong, being based on greed. Fear has become misplaced in the human mind, instead of being one of the natural impulses of the body beautiful."

When Dora had gone, Hetty felt lonely, almost depressed. She struggled against the fear within herself. She wanted her baby to be both beautiful and calm, and so she tried to still her fears and apprehensions, to forget what bad things she had seen and heard, and to replace those impressions with happy feelings and thoughts. She was relieved when, the next afternoon, Mrs. Mundy the vicar's wife had unexpectedly called; and when she had gone, Hetty went for a walk on the Hill, under the tall elms where rooks cawed and fluttered, and strolling along the crest, she tried to imagine the sun shining on the Channel waves, and breaking white over the groins lying out from the shingle beach. Returning in the chilly mists of the winter afternoon she strove to make herself see that the weak red ball of the sun going down over the railway cutting at the end of Comfort Road was the changeless sun she had been conscious of in childhood, and though it was winter now, the spring would come!

And yet, once again within the house, as the last of the blackening redness disappeared behind the fields across the cutting, Hetty's spirits sank, and she tried not to feel overcome with loneliness. For the sake of the life within her she smiled to herself in the mirror, so that her baby should be a happy baby, with a beautiful mind like Dora's. Dickie had fine thoughts, too, only he scoffed at them as sentimentality; but that was only, Dora said, because he had been such an unhappy little boy at home. The elder Maddison children had all suffered from the unhappiness between father and mother, said Dora; but she, the youngest, had been fortunate, for her mother's maid Minnie had been her nurse, bringing her up within a cell, as it were, of affectionate and emotional stability within that distraught household. Dearest Dora, she had promised to be godmother to the baby.

Both women hoped it would be a boy, who would grow into a fine man, to help in the making of a better world. Hetty hoped he would have the light brown hair and fine blue eyes that both Dora and Dickie had; and it was at this point in her meditation beside the tea-tray that the hoarse voice had begun to call down the street, and as it came nearer and nearer, crying *Engasboll Sawbones!* she got up from beside her tea-tray, and saw a ragged man who, perceiving her at the same time, promptly came to the door and knocked.

While she was waiting in the hall, unable to summon up courage to put up the chain, open the door, and say, as Mrs. Cummings had advised, "Nothing today, thank you," and then close the door again, the sound of voices made her creep into the front room, and peep round the lace curtains. The hawker was talking to Mr. Pooley, the very old man who lived with his grandson and daughter over the way. There he was, standing at his gate and smiling at the hawker, who was scratching his shaggy head underneath his cloth cap, and grinning at the old man. They seemed to be friends.

Hetty was relieved, for Mr. Pooley was a dear, with whom she had exchanged remarks about the weather several times since she had come to live there. Mrs. Feeney said that he was over a hundred years old, and had had a telegram from the Queen on his hundredth birthday. He had been working on Bridge House Farm when Napoleon was preparing to invade England. Mr. Pooley spent his time growing vegetables on the level patches of the waste land above the railway cutting. One day he had brought Hetty a bunch of lavender, taken from the twisted bushes which grew among the long yellow grasses and briars beyond his cultivated patches. He had a wrinkled face and weak rheumy eyes, which Mrs. Feeney said had come from working on yellow Kentish clay all his life. Once a week, on Saturdays, he took his vegetables round the streets for sale, on an ancient barrow-cart drawn by his donkey.

Reassured by Mr. Pooley's presence, Hetty opened the door. The old-clothes man hastened across the street to her.

"Got any ragsbollsawbones lidy? Any old clo? Jemjars lidy? Is yer farver in? Kenne spare a pairo ole boots? Me lilpigs gornter market wonst too often, lidy."

With a grin he held out a foot, wriggling red toes in a broken boot.

"Want a nice wallable fern, lidy, take yer choice, water it well and it'll last a lifetime, lidy. Nah then, got anyfink in my line o' ragsbollsawbones, lidy?"

Hetty hesitated. She could only think of her corsets, which Dora had said were the equivalent of a slave's cage, anyway they were far too small for her now. But how could she offer him such a thing, even wrapped up?

The rag-and-bone man seemed to read Hetty's thoughts, for he said with a grin revealing white and splendid teeth, "I buys lidy's apparel, swell's gents, lidy. My ole ooman's your size, lidy, like as two peas. Blime, you're posh, ain't you? 'Ullo, ere's Carlo, come wiv 'is li'l tuppenny."

An Italian organ-grinder, followed by a small girl wearing a scarf and gaily-coloured loose clothes to her ankles, was hauling a barrel-organ down the street towards them.

"I'll go and see what I've got," said Hetty, trying to make up her mind.

"That's right, lidy, gor bless yer. All alone? Don't yer fret, lidy, put up the ole Abel and Cain, an' satisfy yerself." He pointed to the chain, and grinned. "You fink I'm one of 'r rough 'uns, don't yer, lidy? I aint, lidy! They all knows me rahnd 'ere, lidy, I'm a reg'lar, lidy, I come from the tottin' market dahn Dep'ford."

Hetty softly closed the door behind her, and went upstairs to fetch the corsets and an old pair of boots which Dickie had several times said he would never use again. They were heavy walking boots with nails in the soles and on the heels in groups of three, like shamrock leaves. He had last worn them years before, he had told her, when his brother John, accompanied by some of his friends, had taken him on a walking tour in the Lake District.

Dickie had said they had never fitted him properly, that they stubbed his big toes. Several times since they had moved into the house he had picked them up, saying he must get rid of them; but each time, as he spoke of the walk around the lakes of Windermere and Coniston, he had put them back again on the ledge under the kitchen dresser, called the pot-board. Yet the continued sight of the boots there irritated him, she knew.

Now there was a chance to get rid of them, once and for all. Dickie would be glad to learn that in future they would keep dry the feet of the poor man who had said, so bravely and gaily, that his little pigs had gone to market, since Dickie had condemned Papa's treatment of the man who had carried his bags to the station, and been given only the stump of a cigar for payment.

Wrapping the corsets in a piece of brown paper, together with the Deeandjay combinations, which she had never liked, and carrying the heavy boots with their clusters of rusty nails in her other hand, Hetty went to the front door to see with relief that the totter was standing outside the iron gate. He came quickly to her, took the boots, looked at them critically, pursing up his mouth, then giving her a sideway glance, asked what she wanted for them, adding with a laugh that they must have come off a proper ole clodopper.

"Oh no, on the contrary," replied Hetty, "they are the best walking boots. Please accept them as a present. And also this parcel, but please do not open it until you get round the corner, will you?"

"Cor!" ejaculated the totter, feeling what was through the paper. "If this ain't me lucky day. 'Ere, I'll tell yer what! I'll give yer me two best ferns, complete wi' pots!" He darted back to his barrow, and returned with the aspidistras.

"Oh, you are so very kind, thank you very much! Are they really for me? They are lovely ferns."

"'Ere, can you read? I've got a book I'll throw in wiv the ferns, lidy. 'Ere y'are!" And he gave Hetty a dog-eared copy of *The Diary of Samuel Pepys*.

"Thank you!" said Hetty. She had once begun to read the book, finding it in the drawing room at home; but Papa had taken it from her, saying it was not fit for a young girl to read. What fun, now she could read it!

"That's all right, lidy. Arternoon, lidy. Blime, I ken see my old 'ooman doin' the barn dance in them unmentionables on Saturday night rahnd our kitchen table!"

Thinking that she would give one of the ferns to Mamma, Hetty put them side by side on the window shelf. She stared at them happily, imagining that they were brother and sister; while from down the road floated the raucous cry of the totter going away. Then the barrel-organ began to play.

It was by the clock on the shelf a few minutes before the hour of four, and by the waning light nearly time to light the gas-jet. Mrs. Mundy would not be coming to call now. As she decided to make herself some tea, Hetty heard the barrel-organ outside changing a tune, and looking through the curtains, she saw the Italian turning the handle while the little girl was dancing all by herself on the pavement waving a tambourine. The Italian looked such a comic sight, with his black bowler hat low over his ears, and a curling black moustache hiding most of his small brown face. The child could not have been more than seven or eight, and had the serious and wan look of one who had never had enough food to eat. Poor little mite!

Hetty felt in her purse for a penny. The kettle was steaming on the hob, ready for the boiling water to be poured into the tray-kettle; she had gone over in her mind everything she would do when Mrs. Mundy came. Now that Mrs. Mundy would not be coming, dare she offer a cup of tea to the Italian and his little girl? They must have come a long way from "Little Italy" in Deptford. But supposing Mrs. Mundy *did* come?

Undecided in her mind, but following her impulse, Hetty fetched the china teapot from the kitchen, and put in three tea-spoons of tea, one for herself, one for the organ-grinder, and the third for the pot and the child together. When she had poured in the boiling water she glanced at the clock, more for reassurance that Dickie would not get home yet awhile than for wanting to know the time. When the pot had stood a minute she poured tea into a jug, added milk and sugar, and with the cups and a plate of bread and butter went to the door. "Oh, how very silly of me," she said aloud, for she had to put down the things before she could open the door. But she was quick, and was on the threshold as the child arrived at the gate, gravely holding out her tambourine and lisping, "Grazie, Signorina."

With a quick glance down Comfort Road, seeing with relief that it was empty, Hetty felt in her purse. She wanted to put two pennies into the tambourine, but she knew that would be extravagant, with so much extra expense to be faced in the coming months. The Italian was profuse in his thanks, repeatedly removing his bowler hat, grinning and bowing as with a hand like a brown claw he took a slice of bread and butter, and gave it to the child who snatched it hungrily. "No eat today, bambina," he said. "Bambina eat tomorrow, no turn eat today, but now, si! si! molte grazie, Signorina!" He spoke rapidly to the child, who with her mouth stuffed full made a low curtsey to Hetty. "Tanker you molto, kinda lady!" said the father, raising his hat again and bowing. The child made wheezy noises as she tried to swallow.

He put his own slice of bread and butter in his pocket, and sucked in the tea, while blowing on it vigorously. "Nice nice, molto hotta, si si." When the child had drunk, he took the cup from her, shook out the tea-leaves, wiped the inside with his fingers, and with a bow gave it back to Hetty. And having done the same thing to his own cup, he returned to his barrel-organ, and began to turn the handle faster than he had turned it before. Hetty waited in the cold until *Il Trovatore* had ended, then with a smile, and a wave of her hand, returned into the house.

The Italian played two more tunes, then crying in his thin high voice, and waving a hand, "Goodby-ee! goodby-ee! Grazie, buona notte!" he turned his cart round and hauled it to the corner, the child trotting by his side.

Hetty sat by the fire, seeing in her mind's eye the little face, hearing again the wheezing noise of swallowing as the father said that it was not her turn to eat that day. Perhaps there were other children at home, and they too ate only every other day. It was all very sad; but then, there was a hidden purpose in life, which was not for people on earth to know.

She remembered the aspidistras, and went to pour half a cup of warm water over each. She washed the dark green leaves, and the rim of each pot; then returning to the kitchen, found two odd saucers in which to stand them. They looked so nice, she was sure they were brother and sister; and at the thought she remembered Hughie, and wondered how he was getting on, living in a room in London by himself. It was sad how things changed when you grew up.

Outside in the street twilight was come. Over the railway embankment and the field beyond massive dark clouds compressed a smoky red streak of sunset. She heard the friendly footfalls of the lamplighter as he stopped by the lamp-post at the corner; then at the slight clank of the opening door of the lantern she jumped up to watch from the window.

There he stood in the sad light of the dying day; but a blue and yellow flame fluttered to greet the darkness; the door was shut, and the pole drawn down. One more night had come! With regular footfalls the lamplighter walked away, as he had walked away every afternoon, a minute or two earlier every day, since she had come to live there. Hetty always felt glad when she heard him coming, and a little lonely when he had gone again. He looked such a nice man, so neat and tidy.

Now for some reading, with Pepys' Diary to keep her company! First she must light the gas and let down the venetian blinds, and lay the table for supper. Dickie would not be home for some time yet; usually he came at a quarter past seven. To-night she had some nice brawn for him, with some vegetable soup first, and then his favourite apple dumpling. She had got a treat for him that evening, a twopenny jug of cream to go with the dumpling. He needed it, for all he took for luncheon was some brown bread and butter sandwiches, spread with marmalade, in an old tobacco box, the lid held on by a rubber band. He would never take anything else, saying he could not afford more.

Hetty lit the gas, and then with a feeling that someone outside was looking in, hastily she unwound the cord from the brass knob and let down the wooden slats of the blinds. She pulled another cord, making them lie flat; then set about taking away the tea-things. While she did so, the awful thought grew in her mind that Mrs. Mundy had not returned her call because in the first place Mrs. Mundy had not been calling; she had been *visiting* in Comfort Road, visiting old people and the houses of some of her husband's parishioners, and probably *had not for a moment* expected that anyone living there would have the presumption to think that it was a call! How stupid she was, how very very stupid to make such a mistake! She had even told Mrs. Mundy that she hoped her baby would be a boy, who would turn out to be a poet! Of course, people laughed at poets!

Oh, what must Mrs. Mundy be thinking of her? But Mr. Mundy would understand, for he preached such wonderful sermons, how our dear Lord had found His friends among the outcast and the destitute: and how all the brilliance and cleverness of the talented and the successful, even of men of genius, was as nothing unless there was also charity. Hetty stood still a while, thinking of Jesus lowering His head before Pilate's question after the agony of Gethsemane, and of the scene a few hours later upon Golgotha. Dora had said that the cry from the cross was the most poignant in all history; a cry at the breaking-point of the old world, which all men must first lose if they were to find the new world of Truth. This was the theme of all great literature, declared Dora, for example Shakespeare's *Hamlet*, where at the crucial moment of the Prince's life Horatio said, *Now cracks a noble heart*, and then *Good-night, sweet Prince, may flights of angels sing thee to thy rest.* All literally true, said Dora, for great poetry was clairvoyant. Life seemed so beautiful and simple when Dora was with her.

And thinking of her friend, Hetty felt herself suddenly to be buoyant and happy. It was a world truly made by God, though there were other forces in it, and acting through people sometimes, which were opposed to God. And smiling to herself, Hetty clasped her hands before her, bent her head and closed her eyes, and with a tremulous smile whispered, "God, help me to be true to Thee, for the sake of my baby."

With sudden happiness she put a lump of coal on the fire with her hand, glad that Dickie was not there to see her do it, for he always insisted on using the tongs. She must lay supper, but keep the brawn in the larder until the last moment, to be fresh and cold. Would it be nice with some mashed potatoes? Yes, she would do a few potatoes. And remember to mix some fresh mustard, and only a little, not to waste any, Dickie liked mustard always fresh. Thank goodness she had the brawn, and it would not be boiled eggs again! That look on Dickie's face when he had opened the first egg, and found it bad; and then the second egg, and that was bad too. He had exclaimed, "Beastly Free Trade Chinese eggs!" and *she had laughed.* She had imagined Sidney Cakebread saying, "What, is a general election in the offing?" and it had seemed so funny; but Dickie had got up, put on his coat and cap, and left the house without a word, to return an hour later with pinched face, his boots muddy from walking on the Hill. She must never laugh again at the wrong time.

Hetty went to the larder, lifted the mould of brawn off the shelf, and sniffed it anxiously. Could it have come from China, where, Dickie said, the pigs fed on human corpses? Satisfied that it was still fresh, she put it back on the shelf and set about making some vegetable broth of carrots and some celery, which she had been lucky enough to buy in a shop. These she chopped up and put in a pot that had been on the hob all the morning, gently simmering with some scrag of mutton, to make stock.

She had removed the pot to the kitchen before getting the afternoon tea-tray ready; now she took it back and put it on the hob. When she had laid supper on the oak three-legged table covered by a cloth, she went on with her knitting. Soon her high button boots began to feel hot, so she took them off and put on her slippers; and remembering Dickie's slippers, she fetched them from among his other boots standing in a row on the pot-board in the kitchen, and put them by the brass rail of the fire-guard, ready for when he should come in. It was getting on for six o'clock; she had an hour and a quarter before he would be back. Now for the Diary of Samuel Pepys!

As she sat by the fire she heard a dull report, then another, coming from the railway cutting. She knew them for fog signals, and wondered if his train would be late. Noises of trains puffing slowly up the incline of the deep cutting could be felt in the house through the walls and chimney. Mr. Pooley had told Dickie that when he was a boy there had been a canal where now the railway ran, starting from the River Thames by the Isle of Dogs, and barges had been hauled by horses all the way to and from Croydon. To overcome the gradient there had been twenty-three locks between the market garden and the land below where the Crystal Palace now stood. The canal being very deep there, it had held some fine fish, roach and pike and once a salmon had been caught opposite the house "by a gen'elman a-whippin' water." Dickie had been delighted by the information, and had spoken quite a lot to the old fellow about fishing. He had given him some Cavendish tobacco, part of a present he had received the previous Christmas from Doggett's. Hetty had kept the little wooden tobacco barrel for her buttons, after the Cavendish had been given to Mr. Pooley. The old man smoked it in a clay pipe quite black at the base of the bowl, sucking with his cheeks to keep it going after he had lit it; for the poor old fellow had no teeth left.

Hetty sat by the fire, knitting and reading, while the engine puffed away up the incline. Other dull reports came from the distance. Rising to lift a slat of the blinds, she saw only the faintest haze on the top of the lamp-post. The window pane on her cheek was like ice, and even as she stared the haze turned dim and then dark. Yellow fog was drifting down Comfort Road.

She went upstairs to close the bedroom window, which was usually left open two inches from the top, as Dickie was what Hughie called a fresh air fiend. Coming downstairs again, she made sure that the back-door, which opened on to a brick-paved yard and a small narrow garden, was both locked and bolted. She tried the hasp of the kitchen window, and saw that the smaller hinged window in the scullery, scarcely big enough for a cat to creep through, was shut.

Muffled thuds of fog-signals came at intervals down the chimney as she sat by the fire, waiting and knitting, and trying to remember if she had forgotten anything. She sat with her back half to the door, which she had left ajar to stop the smoke from the fire coming out into the room.

The vegetables in the pot began to bubble; and at the sound she got up and stirred the soup with a wooden spoon. After a few more minutes of knitting and stirring her feet felt the draught, and she got up to push the door almost closed. The hinges were worn, for the house had been built before the coming of the railway, when Comfort Road had been extended. They were also stiff, and at one particular position the draught to the small fire, which had an ordinary brick at the back of the grate to save coal, was not strong enough to move the door.

It was possible, Dickie had said, to leave the door nearly shut so that the draught was not felt upon the feet, and at the same time the pull from the fire would not open it wider. Trying to find the exact position, Hetty felt the air from the passage outside chilling elbow and shoulder and ribs under the cloth of her high-necked jacket; and as she closed the door gradually she fancied she could hear it sighing past her. There, she had found the right place! The door remained still, a quarter of an inch from the jamb. Pleased with herself, she sat down again, and went on with her reading and the making of the baby's coat, getting up periodically to stir the soup.

Sitting down after one such stirring, she fancied she saw the door moving slightly; and as a cold shiver struck through her, she remembered that she had not put up the chain after saying good-bye to the Italian organ-grinder. Perhaps she had even left the front-door ajar, and the wife-beating man at the bottom of the street who had called Dickie that terrible name had crept into the hall and now was waiting there to stab her as she went out to fetch the supper things.

Finding it hard to breathe, and knocked as though sideways by her thudding heart-beats, Hetty sank into the chair. She tried to force herself to seize the poker, but she could not move. She saw in her mind a fist coming down on her forehead, and closed her eyes in terror of the thought. Recovering after a few moments, she opened her eyes and stared at the door. It was moving ever so slightly. She tried to make her voice say, Come in and sit down if you are cold, I shall not mind, but her throat had gone dry. She could not even make herself swallow and so moisten her throat for speaking. She clasped her hands, and tried to pray, but only wild and incoherent images broke against her fear. Perhaps she was going to faint.

And staring desperately at the door, she saw it opening slightly, and at the base of the door something ran swiftly over the oil-cloth to the woollen rug by her feet. Her relief was great, for it was a mouse! A little mouse! Hughie had kept white mice, and so Hetty had no fear of the mouse as it sat upright by the fender and washed its face with swift tiny movements. The toilet over, immediately it started to work. She watched its head vibrating as it pulled at the worsted of the rug, and realizing that it was gathering wool for its nest, feelings of tenderness and relief arose in her. There was a mouse-hole by the gas-pipe in the kitchen, through the wooden floor by the side of the cupboard, and the mouse must have come all the way from there!

The mouse had a sharp nose, transparently large ears upright on its head, and bright beady eyes. It worked fast and earnestly. She could hear the noise of its teeth as it tore and snapped at the blue and yellow hairs of the worsted. Then it gathered them together and running ever so fast was gone across the floor and through the crack of the door. A little mother mouse, gathering materials for her nest! Hetty was so relieved that she wept with happiness, sharing the funny side of it with an imagined Dora. With a light heart she went to hide Pepys behind the row of boots upon the pot-board.

At a quarter past seven o'clock all was ready for Dickie's home-coming. She waited for his whistle, and then the knock on the door. The clock ticked on, a little louder than before. Slowly the minute hand came to the half hour, and moved to the Roman figures of seven, eight, nine, ten, as though in response to muffled thuds of fog-signals outside.

The fire in the front room fell low and was made up again, sending its smoke to add to the hundreds of tons of soot from innumerable chimneys blending with the mists rising from what once were marshes beside the Thames.

At ten o'clock, nearly three hours late, came the welcome treble knock on the door, but not the whistle. She knew he was tired, and running to the door removed the chain, and opening it wide cried, "Oh, I am so glad to see you, dearest!" as she stepped back for him to enter.

"Hullo," he said, shortly, closing the door behind him. Then he wiped his boots carefully on the mat, as he always did, whatever the weather. As carefully he put down the black bag he carried, hung up his umbrella and hat, removed his overcoat and hung it on its usual peg, shook his sleeves to get down his starched cuffs, and taking up the black bag again, went into the sitting-room. For a while he stared at the fire, and she knew that he was thinking that the lump had been broken by the poker instead of being left to burn more slowly by itself and so to economise on the coal-bill.

Richard was thinking that the end of the poker was discoloured where it had been in the flames, superstitiously "to draw up the fire." He decided to say nothing about it; if she wanted to ruin him by lack of economy, she must do so; he felt entirely defenceless; nothing to eat since the marmalade sandwiches and a glass of milk at midday. He would work half the night on the envelopes to make up for her extravagance, that was all.

Hetty stood by the door, uncertain what to do. She had meant to put her arms round him and kiss him, but his mood checked her. She managed to say in a cheerful voice, "Would you like your supper now, or will you rest a while, dear?"

"Oh, do not bother about me."

For the past two hours, during the prolonged wait in the cold carriage, Richard had been sitting uncomfortably with other men silent like himself, thinking of the return home to a warm and bright room, his slippered feet stretched out before the fire. He had not imagined food, being too tired.

"It's a terrible fog, I'm afraid," said Hetty. "You'll feel better after some food, dear."

"You have had yours, I suppose?"

"No, Dickie, of course not. I waited for you."

"But surely I have asked you again and again not to wait for me, when I am late? You should keep to regular meal-times, have I not told you that before? There is no sense in two people missing their meal-times, and I cannot help myself, can I?"

"I wasn't very hungry," Hetty replied, apologetically. "And I had a lot to do, and the time simply flew, I hardly noticed the time, dear."

"I suppose you never gave your husband a thought, you were so occupied in your mind with other people." He was half inclined to believe what he had said, though he had not meant it. The sulphurous fog had made his eyes smart, and his throat sore.

"I am always thinking of you, if you did but know it. I'll get your supper," and she turned away, to go into the kitchen, and wipe her eyes quickly on the drying-up cloth, while telling herself that he was very tired, and that she must not allow herself to take any notice of his moods, as Dora had advised her.

Oh dear, supposing the soup was burned! She ought to have tasted it before. But it was too late now. She poured a little cold water from the tap into the bowl for him to wash his hands, then hurried into the sitting-room with a small brass hot-water can, meaning to fill it from the kettle.

While he was washing in the kitchen, she ladled out some Scotch broth into a bowl, and taking too hasty a sip, burned her tongue. Oh dear, she could not possibly tell now! She could taste only her stinging tongue. Oh, pray that it be all right, she cried within herself.

Richard came and sat down at the table. He broke his bread into the bowl of soup; then putting his nose almost into the bowl, blew softly for the steam to warm his face. She watched anxiously while he took a cautious sip from the side of the spoon, and with much relief heard him say, "Ah, this is capital soup!" When the bowl was half empty he smiled up at her. "Your broth is as good as Mrs. Cummings', I do declare. Are you not going to have some, too? Come on, Hetty, sit beside me and be sociable."

"Yes dear, of course I will keep you company."

"Good," said Richard. "Do you know, I look forward all day to having supper in our little room, by the fire. Thank heaven the cold spell has gone. There will be no skating on the Thames this year, as in the great winter fourteen years ago. I remember my father coming back from London and giving us a graphic description of the crowds on the frozen Thames, and an ox being roasted there."

When the supper had been cleared Richard fetched his black leather bag, and taking out envelopes and lists of names and addresses settled down to work upon the three-legged table. At eleven o'clock Hetty filled the copper canister with hot water from the kettle, covered it with its woollen protector, gazed at the head bowed over the table, and murmured, "You won't sit up too late, dear, will you, and try your eyes too much?" He lit the dark lantern, and turning out the gas, told her to go and keep the bed warm for him, and not to worry her little head.

Hetty stood still, holding the wrapped hot water canister under one arm, and the American alarum-clock in her hand. As she did not move, he said:

"Well, what is it now? Afraid to go upstairs in the dark?"

"No, of course not!" Overcoming her deep shyness, she said hurriedly, "The baby is moving about inside me."

"Moving? Great Scott, it is not coming already, surely?"

"No, Dickie. It's only moving."

"Where is it moving to? Does it dislike Comfort House so much?"

"It's just moving about, and giving kicks."

"Playing footer already." He smiled suddenly up at her, and at the concealed desperation in his eyes, the tears came into her own. Ah, she understood him! Papa had said he was shifty, because he never looked anyone in the eyes; but she knew how he felt, he was so different in outlook to other people.

She stroked his head. "Do not be too late, dearest, will you? You work so hard, you are so good really—almost too good. So conscientious." She felt at that moment that she could embrace, like Dora, all the unhappiness in the world.

"The footballer will require boots and socks and other things, you know."

Hetty touched with her lips the light brown hair of the head bent over the work, the brown hair looking so wavy and soft in the light of the lantern. Poor Dickie, she wasn't very much of a help to him. Had she not been the cause of him losing his good position in Doggett's? Now he had to address envelopes after a long day in the City, thousands and thousands of envelopes, to make up for it. The Bank was keeping him on until the New Year when the books were balanced.

"Do not be late, dear, you must have proper sleep, you know."

"Oh, I am all right! Work never killed anyone yet."

Hetty had been in bed about half an hour and was nearly asleep when suddenly she lifted her head off the pillow to listen intently. Downstairs there was a noise like stamping, and then of feet half running in the passage, ending in a bang on the kitchen floor. Soon afterwards she heard Dickie creeping up the stairs and at the open door he whispered, "Are you awake?"

"Yes, dear. Is anything the matter?"

"I was after a mouse! And would you believe it, it had the cheek to sit up and wash its face in front of me, before it started to nibble the rug! We shall have to get a cat."

"Yes, dear," said Hetty, hoping the mouse would go elsewhere first. She must stuff the hole by the gas-pipe with a cork. "You will come to bed soon, won't you?"

"Yes, I think I will, I am rather fagged," the weary voice replied.

Chapter 20

GOOD TIDINGS ON CHRISTMAS EVE

NIGHT AFTER night Richard continued to address envelopes, beginning at nine o'clock, when Hetty went to bed, and working until midnight. He sat in the kitchen; the fire in the front room was lit only on Sundays. As Hetty's footfalls went up the stairs he took down the dark lantern from its place on the kitchen shelf beside the tea caddy, lit the wick and turned it down, laid out envelopes, blotting pad, and postal lists on the table, turned out the gas, drew up his chair, adjusted the wick of the lantern; and after this meticulous ritual, he began the nightly three hours' writing.

It was still and warm in the room, and he settled to write with a feeling of quietude and peace. He wore his favourite tweed jacket, threadbare at those parts of the sleeves which were regular in movement upon the ribbed surface of the scrubbed deal table. The bull's-eye lens of the lantern was swung back on its hinges so that the polished reflector threw a yellow light across the table and upon his hands. The kitchen was in shadow, the dresser, shelves, and rows of canisters insubstantial; and until midnight every evening he sat there, in the voiceless space about him. Each envelope was addressed in a clear and bold handwriting, each letter carefully formed, each comma and stop scrupulously inserted. The work with a quill pen took him almost twice as long as it took others hurrying to get through their lists with legibility only as their standard; nevertheless, just before the beginning of Christmas week he had carried to the basement office in Old Broad Street eighteen thousand envelopes, and received for them in payment a sovereign, three half-crowns, and the praise of the amiable little Jewish clerk of the bucket shop.

Each night, before he began work, he entered into his notebook details of daily expenditure. Two days a week, on Tuesdays and Thursdays, his lunch cost twopence; for on those days he had a bath-bun with his box of sandwiches and glass of milk. On the other days he had only the glass of milk. He had given up riding by omnibus, and was curious to know how much he would save by this economy, after allowance had been made for the extra wear-and-tear of boot-leather. *The Morning Post*, bought from the newsman with a wooden leg outside the station every day was, he considered to be in the nature of a luxury, but the reading of it was almost his only relaxation, especially the articles about the countryside and rural pursuits. His boxes of butterflies and moths had not been opened for months. As for the 'cello, that never moved from the end of the passage.

There was one extra item for food recorded in the notebook at this time, a hot potato. It had been purchased from a man standing in the gutter of Leadenhall Street beside a coke-burning canister on wheels. Richard had taken his purchase into the Golden Grain Company's shop, but the waitress from whom he had ordered only a glass of milk had looked at it pointedly once or twice as he was eating it, and he had left the shop determined never to go back there. Thenceforward he was a customer of the Aërated Bread Company; but never with a potato again. The purchase was duly entered into the notebook:

1 *Hot Potato*—½d.

One evening about ten days before Christmas Hetty saw the entry in the book (she dared to take a peep at it while he was in the lavatory) and the pathos of it decided her to write a letter to Mr. Roland Tofield, at his address in London, asking if he would help in recommending her husband to a post. She explained the circumstances, and begged him to keep her letter secret.

In due course Mr. Tofield replied that he was delighted to be of service to her, that he would do what he could in the matter of an introduction to a City house; adding that he knew he could rely entirely on her discretion, and to regard in the strictest confidence anything he might be able to effect. Hetty read his letter many times, praying that something would come of it. She hid it in her Bible, as being the least likely place where Dickie would look.

Thereafter, every time the postman gave his rat-tat on the door she hastened to the mat to see what might be lying there.

Three days before Christmas a letter fell upon the cocoanut mat, as though detached from the door by a loud double knock.

She ran to pick it up. It had a London postmark, and an embossed smiling face of a moon on the flap. It was addressed to Mr. Richard Maddison. Oh, her prayers had been answered!

"Well, I be jiggered!" exclaimed Richard, upon opening it that night. "I meant to write and apply for a post with the Moon Fire Office, and here they are requesting me to present myself at my early convenience, in the matter of 'an application for employment'! What does it mean, I wonder?"

"Perhaps you have friends at Court, Dickie. I mean, of course, perhaps the Secretary of Doggett's knows the Secretary of the Moon." She laughed, it seemed so funny the way she had said it.

"Well, I will not let the grass grow under my feet, you may bet. I shall reply this very evening after supper and catch the late post in the box outside the station."

Almost by return of post came a reply written, like the original letter, in copying-ink, requesting Mr. Richard Maddison to appear at noon precisely on the 24th of December at the Head Office in Haybundle Street, for an interview with the General Manager.

Richard obtained leave for the appointment, and in due course reported as various City churches were striking the midday hour. A long-haired junior, impressed by his appearance, took him up the broad carpeted stairs used only by the directors and the three senior officials of the Company, past the alarming Board Room, to the General Manager's Office. There the junior pressed back the wings of his Gladstone collar, ran his fingers through his hair, coughed, and knocked timidly on the door. Bidden to enter, he stood just inside, said, "Mr. Maddison, sir," and departed with relief.

"Come in, Mr. Maddison."

Richard, faint with suspense, did as he was bidden. He crossed the room on a carpet into which his feet appeared to be sinking as he approached the big mahogany desk where a frock-coated figure was seated, another standing beside him.

"This is Mr. Maddison, sir," said the Secretary, who was standing.

"Good morning," said the heavy-bearded figure at the desk, fixing his eyes upon the tall young man before him.

"Good morning, sir," replied Richard, bowing, and awaiting the end of the inevitable scrutiny.

"I understand you wish to be taken on the indoor staff of this Company," began the General Manager, impersonally. "You will have realized, of course, that you are beyond the age when this office usually takes on its officials, who commence generally at the age of sixteen years at a salary of thirty pounds per annum."

"I understand, sir."

"Where were you educated?"

"First at Mr. Hawtrey's at Slough, sir, for the Navy."

"Why were you not admitted to the Navy?"

"I was ploughed at the medical examination at Greenwich, sir, owing to a defective right eye."

"Did you not know of that defect before you went for examination?"

"My other eye is strong, and I hoped it would be sufficient, sir."

The thirteen-year-old boy had returned home after that failure, to be called a one-eyed misfit by his father. He had been removed from the preparatory school, his parent declaring that it was a waste of money to send him anywhere else. Thereafter the idea had been to educate him at home. This had meant an unpaid job as messenger, office boy, and clerk in the Estate Office, as the room was called where the accounts and various japanned boxes were kept in a state bordering upon disorder, upon a large table and on various shelves. There was no other staff to this office—there had been a steward years before, until Captain Maddison, retiring from his Lancer regiment, on the death of his father, had decided to manage his own properties.

It had been a miserable time for Richard. The boy had been supposed to know all that his father knew: which in turn had meant condemnation, exhortation, recrimination, and occasionally flagellation.

At sixteen years of age he had run away from home; and helped by an uncle, had been found a post with Doggett & Co. Ever since it had been Richard's fear that others would find out about his early circumstances. Now, as the General Manager of the Moon Fire Office asked his pertinent questions, he felt himself to be hopelessly an object of contempt. To his great relief there were no further questions about his education—or lack of education.

"I understand that you have been employed by Messrs. Doggett and Co. How long were you there?"

"A matter of ten years, sir, since just before my seventeenth birthday."

"Are you married, Mr. Maddison?"

"Yes, sir."

"What salary were you in receipt of at Doggett's?"

"One hundred and twenty pounds per annum, sir."

The General Manager took up an ebony ruler, and balanced it in his hands. He regarded the aloof figure standing before him once again, while reminding himself that the introduction had been given to him by no less a person than Sir Roger Tofield himself. He decided not to enquire further into the young man's affairs.

"I am happy to tell you, Mr. Maddison, that we are prepared to give you a trial in the Town department for a period extending to the Ladyday quarter, at a commencing salary of ninety pounds a year. At the end of the period of probation, we will review the position, with a view to taking you on the permanent staff, if this should meet with your agreement."

Richard managed to say "Thank you, sir."

"And I wish you a Merry Christmas."

"Thank you, sir. And if I may be permitted, may I wish you the compliments of the season."

"Thank you, Mr. Maddison."

The General Manager replied to his bow, by half raising himself from his chair; then turned to the Secretary and asked him to arrange the details with Mr. Maddison; whereupon the two left the room across the heavy Persian carpet and proceeded to an office in the mezzanine room between the first and ground floors, connected by an iron stairway. There it was decided that Richard should commence work after the New Year.

"Ninety pounds a year for one with wife and family will necessitate some economies," remarked the Secretary, as he was leaving. "But at Ladyday the position will be reviewed. You will appear here, then, on the morning of the second of January at nine o'clock? Very well, we shall expect you, then—and may I add my wishes for a Happy Christmas?"

Richard went through the massive mahogany and brass door in jubilation. In his relief he felt reckless, and very nearly took a cab; but commonsense prevailed, and he waited for the halfpenny 'bus down Ludgate Hill and Fleet Street to the Strand. Punctilious as ever, he determined to return to the bank without taking lunch, deeming that he owed it to his employers to make up for the time they had allowed him for his visit to the City. He had the top of the 'bus to himself, and as he sat astride the knife-board he imagined he was mounted on an Arab steed, bearing the good news to Hetty. What a wonderful thing had happened! And on Christmas Eve, of all days! He must call in at Leadenhall Market and buy a duck, or a cock pheasant, perhaps even a hen and cock! Honk! he cried jubilantly, to an imaginary Hetty. Honk!

"My beautiful, my beautiful,
Who standeth meekly by
With humhum hum
And humhum hum
And proudly flashing eye."

Alighting at the stop near Doggett's, on impulse he went into the adjoining building, the Canterbury Tavern, and asked for a glass of brown sherry. He would drink a silent toast to Hetty, and the future.

The Canterbury Tavern was dark with wine-tuns and oak benches, a-gleam with polished copper, verdant with green baize aprons of cellarmen, noisy with theatrical roysterers. Among one such group, seated round a barrel on champagne boxes polished by the trousers of comedians from the Tivoli music-hall nearby, Richard saw Hugh Turney. Not wanting to meet him, and certainly not to be involved in the sort of company he was keeping, Richard drank the sherry with his back turned to the noisy table, before going out of the place; and after crossing the Strand, walked a hundred yards on the pavement, crossed again, and entered the portals of Doggett's.

As he was seating himself at his desk the Registrar came over to him and said, "The Secretary asked me to tell you he would like to see you when you should return, Mr. Maddison."

"Thank you, Mr. Eliot. Shall I go straight in?" The older man nodded. Richard knocked at the door, and entered.

"Well, Mr. Maddison, I have some good news for you. I will come direct to the point. Her Ladyship has interested herself in your case with characteristic broad-mindedness, and the Partners, after due consideration, are willing to overlook the matter of your marrying without their permission, in view of your good record.

Now if you like to reconsider your resignation, I think the matter might be adjusted without any entry being made into the Minutes. Your salary is to be raised to one hundred and forty pounds per annum, so that the matter of your marriage no longer arises." He smiled at Richard. "I am sure you will appreciate the generosity of the Partners."

Richard wondered if he were really hearing and seeing normally, or was he under hallucination from the stoup of sherry he had just drunk on an empty stomach? His perplexity showed itself in his face: it was so unexpected that he could not think what to say: and then it was being said for him by something inside himself, an impression of boyhood, connected with his grandfather, the small boy's hero in default of his father. *An Englishman's word is his bond.*

"I am deeply grateful for the—the very great generosity of her Ladyship, sir, and for the magnanimity shown towards me—but having just accepted a post elsewhere—only this past half hour—I feel I should not go back on—my—on the acceptance."

"The decision reflects credit upon one who has received his training in the Shop; but perhaps you should have time to think it over. Shall we leave it like this then: that should you care to return after Christmas, to continue your duties as before, the way is clear for you."

There was a knock on the door. "Come in!"

A junior messenger, one of the liveried staff of Doggett & Co., entered and bowed. "Sir George Llewtis's footman has arrived with Sir George's compliments, sir, bringing a Christmas hamper."

"Oh yes, I'll come down at once. Well, Mr. Maddison, give it some thought over Christmas." He was dismissed.

Sir George Llewtis was one of the many aristocratic customers of Doggett & Co., "bankers in the Strand at the Sign of Three Swans next door to the Canterbury Tavern." Doggett's was a *private* bank in every sense of the word; and one of the first things to be impressed upon the young clerk was that on no account must any name or any transaction connected with the bank be mentioned outside its doors. Doggett's had its vaults and strong-room—known as the Iron Chest—for bonds, securities, deeds, jewellery, plate, and coin; and Doggett's official mind, shared in varying degrees by those who worked within its walls, was likewise closed, barred, and locked as far as the outside world was concerned. Nevertheless the appearance and habits of some of the more outstanding customers were known, if not discussed, at the various desks and tables. Of these, Sir George Llewtis, an artistic *dilettante* of great wealth and position, was the most liked—if liking was the word to express the mingled awe, wonder, admiration, and pleasurable respect shown in the presence of one from the inaccessible world of fabled splendour and ease beyond imagination. Owner of thousands of acres in the Black Country—many of them disfigured by slag-heaps and pit-head habitations, the wealth from which had enabled him to rebuild the house of his forebears into a mansion of such taste and efflorescence—Sir George Llewtis, cumbered as he was with a chateau in Provence; with deer forests, moors, and lochs in Scotland; a town house in Upper Brook Street; a tenement-castle in Italy; other properties in Ireland and elsewhere—nevertheless in the tradition of *noblesse oblige* did not fail to remember any of those numerous and recurring occasions when one gave of one's substance to others. Thus on Christmas Eve one of Sir George's maroon and black carriages invariably drove down to the Strand, to be delivered of several large double-handled hampers of wickerwork, their lids sealed with wax, their interiors filled with gallon jars of whisky, caskets of tobacco, boxes of cigars and other presents to be distributed among the staff at the discretion of the Secretary.

At four o'clock that afternoon Richard left with others of his colleagues, after shaking hands with them and exchanging the season's greetings. He had made up his mind not to return; but to write a letter on Boxing Day to the Secretary. And with feelings of freedom and adventure he walked down the Embankment to Blackfriars, carrying a casket of cavendish tobacco under the arm upon which his umbrella was hung, and thence along Queen Victoria Street to Cannon Street and onwards to London Bridge animated by the spirit of Christmas in the dancing lights on cab, carriage, cart and omnibus. He had thought all the way of a present for Hetty, but so far he had managed to buy only a pair of nail scissors, constant sight of which he hoped would make her tend to forgo the childish habit of biting her nails.

After all, he said to himself, so far in her life nobody had ever thought of giving her a pair of nail scissors.

That evening as he walked home up the high road shortly after five o'clock he was in settled mood, having acquired a feeling of self-respect in his determination to stand by his bond. He would make a fresh start in the Moon Fire Office, despite the loss of fifty pounds per annum.

The early whistle and knock surprised Hetty, who had been reading absorbedly in Pepys' Diary, comfortably ensconced in the "Sportsman", which had arrived by Carter Paterson's Express van half an hour previously. Hide the book under the pot-board, quick! And oh, his meal was not ready! And oh dear, she had meant to slip out and get the chicken she had bought, with her own money, as part of her present to him, which Mrs. Feeney had promised to draw and truss all ready for the oven. Goodness gracious, she had not tidied up, either! She opened the door with a trepidant smile, and with relief heard him say, "Well, I am home early for once in a while, but do not let me put you out."

"Oh *no*, dearest, of course you could never do that! I will soon get you a cup of tea, and now pray sit by the fire and read your paper, while I find your slippers."

"No, you sit down, I will find them, why should you be my valet? You are my Valentine, are you not?"

She kissed him. "Now don't you go into the front room, I am still decorating, dearest, it is to be a surprise for you!"

"I have got a surprise for you, too! But I think I will keep it awhile." His ease of manner encouraged her to say:

"Have you found a billet? In the Moon?"

"What do you think? I will give you three guesses."

"Oh, I daren't think you have, if you haven't! I do hope so, anyway."

"Well, I will not beat about the bush, although I am the new man in the moon," he laughed. "I have secured a post there! But at a smaller salary, and so we shall have to draw in our horns."

"Of course we must, dear!"

Hetty began to laugh, seeing a picture of long horns on Dickie's head slowly receding inch by inch into his head, until only two small nobs were left. Her own horns would be black and curled up, or perhaps with a little wriggle, like a corkscrew. Hetty laughed and laughed, leaning on the table. A little man inside Dickie's head was winding in his horns, turning a handle. The man in the moon!

"Oh come, share a joke with a fellow, do!"

"It's nothing, Dickie, really, it's so silly!" And she had to sit down, for she was aching with laughter. The man in the moon, beating about the bush, with his lantern and doggett! Doggett, a little dog! Oh, she was so relieved that he had got a post, she could laugh at anything!

"It is no laughing matter, really, as you'll find when your housekeeping allowance is reduced. You *are* keeping your accounts, are you not?"

His tone sobered her. "Oh yes, of course, naturally, Dickie."

"I shall have to audit them for you one day." At this Hetty felt a stir of fear. She knew that arithmetic was not her *forte*, and also she had mislaid her penny account book.

"Now share the joke, do!"

At that moment there was a loud thump on the door. Richard went, and there stood a boy with a peaked cap on his head, holding out a rush basket sewn up with string. "Sign, please, guv'nor." It was a bird, possibly a turkey, by the feel of it in the dark. He gave the lad twopence for a Christmas-box and returned into the kitchen. Opening the bag, which had come by rail from Diss, it was seen to contain a goose.

"Whoever can have sent it, I wonder? *I* know no one at Diss! Where is Diss?" He examined the label. "Great Eastern Railway, h'm. Do you know anyone in Diss?"

"No, Dickie." Hetty was equally puzzled.

"It may be brother John," he said. "He is on the Eastern Circuit, he may have been passing through. But how does he know my new address? I have not heard from him, or written, for some months now. Well, it is a good thing I did not go to Leadenhall market as I'd intended, to buy a duck or a cock and hen pheasant." He held up the bird. "We must have apple sauce with it."

"I have bought some apples. And some nuts—but that's part of my surprise, Dickie."

"Nuts, eh? Monkey nuts, perhaps? Oh well, joking apart, do not let me enquire too closely into the commissariat department on Christmas Eve. Now what about feeding the inner man?"

"Yes, dear, of course. Could you eat eggs and bacon? The eggs are from Joy Farm, so they will be fresh. And tea, or coffee?"

"Coffee, have you some? I am as hungry as a hunter."

After a meal by the kitchen fire they decided to go down into the high street to see the sights. But not over the Hill and down by Botany Bay this time! It would be longer round by Charlotte Road to the hamlet of Randiswell, over the humped-back bridge crossing railway and brook, and so to the trees and shops and horse-trams, but what did that matter?

After the meal they set out, in a spirit of adventure. Walking downhill arm in arm, they came to the main row of shops, where the street widened and stalls were set up on the waste ground on the edge of the side-walks. Normally shops closed at ten o'clock on a week-day, but on Saturdays and Christmas Eve they kept open until midnight. Here amidst noise and light thousands of faces were passing and gazing, small children and ancient men and women, soldiers in scarlet jackets and sailors in the uniform of the Royal Navy, girls in pairs being followed by keen-eyed youths, or giggling in little groups; while in the flaring of naphtha-lamps traders yelled and chanted their wares. Butchers wearing their best straw hats and blue aprons urging to buy-buy-buy, while housewives clutching purses waited for the prices to drop. Greengrocers; men with birds in cages; a Father Christmas standing by a bran pie, pay your penny and take your luck, only a penny!, watched by children who hadn't so much as a far'dn between 'em. Pubs roaring with song and shrill cries; more small children sitting patiently on the steps outside, some nursing babies wrapped in many layers of rags. Christmas Eve! Little Jim selling lace curtains, great attraction was Little Jim, a small, clean-shaven man with a mighty voice coming out of his diminutive grey frock coat and silk hat thrust like the Mad Hatter's on the back of his head. While an assistant at the stall held up the foamy white drapes he cried that they were as supplied to Windsor Castle and all the crowned heads of Europe, what will you bid? Thirty shillings? Twenty five? A pound? Well, he was giving away Christmas presents, so he would give them away. Fifteen shillings the pair, twelve, ten? *Bang*! went many rolled newspapers in his hand. Eight! *Smack*! Six! *Crash*! FIVE SHILLINGS! *Crash bang wallop* on the table, as his frenzy increased to a crescendo and with arms upheld to heaven and eyes closed Little Jim gave away his curtains for three and six, *smack*! *smack*! *smack*! and in a voice suddenly calm and winsome, confidential as he leaned forward smiling, "Three shillings only!" He fixed a stern eye on Hetty—"Do you know what they cost in the shops, madam? Three and eleven three, madam! Three shillings, eleven-pence and three farthings, madam! Can I wrap them up for you, madam?" And as Dickie and Hetty moved away, a little scared by this attention from the magnetic little man under the flares, another curtain was already being displayed, and Little Jim's voice was mounting in pitch and volume over the new wonders, the froth gathered at the corners of his mouth, and *smack*! the hoarse voice was shouting it all over again.

"He must get very tired, Dickie, I hope he sells some tonight, of all nights."

"Oh, he is always there, so he must get a living. I expect the curtains are throw-outs from the Nottingham factories."

Mamma paid fifteen shillings a pair for mine, thought Hetty.

"Are you tired, Hetty? Can you walk round by Pit Vale, and home by the Lane?"

"Oh yes, dearest, I am wonderfully happy with you. It is such good news about your new post."

"The odd thing is that the Secretary of the Bank could not have put my name forward——" He checked himself from saying anything further.

They entered a congested avenue of fire, faces, and happy noises. On the one hand were the shops with their gas-jets; on the other the kerb-side stalls, displaying in the light of flares all sorts of things—a wonderful sight to Hetty, who had never seen a street market at night before, except for the glimpses she had got when driving away from her home ten weeks previously. There was a stall displaying lurid sweetmeats and great bars of pink peppermint rock; a sarsaparilla stall; a colporteur's stall with rows of religious books and texts; the stall of someone calling himself The Apothecary of the People, a man in a silver hat with blue and red stripes painted on it, selling pills, lozengers, licorice and gregory powders, ointments, unguents, and carminatives to cure everything from barber's rash to goitre and the bite of a mad dog; an oyster and cockle stall; another with ginger snaps, cheese-cakes, and Christmas puddings; then a stall selling saveloys and pease pudding; a coffee stall, beside another with toys. Among them moved beggars selling matches, bootlaces, and packets of lavender. Peace and Good Will toward men! Arm in arm they moved through the press of people, passing a Salvation Army meeting idly watched by apathetic faces while shrill voices in disharmony with a ground bass of men's voices cried out:

> "Fling the Lifeline!
> Fling the Lifeline!
> There's one more sinner to be saved!"

The tune was somewhat disturbed by the mechanical notes of *Il Trovatore*, for next to the Salvation meeting was the Italian organ-grinder, his little girl dancing with the tambourine, while her mother stood in the gutter, holding with one hand a small boy, and with the other a black-eyed mite scarcely able to stand on its rickety legs. In a baby-carriage adjacent to the barrel-organ two dark-haired babies were asleep in company with a diminutive monkey wearing askew on its head a pillbox hat, while its body was covered with a green and red waistcoat and a pair of trousers. The monkey also was asleep, a tiny tin begging-mug still clutched in one paw.

"Poor monkee worka hard," cried the grinning Italian, raising his black hat while his other arm ground out *Il Trovatore*. "Tanka you lady, molto grazie, you ver' kinda lady," and with his wife also bowing and smiling to her, Hetty moved away. She had given her last three pennies to the girl with the tambourine, immediately afterwards hoping that Dickie would not be angry with her.

Richard was not angry. He had been touched by the sight of the diminutive monkey sleeping with the babies, while thinking that it was hardly healthy. Still, it was no affair of his, so he would not remark on it. Moving on through the crowds, they passed a phrenologist, who was yelling that he would forecast anyone's character and fate for a penny after feeling the bumps of his head. "Do have your bumps told, Dickie!" He gave her a disapproving glance: had she not heard of pick-pockets? A gipsy fortune-teller; a peep show; a man chewing fragments of a glass tumbler while holding a florin-piece in the central frown of his forehead; a Scotsman playing the bagpipes; a quarrel between tipsy men developing—"Come on, Hetty, never be where trouble is"—passing shops with chanting salesmen under flaming gas-jets, past pale silent children with their faces pressed against glass behind which were pies, cakes, bottles of lemonade, sausage rolls, pig's-trotters and tails. A lost child sobbing to an old woman trying to comfort it; an older boy broken-hearted beside fragments of a glass jar and yellow pickles, clutching his private parts in terror, unable now to go home on Christmas Eve. With a backward hurried glance Hetty passed by, then—"Wait a minute," said Richard, feeling in his pocket. He found sixpence, went back and gave it to the boy, who snatched it and fled. "There you are, there's gratitude for you," said Richard; but he did not see the gratitude in Hetty's face.

At one stall, near the bridge over the river where the horseless carriage had been bombarded, were some Christmas trees, sapling spruces standing among yellow and red globes of paper like monstrous cockchafer grubs.

"Oh do let us buy a little tree, Dickie, I can stand it in a flower pot, and it might grow in the garden afterwards!" So they bought a penny Christmas tree, about eighteen inches high, and Richard bought also thirteen Japanese lanterns for a shilling. Folded flat, they were easily carried.

"An extravagance, but they can be used over and over again."

Coloured balls hung among the lanterns, two for three ha'pence.

"Might we have three?"

"Why three? Oh very well, as you please."

Hetty chose two blue ones, as blue was the colour of Dickie's eyes, and a red one for herself. She hoped the baby would have his father's eyes.

Now the light and movement was behind them, and the ascent from Pit Vale lay ahead. Carrying their purchases they went slowly up the slope, and walking onwards under the wayside trees, came to the lower end of Twistleton Road, wide and quiet, with its large houses on either side, a peaceful road lined with trees, and sounds of merriment coming from some of the tall and lighted windows beside the steps. They passed the church of St. Simon, wherein candles burned, for the midnight service to be. Hetty clung to Dickie's arm, thinking of her awful stupidity in leaving cards on Mrs. Mundy, when she had not called on her in the first place.

Before them in Twistleton Road shone the lanterns of a party of carol singers. The voices were so beautiful, thought Hetty, as they drew nearer. The Vicar was with them, she recognized him by the peculiar wide-brimmed straw hat he always wore.

Good King Wenceslaus looked out
On the feast of Stephen . . .

How beautiful were the voices; but oh dear, she had given her last penny of that week's housekeeping to the organ-grinder. How awful if they were recognized, as they passed without giving anything! But of course she was worrying for nothing, for Dickie was feeling in his pocket for a coin.

"A Merry Christmas to you both!" cried the Vicar, raising his hat as they passed. So friendly was the greeting that Hetty, who had been holding her face against Dickie's shoulder, leaned forward and said, "And a Merry Christmas to you all!" They walked lightly down to the high road, while Hetty knew that it was going to be ever such a happy Christmas.

Chapter 21

BUTTERFLIES AND SNOWFLAKES

It *was* a happy Christmas. Mrs. Feeney came in to help in the kitchen, delighted with the present of the chicken. ("But don't tell Mr. Feeney where it came from, will you?" Mrs. Feeney understood.) Dickie suspended the Japanese lanterns, crossing the ceiling of the parlour from corner to corner, on copper wire, in case of fire. He expressed delight at the wonderful armchair in green leather, but suspecting where it had come from, insisted that she must use it. Hetty said that she loved her low little wicker chair, but to please him, she would rest in the armchair during the day, as he had asked her to, and he must use it at night.

She hung the blue globes on the Christmas tree which now stood in earth within a pot, and watered, beside the aspidistras—one blue globe for Dickie, the other for the baby, and the red one for herself. By a coincidence she had bought him a pair of nail scissors for one of his presents—the others were socks, a pair of mittens, and a long woollen scarf which she had knitted herself. The nail scissors were of a pattern identical with those he had bought for her. His other present to Hetty was a gold half sovereign wrapped up in tissue paper; he was apologetic about this, but she threw her arms round his neck and kissed him, tears coming into her eyes as she thought of his daily luncheons. He was a wonderfully kind man, really, he was her dear, dear husband.

While Mrs. Feeney basted the goose in the oven, Dickie and Hetty went to church at eleven o'clock. Afterwards they walked on the Hill, and looked at the ewes in the fold, Richard as usual pretending that he was a farmer, and what he would do if the land were his. At five and twenty past one they returned home, and when Mrs. Feeney had departed, they sat down to their Christmas dinner. There was apple sauce, roast potatoes, brussels sprouts, sage and onion stuffing in the goose, followed by pudding and mince pies. And of course a bottle of Stone's raisin wine, with almonds and Carlsbad plums, oranges, nuts, figs, dates, and tangerines, with a jar of Chinese ginger in sweet syrup. Hetty looked happily at Dickie stretched out in the "Sportsman" afterwards, feeling that this really was their home now.

Later in the afternoon he opened his boxes of moths and butterflies, and looked at those talismanic emblems of vanished summers, of faraway sunlight and starry nights in meadows and upon the hills. With wings extended, quivering to his breath, though but mummies long since dead and spiked through the middle, these tokens of warmth and light and colour were to him the essence of his own life. Sibellicae and Napeae, the Vanessas and Sphinges, Nocturni and Bombyces—all classified and set in rows—Orange Tip with undersides of lower wings mottled with green; the deep yellow of the Brimstone, with a little orange spot on each sharply-angled wing; Clouded Yellow, most beautiful at summer's end, a hibernator, feeding on clover; the Fritillaries, their underwings of burnished silver spotted and splashed, *argynnis* the shining one: six shining Fritillaries of summer, some with underwings of silver leaf, others of silver dust as though sprung from the Galaxy crossing the night sky seen from the downs. The Comma White, which fed as happily on elm as on currant bush; Tortoiseshell, eater of nettles, hundreds of caterpillars within silken hammocks on the nettles of the ditch side. The Vanessas—Red Admiral with the graceful flight of Atalanta—Painted Lady which came over the sea in little clouds just before the corn was ripe—Vanessa Io the Peacock, like a dead leaf when resting or hiding, its wings held close together and upright; and the rare Purple Emperor, sipper of the juices of the dead. This one had come to feed, again and again, on the corpses of stoats, weasels, and hawks on one of the keeper's vermin poles in the woods, until Father had caught it, and Lethe-wards 'twas borne, as he used to say, within the bottle of crushed laurel. Marbled White, of the family of Satyrs, probably blown across the Channel from France; Meadow Brown, Grayling, Wall Butterfly and Ringlet; the Blues, the Coppers, the Hair Streaks and the Skippers—every one a memory.

There were two kinds of Swallowtail, but not English butterflies: his grandfather had bought them from the Continent. Once he had thought he had a chance to add one of his own taking; for a year or two back Richard had found a slug-like caterpillar feeding on the leaves of a great water-dock under the banks of the Randisbourne; it was green as the leaf of the dock, with a black bar on each segment of its body, and orange spots. He was sure it was the larva of a Swallowtail, which had been extinct for nearly half a century in England. When he had returned thither with a perforated tin the next evening it was gone, and white ducks were quapping in the mud under the banks.

In another case were the smaller butterflies, many of them collected by his grandfather: Clifden Blue, the Blue Adonis, a cerulean hill-butterfly found only on chalk; the Golden Tail, Ermines, the Gipsy, and Black Arches; Silver Ground Carpet and Royal Mantle, Flame Moth and Shoulder Stripe, Iron Prominent and Lobster, the Buff-tip, the Puss, and the Common Chimney Sweeper which fed as a larva on the earth-nut. The Herald Moth which came to announce summer's end; and the Clifton Nonpareil; the Veneers, Pearl Streaks, and Rusts; a rare Wainscot taken on Whittlesea Mere; the Honeycomb Moth, the Twisters and Notch-wings, the Blotches, the Blushes, and the Snow-white Phantoms.

There was a case entirely of Hawk Moths. Along the top row, taking pride of place, were specimens of Acherontia Atropos, the splendid Death's Head with thick and heavy body, wings a warm brown with bands and mottlings of a darker hue, and a small white spot on the disk. Its thorax was soft as a mole's skin, deep brown, in the middle of which was the yellow mark of a skull and two collar bones. Then came the Elephant and the Humming Bird, the Convolvulus, the Privet, and the Lime. And so to the last case of mixed butterflies, the rare Merveil du Jour with its bright green wings, white-striped and crossed by black jagged bars; Yellow Underwing and Angle Shade, Burnished Brass and Gold Spangle, all mementoes of hundreds of wonderful days and walks and expeditions which would never never come again . . .

He closed the last case, and put it on the top of the pile beside him. Well, now he supposed he ought to address envelopes; but he was dashed tired, and so he closed his eyes, stretched his legs to the fire, and breathed deeply, thinking of his mother and sisters and brothers long ago at Christmas; and sighing as the dew of memory fell gently upon his eyes. Hetty knew what he was feeling: and passing by, bent to give him a kiss on his forehead, as light as the touch of antennae.

So the afternoon was for rest and peace; toast for tea, with his favourite patum peperium, and the Japanese lanterns glowing under the ceiling. More lazing in the green armchair; reading old stories of Sherlock Holmes in blue-covered *Strand Magazines;* then supper, plates of cold goose and sausage and bread, eaten before the fire. Lazily the hands of the clock moved on towards midnight.

Doors and windows inspected, seen to be locked and fastened; and so to the routine polishing of boots for the morrow, another whole holiday, and a walk with Hetty into the country. Christmas was nearly over, but at least the days were now beginning to grow longer!

New Year's Eve, and goodbye to the fellows in Doggett's, a very decent lot, all told. Towards midnight Richard went for a walk on the Hill, to clear his mind, as he put it; and while he was there all the bells in tower and steeple for miles around broke into the starry night, and to his dismay he found that his watch had stopped: he had forgotten to wind it that morning, whatever had been the matter with him? Having told Hetty that he would be back for the New Year, he ran all the way down the slope and along Charlotte Road, hastening with long strides up Comfort Road, arriving out of breath, but to the continuous pealing of the bells. Happy New Year to you! And a Happy New Year to you, too, Dickie! Absent friends, Hetty. Yes, Dickie. Richard filled their glasses with more raisin wine, and they drank the toasts. A New Year, a new beginning!

Richard's first day's work in the Town department of the Moon Fire Office was a pleasant one. He liked the quiet informality of his colleagues, and the general air of being left to work on one's own. In the Shop only quill pens had been permitted; but here the choice of quill or steel was left to the individual writer. The work was simple; and Richard, whose mind was not cast in a mathematical mould, found it a relief after the day-long casting of figures of his former living.

His remark to Hetty that there would be no skating on the Thames that winter seemed to have been borne out during the week following Christmas: but on New Year's Eve the mercury dropped to freezing point, and stayed there during the following sixteen days and nights. At least there was no yellow billowing pea-souper to delay the journeys home at night. He caught the same train as before, arriving home at a quarter after seven o'clock, to wash and have his supper, and read *The Morning Post* in slippers in front of the kitchen fire before starting the night's work. .

On the sixteenth of January the mercury rose above freezing point; but at the beginning of the third week of the month snow fell heavily one night. It was soon shovelled from the sidewalks and centres of the streets by the out-of-works, but another fall of twelve hours covered the world again, soon to be pressed by leather sole and iron hoof into ice. Then came a blizzard lasting throughout the darkness, hiding all things to a depth of nearly eighteen inches, making movement on foot and awheel laborious and at times precarious. At the tail of the blizzard came a frost-wind from the south-east which sealed the weather. The out-of-work men rejoiced; snow meant a little money for food for the wife and nippers. For others, the snow was discomfort. Travelling by train became the more uncomfortable as boots were thumped on the floor of carriages and the interior of window-panes were solid and opaque with iced human breathing. Across London Bridge an up-river wind whipped sleet into the eyes, while mittened hands had aching fingers.

There was some warmth from the big pot-bellied iron stove in the great room of the Town Department, but the desk which Richard shared with a clerk of about his own age called Journend, a quiet and kindly fellow, was farthest away from the stove, near one of the many tall windows with their lower panes of darkened glass screening the view of the pavements outside. It took much blowing upon the fingers to thaw them out, in order to hold the long black pen with its Waverley nib and so to inscribe the policies printed on laid paper, each about three square feet in area, with the name and address of the insured, the particulars of the goods covered and their values, premiums, and renewal quarter; but all day the feet remained frozen, so that of the forty-five minutes permitted for luncheon Richard spent about twenty in walking about as rapidly as he could, in order to get his circulation going.

Looking at the names of the Directors of the Company one morning, Richard saw among them the name of Sir Roger Tofield, Bart. He started; stared at the name. Was *that* how he had received the letter to present himself before the Manager? His father! Could it be? Had Father found out about his marriage from the Secretary of Doggett's, and knowing of his resignation, asked Sir Roger Tofield to help his son? Father! That could be the only possible explanation. Father had sold some of the land to Sir Roger Tofield.

The frost penetrated deeper into all brickwork, wood, glass, and human flesh covered with black clothing. Bleak January passed into bleaker February. The kitchen of the Maddison household was now the living-room. There were two reasons for this. Richard was determined that he must do all in his power, as he expressed it, to prevent the water pipes freezing, and also it was incumbent upon Hetty to economise in coal. The hard winter was general upon all England, and coal stocks were running low owing to frozen pit-heads and the delay in waggons. So they must have but one fire only in Comfort House, and that must be the kitchen fire.

Every night when Hetty had gone to bed Richard lit the hooded lantern, and thereafter his pen made its spasmodic whispering upon the foolscap envelopes. He wished that he could take the lantern, whose steady-streaming warmth from the peaked and crenellated cap of iron had fostered an affection in him, to the office, to be stood between his feet under the knee-hole of the desk, to radiate warm air upon his legs; but the idea was quelled as soon as it arose, as inadvisable. A fire office official acting in such a manner as might cause the headquarters of the insurance company to burn down! But he did wrap brown paper under his trousers around his legs below the knees, the paper being secured by tapes which Hetty sewed to his woollen combinations. No one might object to that, provided the dashed thing did not fall down!

Others in the City had the idea of brown paper, too. One lunch-time Richard caught sight of a short and sturdy figure with a black portmanteau walking down Haybundle Street in the direction of Liverpool Street Station; and immediately he bent down as though to tie his bootlace, for Mr. Thomas Turney, around whose trousers on the outside several wrappings of brown paper had been enwound with string, was the last man in the world Richard wished to come face to face with, unless it were his own father. With relief the figure trod past him on the slippery pavement, not having seen him; but all that afternoon Richard had indigestion, though it might have been the cup of coffee, made from chicory, and diluted with blue watery milk, together with the unfamiliar cake he had bought instead of his usual bath bun —an affair festooned with thin feathery strips of coconut, called a cheese-cake—that "sat on his tummy all the afternoon like lead", as he told Hetty that evening. Hetty did see that he had a good breakfast and supper; but no greenstuff was to be bought in the shops now, or indeed any vegetables except potatoes, owing to the frozen state of the fields.

Every evening from nine o'clock until midnight the lantern cast its splay of soft light upon the kitchen table, revealing the long and slender fingers, the brown beard trimmed to a point, the long straight nose and fine nostrils, the blue eyes now easy and gentle, the tall forehead with its wave of light brown hair—the head forward between the rounded shoulders, the eyes peering, scrutinising, translating: the scratching whisper of the pen, the pause for checking with the least sibilance and movement of the lips—one envelope after another laid neatly on the pile.

When the night's work was finished the container of the lamp was withdrawn and refilled with colza oil, the wick was trimmed; and with the flame turned low the shutter was moved behind the bull's-eye lens, to contain the heat for the hooded lantern to act all night as a radiator under the water-pipe in the scullery. According to Mrs. Feeney, there were many frozen pipes in the neighbourhood.

One Saturday afternoon in the second week of February—the half-quarter day on which he had received his first payment from the Moon Fire Office—Richard took Hetty for a walk to the Hill. The white slopes were scored and trodden by dark figures dragging up toboggans and sledges; others were descending with cries resembling those of the old town-criers—"Oi-yoi-yoi-yoi-yoi"—to give warning of imminent approach. They trudged up the slope to the elms on the crest, where about a snowman many boys and girls were gathered, some dragging home-made sleds, others carrying iron trays; while one group of young people had a gaily painted Norwegian frame.

A figure in black breeches, with black gaiters usually seen on the legs of bishops, black coat and muffler, and on his head a wide-brimmed speckled straw hat, was the centre of the group. It was the vicar of St. Simon's. Seeing that Mrs. Mundy was of the party, Hetty concealed herself behind Richard. "Walk on, Dickie, do, and pray take no notice," she whispered. With a serene expression on his face, Richard walked on as though the gay and laughing party was not there. "What a scared little thing you are, to be sure," he murmured, behind the elm-tree whereon he had seen the rare butterfly. "Anyone would think that they were going to eat you."

"Now then!" said the vicar, who evidently enjoyed an audience. "Now let us see how dangerous are the slopes of Vicar's Hill, as our glebe land has been called since before the time of good Queen Bess!" Whereupon the black figure, with ruddy clean-shaven face dominated by a long upper lip, cried out, "Since we have an authority no less distinguished than Sir Isaac Newton to inform us in effect that all which comes up sometime or other has to descend, let us waste no more words but take the plunge in practical demonstration of the Law of Gravity," and so saying, the figure in black ran forward with what agility his happy corpulence allowed, and falling forward upon the light framing of curved steel and ash-wood, proceeded down the slope at a rapid rate, crying, "Oi-yoi-yoi-yoi-yoi!" the while his pied straw hat, lifted off his head by the wind of progress, rolled down the slope behind him.

At the bottom of the hill were the houses of Charlotte Road. By using the toe of his right foot the vicar managed to avoid death up against one or another set of iron railings by changing course to the right, and so gliding out of sight round the bend.

"A sporting parson indeed," remarked Richard, half-admiringly. "He must be turned of fifty, too."

"What a strange hat he wears, Dickie. He has always been wearing it whenever I have seen him."

"I fancy those are the Wykehamist colours on the band."

"A religious order, perhaps."

"It was originally," he replied. "Now it is a school—my grandfather went to Winchester."

"Oh yes, Winchester College, how silly of me."

Other sleds and a trayful of children were going down, amidst cries and gleeful shouts. "I wish I had a sledge, Hetty," he went on. "As this weather is likely to hold, it might be worth while making one. I have some wood planking." He took her arm, fondly.

"Oh do, dearest! I would love to see you enjoying yourself like the others here! You work so hard, you are so good, and if it hadn't been for me, you would now be having a good time, no doubt, with someone more suitable to you."

"Do not delude yourself," he replied. "I should have been just where I am now, for no other woman has ever showed the slightest interest in me. I know very well that I am but a misfit."

"You're too good, dearest, in many ways, for most people."

"No, I am just an ordinary failure."

"I won't have you saying such a thing! Oh look, there is Mr. Mundy returning round the corner. I am glad he wasn't hurt, he is such a beautiful preacher."

"He has missed his vocation, he should have been a clown."

"Oh, but you haven't heard him preach," murmured Hetty, half to herself.

The vicar energetically hauled his sled to the crest of the hill, on the way up recovering his hat from a small boy who had been waiting expectantly to return it to him. The small boy, his eyes shining with the attentive way he had been thanked and patted on the head, followed the sled being hauled upwards towards the group under the elm-trees. Richard and Hetty were waiting by, to watch another descent; and as the trudging figure approached, smiling widely, Richard saw with alarm that he was looking directly at himself. He changed course towards them, and as he drew near called out, "Come and have a go, won't you? The finest exercise in the world to commote the liver!"

Richard was discomposed, suddenly to be so prominent. He was out of practice in such things, he told himself hurriedly: those iron railings at the bottom—and Hetty to be considered, his work being the mainstay: the vision of himself thrown asprawl to be jeered at by small boys.

"How d'ye do," smiled the vicar, raising his hat and bobbing to Hetty. "There were nineteen degrees of frost registered at Negretti and Zambra's in London last night, a Friday. Today is Saturday, and my name is Mundy, while tomorrow is Sunday, but that has nothing to do with the point: which is that, since contrast is the spice of life, do you try a descensus in avernum, it is jolly good fun." He swung round the painted frame of ash and steel, and with a sweep of his hand, indicated that it was at the disposal of Richard.

It was an alarming invitation. The effect of many sedentary emotions conflicted within Richard; but his natural impulse to action was not entirely subjugated. Morning exercises had helped to keep a hopeful zest in his otherwise confined living.

The vicar saw the doubt on his wrinkled brow, and coming near to Hetty, he asked her if she had ever been tobogganning. "M'boy'n' gel have gone home to fetch ours, and you must ride down with 'm, m'dear. I've seen you before, surely? Perhaps at our church of St. Simon?"

"Yes," replied Hetty blushing. How awful if Mrs. Mundy should see her, and discover that she was the one who had left cards. Thank goodness there had been no address on them.

"Have you met m'wife?" went on the vicar. "Like the huntsman who knows every hound in his pack, so the parish priest knows his parishioners by their faces." As this was an obvious lead to enquire their name, Richard said that it was Maddison.

"Yes, m'wife has spoken to me of you. You've just come to the neighbourhood, haven't you, and taken that charming little lock-keeper's house at the end of Comfort Road? Now you, sir—" he continued jovially to Richard—"while you are breaking your neck, I will take good care of your lady."

Dumb-bells gripped and thrown out and pulled back, Indian clubs cautiously swung under low ceilings and between narrow lath-and-plaster walls during five minutes of every morning did not compensate entirely for the mental habits of a sedentary and until recently, a solitary existence. Nevertheless Richard, concealing his reluctance and assuming an attitude of modest bravado, took off his overcoat and gave it to Hetty. Without a word he picked up the sled, ran forward with short hesitant steps, and at the brow of the hill threw himself upon the painted seat. He was committed! With long legs held out behind he slid more and more rapidly down the slope with an expression upon his face corresponding to his thoughts that in but a few moments, and with a sickening thump, he would be projected upon those iron railings.

The steel-shod runners slipped with terrifying speed, the light frame took the uneven places with a series of little hops that were left far behind before they rebounded upon elbows and stomach. Head first he rushed down the slope, slipping past others hauling up their home-made sleds, while the wind tore a succession of tears from his eyes. As the speed increased near the bottom of the slope and the houses of Charlotte Road loomed in front he told himself that nothing could prevent a smash now; but if he escaped with his life never again would he be such a confounded fool as to allow another to make him do what he did not want to do. Desperately he clenched his teeth; his nostrils opened with the imminence of danger; and then, imagining himself steering a canoe on the Long-pond under the beechwood at home with a paddle, he touched the snow with his right toe and at once his fear left him, giving way to exhilaration that he was in control of his own movement. A baker's van in the road on one side and a milk-float on the other were two objects to be avoided by his own skill; and the sled responded perfectly. The impetus took him half way to the high road, and as the steel runners ran smoothly, glidingly, he felt them to be making electricity in friction with the icy surface, and sparks of joy were passing through his body. Wonderful! It was simply wonderful to be alive!

That very evening he would set about making a sled for himself!

He took the frame back, pulling it effortlessly on its raw-hide thong, and when he got to the top of the slope once more he was glowing with warmth, feeling a lightness and freedom that showed itself in his face, and Hetty standing with the others felt proud that he was so tall and handsome, so pleasantly at ease as he chatted with Mr. Mundy.

It was now the turn of the vicar's son to descend. When he had thrown himself down the slope Mr. Mundy turned to Richard, and taking his arm with the confidence of an old friend, he said, "You know, the people of this neighbourhood have been doing this sort of thing on Vicar's Hill probably from before the time of Wakelin de Maminot in the reign of Henry the Second. You have heard, of course, that the alien authorities of London propose to call our Hill a 'recreation ground'? A monstrous suggestion of the half-educated!"

Richard nodded in sympathy: though he felt himself to be one of the half-educated. He began to dread lest the vicar should ask him where he went to school.

"However, to our history, about which the records reveal a curious thing," went on the vicar. "Wakelin granted the manor—though the title of manor is still a matter of dispute—to Michael de Turnham, who then sold it back to Juliana, the wife of Michael who had given it to Michael—no no, what am I saying, it was the other way about; well, my boy, what do you want?"

The hat-retrieving boy stood hesitatingly near. He wore a dark blue uniform skirted to his ankles, and leather-belted around his middle; his stockings were mustard-yellow, worn with black buckled shoes.

"Please sir, will you fill a page of my book of confessions?"

"You are at Christ's Hospital, I see, m'boy. Now tell me, did you have a presentation, or a nomination to the Bluecoat School?"

"A nomination, sir."

"Then you must be a good scholar. And you have good manners, not to interrupt others, whether older or younger than yourself, when they are speaking."

Hetty, smiling at the boy, thought how nice it would be if her son could go to the Bluecoat School, and wear such a picturesque uniform.

"I will fill in a page for you, with the greatest of pleasure, my boy."

"Oh, thank you very much indeed, sir!"

"But not just now. You shall know my favourite flower, my favourite poet, and quotation therefrom, the colour of my eyes, my birthday, my dearest wish—h'm! well, perhaps not that—my favourite pudding, and the brand of soap I use—ha ha ha!—you shall be acquainted with them all, in due course, m'boy. Such confession requires the deepest cogitation. I will give you back your book after Evensong tomorrow evening, at the vestry door of St. Simon. May I keep it until then?"

"Yes, indeed, sir, if you please."

"Miss MacIntosh, my secretary, shall hold it safely meanwhile, shall you not, Miranda?"

"Yes, Vicar."

A tall young woman with red hair and white skin, who had been standing near, came forward, and took the book into her muff. Having patted the small boy on his close-cropped head, the vicar turned to Richard, and said, "Where were we? Oh yes. Michael, Juliana, Wakelin! Juliana bought the manor—the supposed manor, that is—from Michael. Perhaps she was a strong-willed woman, determined not to be frustrated by a mere man, like some of our modern young ladies!" Here the vicar's eye glanced at the tall, red-haired young woman. "But that is mere presumption! *What we do know is*, that Juliana founded a religious house of the order of the Premonstratensians, but whether or not it was her intention to build an Abbey here on Vicar's Hill, we shall never know, but she certainly built one in Sussex. All we got was that red brick building over there, the West Kent Grammar School!"

"Yes, I have often passed it, sir," said Richard.

"Yes indeed," went on the vicar, warming to his subject. "The Premonstratensian settlement at Ottham in Sussex was given our glebe, as it afterwards became, for an Abbey, but Begham in Sussex was shortly afterwards conferred upon them, and there they built their Abbey, dwelling therein until the days of Henry the Eighth! And then of course the blow fell!"

As the vicar looked at him with such earnestness Richard took this news with some attention.

"He was no lover of monks, was he, sir?"

"Ah, my friend, we are a little previous! Permit me to go back a short while in time, before replying to your most interesting observation," went on the vicar, waggling a finger at Richard. "It is on record that King John confirmed the Premonstratensians in their local possessions—our Hill, as we might say—in the year 1208, and for all of three hundred and eighteen years they enjoyed what peace and order came to them. And then, as we have remarked, the blow fell!"

Out of the corner of his eye Richard saw an iron tea-tray piled with children disintegrate into laughing individuals. Hetty laughed, suddenly.

"Yes," declared the vicar. "Cardinal Wolsey, who later was to suffer retribution for his secular zeal, suppressed the Abbey, and the lands were settled on his new College at Oxford University. Three years later he was attainted, and his estates came to the Crown. But—and here is the point, my friend!—mark it well, for it has a bearing on what is to follow!—yea, verily, it has every significance now that Conglutination threatens us!—ever since the recorded memory of man this glebe land has been known as Vicar's Hill, and Vicar's Hill it should, nay it shall, remain! Despite the machinations of the Black Boa Constrictor, the London County Council!" He turned to Hetty. "Now tell me, what do you think about it, my dear?"

"Yes, conglutination, of course, naturally!" said Hetty, wisely. "Isn't it, Dickie?"

"Yes, I recall to mind the connexion, now that you mention it, Hetty." To the vicar, "I saw the cartoon in *Punch*, sir. London is to swallow the countryside all around, including this part of Kent. I hear that Vicar's Hill is to become like the Randiswell Recreation Ground."

"And what a name, 'Recreation Ground', Maddison! In Doomsday the reference is, *Ibi triginta acrae prati*, so the reference is unmistakable: Here are thirty acres of meadow. It is interesting further to note that there were great woods of oak and beech at that time, for the very next entry in Doomsday declares *De silva quinquaginta porci de pasnagio*. The woods as you know were assessed by the number of swine which the tenants gave to the Lord of the Manor for the privilege of fattening them there. Fifty hogs from the *pasnagio* or *pastionaticum* as little boys in the modern school yonder would have us call it."

Richard saw Hetty turning away, saw her shoulders shaking; she was in one of her idiotic laughing moods, he could see. To Richard what the vicar said was interesting; especially when the mention was made of swine in the forest feeding on beech mast. Rookhurst Great Forest at once came into his mind, and himself as a small boy talking to another small boy who minded the herd of black pigs there, at the fall of mast and acorn. A bit tedious, the old fellow, somewhat absorbed in his subject, but at least he had a sense of history and tradition, unlike the rootless urban industrial mind which for him was so detestable, product of bricks, mortar, and money: typified with the prejudice of his mind in the image of his father-in-law, Thomas William Turney.

And here was Thomas Turney's daughter finding comic material for her mind in the remarks of a vicar whom she professedly admired as a preacher, while she lacked the breeding or stability to comport herself with common civility in his presence.

But Hetty had not been laughing, or even smiling; she had been trying not to sneeze, and having left her *mouchoir* at home, she felt dreadful. First calling on Mrs. Mundy, then meeting her without a *mouchoir*. Oh dear, what would Dickie think of such behaviour?

Then to her horror the desire to sneeze grew stronger than ever. So strong that she could not help closing her eyes, and then, waiting in an appalling drag of time, while the sneeze grew up her nose like pepper, she bent down and exploded.

"Bless you, my dear!" cried the vicar. "There is nothing I like more than a good sneeze. It clears the head as a good game of lawn tennis clears the pores. You do play lawn tennis, of course?"

to Richard. "Good man. We have a pleasant little club opposite the parish church, where we meet on summer evenings and Saturday afternoons as well. A modest subscription of five shillings for the season. We shall hope to see you, then, in the coming months! Now you must both come with me and meet m' wife."

With an arm through each of theirs he led them to Mrs. Mundy, who was standing with several young people by a big Canadian toboggan. After greetings, the vicar proposed a descent on the toboggan, which would carry six, he declared. Mrs. Mundy said that she was a little chilled, and a walk around the Hill would be the very thing, and would Mrs. Maddison care to accompany her? And perhaps the run down the other slope of the Hill, the shorter and steeper slope into the Warm Kitchen, would be safer for the big toboggan? She suggested these things in a pleasant, conversational voice, while linking her arm through Hetty's, and saying afterwards, "I am taking your wife with me, Mr. Maddison, to prepare tea; you'll come back with us, won't you?"

The party walked across the snow eastward, and after a few minutes came to the lesser northern slope with its distant prospect of houses massed upon the Thames-side levels under smoke in layers extending above the vast drabness of the frozen scene.

"It's not a bad run, and at least we won't smash up anyone," said Mr. Mundy, half regretfully, as he pulled a watch from his waistcoat pocket. "We'll be back for tea at five o'clock precisely, m'dear," to his wife. "There's a full moon tonight, and the young people will want to enjoy themselves out here, I expect. For me, I have m' sermon to prepare."

Mrs. Mundy took Hetty home, and when the others came in shortly after five o'clock there were poached eggs on muffins, buttered toast, scones with clotted cream and apple-jelly with other good things to eat, all set out upon the big mahogany table, with a tea-urn on the sideboard. Hetty felt ever so happy; she had a different look in her eyes, which were filled with the soft childlike wonder that, when first seen by Richard, had stirred such hopes in him. They sat on opposite sides of the table, Hetty next to the vicar, and Richard on one side of Mrs. Mundy.

Soon the vicar had Hetty talking easily to him. He appeared to be much interested in her life while never asking personal questions, and was, she thought, ever so kind.

"How jolly for you it would have been, had you been living

where you are, Mrs. Maddison, about fifty years ago, when the Sydenham canal was drained, and railway lines were laid on the old bed! The engines did not puff steam or throw out smoke in those days, but ran by atmospheric suction, the air being pumped out of a pipe laid between the lines. I expect you have met Pooley, the 'olde, olde man' who lives opposite to you, and who potters about among his vegetables above the cutting? He is a fount of information about the past. Another good friend of mine is Feeney, the Crimean veteran, your near neighbour. His wife is a fine woman, always cheerful and daunted by nothing. Now let me give you some more tea—oh thank you, m'boy——" for his son on the other side had got up at once and with a smile and inclination of his head had taken her cup.

An hour later Hetty and Richard walked down Twistleton Road arm in arm, talking about the nice people they had met. "And to think, Dickie, that all this time I have been worrying myself, that Mrs. Mundy thought me presumptuous in regarding her visit as a call! Why, she never once referred to it, but treated me as though she had known me all my life. She's not in the least stuck up, and her daughter is like her, too, she was ever so friendly, putting on no airs. Mrs. Mundy said she so admired our little house, particularly the spray of leaves cut in the stone above the front door, with the name."

"I suppose I shall have to accompany you regularly to church now."

"Mr. Mundy is a wonderful preacher, Dickie."

"I am sure he is. He is a real countryman."

"You'll come then?"

"We'll see."

She hugged his arm.

"I must make a sled while the snow lasts. What a pity you are not able to join in—but there, when you have the apple of your eye, you will not need me at all."

"Of course I will—always, Dickie."

They called in at the ironmonger's to buy a length of barrel-hoop iron for the runners of the sled, and a pound of two-inch nails.

When they got home there was a letter lying on the mat behind the door. Richard picked it up. It was a foolscap envelope, the flap of which was embossed with the badge of the office, the smiling lunar disk.

"Oh lor'," he groaned, with an expression of gloom that was not all pretence. "Oh heavens, I dare not open it." He looked unhappily at Hetty. "Now I shall know my fate. Why did that confounded fog have to come when it did? I was twice late during January."

"Perhaps it isn't so bad as you think, Dickie. Surely they would not have held that against you! No one can help fog."

"I should have caught an earlier train."

"But you have worked until midnight almost every night for weeks now."

"That has nothing to do with it," he exclaimed, his face now strained, his voice higher in pitch. "If I choose to work all night, on outside work, that is nothing to do with my employers! I should have got up earlier, and caught the seven forty-two on those foggy mornings."

Hetty did not wish to say anything to cause him further upset, but as the envelope was lying unopened upon the table, she dared to suggest that perhaps the letter contained good news.

"Very well, you shall see for yourself," he cried. "Open it, please. Here am I, fooling about with sleds, things which belong to the dead past as far as I am concerned, when for all I know, I am one of the workless!"

Desperately he thought of the missed chance to remain with Doggett's.

Hetty tore open the top of the long envelope. Richard cried, "No, not like that, please! Where is the paper knife?"

This relic of deer-stalking days in Scotland had belonged to Richard's grandfather who had always shown much consideration and sympathy for the small boy. As he always spoke so affectionately of his grandfather, and showed such concern for it, Hetty regarded it through his eyes. Even so, with her part-urban sense of fun at times she saw it as a comic object with which to open letters. Rather like Punch's stick, with which he belaboured poor Judy in the peepshow! And now, as Richard inserted the rounded end of the blade with such care into the breach she had made, with the deer's foot handle nearly two feet away from the little envelope, it seemed so funny that she could not help laughing.

Her merriment, though suppressed, at once chilled the inner glow of companionship that Richard had felt during and since the tea-party at the Mundys'. Again he associated what he considered to be her inherited Turney insensibility to other people's feelings with the courteous behaviour of Mr. Mundy and his son during their visit to the vicarage. This misinterpretation of Hetty's laughter made him withdraw into himself, and when he read the contents of the letter—the Secretary of the Moon Fire Office informing him that his work during the period of probation had been satisfactory, and therefore the General Manager had decided to confirm his appointment in the Town Department at a commencing salary of one hundred and thirty pounds a year from the forthcoming Ladyday, with an annual rise of ten pounds—he folded the letter and replaced it within the envelope and then sat down in the chair before the cold grate with his hand over his eyes, momentarily overcome.

Feeling guilty and depressed, Hetty went into the kitchen, and sitting on the edge of the table, tried to stop her tears. Oh I am bitterly disappointed with myself, she cried voicelessly: poor Dickie, I am no help to him in any way, always doing the wrong thing. I will never, never, never laugh again.

Hearing Richard coming, she quickly dabbled her eyes with the drying-up cloth, and pretended to be looking at the fire. He stood behind her in the darkened room for a moment, then said quietly, "Aren't you going to light the gas? Or do you prefer this Stygian gloom?"

"Yes, of course I will, dearest. I am so sorry I laughed at the wrong moment."

"Well," he replied. "Apparently I am taken to be on the permanent staff, so you were right after all."

"Dickie! Oh, Dickie! Oh, I am so glad!"

He caught her as she swayed before him. "There now," he said with awkward gentleness. She was pale. "There now, Hetty. We are going to be all right now, I am sure. They have increased my salary, too. Now dry your eyes, and I will light the gas. You need to look after yourself, you know, now there are two of you to consider. Would you like some of that Raggett's stout?"

"No, thank you, dear, but you have some. It will help fortify you against the cold."

She knew that he would not take any of it, because it had been given to her. And, as she had anticipated, he shook his head.

Chapter 22

BLUE MOON

THAT EVENING Richard opened his chest of carpentry tools and with saw, tee-square, plane, nails and claw-hammer, set about building a sled of some wood left over from the making of a cupboard. The runners were four feet long, eight inches deep, and an inch-and-an-half thick, curved in front. These two stout pieces of wood were held in parallel by boards nailed across them with a foot rest in front; while a hole through each curved prow was bored to take a length of clothes-line for hauling. When all the rough edges and surfaces of the wood had been planed smooth, he nailed the hoop-iron to the runners, and at half past nine the sled was ready.

He took it outside, to see how it would slide on the trodden snow of the street. A little push sent it a long way. He would take it on the Hill that very night.

Hetty said she would not mind being left alone. She was only too glad that he should enjoy himself. "You deserve a little rest from your writing, Dickie. I'll have some nice hot cocoa for you when you come in, but don't hurry. It will be such fun for you, and I am only sorry I cannot come with you, dearest. But you will see the Mundys again. They'll be home before twelve, won't they, as it is Sunday tomorrow."

She thought what a pity it was that Hughie was not nearer, so that he and Dickie could go together; Hughie was a wonderful companion, and this might have been an opportunity for them to become friends.

"I ought to wear my stout walking boots," said Richard. "But they will pinch a bit, so they will need dubbin on them first. I shall wear them tomorrow. Will you dubbin them for me, Hetty, but do not put them near the fire, will you, as leather is easily cracked by excessive heat."

Hetty's heart missed a beat. She had given the boots to the rag-and-bone man.

"I shall put on my old pair of trousers, over these," went on Richard. "They will at least keep out the snow."

Should he take his lantern? Deerstalker, yes; grandfather's old deerstalker was proper to the occasion, to the excitement and romance of the dim white silence of the night. He saw in his imagination the lanterns on the frozen Longpond at home; the ice-blink when one knelt down and looked along the ice; the merry skating parties, the young moon like a sickle over the beechwood; Orion hanging low in the south-east, Mother and Father so happy for once, all the children so happy, for the coming of snow and ice brought another world, Santa Claus and holly and everything so jolly. Grandpapa with his long eight-bore goose-gun, and hat with flaps which could be tied round the chin and ears, and so to keep the cheeks from the icy augurs of the north wind! Richard looked at Hetty with bright eyes and smiling face.

"I must wear my deerstalker! Of course!"

"Yes, dear, it will keep you nice and warm."

"But we shall not hear the geese flighting over——. Ah well, one must make the best of the present!"

In high humour he went to kiss Hetty. "Well, au revoir, dearest, I shall keep to the northern slope of the Hill, it is dangerous the other way tonight, so do not worry your little self on my account."

"Of course not, Dickie."

He put on the extra pair of trousers, the old double peaked cap, and woollen gloves; and thus equipped, set off into the night. At the open door he said, "I did think of taking the lantern, but on second thoughts, I do not think I will. It is bound to fall off, and be stolen, like as not."

"Yes, I think you are wise not to, Dickie. Now have a good time, and enjoy yourself. I shall be quite all right."

"Do not forget to put the chain up!"

"No, dear." She laughed, thinking of the totter's description of it, *the old Abel and Cain.*

"Oh, you may laugh, my girl, but you do not know this district as well as I do," he replied, half-seriously.

"Oh yes, of course, naturally." Hetty closed the door when he had gone down the road, and slipped the dog-head of the chain into the slot. The dog's name was Abel, how funny! And she laughed again.

Richard went on down the road. Movement over the snow lying upon street and side-walk was silent save for the cautious muffled foot-falls and the soft slur of the sled runners. No one was about in the high road where the elms held up black leafless branches among the stars. He looked for Orion, but the lower southern hemisphere was dimmed by frozen mist and smoke. He turned into Charlotte Road—houses built in the reign of George the Fourth, intermediate in size between those of Comfort and Twistleton Roads—and quickened his pace as he heard the distant cries coming from the slopes of the Hill in the distance. Wonderful the white silence, the winking lines of street lamps, the stars overhead! He trudged on, expectantly.

Here and there a glint of light in the house-fronts, set back beyond gardens, showed where a family was seated round the fire. Richard imagined family after family in a row, reading or sewing or playing quiet games upon the plush or heavy patterned cloth covering a mahogany table, while the father of the house, in the best horsehair-stuffed armchair, of course, read *The Daily Telegraph*, or *The Daily News*, or *The Chronicle*, or *The Times*, or (improbably) *The Parish Magazine of St. Simon Wakenham*, or (more probably) old copies of the *Strand Magazine*, with its pale blue cover opening upon the advertisements, a few to be glanced at, some to be dwelt upon—he knew them all by heart—Hinde's Hair Curlers, Monkey Brand Soap, the Waterbury Keyless Watch, Nixey's Black Lead, Epp's Cocoa, Liebig's Extract of Meat, Horniman's Tea, Gerandel's Pastilles, Dr. Rudolf St. Just's Rupture Adjuster—what a tongue-twister—and the rhyme made familiar by advertisements on large enamelled iron sheets on the sooty brick walls of London's railway termini:

They come as a boon and a blessing to men,
The Pickwick, the Owl, and the Waverley Pen.

—all the looking-at-advertisements, of course, but to delay the pleasure of the unsurpassable moment before turning the first real page, and so to come upon one of *The Adventures of Sherlock Holmes*, that supernatural being who had caused the greatest shock to sedentary black-coated lives, himself among them, when exactly a year ago, in the previous Christmas number, he had disappeared over the precipice in the Alps, along with the terrible Dr. Moriarty! Richard exulted within himself: wonderful fellow, Conan Doyle!

All the same, what *had* happened to Sherlock Holmes? For of course he *could* not die!

Coming to the end of the double row of houses with their black attic star-reflecting windows, Richard's anticipation quickened as he saw before him the white slopes of snow glimmering under the moon which looked to be so small and bright. Gazing into the sky, he saw that the moon had a sheen over it like that upon steel—it was that rare phenomenon, a blue moon!

As he hauled his sled up the slopes a pleasant warmness grew upon him, and with sweat beginning to open his pores, he began to feel extraordinarily free and happy. Golly, one hundred and thirty pounds a year! Hetty would be able to have a good doctor, and Mrs. Feeney could help her for an hour or two every morning with the heavier work. Sixteen sovereigns and a crown piece next half-quarter day! Even so, he would have to practise the strictest economy, to make up for the savings he had been forced to call upon lately. He determined to keep on the night work of addressing envelopes, though he would ease up on that, lest he develop a tendency to writer's cramp, and the sharp pain which he had felt so often in his neck become serious. If he fell ill, both Hetty and the coming little one would be the first to suffer.

The vicar had spoken of a lawn tennis club, and this should provide some good exercise during the summer evenings, and on Saturday afternoons. Then there was the Rover, and the possibility of fitting upon it some sort of box to take his silk hat, so that he could in fine weather cycle up to London Bridge, lodge it somewhere during the day by paying a small rent, and return awheel down the Old Kent Road in the long light evenings.

Toboggans and sleds were moving down the slopes, at varying speeds, with the warning cries of the travellers. *Oyee-oyee-oyee-oyee-oyee*! The southern slope gave an infinitely better run; but the thought of his responsibility to Hetty made Richard trudge across to the safe descent into what the Mundys called the Warm Kitchen. It consisted of about eight acres of sheltered level land, with a deeper top-soil over the yellow clay, which yielded well in corn, and roots for the lambing fold in former years, Mr. Mundy had told him during tea.

Richard went down into the Warm Kitchen, sitting on his sled with his feet braced against the cross bar in front. It slid fast upon the snow hardened by the passage of many other runners going down, and feet tramping up. Several hundred people, many of them boys, were on the slopes, and a descent was hazardous and stimulating. *Oy-oyee-oyee-oyee*! Look out! A near shave, that one. *Oy-oyee-OY*! *Billo, mates*! followed by laughter as a home-made contraption, packed with boys, turned over, the crew preferring to abandon ship at the last moment rather than to face collision.

One such excitement occurred about half an hour later when Richard, sorry for the number of poor Pit Vale boys who had nothing on which to slide down, called out, "Come on, I'll take two of you down with me." Immediately there was a rush forward, and then the struggle began for supremacy.

"I was fust! No, you wasn't! Yus I was, warn't I, Billee? Yus, I seed you. You shut yer bleedun jaw, afore I shuts it for yer! Now then, boys, no swearing, or I won't have any of you! Aough, 'e bit my ear-'ole, guv'nor! Come on, sit down, and hold tight! 'Ere we go, chaps! There's too many of you, I say! Take your hands off my throat, did you hear what I say? Look out! Cor, ain't it some sport, mister! *Oyee-oyee-oyee-oyee*! Billo, billo!" and the sled, with a mass of boys piled chiefly upon Richard, who wondered how many fleas would transfer themselves to him, started to move down the slope.

What a fool he was, to be sure! The thing had started before he was ready. The sled was only four feet long, but three boys were in front of him, perched upon and clinging to his legs and to one another; while a bold rascal, not to miss the fun, at the last moment had sprung upon his back, found a toe-hold on the edge of the rear cross-piece, and clinging with his hands to the flaps of Richard's deer-stalker, bawled out an *Oyee-oyee-oyee-oyee*! in hoarse triumphant tones like those of a game cockerel.

The unbalanced weight made the sled slip off its course; no one was steering, for Richard's legs were pinned down; the boys in front began to yell, for they were descending diagonally at an alarming rate into a toboggan being hauled uphill by two youths amidst others of its crew.

The weight of the sled was now greatest at the rear end, and as it started to move down it began to slip sideways; and this movement was hastened by the action of the boy behind who, leaning backwards with his paws now upon the lapels of Richard's coat, caused it further to rotate on its axis until, with gathering speed, the sled was shooting downhill backwards.

Warning shouts of "Billo! Look out!" and an ironical jeer of "Whip be'ind, guv'nor!" came from the more nimble of the smaller spectators, as the loaded vehicle bore down upon the big Canadian toboggan. "Crikey, boys, 'op it quick!" screeched the urchin who by now had his arms wrapped round Richard's neck, as he dropped off, to be followed involuntarily by the crew. The sled turned over, the designer with it. No harm done; brush off the snow; quite an adventure! "So nice to meet you again, sir"—it was young Mundy speaking, a tam-o'-shanter on his head glowing a dark warm red in the moonlight.

"I say, sir, very sporting of you, if I may say so," was his remark on the attempt to take a crew of small boys down the hill. "And you made your sled between now and leaving us after tea? Surely that must be a record."

"Oh, it is only a rough and ready affair."

"Shall we have a race, sir? You with your team on—has your sled a name?"

"'The Backslider'," said Richard, and after the laughter, it was agreed that they should have a race, each with its team of small boys. "Only no cussing, you boys!" said young Mundy, with amiable truculence. "You shall haul up 'Backslider' and 'Buffalo Bill', that'll sweat the vice out of you."

"I say, have you noticed that it is a blue moon?"

They all looked up into the sky, at the hard bright disk of the moon above a flocculence of small frozen clouds. Was it green or blue, riding with serene timelessness among the winter stars? The Pit Vale boys stared, the one called Billee saying, "Cor, ain't it grand, mister". The others, instead of jeering at Billee (who was one of the smaller boys running beside the sledge) allowed themselves to echo the mood of the toffs around whom they clustered the closer as they went on up the hill. Richard found to his amused embarrassment that several were vying with each other to walk beside him, while others, including Billee, were hauling on sled and toboggan with a pathetic determination to please. Poor little devils, he thought to himself, while removing his gloves to feel in his pockets to discover if he had left in them anything likely to be stolen. Then he thought of his grandfather Maddison, and how he himself as a small boy had wanted to do everything he could to please him—the only man who had treated him as an equal, thereby inducing in himself an immense desire to be good, to be worthy of the trust. Perhaps these boys—but one must not be sentimental—no, these boys were different. They were by nature incapable of feeling like boys brought up differently. Give them an inch, and they would take an ell. What a good thing he had not brought the bull's-eye lantern: by now one of them would have been halfway to Deptford with it.

At the top of the slope, when sled and toboggan were turned round, he was already regretting his impulse to give the boys a ride. They were quarrelsome little brutes, those who had walked beside him and the haulers forming themselves into one camp, and immediately seating themselves on the sled, while the others raucously declared that they were being done out of their turn. A fight seemed inevitable, until Richard told them that if they didn't behave themselves, not one of them should have a ride.

"I am dashed if I am going to be told what I am going to do with my own sled," he declared, to a silent assembly of odd-sized boys. "Now, all of you behave yourselves, otherwise no one will go down with me." By now other boys had come along, and there was a small crowd.

"If I may make a suggestion," said young Mundy, "and that is that Buffalo Bill can take the amateurs, the more the merrier, or rather the faster, for it's a somewhat slow old hearse unless loaded to the gunwales."

"Then I must insist that you and Miss Mundy come with me," replied Richard. Immediately as doubt came to him that he might be intruding himself, he said, "Perhaps you and Miss Mundy would care to try it yourselves, with your friends?"

"Oh no, you must be skipper," replied Mundy. "How about that race? Good, it will be fun. Now lads, pile up on the toboggan, as many as you like, but mind what I said. No cussing! I'll give you the word to go! How about that, sir? The Blue Moon Bumpers, versus The Pit Vale Scramblers?"

The boys clambered upon the long toboggan, frantically arguing among themselves who should sit in front, in the middle, the back, who should steer, etc. "It steers itself, you oafs," cried young Mundy, "so get on, for we are about to start!"

Richard, with Miss Mundy in front, and one of their friends fitted themselves on to the Backslider, while young Mundy cried, "One to be ready, two to be steady, three to be off!" and then, giving the Backslider a shove from behind, he sprang on the back, crouching down, and "Oyee-oyee-oyee-oyee!" they were slipping down the slope, faster and faster, while cries and shouts from behind told them that the more cumbrous Buffalo Bill, with its flat but shiny bottom, was following. "Oyee-oyee-oyee-oyee!" down into the Warm Kitchen, and across the level acres.

After the first run the boys became more amenable, and arranged themselves, though noisily, into turns, and during the subsequent races Richard rode on Buffalo Bill, in the general feeling of friendliness forgetting his concern lest his sled be stolen. But Billee had appointed himself its guardian, and brought it back to the owner. Richard thanked him, not recognizing the boy who had accompanied the two others during the stone-throwing incident which had ended in Greenwich Police Court.

At half past eleven he went home, taking the Backslider some way down the southern slope, and then riding on it feet-first into Charlotte Road. It was so light that he could see dark figures several hundred yards away, and his previous caution now seemed unnecessary. He must take more exercise, and not slip gradually into the alienation of middle age. Routine was all very well, but one must never get into a rut.

To prove to himself that he could do what others were doing he hauled the sled to the crest again and setting off between the elms, with their rooks' nests black against the sky milky with stars, went down head-first. Steering between several groups with his toecaps, he slid on down Charlotte Road, coming to a standstill a hundred yards or so from the high road. Dear little sled, it ran true, without crank! He had libelled it, giving it that name! It should be called The Pathfinder, after the wonderful story by Fennimore Cooper.

Hetty was waiting up for him, a saucepan of cocoa on the kitchen range. She was mending his socks by the sunken embers of the kitchen fire. She looked pale; and at once he asked her why she had not gone to bed. It did not seem fair, that she should have to be deprived of sleep on his account; why couldn't she be sensible, instead of always showing such concern for him?

"Well, dear," she said. "How did you get on?"

"Oh, all right. But you need not have waited up for me, you know."

"I've been busy, dearest. Would you like some cocoa? I've kept some warm for you."

"Thank you," he said. "Well, how have you been? Anything happened?"

"No, everything has been quite all right, dear."

The only thing that had happened was the appearance of the mouse from the hole by the gas-pipe. This hole had been plugged by Richard with a cork, but unknown to him Hetty removed it at times, and placed scraps of bacon and cheese rind near it, her idea being that if she fed the mouse there it would not dig a way into the larder. Also, during the cold weather it must be hungry, with a family to feed. The mouse was by now half tame, and made its appearance on the oil-cloth by the hole within a few moments of the cork being removed; it seemed to know that it was on sufferance, for after an inspection of its benefactor with its black-currant eyes, it withdrew the length of bacon or cheese rind into the hole with surprising speed. Whereupon Hetty usually replaced the cork. But this night, due to her preoccupied thoughts, she had forgotten to put it back.

While Richard had been on the Hill, Hetty had been wondering how best she might tell him about the boots she had given away. Towards eleven o'clock anxiety had given her a headache, and by the time he returned she felt sick. Oh, how could she tell him? She would do anything, rather than see him upset.

Having removed coat and extra trousers, Richard stood and sipped his cup of cocoa. Hetty's thoughts usually affected him, but tonight, after the exercise, he felt easy and tolerant as he reflected upon the absence of the boots by the fire. "Did you forget to put the dubbin on them?"

"Oh no, Dickie. I mean, yes. Oh, I couldn't find them."

"But they are surely on the pot-board, where I left them?"

"I don't think they can be, Dickie," she replied faintly.

He went to look and found the volume of Pepys' Diary. "I think the last tenant must have left this here," he remarked. "Why, what is the matter, you look pale, Hetty! You should have been in bed a couple of hours and more, you know. Oh dear, cannot a fellow go out and enjoy himself for once in a while, without a feeling of responsibility for his wife's actions?"

He put down the book upon the table. "Oh please!" he said. "Must you cry, just because I speak to you? To cry is surely unfair, for it puts the onus on me, for being an unpleasant complaining person! Oh well, I suppose I should never have thought of going out, and leaving you alone like this, if you cannot be sensible."

He saw the cork, which Hetty had forgotten to replace, lying on the oil-cloth by the mouse-hole. "Hullo, what has happened here? Did you remove it? You did? Why, may I ask? What —in case the mouse is suffocated? Am I hearing rightly?"

He sighed. "Oh well, if you will do such things, I suppose you will. It's beyond me." He stared unhappily before him.

Hetty tried to explain. "I gave it only bacon rind, so that it should not get into the larder, Dickie, that was all. And I couldn't bear to think of it being suffocated."

"Well, why did you not say so in the first place? It is the sort of thing you would do, but at least it had a good intention behind it. Suffocated! Do you not know that mice bring disease—the cholera in the East End thirty years ago was probably brought by rats—or mice, the same thing? You are a silly, you know."

He sat down to unlace his boots. Half way through one boot he looked up, saying, "I suppose the truth is, that you have given away those boots of mine to Feeney, or some such person? Please do not bite your nails! You make me nervous, so that I do not know where I am with you."

"Oh Dickie, please don't go on so! I am sorry, truly I am!"

He looked as though he were going to speak; then bent to the unlacing of his other boot. When his boots were off, and slippers on—the old pair of trousers hung before the fire—he said to her, not unkindly,

"You know, Hetty, your nail-biting, and keeping things from me, and sentimentality about mice, is all part and parcel of the same condition. It is your—well, you know——" He was going to say "bad stock", but checked himself in time, not so much out of consideration of her feelings, as from a connection with those words and his own father. He sighed. "Look dear, if you would train yourself to be factual, and incidentally tidy—for they are the same thing in the end—you would cure yourself of much that hampers our relationship, I can promise you that. Read this book—Pepys deals with facts about the world as it is. I am told it is most interesting, I must read it myself when I have more time. Come now, make a clean breast of it, what did you do with the boots? No need to look on me like a schoolmaster, you know."

"Yes, Dickie. I gave them to the fern man whose boots were

broken, and his toes sticking out. I also gave him my old corsets, and he gave me those two aspidistras for them."

"Well, why did you not tell me so at the time? I did not particularly want the beastly boots, and told you so; though you should, merely as a matter of good manners, have asked me first. I would not give away or otherwise dispose of anything of yours in an underhand manner, and that should apply equally with you. Now dry your tears and tell me—did the fellow put on the boots, and then the corsets?"

Hetty smiled through her tears; and all was well again—she tried to believe.

"Would you like some more cocoa, dear? It is warm on the hob. Oh, I forgot to tell you—the fern man gave me that book, it is about old London, and I am sure I shall like it."

"H'm. If I were you, I should bake it in the oven, first. You never know what germs there are in such things, coming from an unknown source. Baking will kill any germs."

So Pepys was put in the oven, and left in there, as Hetty forgot all about the book. On the Monday she had a good fire, it being washing day; and when she did open the oven door, to put in a shepherd's pie for Dickie's supper, there lay Pepys, browned at the edges, and brittle. Hetty opened the book, and seeing that it was burnt most of all at the description of the Great Fire of London, she laughed until the tears came into her eyes.

Chapter 23

CELESTIAL EVENTS

As THE cold weather continued, many water-pipes froze in the houses of Comfort Road, but the warm air arising from the dark lantern placed at night on the kitchen floor, directly under the iron piping, kept the water flowing in Comfort House. One by one the neighbours came with pails in the mornings, and to them all Hetty gave a smile and said that of course they were no trouble. She was glad to be of help to them, and everyone was so nice, she thought. First old Mr. Pooley came from the little cot built on to the house opposite, then someone seven doors away, until in the third week of February nine houses were being supplied. Hetty did not tell Richard of this, as she thought it might worry him on her behalf; and the callers understood, and made their last visits of the week with their pails on the Saturday morning, saying that they "would not disturb the master" on Sunday.

Richard continued to leave Comfort House just after eight o'clock as usual in the mornings. On two occasions in the high road he was the target for snow-balls; and the second time, the boy who had thrown one of the harmless powdered handfuls—for the intense cold prevented the snow from binding—was unexpectedly set upon by two other boys, and his head held down and bumped into the snow, until he arose with bloody nose, bellowing. The two avengers had ridden on Richard's sled that Saturday night, but he did not know this. He thought they were merely horrid little bullies.

After his first night's sledging on the Hill he had not gone again, as he did not want to spoil his city boots; but during one luncheon interval he went to a shop in Aldgate Street and bought himself a new pair, size eleven, for the former pair had been a ten. These boots, worn with an extra pair of socks, were warm and comfortable; and having been thoroughly dubbined, on the following Saturday afternoon he took his sled, which had been painted a pale blue, upon the Hill for the second time. Hetty, in her sealskin coat and cap and muff, and dubbined button-boots, went with him.

This was a memorable occasion, for about four o'clock Sidney Cakebread turned up, accompanied by Theodora. They had walked over from Brywich village, where Sidney lived. Theodora was spending the week-end with Dorrie. They had called at Comfort House, to be told by Mrs. Feeney that Mr. and Mrs. Maddison were on the Hill, with the sled.

Theodora did not ride down on the sled, because she knew that her brother did not think that it would be proper for a woman in skirts to do such a thing, and so she made the excuse that she and Hetty had such a lot to talk about; and while the two men were enjoying themselves, they went for a walk around the Warm Kitchen. Hetty thought there could be no harm in telling Dora that Dickie had been taken on the staff of his insurance company, though naturally, she told herself, she would not dream of mentioning anything to do with money. Theodora told Hetty about Dorrie and the children, and her own work and affairs, while all the time at the back of her mind she was seeing the face of Hugh Turney.

"I went down last night to stay with Dorrie," said Theodora. "And who do you think I met on the train, but Hughie."

"Oh, do tell me about him," said Hetty. "How is he? I had a letter from Mamma at the beginning of the week, but beyond saying that she had been to London, and had seen him she said little, except that he was not very well, and had rheumatism rather badly."

"Yes, he was looking poorly, I am afraid," said Theodora. "And hardly spoke to me as we walked together from the station to Dorrie's. He was in some pain, I think, and walked with difficulty, with the aid of a stick."

"Poor Hughie, I suppose he has not been feeding properly, perhaps he has got wet, he never bothered to change his damp clothes when he was a boy, unless he was made to by Papa."

"He has brilliant gifts, Hetty, and I am so worried about him. His manner to me was evasive; I am afraid he still feels much as he did before. I am fond of him, as you know, but I cannot give him what is not in my power to offer him. Do you think that can be at the root of the matter? You won't think me conceited, will you, Hetty; I do assure you that my interest in him is purely platonic."

"Of course, dearest. Is he staying with Dorrie?"

"No, he left without even having supper, last night. Indeed, I noticed that he wouldn't even take off his gloves. I think he came to talk over something with Sidney, for they were together in another room for a time, then Hughie came in, with a peculiar smile on his face, and said he must be off. He wouldn't accept even a cup of tea, nor would he sit down, and waved little Bertie and Ralph and Gerry away, when they went up to him—you know he loves playing with them as a rule. Then with a 'So long' to his sister, he went away. Without so much as a glance at me."

"Oh, I am sure Hughie is in trouble!" cried Hetty. "That isn't like him at all, to act so. Perhaps he is in money difficulties. How did Sidney behave to him?"

"With his invariable good-natured manner, Hetty. Well, one must not enquire too closely into the affairs of others, but I cannot help feeling a little guilty in the matter. Oh, this falling in love is a delusion, I am sure. And our civilization is so unnatural, it causes people to behave strangely at times, in variance with their real nature." Theodora sighed, then taking Hetty's arm, she pressed it warmly. "Well, dear child, tell me that you are happy!" Theodora was some years younger than Hetty, but always she had been like an elder sister.

"Yes, I am very happy, Dora," replied Hetty, with her little laugh. "Dickie is splendid, he works with such patience and is so steady and persevering. He deserves his new post, if ever a man did. Look, there they are, isn't it a lovely sled he made, it runs straight as an arrow. And he made it all in just under three hours, last Saturday evening, after we had come back from having tea with Mr. and Mrs. Mundy, at the Vicarage."

"So you have been making friends with your neighbours, have you?"

"Yes, and Dickie goes with me to evening service at St. Simon's. Mr. Mundy preaches such a wonderful sermon, and is so jolly. He is ever so popular in the neighbourhood."

"You are indeed fortunate, Hetty. I thought you might be lonely here, after I made my first visit to you—but people are generally pleasant when one gets to know them. Poor people, you know, help one another wonderfully, especially when they are in trouble. That is why I love the mission work in the East End, slight as is my contribution to it. The sincerity of the women is most touching, and when they have the franchise, they will sweep away much that at the present time is accepted as inevitable." Theodora clung closely to Hetty's arm. "I am sorry to say that many little children and old people have died recently, in this bitter weather. They have not enough warm blankets, or proper food, in their wretched sunless homes."

"It is very, very sad," murmured Hetty.

"The wonderful thing is that one hardly ever hears a word of complaint from them," said Theodora, smiling gently, her eyes bright. "Now how are you, Hetty? Here I am, selfishly involved in my own doings and concerns, and not a word about how you are getting on! You look extremely well. How do you like your new little house?"

"Oh, I love it!" exclaimed Hetty, and told Theodora about the rag-and-bone man, and how she had given him the boots and Dickie had been so very very kind about it; and the Italian organ-grinder and his little girl, who came once a week, and all for a penny, and a cup of tea and some bread and butter, dragging the barrel-organ through the snow. She told her how Dickie had made friends with some poor boys, and had taken them for rides on his sled, and how clever he had been in keeping the water in the pipe from freezing. She told Theodora how nice Mr. and Mrs. Mundy were, and also Dr. Cave-Browne who lived at the corner house in Charlotte Road, just before the beginning of the Hill. Then the Feeneys, and Mrs. Birkett the midwife whom the doctor had recommended, and as Mrs. Cummings also said that she was the best in the district, she must be good.

"And Mamma writes that Papa is coming round—metaphorically speaking, of course—Mamma thinks it would be best if he waited to visit us after the baby is born, Dora. So things will be all right in the end, I am sure."

"Of course they will," said Theodora. "It is ever so much better for everyone when people stand up for themselves. Parents often allow their genuine concern for their children to overrule their judgment. So few people think with their heads, I find. Emotion is a snare like birdlime, in which reason becomes hopelessly entangled. But here I am again inflicting my ideas upon you, who have your own problems and worries. Oh, the beautiful sunshine!" And Theodora extended her arms and ran forward, her eyes closed, feeling herself to be Icarus flying up into the sun.

She returned soon to Hetty, saying that she had cast off her earth-bound self.

They walked around the Warm Kitchen, with its dazzling white expanse; and climbing the slope again they came to where Richard and Sidney were preparing to make another run. Sidney wore what he considered to be a very dashing hat, one of a special design, he declared, made by the successors of Mr. Bowler, the hatter of Houndsditch, who made the hats of the senior partner in the family firm of wine-merchants for whom Sidney worked. It very nearly resembled the pattern blocked for that distinguished personage, Sidney admitted; but in fact, it had been made to his own design. It had a brim both curved and curly beyond the usual, and since it might be taken to resemble the hat made for the senior partner, Sidney did not consider it proper to wear it in the West End; but only on the Surrey side of the river. He held it on his head during the rapid descents into the Warm Kitchen, lest it be lifted off by the wind and damaged in the snow, perhaps even to be run over; and since it had cost all of a guinea, this fate was unthinkable.

But all was well; the felted cork bowl, silk-lined, took neither crack nor crenellation, and duly appeared on its owner's head at the correct angle, slightly jaunty, all the way down Vicar's Hill and half way along Charlotte Road, by way of the sled; and thence to the corner of Comfort Road, where the Reverend Mundy met them and raising his pied straw with the wide brim, enquired blandly as he raised it, "Sherlock Holmes and Dr. Watson, I presume?" to deer-stalker and bowler respectively.

After tea in the parlour Theodora helped Hetty wash up in the kitchen, and then said goodbye, for she and Sidney were to walk back to Brywich. When they were gone, Hetty felt that the house was empty, almost sad without them, as she put the best china pieces on the tray, to carry them back to the glass-fronted corner cupboard in the sitting-room which her mother had sent with the other pieces of furniture. Dickie had cleared the table, after shaking the crumbs carefully into a newspaper, for the birds out in the garden, and was preparing to do some writing.

He had intended to give up the addressing of envelopes, and had said so when he had taken the last batch back to the basement office in Old Broad Street; but the amiable little Hebrew clerk had asked him what he wanted to do that for, just as he had made up his mind, he said, to mark the price up in accordance with the rising cost of living. He held up two fingers. "Vell den, how about anodder sixpence?" Richard said, No, he thought he would give it up, for a spell at any rate. More amiable than ever, the little clerk said, "Half a crown, mister, and you wouldn't want to 'urt me no more, would you now, a nice gén'leman like you, eh?"

Richard took home another black bagful of foolscap envelopes and postal lists, and settled down to some hours' writing before supper. The parlour fire had been lit for the guests; and as the kitchen fire was also alight, some economy had to be made, for apart from economy for its own sake, the coal cellar held only little more than a hundredweight, and supplies were more uncertain than ever, owing to the continued frost. So he removed the coals of the front room fire to the kitchen; and putting on his overcoat, and lighting the lantern, closed the front and let it heat its metal frame before turning the dark screen round for the beam to play upon part of the table before him.

Hetty sat before the kitchen fire, writing a letter to her youngest brother Joseph at school, while reliving happy scenes of her former life; Richard, content in the security of himself, settled at the three-legged table in the parlour. Three pence for every hundred envelopes was a fair rate of payment, he considered; and that the work was no longer a matter of compulsion, was an added satisfaction. With blinds down and curtains drawn, he felt safe in the semi-darkness of the room which was entirely for himself. He was alone with the warm and friendly slant of light illuminating his hands, the pen, ink-bottle, blotting-pad, the two piles of envelopes and the lists of names and addresses. These were his companions, who responded perfectly with him in his work. He settled himself to write for three hours, happily in the room warmed and lit and sheltering him by his own efforts, by his own mastery of life.

He had been sitting there a short time only, when a sound above the whispering of pen to paper, above the occasional rustle of the lists pinned in folio, made him raise his head and stop his breathing while he listened. Was someone playing a trumpet in the distance? There was more than one instrument: the sounds were varied, but continuous: could it be a German band? If so, the poor devils were not likely to get much out of a visit to the neighbourhood, especially in such weather. He listened again: the sounds or noises were clearly those of a band, but played so badly that surely the instrumentalists must be tipsy. So startling and unusual was the noise that he got up, withdrawing his chair carefully lest the table-leg be moved, and opening the door, went down the passage into the kitchen.

"Do you hear anything, Hetty?"

"Yes," replied Hetty, standing up. "Whatever can it be? It sounds like a sort of concert somewhere."

"Perhaps it is Mr. Mundy leading the Band of Hope."

"Or the Salvation Army Band, while the onlookers are sucking lemons!" That is what Hugh and Sidney had once done; and the music of the Salvationists had gradually become watery.

"I must go outside and find out. Put on a coat when you come, Hetty."

Sliding back the chain, Richard opened the front door, and at once the cold struck into him; but immediately he was unaware of himself as, looking up into the sky, he realized with joy that the cries he had heard were from many geese flying over from the direction of the Thames estuary, and migrating to the south.

"Come here quickly!" he called to Hetty. "Wild geese! Are they not wonderful! Think of it, from the frozen north!" He put his arm round her shoulders, to draw her to him in the sudden warmth of companionship.

"They used to come to the Longpond, years ago, and flock to the middle of it, resting there by day for safety; and then flighting in the evening to their feeding grounds. But when the Longpond was frozen over, and the ice strong enough to support skaters, they went elsewhere. We boys used to hear them honking just like they are now, as we lay in bed at night."

"Oh, I would like to fly with them!" cried Hetty.

Mrs. Feeney's door opened. "Oh my!" her voice exclaimed. "Did you hear it, ma'm? I thought it was election night all over again, at first. Then Feeney woke up and said it was the geese flying over."

"Arrah!" said Feeney, over her shoulder. "'Tis the gayce I'm thinkin' that is departin' with the souls of the slain. 'Tis the grey birds returnin' wance more wid the souls of the bhoys of Inkermann and ould Ireland." Feeney had been spending some time that day at the Jack, an old inn near that part of the high road known as The Rise.

They went back into the house; and coming out ten minutes

afterwards, to listen again, Hetty saw that the sky had turned green. When she saw it was that colour she was startled: then she was alarmed. Was she ill, was she going to have a fainting fit? Richard heard her draw a deep breath and was about to ask her if she were cold when Hetty gave a gasp and exclaimed, "Oh, it's red now." Forcing herself to speak lightly, she said, "Dickie, does the sky seem a strange colour to you?"

Richard looked up. "Good heavens, there is a fire somewhere!" he exclaimed, and stepped back in order to see a wider expanse of sky over the roof-tops. "Why, it is green, too! Like the flames from molten copper. The Northern Lights!"

Feeney stumbled out of his gate and stood near Richard, slightly unsteady on his feet. "Mother o' God," he said. "Sure it is the dade turnin' out of their graves and away flyin' with the souls o' them inhabitin' the wings o' birds. I did see that wance before, in the threnches o' the Crimea. 'Tis phwat they do call a roarin' bawlin' ale-house."

"The Aurora Borealis!" said Richard, aside to Hetty. "Just look how the pillars of light are shifting!" They stood gazing awhile, then Richard and Hetty, saying goodnight to their neighbours, went back indoors. Aurora Borealis! The dawn of the winter-god, rising above London!

Richard came out again about ten minutes later, gloved and cloaked, carrying his sled. Such a wonderful occasion must not be missed. Green and crimson bands of light were now arising like spokes of a wheel over the roof-tops and chimney stacks. When he turned the corner into the high road, the rays had become zones, one merging into the other, patches of colour shifting and dilating to the zenith. He hastened along Charlotte Road, eager to see the full wonder of the sky from the Hill.

Others were looking up from street and sidewalk, to behold the glory of the northern dawn above the dark silhouettes of houses. Sidney Cakebread and Theodora Maddison, having walked through the muffled pallor of the Rise, with its friendly rows of street-lights winking ever brighter in the sharpening air, and up to Berehill, heard the geese at the corner of Ladyship Lane. They had stopped by a glowing coke-canister at the kerbside to buy two hot potatoes from the man who had been standing there when they had passed by in the early afternoon. Recognizing the sounds, Theodora threw up her chin and an ecstatic look came over her face. Sidney saw her face in the gas-light, and at that moment he felt a piercing sweetness that alarmed him, for he knew what it meant. Up to that moment he had found a pleasant stimulation in the personality of Theodora, coupled with a feeling of pride and contentment that she had seemed to find him easy and amiable to talk to. Hitherto Theodora, in Sidney's opinion, had been a personable young woman, who at times of animation could look extraordinarily lovely; and his respect for her ability and coolness had been gained on the night that Old Man Turney had thrown one of his blistering rages and knocked down poor little Hetty.

Until that night, and its revelation that she had been married some time to Richard Maddison, Hetty had been Sidney Cakebread's ideal of budding womanhood, and his oft-repeated phrase, "pretty as a peach", had expressed his open and affectionate delight in her company, an attitude which Hetty had reciprocated. Sidney was "ever so nice", Sidney was kissed impulsively and freely in a way that Hetty could never kiss Papa; or Dickie, even when they were alone.

After that unhappy night, the old spontaneity of feeling between Hetty and Sidney, or rather from Sidney to Hetty, had gone. Sidney was kind and affectionate as ever, but the ideal of his mind was no longer centred upon Hetty.

Beside Theodora he walked on down Ladyship Lane, carrying a large hot baked potato first in one hand, then the other. Sidney had suddenly found himself unable to say anything; and Theodora also was withdrawn into her own thoughts. Sidney, to his consternation, began to dread the end of the walk together; and as they came nearer and nearer to his home, he thought blankly that Dorrie his wife had never been, and never could be, any sort of companion. Dorrie had no interests outside her home, and the children. This was as it should be: a woman's place was the home, and nowhere else: but one needed more than an acquiescent wife. And he had once described Theodora to himself as a bluestocking!

It would be a lucky man to whom Dora gave herself: that warm and eager body, that mass of glossy fair hair, that tender, mobile mouth, that sudden eager smile! No, no, no! Sidney Cakebread tried to dissemble to himself his feelings—that uncorseted figure as she had sat on the floor and played with little Bertie and Ralph, the soft outline of those virginal breasts, the long white neck—he dismissed the critical thought of Dorrie's figure, loose and infirm after two children, and heavy with another on the way.

Then, as they were turning into the village and the dull approach to home, Sidney saw the Northern Lights in the sky over London; and his thoughts were lifted into the air above. Theodora, too, felt exaltation: she felt the strength of the starry universe in her mind, the power of infinite Mind above the little history of stars and planets in their circumscribed ways. She was sure that with only a little more consciousness she would be able to feel herself lifting away from earth and rejoining that Mind which had determined to uplift man long before the evolution of species. That was the Polaris of truth, the steady immortal star of truth by which man alone could find his earthly harmony. It was while she was looking up into the sky that Sidney kissed Theodora, very tenderly, on her cold, soft cheek.

Northwards of where Theodora stood, with shining eyes, thousands of skaters on the Thames stopped to watch the strange lights in the sky; then pushing off again into the keen unknown, the skaters upon the face of the river—frozen over above the bridge at Staines—felt themselves to be part of a marvellous electrical universe as they swooped and curved and their feet of steel scored grey and winding tracks under the spectral sky. Farther east, where the tidal flow had been pressed back by thousands of tons of plate-ice uptipped at all angles and welded by frost into barrier after barrier upon the piers of the bridges of London River, innumerable adventurers paused to regard the mystery of the heavens.

Upon the stony foreshore near Blackfriars Bridge, suspended on an iron rod hung across two great trivets, its limbs bound by iron wire to its skinned body, its glazed eyes staring from its horned head, an ox was roasting above the tide lapsing with riding ice, while the fat dripped from the colourless carcase and splashed to flame in the embers glowing on an iron plate beneath—watched curiously by the more venturesome, among them Hugh Turney, who with pale indifference considered that if the tide suddenly were to rush them all away to oblivion, it would make not the least difference to the nihilism of life.

Distant by less than a dozen miles as the geese had flown, Polly, the country maid in the service of Mrs. Turney, was sitting by the light of a candle beside her attic bedroom window, her thick red hands covering her wet cheeks. Polly had just had another fit of sobbing, for she was departing the next morning from the service of Mrs. Turney; and even two months' wages of two pounds, thirteen shillings and fourpence in lieu of notice was nothing to the desolation in Polly's heart.

Mrs. Turney had told Polly again and again, and Cookie had told her also, that she was in no way to blame for what had happened, or might have happened; and that when she had had a holiday at home, during which time Mrs. Turney had promised to find her another situation, she would be as happy as she had ever been; and she would be given the highest references. Even so, Polly was ashamed, hurt, unhappy, and afraid.

When she saw the colour of blood in the sky through her attic bedroom window, Polly gave a cry and hurried as fast as she could down the stairs; and so great was her agitation as she passed the sitting-room door, behind which Master and Missus were sitting, with Mr. and Mrs. Mallard, playing whist, that she let out a great screech. And then her feet were thumping down the wooden stairs into the kitchen.

The tension was relieved a little when Cookie, knocking on the sitting-room door, went to tell Mrs. Turney that there was a great fire in the sky, and maybe London itself was in flames. Mr. Turney and Mr. Mallard went out into the drive, and the two women followed the men soon afterwards to the railings beside the pond, Sarah in a shawl, and Mrs. Mallard in a velvet cloak. Others were gathered beside the ice-covered sheet of water, while to a little group Mrs. Mallard remarked that it must surely be one of the Seven Wonders of Nature.

Thomas Turney made a point of going through his gateway and in a cordial voice of inviting both Cook, standing outside the hall door, and Polly half-concealed behind her, to come into the road and see the Northern Lights. "You don't see them but once or twice in a lifetime from southern England," he exclaimed. "They are only electrical discharges, all nature is energy, you know, and this is a sight not to be missed." Thus encouraged, the two women followed at a respectful distance, and by the green and rosy ice looked up at the pretty colours.

"Well, Sarah my dear," remarked Thomas Turney, when once again they were sitting before the blazing coal fire, their guests having departed, "I can't say how sorry I am for what happened last evening, it was a moment's passing madness, I intended no harm, I don't know why I did such a silly thing as to enter the girl's bedroom at all. She's hysterical, of course, screaming as she did, and better elsewhere. D'ye think she'll talk, eh?"

"Why, no, Tom," replied Sarah, softly. "We all understand, I am sure, how worried you have been, my dear husband, so let us forget it, shall we? We must all love one another, as the Good Book tells us." Then Sarah, with a calm that surprised herself, said something she had been awaiting the right moment to say. "You will forgive Hetty, dear, won't you, as we all expect to be forgiven our little peccadilloes at the Judgment Seat?"

"Forgive her? Why, it is for the dear child to forgive me, in my opinion," declared Thomas Turney; and after Sarah had risen to kiss him on the brow for his generous attitude, and was wiping her eyes in thankful relief that her prayers had been answered, Thomas Turney went into the dining-room to his cupboard and poured himself out an extra measure of whisky, for an extra glass of good stiff grog—to keep out what might have been a cold draught, he-he-he.

Part Five

DEATH AND RESURRECTION

Chapter 24

THE MAN WHO LOVED PARTRIDGES

ON THE fifth day of March the thaw came. By evening of that day the interiors of windows in the trains from London Bridge and Cannon Street were streaked with melted moisture and the wooden floors of carriages were wet with dissolving wads of snow cast from sodden boots. But the sky was blue in places. Spring was coming!

Richard, wearing his stout new boots, felt happy and secure as he crossed streets dirty with slush and broken straw. In the morning and again in the evening he saw the icicles dripping and diminishing, the Thames swirling under London Bridge with its press of muddy waters, the gulls hovering and screaming above the parapets for fragments of food—a new sight for Londoners that year—becoming fewer as many departed, with new black polls, for the estuarine marshes where they nested every spring. Mist and fog succeeded sub-arctic air; but spring was on the way!

Crusts of snow and melting cornices slid and slattered from roofs; ruts and plashes in the high road reflected the sky; water-pipes, opened by ice so long bulging at the seams, hissed and spirted their fine spray under pressure. The lavatory pan leading off from the back porch of Comfort House, frozen solid during the past three weeks, suddenly fell apart when nobody was looking, said Hetty.

H'm, replied Richard, very fishy. Had she been pouring down boiling water, despite his repeated warnings? No, Dickie, really she hadn't.

Nightly Richard continued to carry the slop-pail to the waste-land of the embankment, and to empty it in a bed of nettles, intending to cover the deposits when the thaw had dried out of the land. This, with due consideration for propriety and health, he did; while too many times in his mind arose the mental picture of Hetty with a kettleful of boiling water, of Hetty afraid to tell the truth, of Hetty—a Turney—causing the pan to crack.

He had put away his sled after greasing the iron-banded runners. He said to Hetty that the next time the snow came in such quantity to make sledging possible he might be taking her son for his first run on the Pathfinder. Hetty's face lit up at the prospect; but oh, if only he would believe her, that she had never never *never* poured boiling water down the pan. It *had* simply fallen apart, all by itself!

"Well," said Richard. "I rely on you to tell the landlord, when you give him the rent, to have it replaced at the earliest possible moment."

The sun was now visible often over the roofs of a morning. It rose aslant the window of the little north-eastern room that Richard used for dressing. Thrushes and blackbirds sang in the trees, and tomtits seemed to be ringing little hand-bells. Boisterous winds dried roads and side-walks under the elms along the high road. Their branches were reddish-brown with opening blossoms. Richard swung his umbrella as he walked to the station of a morning, and sometimes carried his hat in his hand, to feel the air on his brow.

One Saturday morning towards the end of March Hetty received by the eleven o'clock post a letter from her father. After some agitation caused by the sight of the handwriting, she opened it and began to read with a dry throat, until in great relief she realized that it was the opposite of an angry letter. Upon recovering her equanimity she had sung while doing the housework. It had never seemed so light or easy before.

Thomas Turney in his letter had sent his kind regards to Richard, and referring to his own beginnings in business with the help of his dear wife, had asserted that if a man worked hard and well, "the cobbler sticking to his last," he would be a success; for, wrote Thomas Turney, "a good man cannot be kept down".

When Richard returned from the City that afternoon Hetty did not mention the letter, for once again she had not managed to get a definite promise from the landlord about a new pan. She waited for what she called to herself a favourable moment. That afternoon they went walking on the Hill, where the trodden and yellow herbage was being pierced with thin points of new green grass. So severe had been the frost that reservoirs supplying London had borne layers of ice twenty-five inches thick, Richard told her.

Atop the row of elms rooks were busy at their nests; but where in former springtimes a hundred and more were to be seen fluttering, cawing, and gossiping, now there were less than half that number.

"Even they have suffered in the hard weather."

As they watched, one of the rooks started to caw in a different voice. Looking down the slope, Richard saw a kestrel poised over the grass where his sled had once slipped so fast. *Hawk! Hawk!* one of the sentinel rooks cawed. Soon several birds had risen into the breeze and were flying in pursuit of the little falcon. They chased it over the houses west of the Hill, but almost at once the sentinel rook which had given the alarm turned back. Slipping among the branches it seized a stick from an unattended nest, hopped and fluttered to its own nest and apparently laid the stick upon it.

"Now did you observe that? There, plain as a pike staff, is what nature is, including human nature! If a man does not constantly look to his own, he'll be rooked! Do you hear that different note? That was the sentinel rook uttering a croak of approval that the rookery is once again safe from the invading hawk! All a subterfuge!"

"Surely he did not do it just to steal a stick, Dickie?"

"I am not so sure! The kestrel never interferes with rooks, being far too small. He eats the same kind of food, it is true, beetles and worms as well as small birds and mice, so rooks drive him away from their territory."

"Are the sentinel birds by the nests the father birds, Dickie?"

"Yes, I think they are. The hens go out for material, while the old Feeneys sit by the fire and keep it warm for Mrs. Feeney when she comes back. That reminds me, did the landlord say anything about replacing the broken lavatory pan when he called for the rent this morning?"

"I did mention it, dear, as you asked me to, and he said the same as last week, and the week before: that the builders were busy, with so much damage to repair owing to the weather."

"And I suppose you agreed with him, instead of getting him to agree with you that it should be done at once?"

"He said he would see to it as soon as possible, Dickie."

"That is what he said last week, and the week before."

"I did my best, dear."

"Well, you must try harder, that is all. Where would I be now if I hadn't gone on trying, despite every discouragement, to get another post? You really must learn to take your proper share of responsibility in our life together. What irony! for you think, with the crackpot Dora, that women should have the franchise! Look at the rooks up there, and take a lesson from them."

"Yes, dear, I will. I think they are such comic birds, always cawing."

"Well, it is part of their nature. And at least they share a life together equally, vote or no vote. Just supposing the bird on guard felt sorry for the pair at the next nest, and let them help themselves, there would soon be chaos. Well, Winner the landlord takes the rent, while not returning value in the shape of a new pan. And as I am not at home when he calls, you should see to it. That is my point."

"I'll try to be more like the rooks in future, Dickie." She began to laugh.

Richard, keeping a straight face, for the principle of responsibility was one that he considered Hetty needed to acquire, said: "Well, perhaps it is not entirely your fault that nothing has been done. These petty landlords have not the slightest idea of the responsibilities attached to the owning of property."

"Yes, dear, I'm sure you are right."

"Good, then we are in agreement!"

"Of course, dear, naturally."

The kestrel flew high over the rookery, its wings a brownish pink against the clear blue sky. It uttered a cry, plaintive and wistful, *kee-kee-kee*, almost a whistle, before it turned round in the breeze and hung poised, on fluttering wings, farther down the slope.

"They are pretty little falcons," said Richard. "I used to have a tame kestrel when I was a boy. It was never caged, but flew about at will, always coming to one of us to be fed. We boys had many such pets. Hullo, see that pair of partridges! Fancy, they still come to this place! Do you know, my Father once had an entire covey, or rather nid of partridges, as pets!"

"A whole covey, Dickie? They are such wild birds!"

"Yes, but they were quite tame, following him everywhere. They were very small when he got them, in fact not hatched, for a mower had cut off the head of the hen bird as she sat close in the mowing meadow. There she was, a rounded mat of dead leaves in the grass, her back feathers ruffled by the close sweep of the scythe."

"The poor thing."

"Under her were twelve eggs, chipping. Father took them and put them on flannel kept warm over a dish of hot water heated by the very self-same dark lantern I now possess, yes, my dark lantern!

They hatched off, too, and when they had dried, and were lively, he fed them on minute pieces of chopped-up yoke of hard-boiled pigeon's eggs. I remember we had to climb many holly-trees to get the pigeon's eggs, two on every raft of black sticks."

"Did they all live, Dickie? They must have been even smaller than the chicks of Mamma's bantams."

"They were scarcely bigger than humble-bees. At night they crouched round the lantern, their foster mother, only the lantern was inside a glass cylinder, and the chicks were in a box hung inside with strips of green baize, so that they were warm as under a hen's wing. As they grew, so they ranged abroad. Whenever they saw Father they simply flew at him, cheeping and clustering round his feet. They followed him on the lawn, taking grass-seeds and insects. They soon cleared any ant's nest in the flowerbeds when they found it."

"But didn't a cat get them? Or an owl at night, when they were bigger?"

"No, for they slept where Father was! They followed him into the house, and always settled round his boots. Father had an instinct for birds and animals, and taught us boys a lot about them. I can see the little partridges now, running ever so fast after him, scarcely so big as sparrows as they fluttered up the stairs after him into the laboratory, as he called his study on the first floor. When he sat down they settled on the carpet in a ring and went to sleep around his boots, while he read his newspaper."

Hetty had never seen Richard so animated. His eyes looked a deeper blue, he was smiling. Impulsively she cried:

"What a lovely man your Father must be."

Immediately he became silent. "Well, let us walk on," he said presently. "It is cold up here, when one stops walking. These March winds may be worth a king's ransom, to a farmer of heavy land, but they can be treacherous. And I must get on with my envelopes. I lost much time last month."

They walked in silence down the slope, and so to Charlotte Road.

"What I was going to tell you," he continued, "was that one day my Father stole away, while the chicks were asleep, and left them there on the carpet, after closing the door, in case the cat found them. And dash me! do you know, when they heard his voice a few minutes later in the garden, where he stood on the lawn with old Fritz, his black Labrador retriever, all of a sudden they were on the sill of the open window above, and altogether they flew down and pitched at his feet, just as though his two boots were their parents."

"Oh, I would give anything to have seen them!"

"My Father gave up shooting soon afterwards, I recall."

"What happened to the little partridges, Dickie?"

"They wandered off as they grew bigger, but they knew him from anyone else, and always flew to him whenever they saw him. They often came at dawn to the lawn in front of the house, and called. But after harvest they strayed away on the stubbles. I was only small at the time, and went to school at Slough that September. It was about the start of the depression in British farming. Soon afterwards several of our farms were sold, and that was the beginning of the general break-up. Father had put all he had into the estate. I know it is true, because I helped him with his affairs for a year or two, before I went away to work in Doggett's."

Hetty did not say anything. She noticed that his hands were clenched, where before during the telling of the partridge story they had been open and expressive of his happiness. She had particularly noticed this because she admired his hands, with their long and slender fingers and filbert-shaped nails, and was often saying to herself that she hoped her baby would have hands like Dickie's.

She wondered in the evening of that day, when she was resting alone in the parlour and Richard had gone up to London, if there could have been any connection between his thoughts on the Hill about his Father, and the news that Theodora had brought soon after they had reached home that afternoon. Were thoughts in the air, winged like birds, coming home to roost? In all the time she had known him he had made only the briefest mentions of his Father to her, and she had always tried never to mention the subject to him. Mamma's words had been her guide—"It behoves us never to judge a fellow-creature, Hetty."

Even so, Hetty had never thought of Dickie's Father as a fellow-creature, but as a Figure of Awe, one quite apart from ordinary life, as he belonged to another world, and therefore must be quite different. It was strange that Dickie should have spoken so much about him only that afternoon, for just as she was getting tea there had come a little rat-tat-tat on the door, and when she went to open it, there was Dora smiling at her on the doorstep. Richard was in the back-garden, looking at the ground to see if it were fit for digging.

Taking Dora into the parlour, Hetty noticed a fixed expression in her eyes as she sat on the sofa, and on inquiry if she had a headache Theodora said suddenly,

"Oh, Hetty, I am the bearer of serious news. I must tell Dickie—it concerns our Father."

"Oh dear, I hope nothing awful has happened, Dora. Is he ill?"

"Father has had an accident, and is lying in hospital in Agar Street, just off the Strand," replied Theodora, in a low and level voice. "He has been knocked down by a fast newspaper gig, and the wheel of a heavy dray went over him before it could stop."

Theodora could not bring herself to say that it had been a brewer's dray; she flinched from the connection because it added to her inner anguish.

"Oh, how terrible!" cried Hetty. "I am so very very sorry, dearest Dora. Now is it not strange, Dickie was only just now talking about him to me. Is he—is Captain Maddison badly hurt?"

"I am afraid it may prove fatal, Hetty dear. He is in some pain, poor man, and since this afternoon has been asking for Dickie."

Theodora's voice faltered. Hetty put her arms round her. Theodora's lips touched Hetty's brow, and she went on in a low tone, controlling her feelings. "He was an unhappy man, always running away from his true self."

"Yes," whispered Hetty, to herself. Her eyes were bright, their sight fixed far away.

"How strange life is, Dora. Only this afternoon Dickie told me of the little partridges. They loved your Father, I am sure."

"We all loved him, Hetty dear, in spite of what he did at times. Well, his fate has met him at last. There is an internal hæmorrhage, and the surgeon has told brother John that it might take a turn for the worse. Father is not unconscious, but when I left him he was growing weaker, and in some torment of soul, saying that he has behaved very badly to everyone."

"Oh, how very very sad! I am sure he was such a kind man, really, from what I have heard."

Hetty saw in memory the figure in the street at Brighton, the

Awful Figure created by Papa's attitude, for she had been a child at the time; but now a tear rolled down her cheek as she thought of a Tender Figure guarding the little partridges, safe and happy around their foster-parents—two boots side-by-side, that would never hurt them. Oh, he must have been good!

"Yes," Theodora was saying with a smile, her gaze upon the ground. "Sometimes he scattered seeds of wildflowers on railway embankments; and hardly a beggar would appeal to him in vain. He was a strange man, paradoxically always thinking of a better world." Theodora reflected awhile, and then looking direct at Hetty, and smiling, she said, "I think Dickie should come without much delay to the hospital, if you will not mind my taking him from you for a little while."

"Yes, dear Dora, of course, naturally. Do you think there is time enough for a cup of tea first? I can have it ready in no time at all. I have got some sprats, they won't take long to fry, and are full of health-giving nourishment. Dickie all the week has only a very light luncheon, he so looks forward to his Saturday tea."

"Yes, he must have his proper meal," said Theodora. "He has a nervous stomach, and needs the right foods, and at the right time. As we all do, indeed. Men particularly are only big children, you know, and need looking after."

"I'll put the sprats on to fry at once, and tell Dickie in the garden that you're here," said Hetty. "Will you remain here in the parlour, then I will tell him you want to see him. I'll just say you want a word with him, leave it to me, dear."

Richard had just come into the kitchen from the garden as Hetty returned down the passage. The kettle was steaming on the hob. He was staring at it. "We cannot afford to waste coal," he remarked, sliding the kettle off the open hole, and putting the iron cover in place with the poker. "This fire is far too big for the time of year."

"Yes, dear, but I was going to fry some sprats, and you like them crisp, like whitebait, don't you? By the way, Dora has just come."

"Dora? Where is she?"

"I left her in the parlour. I'll lay the tea in the kitchen, shall I?"

He was affected by her nervousness; the sight of the patch of weed-grown ground outside had already depressed him. "Where else would you lay it? You know very well there is not a fire in the parlour."

"Yes, dear. Do go and talk to Dora, she wants to see you, I think."

"What is the matter with you? Hetty, are you ill?"

"No, dear. Please don't take any notice of me. Here's Dora."

"Well, well!" exclaimed Richard. "How nice to see you, sister. How are you? Where have you sprung from this time, eh?"

Theodora told her brother what she had told Hetty. He took the news in silence, then sat on a chair and, unlacing his heavy walking boots, placed them side by side on the pot-board under the dresser; and taking the lighter pair he had worn to the City that morning, put them on.

"Well, it had to come sooner or later," he said at last, concealing his shaken feelings. "Now if you will excuse me for a little while, I will go upstairs and wash. I will be down shortly, then we'll have tea, and I shall be ready to accompany you to the hospital." And half-filling a brass can with hot water, he went upstairs.

Later, as they sat at table, eating crisp sprats, sprinkled with lemon juice, with brown bread and butter, and sipping tea reflectively, Theodora said, "Is it not strange how many things seem to be happening all at once? Who may say what is good, and what is bad, at any moment? Six months ago, who could have foretold that Hetty would be in your own home with you, in time to help you, boy, to recover from the loss of your Mother; and now your Father? And soon, another generation, to do better things than the last; for experience surely must mean something, and lead to better things."

"Ah, you should read Thomas Hardy's novels."

"I have," she replied serenely, "but I do not accept all their implications. I have also read Shelley. And while people like Hardy and Shelley are born on the earth, I see cause only for optimism, Dickie dear."

"Have some more sprats, Dora. These sprats"—to Hetty—"are cooked to a turn!"

Hetty thought of the hot fire which had enabled them quickly to be fried; but she said "Thank you, dear," gratefully.

Theodora looked up. Her childlike face, with its wide mouth and slightly protruding teeth of the upper jaw, smiled at Hetty, then at her brother. She had heard what had been said about the fire; she understood his ingrained fear which at times prevented him from awareness of the feelings of others. Poor little brother, he had more to bear in his soul than people knew. Theodora's masses of fair hair were twisted into several knots about her tall neck, seemingly without care; but Theodora had passed the night beside the bedside of her father and the crypt of St. Martin-in-the-Fields, in prayer and meditation. Theodora's lips quivered at the corners.

"Come, Dora dear, do not say you cannot manage some more sprats!" said Richard, peering kindly at his sister.

"Thank you," said Theodora. "May I help myself?" and she got up, taking her plate to the frying pan.

Immediately after tea brother and sister set off to walk to the station. At first, following the path under the roadside elms, they did not speak; but soon their eyes were accustomed to the twilight of the March evening illuminated by smoky lights on cart and waggon moving between the street lamps.

"I think I ought to tell you that there is not much hope for Father, Dickie."

With inner anguish Richard saw the figure of Father coming up the lane to Temperley's Farm, to find him.

Presently he said, "I hope the old home will not be sold. It would be good if John were to live there."

"Poor house, it needs some happiness now, Dickie."

After a while he went on, "Of course, I know nothing of John's intentions. And anyway, the house and what little land remains probably carry both first and second mortgages."

"I do not know, boy. But there is our grandparent's marriage settlement, a trust fund, which is to be divided among the children after the death of both parents."

"It should all go to John as the eldest son, in my opinion. I suppose I am old-fashioned, but I believe in primogeniture. The family place should remain always as a base for the family. The land is the source of everything, though the trouble is that many landlords no longer regard themselves as trustees of their land, but as privileged and selfish individuals."

"I could not agree more with you, dear brother," replied Theodora. "And that is the reason why more and more people begin to feel that there should be one owner of land, to conserve the nation's heritage."

"Oh, socialism! Mob rule! It will be a sad day for England when that happens."

"England should be ruled by the best minds, Dickie—not by those whose sole concern is to acquire more and more money."

"I have seen some of your best minds at work—a year or two back in Trafalgar Square, on Bloody Sunday!"

"They were starving people—with starved minds, Dickie."

The train came into the station. Brother and sister sat silent during the journey to London Bridge. There they had to change to the Chatham line for Waterloo and the iron bridge across the Thames, with its moving lights and melancholy hoots and whistles of river-craft below the open carriage window; and so into Charing Cross station.

"Let me take your arm, Dickie." She saw that he was upset; and taking his arm, guided him with great care across the radiant, jingling, clip-clopping Strand.

The hospital entrance was in a side street. They went up the steps, and through the doors, entering a tessellated hall where several people were waiting. A queue of depressed individuals stood against one wall, and Richard caught sight of a pale-faced young man among them, who recognized him at the same time and immediately turned away his head. It was Hugh Turney.

Richard said nothing; Theodora had not seen Hugh. Then his own thoughts were tremulous as he followed his sister to a porter who, listening a moment to what she said, led them up a stairway to the floor above. They waited in a room together, in an odour of soap and carbolic, until a nurse came to lead them to a door whereon she knocked before opening it and telling them to enter. There, standing side by side, were a man and a woman.

"Dickie! My dear fellow!"

Richard had not seen his brother John or Jenny his wife since the funeral of his mother. On that occasion, when they had seen that he did not wish to stay for a meal in the house, Jenny, as she said goodbye, had pressed him to go and see them in their London apartment, but he had never gone. He had seen Jenny only once before the funeral, on the occasion of her marriage to his brother. The first sight of her had startled him; he felt that she had looked at him and seen deep inside him, so that the memory of that look ever afterwards had come with a longing restlessness. The ease of manner of her people and friends had added to his disquiet, as he contrasted it with that of his own family. They had all seemed to be so happy, and so open and free together; whereas the members of his own family were so apart from each other. His sense of loneliness had deepened, and when he had met Hetty he was at once attracted to her because she had the same dark eyes and gentleness of face as Jenny. Yet he could not bring himself to compare them—his mind turned away from the thoughts of comparison. Jenny was highest in his secret thoughts.

Jenny had liked John's younger brother the moment she saw him. His patent plight and air of loneliness had touched her. Talking to her husband about him on a fishing honeymoon in Connemara, she had learnt that Richard had always been a solitary kind of boy, not easy to understand. "I think he is charming," declared Jenny. "But he is *so* unhappy, I feel we must find a wife for him when we get back to London, darling." She was disappointed when Richard had never written, or come to see them.

And now Jenny smiled her sympathy to Richard, lowering her gaze immediately as John, glancing from his sister's to his brother's face, went forward to break the news to them.

"I am afraid that it is rather bad news, brother and sister."

Richard glanced at Jenny. Meeting her eyes, he felt a pang, a wish to hurt himself by going away and never again to see anyone he knew. John, observing the expression on his younger brother's face, took him by the arm, while his free hand sought his sister's hand, and pressed it.

"Well, Dick and Dora, it has ended. Father is at peace now. His last moments were serene." He breathed to steady himself and said, "He died shortly after five o'clock."

Richard replied, as though half jocularly, "Well, I suppose it is a relief that it is all over, eh?" He looked awkwardly at his brother. "Well, John, how are you?" He shook him by the hand. "And Jenny, how do you do," he said, with an effort to be easy, as she moved beside John.

Jenny took his hesitant hand in both of hers, pressed it warmly, and said softly, "I cannot tell you how deeply I feel for you three—words are poor things—Oh, Dora darling!" for Theodora, standing with lowered head, had turned away, and subdued whimpering sounds were coming from her. Jenny put her arms round the young woman, saying in her caressing voice, "We are all with you, darling, so do not feel alone, will you? Your Father is happier now than he has been for a long time, perhaps happier than he has ever been while he was alive. Now he has brought us all together, and we all love you so, dearest, dearest Dora." She led Theodora away towards the window.

"At the moment one feels these things heavily," said John to Richard. "It has been a time of strain for all of us. Well, how are you, Dickie? I had no idea you had chucked Doggett's. Whatever made you do that?"

"Oh, I resigned and found another billet, John."

"I called in there this morning, hoping to find you in, and they told me you had left after Christmas. Father was in good spirits until shortly after three o'clock, when a hæmorrhage broke internally. Until then it had seemed that he might have a chance of recovery. Fortunately Dora knew your whereabouts, and at once went down to tell you, saying she would get there quicker than any telegraph boy on a Saturday afternoon. Also, that you were usually out walking and she would catch you on your return for tea."

"Yes, I usually go out for a walk, John."

"Well, I am sorry I did not get in touch with you earlier, old chap. I am afraid it was not realized before how badly he was hurt. His heart was as good as one would expect after the shock, but otherwise he seemed fairly at ease."

"What actually happened, John?"

"He fell, and the front wheel of the dray passed over his arm just below the shoulder. He was dragged some little way like that; but the rim of the wheel must have crushed more than was apparent behind the contusion upon the ribs. Fortunately the back wheels of the dray were on skids, preparatory to going down Whitehall—the asphalt there is usually slippery—otherwise the off rear wheel would surely have passed over him in turn. I am told the heavy draught-horses often go down at that particular place."

"Dora said something about him being—well—under the influence of——"

"The house surgeon tells me there is no proof of it at all. We have a complete account of the accident, I think. A witness informed the constable on duty there that he saw him hesitate after starting to cross the street; he turned back, then started to go on again. Apparently he changed his mind once more when a paper boy cut across in front of him, and the hesitation was fatal. It was about the half hour after seven, when the traffic, especially at that place, was at its height. One of those fast gigs belonging to *The Globe* apparently threw out a bundle of papers, and the boy dodged under the belly of one of the dray horses to retrieve it. Father stepped back and was struck by the wheel of the dray."

"Oh dear, was he unconscious when picked up?"

"No, on the contrary. He was articulate and reasonable after being brought into hospital, and said that no blame must be attached to the driver, as it was entirely his own fault that he had stepped back without taking proper care. He spoke slowly as one in some pain, but coherently. So there can be no question of inebriation."

"Well, that is something, John."

"It was an accident of a kind that is becoming, with the increasing pace of modern life, more and more frequent, so the inspector told me at Bow Street Police Station."

"Well," said Richard, with a forlorn smile. "First it was Mother, now it is Father."

"Yes, we must face the inevitable with an equal mind, Dick." John smiled at his younger brother. "We must see more of one another, eh? I have telegraphed to our other sisters. I will attend the coroner's court. The funeral will be at Rookhurst."

"Yes."

"Now if you agree, I think we should pay our respects to the house surgeon on duty, and then take our leave. There is nothing we can do here, for the moment. You must both come with Jenny and me and have some dinner. The Irish are so sensible on these occasions, and give a party for the departed. Let me see, there is the Golden Cross, quite near at hand, a quiet place; or there is Previtali's in Arundel Street; or the Caledonian in Adelphi Terrace. Which would you prefer?"

"Thank you most kindly, John and Jenny, but I think I ought to be getting back. I have some work to do."

"We will not hear of it, will we, Jenny? We seldom have an opportunity of coming together, and this surely is an occasion when the family needs to feel its solidarity, or rather, to demonstrate its unity. And also, as head of the family now, I suppose I should tell you about various things. No, I simply will not hear of your leaving us alone just now! Remember the covey of partridges?"

"Yes! Only this afternoon——"

Richard stopped. He looked at Theodora. She put her arm through his. "Do come," said Jenny. "We should feel so lonely without you." Her hand sought her husband's, and held it. Richard stood looking at the floor.

"I believe Richard is in love," said Jenny.

He did not reply to the lead. Theodora said, pressing his arm, "Tell them, Dickie." And as he did not speak, "Let me tell them, boy. They will be so glad to hear."

"You're engaged to be married?" asked John.

"He *is* married," said Theodora. "To a lovely girl, and my great friend."

"Well, well!" said John. "A dark horse! Let me congratulate you, my dear chap. Do I know her? When did it take place? Why did you not let us know, Dick?"

"There was parental opposition," said Theodora. "And of course, the rules of the Bank."

"Ah, now I begin to see light!" said John. "Well, my best wishes for your happiness, dear boy. When may we meet your lady?"

"Yes! And my warmest congratulations, Dickie, too! Why not bring her tonight?" said Jenny.

Richard did not know what to reply. He felt suddenly fagged out.

"Another time, then," said Jenny. "Now, John darling, the house surgeon may be going off duty, it is nearly seven o'clock."

"Yes, of course, I was forgetting. How does one find him? Is there a bell-pull somewhere?"

"Let me find the nurse on duty," said Theodora.

"Does one call her 'sister'?"

"I think 'nurse' is the higher rank."

"It is as well to know these things."

John looked tired. He was tired. He was thinking of the coroner's inquest, of the arrangements for the coffin to travel by train, watched over by either Richard or himself, or both; of the burial in Rookhurst churchyard, beside Mother. Would there be any complications, any awkward claims on the personal estate of Father, who had been living with a woman for some years now, in Highgate? Then the house, vacant since Mother's death. Perhaps he could get on the Western Circuit, and make Fawley his headquarters. And so gradually build up what had been allowed to decay. And have a family, a happy family, to help atone for the past. Jenny wanted children. A happy family whose laughter would make it up to the house for the unhappiness its walls had suffered during the past years. Then Father would be absolved, Father who had held his hand, and cried out towards the end for Dickie, the child he had harried more than the others, perhaps because Dickie had always been so timid, so sensitive. Should he tell his young brother this, or would it upset him?

Father had asked for his second son Dickie, to hold his hands: and the firmer he himself had held them, as it were by proxy, the more Father had cried, *Hold my hands, Dickie, hold my hands, Dickie;* then, *O Christ, I have been such a bad man*, and *Adela forgive me, forgive me*—again and again, more and more wearily, more and more feebly, until with a long sigh he had ceased, and the lower jaw, falling loose, had been the end. That was the fact; the peaceful end was a fiction, to save the younger ones from being haunted. And Father had been tipsy before the accident, though that was no great sin, except to himself. No, Dickie must never be told, to go away haunted into the darkness; he and his little brother must renew the old feeling of friendship, of open happy brotherliness, and never allow their relationship to become remote and dim again, like ships that pass in the night.

The dead man, already a ghost, soon to be a memory, a name on a tombstone forgotten in the wasting of Time, lay in the mortuary clothed in a new nightshirt, and covered all but bearded throat and face and head by a shroud. His children stood by this effigy, this fount of all life and joy and sorrow to them, and the love which had been dulled within them, the pride that had been abashed, the hope which had been mortified, flowed anew in their tears. Here and now prayer was natural; here was absolution, here were visions of the mind come to elemental, thoughtless truth. They felt forgiven, they felt forgiveness. These two things are of the same quality, sighed Theodora to herself, in a feeling of sublime joy: for such was the love of God.

Chapter 25

MIXED IMAGES

RICHARD RETURNED home that night with new feelings of freedom and exhilaration, accentuated by the wine which he had drunk at supper. He felt he had made friends again with Father, his brothers, his sisters, and therefore with all of himself. The serene illusion remained in the train and during the walk along the high road to the turn into Comfort Road. Then he felt his heart to be sinking.

Hetty was waiting for him. His slippers were by the fire. A big wedge of Canadian cheese was on the kitchen table beside a loaf of bread and a jar of pickled onions. The table cloth was laid with plate, knife, fork, spoon, tumbler and a jug of water.

Beholding the ordinariness of the room he sat down, hoping that Hetty would not begin to ask questions. He sat on the chair in silence for a minute or so, and then, more and more aware of her subdued presence, a vague irritation began to arise in him.

Richard had been thinking much of Hetty during his absence from home. He had imagined her to be like Jenny, a twin of Jenny. The image of the charming Jenny had taken the place of Hetty until he had turned into Comfort Road; and upon entering the little house he had been stricken by acute disappointment, accompanied by almost a physical revulsion of the drab little room, and—but he veered away from the wretched thought. Gone was Jenny, gone the bright picture of the private supper room of the Charing Cross Hotel, gone the stimulating personality of Hetty-Jenny which had brought him out of himself, to be himself fully.. Now his life was dull again.

Hetty had been keyed-up all the evening; she had gone to the kitchen-door many times during the past two hours and held it partly open, hearkening for an imagined key in the front door lock; and all the while a sense of doom and expectancy had grown upon her as hour by hour the clock's hands moved to their steady ticking, and she remained waiting.

Remembering what Dora had said about the importance of the right foods, Hetty had thought most of the time what to give Richard on his return. A sop of bread and milk which would be easily digestible? She had the pot all ready in which to pour the milk. Boiled eggs and toast, which he liked when he was tired? The eggs were there, ready to go into hot water from the simmering kettle. The difficulty was that he might come back in need of food quickly; and again, if she prepared anything light, might he not declaim, as he had once or twice before, on the value of food being wasted by being cooked and kept hot too long? Cheese—was that indigestible late at night? Supposing she made him a cheese sandwich, with thin slices of pickled escalottes between the cheese? He liked that, sometimes, but only when he had been walking. And if he did not fancy a sandwich, it would be stale the next day, and that would worry him.

So Hetty had laid the table, put the slab of Canadian cheese near the loaf and the glass jar of pickled escalottes, and a bottle of Raggett's stout; filled the kettle and set it on the hob; with teapot keeping warm and a saucepan all ready for heating milk should he fancy a cup of cocoa, or for water if he would like a boiled egg. Remembering what he had said about milk going sour if shut-in anywhere, she left the jug in the scullery for coolness; then she had settled down, as much as she was able to with her crowding thoughts, to Pepys' Diary and the knitting of a second woolly jacket for baby.

She felt much alone, for Mr. and Mrs. Feeney next door had gone to the South London Palace of Amusements, near the Elephant and Castle, travelling there with a friend by tram along the Old Kent Road. They would not be back before midnight.

It was a few minutes after eleven o'clock when Richard's key in the front door made Hetty's heart beat faster with relief, but she experienced the slight feeling of dread which, however hard she tried to control herself, always came over her whenever his presence was imminent. She poked the fire, to draw up the blaze, and left the poker in the flames at an upward angle. Then she hurried to the door, to undo the chain. Thank goodness she had not forgotten to put it across!

"Why is the chain across?" asked Richard. "Do you wish to keep me out?" He did not mean what he said; he was half-joking; but he was also, despite his intention, half-serious.

"No, dear, of course not. Only I thought it best, as I was alone."

"Yes, but you need not keep it across when you know I am coming home."

"Very well, dear," she said, sympathetically. How could she have known when he was coming home?

When he had taken off his coat, he sat by the fire, his elbows resting on the arms of the chair, his hands under his chin, staring before him. At last she ventured to ask him what he would like to eat.

"Nothing, thank you."

Seeing from his face that he was tired, Hetty was anxious lest she upset him in any way. Should she warm some milk, without further ado? There could be no harm in that, surely; but perhaps it would be best to ask first.

"Do you feel like a glass of hot milk, dearest? I can easily heat one up for you, you have only to say the word."

"Why do you say to me, 'Do you *feel* like a glass of hot milk,' or anything else for that matter? How do you know what a glass of hot milk feels like? And why in heaven's name is the poker stuck in the fire like that?"

"I put it there to draw up the fire, in case you were cold."

"It is a mild night, and I have walked from the station, so it was improbable that I should be cold. Anyhow, the idea of the poker drawing up the draught, like that, as I have told you before, is foolish, part of superstition. How can a rod of iron cause flames to leap up? If it were very hot, and the fire just starting, it might induce a flow of hot air, or rather warm air, up the chimney, and so help the draught that way; but when a fire already has a good bed of embers, to stick up a rod of iron like that in front of it is about as sensible as praying to an idol."

"Yes, dear," said Hetty, thinking that it *did* draw up the fire.

She stood there, wondering if she should enquire after his Father. It was so very difficult to know what to say, or what not to say, when he was worried or overtired.

Richard was trying to avoid thinking of the contrast between the balance of Jenny, the way she managed to put people at their ease, and—how things were in his own home. He knew that Hetty had not enquired of his Father, because she was afraid of saying the wrong thing. Why could she not learn to say the right thing, like Jenny?

"I think I'll put on some milk for myself, dear," said Hetty, a hurried note in her voice. "I kept the milk outside to keep cool. How did you find your poor Father? I hope he was not suffering much pain, and will soon recover."

Richard drew a deep breath, and breathing out slowly, he said, "My 'poor' Father, as you call him, was dead before we got to the hospital. My sister-in-law told me that he asked several times for me. It is strange, since from the first he never liked me."

"Oh, I am sure he liked you, dearest." She went to him, and stroked his head. He made as if to yield to her, then he moved his head away.

"I am so sorry, dear," said Hetty. "About your poor Father, I mean."

"Why 'your poor Father'? Why not just 'your Father'?"

She murmured, "I felt sorry for him, he was so kind to the little partridges."

"Kinder than I am to you, you 'poor' gravid little hen partridge."

When the milk was hot, but not too hot, she poured out two cups, and placed one in its saucer beside him. He took it, and sipped, while she drank hers on the other side of the hearth.

"That was good," he said, when he had finished. "He is a good farmer, the new man at Joy Farm with the shorthorn herd."

Joy Farm lay to the south of the cemetery. When he had first come to the district Richard had lodged there for a week or two, leaving only because Mrs. Cummings' had been nearer the station, and at Joy Farm his boots got yellow clay on them sometimes of a morning.

On impulse Hetty knelt by his chair, and put her arms round his knees, laying her cheek against them. Richard saw the clustered silken curls, the slender wrist, the shapely forearm encased in brown silk lying across his legs; and then his hand sought the back of her head, and his fingers felt the warm skin of her neck. She turned and looked up at him, and the tenderness in her eyes moved him, the lips slightly parted, the oval face with soft shadows below the moulded cheekbones. What long lashes she had, just like Jenny; she might be Jenny, allowing for the differences of upbringing. He bent over and rubbed his nose and cheek-bone in her curls, and down her cheek until he came to her ear, under the lobe of which the end of his nose rubbed gently. As he did so, he thought of a dog burying a bone with its nose. His teeth nipped the ear-lobe, then he took it between his lips, saying that he was a piglet tugging at its sow.

"Dear little pig," said Hetty, taking his lower arm and hand to her breast. "I love little pigs. Have you noticed how a little pig sometimes trots round to his mother's nose, as she lies on her side, and just touches her nose with his nose after he has fed? I am sure he says thank you to her."

"And for what am I to say thank you to this little sow?"

"I don't know," said Hetty, subduedly. "Sometimes I think I am no help to you in any way at all."

"Oh, come now, you must not feel like that, just because I make a joke."

"Oh, I am not, Dickie! I am perfectly serious when I say that I know I am not adequate for you."

"Well, I have *added quite* to you, have I not, eh?" He laughed at his pun.

Hetty looked puzzled a moment; then she saw the play on the word *adequate* and laughed. "Yes, you have indeed! I felt him moving about a lot tonight while you were away."

"The piglet in the little sow. It is odd, you know, I do not feel in the least like one who is about to become a father."

"Mamma told me that even a mother does not feel anything for her baby until it is born, while the father makes friends with it bit by bit, usually after it has smiled its first smile."

Richard, his thoughts having moved through nearly three decades, sighed. "You are tired, dear," said Hetty, turning round to look up at his face. "Would you like a boiled egg, with some toast? I am still getting the eggs from the Joy Farm milkman, they are so very fresh, so different from shop eggs. Do you feel, I mean to say, do you fancy one, lightly boiled?"

Richard laughed unexpectedly. "To tell you the truth, Hetty, I *do* feel rather like an egg—an old and rather stale election egg! My eyes were too big, I expect, for my stomach. Still, it was a wonderful supper, oysters and smoked salmon, then cold chicken with Burgundy, and afterwards John ordered a bottle of dry champagne, and we drank one another's healths. I do wish you had been there, Jenny is so very kind, she asked after you, and insisted that I must bring you to see her. But that means inviting them in return here, and oh, we do not live in their world at all."

"But would it make any difference to them, Dickie?"

"In one sense, of course not; but after all, I am a poor man, and likely to remain so, and therefore cannot possibly afford to keep up the appearances of their kind of living."

He passed his hand over his forehead, and sighed. "Phew! I have eaten too much. And I have got such a thirst."

"Well then, I shall make you a pot of your favourite Soochong right away! Mamma has just sent me a packet, and I have bought some nice lemons. I'll slice the slices ever so thin, just as you like them."

"Give me the big cup you brought back from France, will you? I could drink a bucketful. It's good to flush the kidneys. Half the illnesses of later life are due to men not sweating enough, my grandfather used to say. Lord, I hope I do not get an aftermath tomorrow."

He passed his hand again across his brow, shielding his eyes from the light. He did not want her to see that they were filling with tears. *Hold my hands Dickie, hold my hands.*

Knowing what he was feeling, Hetty put her hand against his forehead. It was hot. With her other hand she stroked the brown, wavy hair. If only she could act always so that she never did anything to upset the nervous brain under the soft, soft brown hair. In a moving and clairvoyant tenderness she held the head in her hands, and laid her cheek on the hair, turning away lest he see her eyes, which were filled with compassion.

She made the China tea. Richard got a lemon, and opening the largest of the three blades in the ivory-handled pen-knife his father had given him years before, to help make up for his failure to pass into the Navy, he cut several thin slices and laid them in a pattern on the saucer, while Hetty poured the tea into the large earthenware French cup and placed it on the corner of the table near him, in the manner that he liked, without saying anything. Afterwards she poured a cup for herself, and sat on her wooden chair by the hearth, remembering that she must not blow on the tea to cool it before sipping.

He sipped his tea in silence, and when the cup was empty, she refilled it.

"According to Dora's precious theory, we should not be drinking this tea. According to Dora, it is purchased at starvation prices, from Chinese coolies rotted by opium forced upon them by the opium interests in India, financed from the City of London. Have you ever heard such a cock-and-bull story?"

"Dora does get some strange ideas at times, I must admit, Dickie."

"It is rot, of course. Well, I have a secret to tell you. A secret, mind, not to be communicated to your people, or to anyone else."

"Of course not, Dickie. Your affairs are nothing to do with anyone else."

"Well, brother John told me tonight that each of the children are to receive, at a round sum, about two thousand pounds, from the marriage settlement of my grandparents."

"Oh, I am so glad, dearest. Though of course I am deeply grieved by what has happened."

"Well, I am rather fagged out, Hetty. I think we ought to go to bed."

"Yes, dear. You go and wash, and I'll clear these things away."

Richard liked to come down into a tidy room. Remembering what Mamma used to do, Hetty went down to the kitchen and filled the glass carafe with water from the tap, and returning upstairs, put it on the table near the bed-head beside a tumbler, and a packet of seidlitz powders, in case Dickie should wake up in the night and have a sour taste in his mouth after the wine. He was in the scullery, washing and brushing his teeth; she had washed herself all over, with a flannel, before the fire while he had been away in London. She undressed quickly, hung her clothes neatly on the back of a chair, and was in her nightgown and brushing her hair, when he came upstairs. She knelt by the bedside in prayer, while he removed his clothes in one of the two small rooms adjoining. He came into the bedroom in his nightshirt, carrying his folded trousers over his arm, and lifting up the side of the hair-mattress, laid them on the hessian cover to be pressed for the next day.

Until that moment Hetty had been lying on his side of the bed to warm the bedclothes for him. When he turned out the gas she moved over to her side. He settled in beside her, taking some time to tuck the blankets and sheet around his neck; and this being done, she turned towards him, and took his head on her shoulder, to stroke his hair. It was a nightly ritual. He lay inert in her arms for a while, and then turning over, pulled the sheet more securely round his neck, thus taking some of the protection from the small of her back; and putting one arm across his shoulder, so that his hand clasped his collar-bone, he drew up his knees, holding himself close together, in the position of an embryo within the womb. Thus dismissed, Hetty could turn over and warm her back against his back, and settle herself more comfortably and as it were economically under her portion of the protecting bedclothes.

In his curled-up posture, habitual since childhood, Richard hugged himself, and in the friendly state with himself he was able to release his imagination in pictures and scenes passing before his eyes. It was as though his forehead had dissolved, giving place to a sort of luminous screen across which impressions within the mind were impelled into vision by dreads and desires. Tonight, in the Camera Obscura, he saw Jenny's eyes and smiling lips, her hair falling over her white shoulders as she held out her arms to clasp his head upon her breast, his head bowed in adoration as he was enfolded in her warmth and desire, and so absorbing him in shining bliss for ever. Alas, this vision soon dissolved, and in its place came, terribly into focus, Father's face with fallen lower jaw above the white shroud, crying in thin voicelessness for him to hold his hands, while Jenny's remembered words came to him, *You see, Dickie, he really loved you, and all his children.* Other pictures swam into shape and focus, to be dissolved and succeeded by Father carrying him on his shoulders while he picked apples beside Mother, sunshine, ladders, and baskets, all the children happy in the orchard, butterflies and wasps and a big hornet—partridges tumbling fluttering down the stairs into the hall—Father shouting at Mother, rain streaming down the window panes, Father throwing plates on the floor, dashing the teapot against the wallpaper —other pictures, twisting and fragmentary, so that the viewer pressed his thighs against his ribs and a groan escaped him, heard by Hetty lying apart, remote from him though so close in body, Hetty in loneliness of spirit lying with eyes open to the darkness swirling all around her. His cry impelled her to shift around and take him in her arms, to which he yielded with a long sigh; then pulling the bedclothes around him, he exposed her entire back to the cold air of the night.

"There now, dear one," she murmured, feeling his tears on the flesh of her shoulder. "There now, you mustn't cry any more. Hetty is with you and will take care of you. Poor little orphan partridge, Hetty understands." He was a child to her, the constrictions binding him were gone; and with a deep sigh he lay relaxed, his legs stretched out and warm against her legs, his feet moving slightly up and down as though freeing themselves for their own instinctive rhythm, like the tail-wavings of a fish balanced in a stream.

"May I have a little more bedclothes, dearest? I think they must have slipped."

He was eager to cover her back, and leaned over her to tuck in the clothes.

Then with a deep sigh he turned to her and lay in her arms until voices outside and the banging of a door told that the Feeneys had returned from their music-hall jaunt; and turning over once again, with a muttered good-night he fell asleep and knew no more until the sparrows chirping on the gutters above the window opened at the top announced that it was another day—and Sunday, the day of rest, when he could lie in bed an extra half hour before getting up and thinking of a walk into the country, where perhaps they would see those little brown birds so typical of rural England—partridges already paired for the coming of spring.

Chapter 26

NEW PROSPECT

RICHARD OBTAINED leave from his office to attend the funeral of his father, and went down to Rookhurst on the following Tuesday evening. There were no untoward happenings before or after the burial, no irregular claimants to affection or property. After the service in church a score or so of mourners, composed of male relations and neighbours of the dead man, grouped themselves about the grave, wherein after the ritual and its immemorial words his two sons dropped earth upon the flower-laden coffin. About a hundred men and women of the village stood inside or beyond the mossy flint wall of the churchyard dressed in their sombre best clothes, an old man here and there in a smock, his beaver hat carried in thickened fingers.

Among the mourners was an elderly spinster aunt from Bath, whom Richard had not seen since he was a small boy, when she had presented him with a hobby-horse. Then there were his married sisters, Ada and Victoria, accompanied by their husbands. One was the steward, or agent as he preferred to be called, of a noble landed proprietor in Somerset, a connection of Jenny's; the other a member of a firm of London solicitors specializing in that affluent branch of the law known as conveyancing. This married sister lived in a villa in Epsom, a mile or two south of Cross Aulton. There was a third sister, the eldest of the family and unmarried, called Isabelle.

Richard was relieved when it was over; and the will having been read by the solicitor brother-in-law in the hollow-sounding house, the members of the family drove to the white-and-gold painted Spreycombe Arms in Colham for luncheon.

At half-past three, five of the figures in black—Isabelle, Victoria and her husband, Richard and Theodora—were seated in the train for Waterloo.

At first the conversation was general, then it became personal, and lapsed to the desultory as *The Times* was opened, *The Queen* and *Punch*, a three-volume novel by Mrs. Henry Wood, the *Medea* of Euripides in the original Greek, and some manuscript notebooks from the dead man's library. After a while rugs and footwarmers were adjusted, bodies leaned, eyes closed, quiet sighs were released, each personality withdrawn into its own world as the engine, now a-whistle with white plume, now growling out black mechanical thoughts, drew the carriage rocking and shaking on its iron wheels through fields and across streams and under hills, while the shadows of wayside hedgerow timber lengthened upon the yellow green of pastures as they rushed away from the declining sun into the stained air of the metropolis.

At Waterloo, after a cup of tea and bath bun at the station tea-room, Isabelle left them, departing by the Liverpool Street omnibus. She had for some years been a governess in the home of a minor canon of a Cathedral in the Home Counties. Relieved of their eldest sister's somewhat heavy presence, the younger members of the family went back for more tea and bath buns. Victoria, called Viccy, was two years older than Theodora; she had a great admiration and regard for her brother Dick, who had always been so kind and generous to the younger sisters and brother. "Now do keep your promise to come and see us, won't you, Dick? And of course bring Hetty over. Dora, you will keep him up to it, won't you?" George Lemon, her husband, a man with a dark sensitive face and soft voice, repeated the invitation as Richard and Theodora saw them off on the Epsom train.

Then it was Dora's turn to say goodbye. Richard saw her into the omnibus for Oxford Street and Regent's Park, where in between the Cambridge terms she was living with a family, part of the time coaching two small boys in the rudiments of Latin and Greek.

Feeling lonely, and thinking he would like to walk home and so clear his head, Richard set out for the Elephant and Castle and the New Kent Road. After a while he turned in a southerly direction, over high ground and through streets that he knew, having walked and bicycled that way home several times before.

He soon regretted his choice; for owing to the several cups of tea he had drunk at Waterloo Station buffet, he found that he needed a public convenience, and there was not likely to be one away from the main road. He looked about him for a mews into which he might slip; but the row of houses was uniform, so the only hope lay in finding a stables in the street of shops which lay across the crest of the hill before him.

He had reached the street above, and was striding along with swinging step when his nostrils were assailed by the pungent smell of the dung of horses. Several small boys, under the raucous cries of a leader, were collecting the stuff in pails upon the sett-stoned surface. As he hurried on, he reflected that he must have caught a cold in the kidneys, perhaps as he was standing by the grave, so sharp was the effort of having to contain himself.

In desperation he enquired, in a busy part of the street, of one who, with leather cowl and shoulder shield, had his back to him, a sack of coals upon his neck, ready to shoot it into a hole in the pavement. On the other side of the street was a public house, a woman's head in carved wood on its front.

"Excuse me, but can you tell me where there is a gentlemen's lavatory near here?"

"A gent's what?" asked the coalman, turning round and revealing a distastefully familiar face above bandy legs. "Blime, if it ain't li'l ole Tin Wills!"

Richard was taken aback; and stepping well clear of the coal-hole, he stared at the grimy fellow.

"Fancy meeting you 'ere!" said the coalman. "Why, you could knock me dahn wiv a fevver!" He appeared to be friendly, though that might be subterfuge on his part. Richard was on his guard.

"I asked you a civil question, and please let me have a civil answer."

"What's the gime this time, inspectin' o' coal 'oles? Got yer bull's-eye wiv yer? Nice thing on the Hillies, shinin' a light on ter honest blokes and then knockin' 'em on the napper, fancyin' yerself Bob Fitzsimmons! But there, you treated my bit respectable, I don't bear no malice, guv'nor." And a grin breaking over his face, the coalman said again, "Fancy seein' you 'ere, up by the old Nun's 'ead!"

Some of the boys in the street had stopped shovelling and scraping, "Crikey, boys, looks like some sport! A toff in a tall 'at doin' the dags o' a coalie!"

The coalman shot his sack expertly into the circular hole, shook it, folded it, and said, "Whatcher want, guv'nor?" The boys waited for the dags—challenge to fight it out.

"I want to relieve nature rather badly, and I do not know the whereabouts of this district. Can you help me, please?"

The coalman was puzzled. "Blime me, arst me annuvver! What's 'at, guv'nor?"

The boys, not so sure now, came closer. Others hastened up with pails, the smallest one, scarcely four years old, carrying a broken shovel. They gathered round—close-cropped heads; dirty ears, necks, and feet; open mouths; eyes blank, awaiting.

Suddenly the coalman turned, flung his free arm round his neck in imitation of a blow, and shouted, "Gert you!" at which the boys' eyes filled with light. "Shog off, you little bleeders!"

"Gerr! Laugh at 'im, boys! Laugh at 'im! Can't catch us, mister!"

Ignoring the taunts, the coalman turned to Richard again.

"Don't take no notice of them boys, guv'nor, they don't know no better. No 'arm in 'em, like my kids, out fer a bit o' fun, blime, you was a proper Farver Kissmus, you was, to my kids, givin' on 'm rides on yer sledge! Remember?"

"Oh, they were your lads, were they? Now look, I am sorry I have not made myself clear," said Richard. He lowered his voice, not wanting his request to be heard by the pressing heads of the boys.

The coalman listened.

"What, guv'nor?" he asked, mystified. "A ship on top 'v a 'ill? There ain't no such place rahnd 'ere." He scratched his head.

By now quite desperate, Richard used a biblical word which, as a small boy at school, had been pointed out to him soon after his arrival, in the Bible his Mother had given him, declaring that it was his best friend. Now he used the word in some shame, recalling the abhorrence with which he had been forced to read aloud the verse in Isaiah, chapter thirty-six, by the bully of the dormitory.

A light broke into the coalman's face.

"Blime, you want a urinal, guv'nor! Then why didn't you say so? There ain't one rahnd 'ere. I'll tell you what, there's a drain dahn the alley there, the landlord won't say nuffink, though you ain't bin in 'is boozer. Cripes, you toffs don't 'arf talk fancy!"

While Richard was occupied down the alley, the coalman stood on guard. As he came out, the leading boy of the composting party said, "Want to buy a pail o' manure, sir? For yer garding, sir? Make yer roses grow, sir! Only ha'penny a bucket, sir! Carry it anywhere yer like, sir!"

To which Richard gave a polite, "No, thank you."

Whereupon another boy, mocking the tone of his voice, began to chant:

> Not last night but the night afore
> Two tom cats came a-knocking at me door.
> I went dahn stairs to let 'em in
> They knocked me dahn wiv a rollin' pin.
> The rollin' pin was made of brass
> They sat on me and banged my ass.
> I went upstairs to get in bed
> They whirled the charley at my head
> I went dahnstairs to dry my frock
> I fell in the fire an' burnt my——"

then they scattered with jeers of delight as the black-faced coalie, having shot another sack into the hole, made as if to run at them with his long whip. Pausing, at sight of a constable walking towards them on his beat, the coalman said significantly, "You boys got a 'awker's licence? If yer ain't, I hadvise yer to 'op it quick!" at which they hurried away, with loaded pails and broken shovel.

"Haw-haw!" gloated the coalman, "'Awker's licence fer 'orse"—he looked at Richard—"mer-newer!"

Richard gave him sixpence, and having spun it, caught it, and spat on it for luck, the coalman cried, "Blime, you're posh, guv'nor!" and disappeared into the pub, whip and all, for what he called a wet, otherwise a quart of porter, and two packets of Wild Woodbines with the change, leaving Richard to continue his way, relieved and buoyant in his thoughts. Often the figments of that night upon the Hill had arisen to disturb his mind. Urinal—urinare—perhaps a survival of Roman Londinium. Let Mr. Mundy put that piece of historical information in his pipe and smoke it!

People were not so bad when you came to know them. There was Mr. Mundy the Vicar, a thoroughly decent man, and the whist drives in the church hall with Hetty had been enjoyable. Then there was tennis to come, in the club he proposed to join;

and the proximity to London, being also on the fringe of the real countryside, was not without advantages. Nevertheless, he would not be sorry to see the end of Comfort Road. Some new houses were soon to be erected upon the eastern slope of the Hill, just outside the area intended for a public park; and since he was the possessor of over two thousand pounds capital, he was entitled at least to look around! And striding along, he began to hum to himself *The Arab's Farewell to his Steed.*

Turning northwards, he descended to the Old Kent Road again and there took a tram which eventually brought him down Pit Vale and to the tree-lined street where he and Hetty had walked on Christmas Eve. It was a pleasant borough, seen in the clear March evening light, its inns with white posts and hanging signs in the yards in front of them, set with pumps and wooden drinking troughs for horses; the white-and-yellow-painted weather-boarded cottages in rows between the gardens of larger houses hidden behind trees, each approached by its carriage sweep behind tall gates of wrought iron. It was quite a pleasant neighbourhood, though rather noisy with the passing of so many wheels and hoofs, while the clang of the tram bell would in time no doubt come to jar upon the ear.

No, the place to live was upon higher ground, preferably up by the Hill. With this expectancy he got off the tram at the junction with Randiswell Lane and walked westwards to the hump-backed bridge over the brook and the railway lines, and so to the cluster of weather-boarded cottages which was the hamlet of Randiswell, spoiled, he thought, by the vulgar gin-palace erected on the corner before the station.

After leaving the hamlet the lane forked, one turn leading up from the lower end of Charlotte Road, which here curved to the right. The houses had been built on both sides of the road, and trees planted on the sidewalks. After three minutes' energetic walk upwards, the grassy slopes of the Hill came into view, with the elms darkly outlined in the sunset beyond the far end of the crest. Nearer loomed the mass of a square building of weathered red brick, along the southern front of which was affixed a large board with the letters WEST KENT GRAMMAR SCHOOL in gold-leaf, readable in daylight from Charlotte Road three hundred yards or so below. There was a track leading up to the school, and it was to the right of the track that the site for the new houses was being cleared. Piles of scaffolding poles and planks had been dumped there beside squares of bricks, heaps of gravel and sand brought by tumbrils from the pits in Blackheath, together with loads of quicklime not yet slaked for the mixing of mortar.

There was enough light left to read the details on the notice-board at the bottom of the track, where it branched off from the lower section of Charlotte Road. Richard read that "desirable semi-detached villas were to be built for sale on a leasehold of ninety-nine years." The terms could be learnt on application to the builder at his estate office. He stared at the white board with its black lettering with a feeling of adventurous anticipation not unmixed with trepidation, before walking up the track.

The sunset was dying out across the grassy slopes of the Hill. When he stopped to listen he heard the cries of lambs in the fold adjoining the dark school, the answering deeper notes of the ewes, and sometimes the *tinkle-tonkle* of the belled wether.

Away to the right came the last sleepy twilight cawing of rooks. There was another rookery in a group of elms to the east of the track. The moon was rising through them, round and yellow. As he stood there he heard a cock partridge calling in the pasture before him. The call note was husky, wheezy; he remembered Father telling him once that it was just like the turning of the great wooden lock in the door of the Corn Barn. Father! at rest now, beside Mother.

The evening was calm, the air still and yet warm from the day of sunshine, and as he stood there in the half light, while a star-point shone steadily in the height of the sky, he believed for the moment that the dead were at peace. For the moment he was at peace with himself. The reality of two thousand pounds had relieved much anxiety.

He decided to walk up the track, and so to the crest of the Hill. There was no doubt that it was a good position for a house; and though he would have preferred one standing in its own grounds, if only a quarter of an acre, that would be out of the question, since the price being asked for the Hill was said to be fifteen hundred pounds the acre. Smaller lots could not be purchased freehold, but only leasehold.

Even so, a house in that new short road would possess several advantages which would not be found readily elsewhere in the district. The subscription list towards the purchase of the forty acres of the Hill was growing, and under the London County Council it would remain an open space in perpetuity. That would mean a pleasant vista in front of the house, of grass instead of an opposing row of brick. House property was likely to appreciate in the district, and if, as was generally believed, there was to be a general election that year, with Gladstone and his Free Trade radicalism thrown out, Conservatism would return and tariffs help to end the disastrous dumping of foreign goods and food into the home market, which had caused the ruinous condition of agriculture.

A lease of nine and ninety years; a long time before the house would have to be surrendered to the ground-landlord. Ninety-nine years—nineteen hundred and ninety three—why, anything might be happening by that time! A lease of ninety-nine years would see him out, and any family he and Hetty might have as well.

Somewhat alarmed by what all these thoughts were leading him to, Richard increased his pace, and coming to the top of the Hill, turned westward past the grammar school and so down the slope to the continuation of Charlotte Road now marked in the crepuscular night by the steady shine of lamp-posts.

When he turned into Comfort Road his footsteps pressed lighter as he passed the end houses across the way where lived the disreputable families, thought of which was part of the permanent depression of one side of his mind. Still, there was no bad blood now with the coalman—he hoped. Safely past the houses, his stride increased, as he began to think of Hetty, wondering how she had fared while alone in the house. Two thousand pounds! Now for an evening in the green leather armchair, reading.

All was well; and after supping off a bowl of hot milk-sop, so easy to digest when he was tired, Richard sat before the fire in his armchair to read more of his Father's manuscript journal; and closing the volume just before bed-time, marking the place with a woodpigeon's feather picked up in Rookhurst churchyard, he carried out the slop-pail and buried its contents on top of the railway embankment.

The next morning, a Thursday, he set off for the office at his usual time, while hoping that the notice of his father's death, which brother John had sent to the *Post*, would be appearing in that paper that morning, and so settle any possible doubts in the office about the authenticity of the reason of absence.

He read the notice several times in the carriage on the way to London Bridge; and resumed his work in the Town Department the more contentedly that several of his colleagues had come to him and expressed their sympathy. Two more days to Saturday, and then he hoped to cycle out by himself into the country.

Hetty was not looking forward to Saturday. Indeed, she was in such a state of apprehension by the time of the landlord's arrival that she had a nervous headache. Richard had again told her that she must be firm with the landlord, and withhold payment of the rent when he called unless he gave her a "specific undertaking" to replace the broken lavatory pan within one week. She had to give him a message, should he try and avoid the issue, that Mr. Maddison intended to report the matter to the authorities unless he promised to undertake the work immediately.

Hetty dreaded the idea of meeting the landlord, Mr. Winner. He was a red-haired man with a large head. His clean-shaven ruddy face did not smile. He had a blunt, determined manner. When shortly after eleven o'clock she saw his horse and cart draw up by the kerb, her throat went dry, and taking the three florins from the pewter mug on the dresser, she went into the front room and waited there trepidantly for the iron gate to open and the knocker to strike against the door.

When the landlord arrived Hetty at the open door did her best to tell him that the matter of the pan was urgent. She held the three coins in her clenched hand, determined not to hand them over until he had promised to get the work done. She gave him Richard's message, omitting the part about the threatened reporting, while he stood there with stony eyes. She ended by saying that she hoped the pan would be done, for really, it was ever so necessary.

Mr. Winner gave her a glance, and did not reply for a moment. He was a cattle dealer from the Deptford market, and he drove over to collect his rents every Saturday morning in his T-cart, drawn by a broken-winded chestnut horse that had been a hunter. His curt manner and expressionless stare, so dreaded by Hetty, was due to a habit of repeatedly assessing the value of individual bullocks in the pens after unloading from the cattle-boats, and then of bidding for them in bunches, up to his determined price, which he never exceeded. He bought only for resale to butchers. In the same way he sized up men with whom he did business; the quality of beef supplied on the hoof depended on the quality, or otherwise, of the butcher for whom it was bought. Butchers whom he respected for their skill as tradesmen always got the best beasts for slaughter.

He was an honest dealer, and well-to-do; he invested his money in bricks and mortar, for a yield of ten per centum; and he collected the rents himself because he enjoyed looking after his own affairs, for business to him was as the breath of life.

In addition to enjoying his business, the landlord enjoyed a pastime. He did not allow the pastime to come before business, but there were times when business and pastime, at least in the house property game, could be worked together. His pastime was women. He knew the value of ordinary street women: fourpence; but street women did not interest him. Repairs and decorations did; for those who were keenest to keep their places in proper order were also the best in other directions. If a women was nice to him sometimes, he could be nice to her. He was by nature a sympathetic man, with an inner core of diffidence concealed under a face generally expressionless.

"'Ow do I know the pan was not broke by droppin' suthin' into it?" asked Mr. Winner of Hetty as she stood at the open door.

"It's cracked where the ice was," said Hetty eagerly. "The part fell out on the brickwork, as soon as the thaw came. It was impossible to use it when it froze." She blushed.

"Let's have a look."

Mr. Winner's stomach was covered by a large leather satchel with several compartments heavy with coins. He swung the satchel over a thigh, and pushed past her into the passage, pressing himself against her as he did so. He felt her hard roundness under the loose gown she wore, and grunted to himself. A down-calver! And he had never noticed it before! He must be getting old.

Mr. Winner gave the broken utensil but a moment's glance; then returned to the kitchen. Hetty was standing there waiting in the hope that he would see how necessary the work really was. She was in no way apprehensive otherwise, for Mr. Winner's thoughts never showed upon his face.

"'Ow d'yer like livin' 'ere?" he enquired, regarding her fresh and open face.

"Oh, my husband and I find it such a dear little house."

"You kip the place well. Is it done-up upstairs like vis?"

"Oh yes!" said Hetty. "Only a different style, of course. Mr. Maddison and I did it ourselves, we took ten days to do it."

"If you'll pardon the question, you're expectin', ain't yer? I'm a family man myself, got seven."

"How nice!" exclaimed Hetty. "I think it's so much happier for children to have lots of brothers and sisters! Mr. Maddison was one of seven."

He looked at her pink cheeks and bright eyes. She had class. And she wasn't stuck up.

"I'll send a man to replace that pan soon as I can. Act o' God, they call it; act o' Jack Frost I say. Neither won't pay so I will. You ain't got no bust pipes?"

"Oh no," replied Hetty. "You see, Mr. Maddison is so very careful, and all through the cold spell, he kept his dark lantern alight under the pipe." She pointed to the lantern, standing on the shelf over the kitchen range. "Oh, the rent. I nearly forgot it."

"Ta," said the landlord, taking the three florins. "Wish all me tenants were as keerful. Well, I must be gettin' on. I'll send a mason first thing Monday morning. Tata."

When Richard came home at two o'clock, he was met by a jubilant Hetty at the open door.

"Well, you seem to be in high feather," he remarked. "What have you been up to now?"

"Ah! Guess!"

"Mrs. Mundy has dropped some bits of paste-board through the letter-box."

"No, be serious, Dickie."

"Well, out with it. What is the mystery?"

He was standing before her, his face rather strained. "Come on, tell a fellow."

"Yes, dear, of course, naturally. I'll soon have your chump chop fried. The landlord has promised to send a man to replace the broken pan on Monday. He is ever such a nice man, and has seven children, he told me."

"I will bet he only agreed to have the work done, knowing that otherwise the sanitary inspector would soon be after him. I know that kind of customer of old."

Hetty thought that this was not the case; but she said nothing: it was best to keep her thoughts to herself.

Outside the house a barrel-organ began to play *Il Trovatore*. As soon as she had put the chop into the frying-pan, Hetty ran to the door, and opening it saw the Italian in the same oversize bowler hat and curled moustaches, bowing and smiling, while the little girl danced with the tambourine on the pavement. The monkey, in uniform, was perching upon the box. Hetty was overjoyed to see them all, for she had been thinking during the long dreary weeks that perhaps the child or the monkey or both had died of starvation in the cold. She put her penny in the tambourine, and with a wave of her hand ran back into the kitchen. Dickie was upstairs, changing his clothes for the Saturday afternoon walk into the country. He told himself that she ought not to be left alone; and so he had given up the idea of a cycle ride, and instead he would take her to Cutler's Pond, near the Seven Fields of Shrofften.

Chapter 27

THE BIG TROUT

AFTER DINNER they crossed the high road, to walk down the lane beside the cemetery. On the corner was a stone-mason's yard. The lane was enclosed by the wall on one side and the cleft-oak fences of the back gardens of Charlotte Road on the other. The wall led on for a quarter of a mile or so before curving round the lane to another iron gate with another stone-mason's yard, heaped with white marble tombstones and monuments, immediately outside it. Leaving the blank and dolorous sight behind they continued down the lane which led to Randiswell. There was a row of houses on their left, and on the other hand an open arable field where winter wheat was being harrowed by a man with a pair of bay horses. Whenever he had a chance to look at anything to do with farming, Richard usually stopped and watched.

"How long will this land be under cultivation, I wonder? Everywhere money is going into bricks and mortar."

Half way down the incline he stopped again and pointed to a notice board erected at the corner of the field. "There you are, I told you so! Messrs. Antill Brothers have purchased the Bridge House Farm for the erection of modern villas! Antill, what a name! That's just what London Bridge looks like nowadays—a swarm of ants."

As he declaimed, a pair of partridges arose with whirring of wings and glided away over the field.

"Goodbye Perdix perdix," he said.

"I saw a hare on the Hill yesterday, Dickie. I meant to tell you before."

"Yes, I have seen it occasionally. It will not last much longer, I fear."

"Still, the Hill will never be built upon, will it, dear?"

Richard had not yet mentioned the idea of the new house. "You like the Hill, do you?"

"Very much."

He decided not to say anything yet awhile, lest he raise false hopes.

Hetty wondered if it were a favourable time to give him Papa's kind regards; and the message about the cobbler sticking to his last; she had waited during the past month for a favourable opportunity, but so far had not found one.

"The Hill will be such a nice place for children to play on," she said a moment or two later, and blushed.

Richard took her arm. "It must be eight and a half months now, surely? We are in the second week of April, and any moment now your favourite swallows will be coming back. Will they bring a boy with them?"

"I do hope so, dearest."

"Well, do not be too disappointed if it is a girl, will you? D'you feel able to walk so far as Cutler's Pond?"

"Oh yes, I am quite all right, really, Dickie."

"Well, you know, I must see to it that you do not overtax your strength."

They came to the hamlet of Randiswell, beyond which were rows of houses in course of construction. There was also a row of small children sitting outside the "Railway," the public house of industrial-urban design on the corner leading to the station, opposite a mission house. Walking over the bridge they turned down a footpath beside the river, coming to a church and graveyard where old tomb-stones leaned under yew-trees. In front of the church was the high road leading away south into the country.

It was a pleasant walk. Elms and chestnuts lining the road were coming into leaf. They passed weather-boarded cottages and houses set back in spacious gardens behind wrought-iron railings and weathered brick walls—houses dating from Queen Anne and the early Georges. There was a row of Almshouses, built about the time of the Great Fire of London by the vicar of the parish church in those days, according to a stone plaque. Then there was the new Workhouse, or Infirmary as it was called, with its Lunatic and Casual Wards, part of the new growth that was expressed through the Local Government Board.

"This place," said Richard, pointing with his stick across the road, "was until recently the home of Mr. Rowland, the original Rowland of Macassar Oil—to whom many a housewife must owe an oily grudge."

"Oh yes, the antimacassar, of course, naturally!" laughed Hetty.

They walked on, arm in arm. About a mile down the road there was an old inn with a bull painted on its sign. Beyond were the open fields and meadows of Kent. Hetty knew the district by now, and had come to love it, through many walks with Dickie.

It being Saturday afternoon, several people like themselves were walking into the country. The high road was drying after recent rains, but the wide plashes made by so many passing wheels and hoofs still held water.

Larks sang above the meadows on the west of the road, where the Randisbourne, rush-grown below its banks, gleamed along its wandering course. On the other side of the road the land sloped gently to a wooded skyline. Corn, roots, and cabbages grew in the fields behind the thorn hedge. There were raised grassy banks on both sides of the roadway, with cuts through them to draining ditches dug below the footpaths. Richard, exultant at the thought of a day and a half's freedom before him, amused himself as he walked along the grassy bank on the left of the road by trying to determine, after but a moment's glance, which of the cornfields they passed were down to oats, wheat, or barley.

Pheasants were feeding in the fields. Hetty, walking happily by the hedge, was glad to see Dickie leaping the drain-cuts in the bank. He was a boy again. "Hark, a cuckoo! Turn your money, and wish!"

It was the first time that year. Richard stopped, and solemnly turned over all the coins in his pocket; then taking the crown piece from a waistcoat pocket, he gave it to Hetty, with his finger on his lips, lest speech spoil the luck.

Without realizing time or distance they came to the bottom of Whitefoot Lane. Beyond the turning were high brick walls, with tall white wooden doors at an entrance, enclosing a manor house and its garden for a considerable length of one side of the road. Across the way was a group of weather-boarded cottages, among them a tiny dame's shop scarcely the width of a man's arms, with a stone step leading up to the threshold. In the window was a jumble of toffee-apples and arrowroot biscuits, china mugs and balls of string, a child's rag-doll, boys' whip tops, clothes pegs, roots of licorice, a Valentine card, a plateful of big sticky striped humbugs, a strip of leather boot-laces, glass globes filled with water in which minute painted cottages and trees were snow-bound, and strings of red Chinese crackers. These and other objects were fascinating to Hetty, who stared at them, imagining herself to be a child again with her first penny. Such treasures behind the little bow window! She had looked into it with Dickie on several previous occasions, and each time he had made, more or less, the same kind of remark, "You must bring your son, one day, to my especial shop. Many's the time I have bought humbugs in here, and arrowroot biscuits, and ginger pop." He tried the brass latch. "M'dame is out this afternoon! Bad luck!"

Walking on, they came to a mill at the lower end of a pond, with its row of white oak posts and railings protecting it from the road. The mill-house was forsaken, the glass of its windows broken, while upon its walls and roof were clusters of ivy, many of the sprays of which, killed by the recent intense cold, were dry and brown. Sparrows chattered and scolded there. A notice board, covered with the marks of dried mud flung at it, announced that Cutler's Mill was for sale.

Richard and Hetty peered at the brick arch of the tunnel leading to the mill-wheel under the building. Something was floating against the iron bars of the grill placed there to keep back encumbrances which otherwise might clog the wheel when it was turning. It was a sack, tied at the neck to contain an object within. Through a rent in the hessian a slender hairy paw, with pallid pads uppermost, stuck out. Perhaps it had been in the sack all through the winter, lying under the ice—all alone: perhaps even now its ghost was haunting the pond, sadly, waiting for its master to come back to it, and the paw was held out to shake its master's hand. Hetty turned away from her thoughts with a quivering mouth.

Richard noticed the paw, too; his feelings were extended beyond those of pity to indignation and anger, as in his mind he imagined a brutal close-cropped head, a muffler round its neck: and he who had done such a thing ought to be tied in a sack and thrown into the water, to see how it felt to be treated like that. The figment had the face, but blurred, of Thomas Turney.

A water-wagtail with yellow breast was perching on one of the white posts through which the tubular iron railing extended round the roadside verge of the pond. The water glittered with the westering sunshine. Moorhens were swimming around an islet, grown with willows and a wild cherry tree in bloom, in the middle of the half acre of water. The Randisbourne brook entered the upper end of the mill-pond underneath a bridge, and it was this bridge that Richard made for.

Whenever on previous occasions they had walked to Cutler's Pond he had always gone on alone to the bridge in order to look over the parapet into the water beneath. He had never seen a trout there more than ten inches in length, about half a pound in weight; but he had a belief that in the mill-pond were several big fish. Always when he approached the bridge he hoped that he would see one "of aldermanic proportions"; and as he drew near to the bridge that afternoon he warned Hetty not to look over the parapet too suddenly, lest she frighten the anticipated wonder below. "I will peer over this side," he said, indicating the pond, "and do you go and peer over the other side. Slowly, extremely slowly, please to remember!" He considered that no fish of any size would be in the upper stream, so Hetty could do no harm by looking there.

While he was peering over the lower parapet, methodically searching the flow of water past plants of water-parsnip, cress, and brook-lime, Hetty was gazing at nothing in particular from the other parapet, and breathing the sunny air sweetened for her by the gentle rustling of new leaves and the singing of so many birds.

The brook flowed slowly down from the wood of alder and willows. Leaning against the parapet, she listened to the cooing of a dove hidden somewhere among the trees; then quite near to her a chaffinch, gay blue and brown, sang on a bough of hawthorn. From the top of a poplar came the bold piping of a thrush, a bird loved in childhood ever since Mamma had told her one morning that it was singing, *Get up, Hetty! Get up, Hetty!* She stood there, lost in her thoughts, until suddenly remembering her purpose she looked down into the water immediately below the bridge and saw with a start an enormous fish leisurely waving its tail just under the surface.

It was so unexpected a sight, and so near—the black spots were clearly seen, with red among them—and the dark head with pale mouth and red gills opening as it breathed—that she stood staring down at it, feeling it to be almost frighteningly unreal. It was the first trout she had ever been close enough to observe in detail, by herself. She had seen dark movements often in the pond at Cross Aulton, thin remote shadows which were trout; but never had she seen one so close, its eyes clearly visible, every spot distinct, even the red spot on the little fin near its tail.

Quivering with excitement she withdrew slowly and crossed the road, to wait behind Richard's bended back, hesitatingly, lest she disturb him. Peering round his arm, she saw that he was dropping tiny pieces of paper into the water, and watching them ride away with the current.

"Dickie."

"Hullo. Look over slowly. There are a lot of minnows below here, and I do not want them disturbed. Any moment a big trout may dash among them, on the feed! I say! Did you see that? Look, there he goes!"

A kingfisher, uttering a keen whistle, had shot under the bridge. It flew straight over the pond, suddenly to alight with flash of blue and green wings on a branch of willow growing out of the islet. "Isn't he a beauty?"

"Yes."

"Your friend Mrs. Duck, or Mallard, has a hat made of the wings of those birds."

"She isn't my friend, Dickie, really she is only a business acquaintance," explained Hetty. "But I remember that hat she wore, we saw it on our lovely cab-ride together. Ah well!"

"Regretting the old days, I suppose?"

"No dear, not in the very least."

"You look rather pale. What is the matter?"

"Only a momentary qualm, dear, nothing at all really. I think the rhubarb I ate at dinner must have disagreed with me. But there, please don't take any notice, I shall be quite all right. I came to tell you, there's ever so big a fish just above the bridge."

The pain made her feel a little sick, and she was relieved when Richard walked over the road, and creeping to the parapet, gradually insinuated his head over it. Left alone, Hetty waited to feel better; but the next moment he was saying, "I cannot see any fish."

"It was there a moment ago, Dickie."

She crossed the road, and looked down. The stream, about a foot in depth, flowed slow and clear and empty over the green growths on its bed.

"Your fish must have come out of a mare's nest!"

"Really, Dickie, I did see one."

He peered again, searching the flow, his sight adjusted to detect the least shadowy stir or slightest variation of hue in water which might mean the submerged back of a fish.

"That little kingfisher is not likely to have disturbed a trout of any size. I expect you imagined it."

"I did see one, truly, ever so spotty, like currants."

"Are you sure it was not an old currant pudding floating down, thrown away by one of the lunatics in the grounds through which the river flows here? Come now, how big was it, really?"

Hetty held out her hands. "It was quite as long as this, really it was."

"What, you ask me seriously to believe that a trout two feet long, which would mean a weight of five or six pounds, can exist in this little brook! Still, one could live in the millpond, I suppose, and grow to that size. Perhaps what you saw was a pike. I expect there are several in the pond. Do you know what a pike looks like?"

"Isn't it a sort of alligator, or some such thing?"

"Well, an alligator is a reptile, and not found in England outside of zoos and aquaria, while a pike is a fish—though he looks rather like an alligator."

"Yes, dear, that's what I mean."

"Well, you said 'sort of alligator', which means a kind or species of alligator, which has legs; while a fish has fins."

"Yes, of course, naturally," said Hetty. "How silly of me."

"Not 'silly'," replied Richard. "But it is a loose way of thinking, and of speaking. Now you would not call a dumpling a loaf, would you? Though both are made of flour and water."

"Yes, dear."

"Though perhaps some husbands would not be able to distinguish between what was a loaf baked by their wives, and what was a dumpling," he concluded, facetiously. "Well now, where is your famous trout that is a sort of alligator?"

"It was down there," said Hetty, pointing. "I saw it quite distinctly."

"Perhaps it was an hallucination! Perhaps you have caught the habit from the lunatics inside there!" He was joking; but his words terrified Hetty. Something inside her seemed to go thump, as though dropped. She felt sickeningly afraid.

"You are looking pale, Hetty. Do you feel unwell?"

"I shall be all right after a little rest, Dickie. I am so sorry about the fish not being there. Are you serious about the lunatics in the woods here?"

"Yes, it is a private mental home. People suffering from delusions; perhaps your trout is a mental case, too, thinking he is a whale of a fellow."

She had to support herself on the parapet. Had she seen a fish, or only imagined it? Was her mind deranged, from the blow Papa gave her? It was her secret dread that she would become mentally affected, and the baby be born—she dared not think of the word.

"—though with so many people bicycling nowadays, it is not so secluded in summer as it used to be," she heard him saying. "Now I wonder if that fish of yours has his lie under this bridge? It is possible, of course, though his real hide would be in the pond, where he would be safe from eels and otters."

She nodded, not daring to trust her voice.

"Eels eat any fish they can get hold of. They are cannibals, like most fish. I have watched them in packs, attacking a sick pike. They attack the gills first."

Hetty felt detached from the scene about her. Perhaps she was going to have one of her bilious attacks, which usually laid her up for twenty-four hours or longer. Dickie did his best in the house on such occasions, but the worst part of it was that he usually found so much that was wrong in the scullery and kitchen and larder, and he would not have Mrs. Feeney in to get his breakfast, but insisted on putting everything in order himself, complaining as he did so that he would miss his train. Oh, she was silly to have eaten that rhubarb given her by Mr. Pooley, it was not quite cooked perhaps, or the tin inside of the copper pan being worn thin had caused a little poisoning. She must get it seen to by the tinsmith before Dickie noticed it. She felt so queer, like being on board ship when the boat began to roll and pitch at the same time. If only Mamma were there to help her—she felt so strange, so ill—perhaps the big fish—perhaps her brain—a coldness of terror held her leaning upon the bridge.

It was then that, looking up the lane golden-hazy in the declining sun, she felt another deep shock. The lane was half dissolved by the haze; but darkly outlined in it was the shape of a great bear walking upright towards her, preceded by its swaying shadow. A smaller figure walked beside it, casting a lesser shadow.

Dickie was far away, gone across the road again to lean over the bridge. She managed to call out to him in a voice that made him turn round and hurry across the road to her where she clung to the parapet.

"It's all right, Hetty, do not be alarmed, the bear-leader will not let the animal hurt you. Really, you must not let yourself be upset, especially at this time——" Her momentary piteous stare induced in him a trace of impatience. Even the consequent thought that she might be a little unwell did not lessen his intolerance for an almost childish state of mind. It was time she grew up.

"Surely you have seen a dancing bear before?"

"Oh Dickie, is it real? Is it *true*? I thought I was losing my reason! First the huge fish, then the bear. Oh, I am so glad I am all right!"

The bear-leader came nearer. He had on a grey felt hat, a white short cutaway jacket with German silver buttons. His brown knees were bare, he wore short leather trousers, supported by leather braces and cross straps. White stockings with heavy nailed boots completed his garb. There was a concertina slung on his back.

The bear dropped on its four pads, but at a cry from its owner and a touch of the alpenstock it gathered itself upon its hindlegs again.

"I wonder where he comes from," said Richard. "My German is not good enough to ask him." But as the man came upon the bridge, raising his hat, Richard said, "Grusse Gott, Herr Barenführer."

"Grusse Gott, mein herr Englander," exclaimed the other, a wide smile revealing even white teeth under his moustaches. "Sprechen sie Deutsche, mein herr Englander?"

In halting and imperfect German, learned from his mother and from her maid Minnie who had acted also as the younger children's nurse, Richard talked to the Austrian, while the bear sat down on its haunches and scratched. The bear-leader was delighted to find someone who was a link with his own country, and when Richard told him that his grandmother had come from the hills of Wurtemburg, he insisted that his bear perform a special dance for them, then and there on the bridge. And unslinging his concertina, he gave his pole to the bear, and began to play a tune.

To Hetty it seemed a pathetic performance, for though she had not understood a word of German, she knew by the music, by the light in the man's smiling face that in fancy he was back among his own people. She felt sorry for him, and for the bear too, taken from its home in the forest on the mountainside, to be a chained captive wandering from place to place, and made to lumber about like that for its living, while holding a pole in its arms. She was glad when it was over, and when Dickie gave the man a shilling, she was proud of him for being so kind to a poor foreigner.

"I have always wanted to visit my mother's people," he said, when the strange couple had gone away, the Austrian to play his instrument outside an inn across the road called the Green Man. "So many of the peasants simply cannot live on the poor mountain soil, you know, and are driven to seek a living elsewhere. Many go to the United States of America. The Old World is now overcrowded, thanks to the machine replacing handicraft."

"Yes, I suppose so."

"How are you feeling now, Hetty?"

"Oh, quite well, thank you, dearest."

"Fancy being frightened of a tame bear!"

Hetty's dread had been so dark that she had not been able even to confide in Theodora, which was a pity, as Theodora suspected what Hetty must be feeling; but Theodora's delicacy and sense of the privacy of another's feelings had prevented her from speaking to Hetty of it, since Hetty had not spoken first.

A greater happiness, or relief from anxiety, was soon to come upon Hetty: for a short while afterwards, when Richard took a last look over the upper side of the bridge, he gave a low whistle of amazement; and beckoning her with his hand behind his back to join him, he whispered, "Your trout is back again! Look over very, very gradually! Is he not a beauty!"

He was amazed and delighted that such a small stream should hold such a big fish.

"It must be all of four pounds in weight. Quiet now! There is a hatch of fly coming down!"

The fish below slanted up and with a lazy curl of its tail took something just under the surface. It left the least ripple, soon to be smoothed away in the gentle flow of the water. Richard was in two moods as he stared at it: hoping that it would never be seen by anyone else, never be caught; and wondering how such a fish might be taken on a fly. Only by wading in the pond, and casting a dry fly sideways under the bridge. But the mud in the pond must be three feet deep at least! No one could wade there! Good!

The trout must be taking nymphs, he thought, for as he watched, it swung sideways and sucked in something under the skin of the water, not breaking the surface. Then it swung back to its place again. Peering intently, he saw red spots among the black spots on its shoulders.

"This is a wonderful sight, worth all the rest of the walk," he whispered. "It is your fish, you know. You spotted it first. Now do not move your head, whatever you do. I cannot quite see what he is taking. Ah! There's a dun hatching. See over there by that black branch lying out of the water. Oh, that beastly bird has taken it!"

The chaffinch had dropped off the hawthorn branch and, fluttering, had seized in its beak the minute slow rising whorl of pale colour. "It is an olive dun," he whispered. Then, "You have scared it now, you cuckoo!" for only a stir of silt drifting away in the water was left to tell where the fish had been. "Any sudden movement frightens a fish, especially a trout."

"I am sorry, dear, I think the rhubarb has really upset me."

Hetty was gripping the parapet.

"Well, I bet he will not come back now, for some time," said Richard. "I hope those loafers over there outside the Green Man haven't been watching us. They would soon stick a dung-fork into its back, and heave it out for their pigs to eat."

"Perhaps they have children hungry, dear."

"But whatever has that got to do with a beautiful fish remaining in its native waters?"

"I thought that perhaps poor children would benefit from it, dear; surely no one would waste it on a pig?"

"But why should it not be left where it is? I have no sentimental feelings about people being allowed to please themselves, whether they be individuals or big corporations or companies. Look at the mill, shut up and falling derelict. Foreign grain coming in at Liverpool and London and Bristol, steam mills built there and insured for fifty thousand pounds and more. All of England will soon be industrialised, the rivers poisoned out."

"Yes dear, I am sure you are right."

The thought of being so far away from home was almost

more than Hetty could bear. She walked by his side, stiffly.

"Do you feel any better?"

"It's the rhubarb still, I think, Dickie."

"Well, you may walk it off. Try, anyway. Are you tired?"

"I am rather, Dickie. But there, I will be all right. I am so sorry to have spoiled your walk."

"Let us take the horse-tram outside the Bull, if you can get so far."

They walked on down the road; until, realizing that she was really not well, Richard stopped and, showing a concern that he did not really feel, said that perhaps he ought to call the doctor to her when they got home. "Here, take my arm."

"Thank you, dear. I shall be all right, really I shall. I can rest when I get home."

"But you said you had a pain. Now you say you are only a little tired."

"The pain only comes and goes, dear. It is the rhubarb, I am sure."

"It might be the baby, you know."

"I don't think so, dear, please don't worry about me."

"I am not worrying about you. I am only saying what would occur to most husbands at this time. Lean on my arm."

"Thank you, dear. I am so sorry I have spoiled your Saturday walk."

"Now just do not worry any more. Lean more on me. You can spot a trout quicker than I can, anyway."

"I am so glad you saw it, Dickie."

They walked on for a few minutes, without speaking; then realizing the unusual weight on his arm, Richard became genuinely anxious. When she stopped, and with a sickly little smile said, "I think I ought to go behind the hedge, do you mind," he at once looked for a gap, and leading her to it, stood on guard while she went behind the trunk of an elm rising out of the hedgerow.

Along the road fast dog-carts and an occasional racing tandem with rubber-treaded wheels were returning towards London. There had been a football match that afternoon at Stumbleshill, a village distant by a mile from Cutler's Pond, and now some of the spectators from the Royal Military Academy at Woolwich were returning in their sporting turn-outs. While Richard waited, three gigs painted and varnished in varying styles of red and blue, each drawn by a pony racing at the trot with outflung forelegs and followed by a spotted Dalmatian dog, came abreast down the road and dashed past him. He watched the race with mingled feelings of envy and disdain. Chappies with too much money!

The young gentlemen-cadets, moustached and smoking cheroots, dressed in check coats with yellow waistcoats and grey bowler hats, diminished into the distance; to be followed by half a dozen youths on bicycles, bumping and rattling over the rutted grey surface of the road as they pedalled furiously in imitation of the gigs.

After waiting for a couple of minutes, and hearing nothing from Hetty, Richard called out, "Are you all right?" and listened. He heard only the cawing of rooks from the rookery at Cutler's Pond, and the remote clopping of hooves passing away down the high road. Then pushing through the gap in the hedge, he saw his wife with bent head, leaning against the trunk of the elm tree. Going close to her, he saw that her mouth was clenched, and her eyes were shut.

"Are you ill, Hetty? Tell me now, are you in pain?"

She opened her eyes. He heard her whisper, "I want Mamma". Then giving him a distraught stare, she managed to say, with an attempt at a smile, "I am terribly sorry, I think the baby is coming. Oh, please don't be angry with me."

Richard breathed deeply, to steady his agitation; and his deeper self taking over, he said calmly, as he pressed her hand to reassure her, "You will be all right, Hetty. Sit down, put your back to the tree—here, sit on my jacket"—he pulled it off, and placed it on the ground—"now, do not worry, we shall have you home in no time. Be as easy as you can—I will go for help——"

He touched her forehead with his hand and then said, "I do not think that you have got much of a temperature, anyway. Now I shall be on the path only a little way yonder. I shall stop the first suitable vehicle and then all will be well. I shall be within ear-shot," he added soothingly, "now just keep calm. Do you think it will happen soon? Oh Lord, I hope not."

"I don't think so, dear," said Hetty, now smiling, more at her ease. "The pains are better now. You are so kind, Dickie. Please don't worry."

With a wave of his hand, he left her and returned to the path. An old woman with a weather-brown wrinkled face was slouching along a couple of hundred yards away, with a basket of watercress on her arm. "Fine fresh watercreases, my fine gen'elman?" she muttered. His hand waved her away, and she slouched on again.

Nobody and nothing else was in sight to the diminishing figures of the cyclists. It must be after tea-time. He looked at his watch; it was nearly half-past five. He returned to Hetty, relieved to see her looking easier.

"I feel ever so much better now, dear. Perhaps it was the rhubarb after all."

"Oh lor, let it be one thing or the other!" he laughed. "I suppose you have not been eating any tinned stuff?"

"No, dear, of course not. Not since you forbade me to buy it."

"That foreign imported stuff should be prohibited. If we had a decent government in power, instead of kow-towing to Free Trade, which is ruining the real England for the sake of a few jumped-up millionaires. Now——"

Hearing the approaching sound of a trotting horse, Richard broke off his political disquisition and hastened back through the hedge. A T-cart, of the kind used by dealers and publicans, was bowling along the road. As it came nearer he saw it was driven by a red-faced man in a brown coat with a velvet collar, a brown stock-tie, and a brown bowler. Richard stepped into the road, and held up his hand. The driver pulled on the reins, and the horse, making a whistling noise as it breathed, pressed back on its crupper and stopped. Richard raised his cap.

"I must apologise for stopping you," he said, "but my wife is taken ill, she is behind the tree over there. Would you be so good as to take us to the Bull, if you are going so far? I can hire a cab there."

The driver looked at Richard with eyes expressionless as the tone of his voice. "Ill, is she. What's up? Accident?"

"Well, between ourselves, she is expecting, I think that is the term."

"Kid actually comin'? This ain't a hambulance, you know."

"Oh, she is all right so far, the pains are only just starting, I think."

"Your first?"

"Yes, as a matter of fact, it is."

"I got seven. Where d'yer live?"

When Richard told him, the expressionless voice said, "Right-o, get you the li'l lady, I'll take yer 'ome. Don't know me, eh? Never sin me before, 'ave yer? The name's Winner. Mean anything to you, sir?"

"You are not my landlord, by any chance?"

"You've said it, sir. I was at yours s'mornin', arranging about a noo pan. Now fetch the li'l lady, sir. Lucky I come along, eh?"

"Well, thank you very much——"

"Do anyone a good turn. Let's get goin'. Nature works fast sometimes, even the first time."

Hetty was on her feet when Richard returned. She felt better, and was greatly relieved to hear that she was to be driven home by someone she knew already. Mr. Winner raised his hat to her, and held out an arm to help her up beside him. She sat on his left, while Richard sat behind them; and at a spanking pace the light cart went down the road, through the long shadows of the wayside trees.

Chapter 28

MANY APPREHENSIONS

THE DRIVER turned left-handed when they came to the sign of the Bull inn, and passing at a smart trot across a bridge over a railway, and then the river Randisbourne, gave his horse several light flicks with the whip to keep it going up the slope. Hetty began to wonder where the driver was going, but the presence of Dickie behind her was reassuring.

"You will soon recognize where we are," said Richard. "We are about to enter the road we travelled in the cab from Croydon last October."

"Vallable building sites round here," said the driver, who had developed a nervous impediment. "Vere's more money'n bricks and mortar than in meat vese days." He speculated on the idea that the building of new rows of houses would reduce the value of his property in Comfort Road. A moment afterwards he said, leaning back so that his passenger behind might hear, "Well built, vem houses in your road, sir. Better bricks than vey use nowadays, wood better seasoned, too. Slates put on wiv oak pegs, not nails vat rust away after a few years. If you want to make an offer any time for yours, sir, you know vere to find me."

They were going down the beginning of the Rise towards the Jack inn standing in the shade of trees on the left of the road. "'Ighwaymen's pub," remarked the driver, with a wave of his holly whip. "Dick Turpin and 'is pals used to 'ang out there. In vose days it was a forest round 'ere. See the sign? It's painted on a mammov's bone. They found it when they dug out the bed of the Croydon canal. Old Pooley, opposite your'n, seed it dug out. A mammov wiv great big tusks."

"Dick Turpin, and mammoths, just fancy that," said Hetty. "I think olden times are very interesting. Jack Cade's rebellion, I remember that name in a history lesson at school."

"Yes, vey caught 'im near where I picked you up just now, in the meadows. Vey cut 's 'ead off and stuck it up on Lunnon Bridge."

"Poor man. People were very cruel in those days, weren't they? What a fine horse you have, doesn't he step out well, Mr. Winner."

"He carried the first whipper-in of the Old Surrey foxhounds for 'is first six seasons," remarked the driver, not without pride. "Then 'e started whistlin' like a starlin', so vey sold 'im."

The cart passed over a railway bridge, through a cloud of steam. A train was standing in the station below. A magpie flew across the road in front, and perched in one of the elms lining the road. It was building a nest in the higher branches. They were now nearly home, for after a row of little shops Hetty saw the beginning of the cemetery behind iron railings. She saw the white and grey tombstones beyond the hedge of laurel within the railings. There were many new heaps of mounded yellow clay covered with flowers wilting in jampots, and artificial sprays made of wire and marble chip under domes of glass. Among them were older tombs of heavy stone slabs erected within spiked iron fences, to frustrate the work of body-snatchers. Hetty turned her head away from the slow figures standing by an extensive common grave, depressed figures in black. The women were heavily veiled and draped, some of them weeping, flowers in hand, where their children had been buried, after the severe winter.

"Nightingales sing like anyfing 'ere later on," remarked the driver. "They fancy v'nettles to nest in. But they ain't no good in cages." Farther on he said, "They can lay me vere if they like, when my turn comes. Me farver and me granfer before him ploughed there, when it was the Great Field, worked in with Bridge House Farm."

"How very interesting," said Hetty. "I love the nightingales, too, Mr. Winner. I'd like to be buried at the top of a tree."

The driver broke into a chuckle. As they neared Comfort Road, he chuckled again. "You're Irish, ain't yer, miss?"

"Partly," said Hetty, smiling. "I'd like to be always up near the sky, in the wind. Not down in the dark earth. Where I can always feel the sun, and hear the birds."

"I know what you means, miss. Like a bird. Like a jenny-wren!" He glanced at her bright eyes and dark brown hair. He was the landlord again, confident in his best brown bowler, stock-tie, and melton overcoat.

They were approaching a funeral procession. Men on the side-walks removed their hats as it turned into the gates of the cemetery.

The sight of it to Richard was repellent; to Hetty, it was fearful; to Mr. Winner, an occasion for pulling up his nag and removing his hat. The cart waited while the funeral cortège entered the cemetery. Richard had taken off his cap; and removing his gaze, he thought that, instead of a farm-cart or wain bearing the coffin, with mourners following on foot to pay their simple respects to the departed, these townee funerals were ostentatious and vulgar, almost ghoulish.

The hearse was an elaborate affair of decorated plate-glass enclosing nickel-silver railings with scrolls within which rested the coffin, wreaths of lilies laid upon it. The catafalque, however, was hardly to be noticed in the equestrian display of high-stepping horses with plumes of black ostrich feathers on their heads. The black of their coats was intensified by dye mixed with glycerine, the lugubrious effect heightened by caparisons of jet velvet which rippled and flowed to the matched stepping of the pair, their heads held back by martingales attached to spade-bits pressing against their palates, thus to widen the nostrils and also to accentuate the curve of the neck by which the plumes on the poll were made to bob with the restricted motion of each high step. The driver was in deepest black, from tall hat covered half way up the crown with crepe, to his black gloves. Similarly dressed were the mutes standing upright behind the coffin, their shaven faces as expressionless as they were pallid.

The hearse, followed by carriages in which red-eyed female mourners heavily hatted and veiled were seated, turned into the cemetery, watched by a little group holding brown paper parcels in their hands underneath the three gilt balls of the pawnbroker's across the road.

"A lot o' money goes in there," remarked Mr. Winner, with a glance at the cemetery. He shook the reins for the horse to move on. He clapped his hat on his head again.

The cart went on down Comfort Road. Mrs. Feeney's door was open. She looked out, tying on her bonnet. Richard jumped off and helped Hetty down. He took her inside, to seat her on the sofa in the front room. The two aspidistras on the window ledge were like reassuring friends. And when Mrs. Feeney came in, Hetty's relief was complete.

Mrs. Feeney took charge. Lifting Hetty's feet up on a chair, she put a rug round her, then telling her to rest awhile, she went into the kitchen. Richard returned outside to thank Mr. Winner, who waved away his offer of a florin.

"Only too glad to be of help, sir."

"Well, thank you, you are indeed a good Samaritan, Mr. Winner."

With mixed feelings the landlord drove away: he was cursing to himself, thinking that he could buy such people up many times over. Money! They needed it more than him!

In the kitchen of Comfort House, Mrs. Feeney was saying to Richard, whose manner had so discomposed Mr. Winner, "Plenty of hot water is always useful, sir, so I'll bring in one of my kettles, and fill up yours. Mrs. Maddison is a little before her time, but that won't matter. It may be a dry birth. I'll make you and her a nice cup of tea, there's plenty of time, I'll get her up to bed afterwards. Then if you like to go and tell Mrs. Birkett, I'll get the bedroom ready, sir."

"Thank you, Mrs. Feeney. I shall go immediately, in case she is going out tonight."

"I'll have some tea for you when you return. You know the address, don't you, sir, five doors down from Mrs. Cummings'."

"Yes, Mrs. Feeney, I have it in my pocket-book."

Richard went down Comfort Road again, walking with his long stride. His anxiety urged him to hurry, hurry, his mind told him that more haste meant less speed. As he came nearer to the high road his pace slowed somewhat, he walked more upright, his hands clenched in case he should be set upon by one or another, or both, of the blackguards, as he regarded them, who lived in the end houses on the other side. His expression was set, his upper lip held stiffly against the lower lip, so that his face wore an expression of rigid seriousness.

"Tin wheels! Yah, old Tin Wills!"

Two ragged boys over by the cemetery, hoping to get a halfpenny or two from the Saturday afternoon mourners by offering bunches of flowers taken from various graves, had seen him. To the boys he was a figment of fear and hatred, allied with peelers—those dreaded figures who were the enemies of the poor, who strapped men down on stretchers and covered them up, who wheeled them away to that place of final darkness and terror, the police-station.

"Yah! Tin Wills!"

The adenoidal cry, less urgent, less shrill, followed him as he strode on down the high road. His mind became easier as he felt the April breeze on his forehead—he had taken off his cap and it swung in his hand—as he heard the sparrows chirping in the elms under which he walked. One bird flew up from the road, with a long yellow-brown oat-straw in its beak; the fluttered wings could barely lift it; the bird rose slowly into the air towards a leafy branch, but grew tired, and the straw fell to the road again.

He passed strolling couples, seeing them as insubstantial. The sun sunken below the houses on the west side of the road was splashing its radiant gold upon chimney stack and roof-ridge. On one chimney-pot, unseen like a cockney phœnix in fire, a starling was uttering its medley of local sounds and noises: errand-boy whistles, clopping of horses' feet, *milko!* morning cry of milkman carrying his big can and dipper with which to fill the iron milk-cans on the doorsteps, *cling-a-ling!* of muffin-man's bell, bleat of sheep on the Hill, thin imitations of the phrases of the songs of thrushes and other garden birds. If Hetty died, he would be lost, lost as the earth under the yellow clay of the cemetery.

Fleeing from the phantom of his thoughts Richard passed his old lodgings and with faster-beating heart began to count the doors to the number of five beyond the little yew-tree in the garden of Mrs. Cummings'. He counted in a desperate attempt to overcome chaos; to regulate his thoughts; for he knew by the brass plate fixed on the brick wall beside the door where Mrs. Birkett lived, having glanced at the doorway more than a hundred times in passing that way. Shaken by anxiety, he counted to five, using the index finger of his right hand held by his waistcoat to reassure himself against the cold hollow boding of death. Women often did die in childbirth! Childbirth was a terrible experience for a woman even in the best of conditions, especially if she was not broad in the hips. And Hetty was *petite*, with small bones.

Unable to control his imagination, Richard saw bones huddled together in a coffin warped by decay, soon to collapse under the pressure of the clay. Mother, mother! Oh Hetty, I have been too selfish, I have never been able to make up for taking you from your happy home. With trembling hands he put his cap on his head, and opened the iron gate which groaned dismally with rust on its hooks. The front garden was untidy; the brass plate was streaked and dulled with smoky rain. Was the midwife careless, did she wash her hands in carbolic before handling the delicate, helpless body of a new-born babe? Taking a deep breath, he pulled the bell-wire. The bell jangled somewhere within the depths of the shut and silent house.

He waited. Sparrows chattered on the tiled path behind him. A coal cart rumbled northwards, empty, the heavy, hairy horse lumbering at the trot towards the stables beyond the station. The gaunt, black-faced figure of the coalman stood up in the cart, thinking of his meat tea and of quarts of porter in the pub he would drink until one o'clock in the morning. He saw Richard, and waved his whip in salute. "Whatcher, guv'nor! Nice day!"

Richard raised his hand.

"Good luck to the missus!"

"Thank you!"

The coal cart rattled away toward the station.

How quickly people learned of what was happening.

It was clear that the midwife was out, perhaps for the evening. He pulled the bell once more, and listened. No answer. He went back the way he had come, and on impulse turned into Mrs. Cummings'. That good woman was reassuring, telling him that now that Hetty was home, she was safe, and if things happened quickly, Mrs. Feeney was quite up to dealing with them. When he suggested that he should go for the doctor, Mrs. Cummings declared that it was not necessary, and only extra expense to fetch him that early. Let him not worry, Mrs. Feeney was quite capable of looking after everything for the moment. Would Mr. Maddison stay and drink a dish of tea with her?

Richard said he would be getting back, to see how things were; and forgetting to thank her, he hastened away. His haste was unnecessary, he realized as he entered the front room, for Hetty was seated there as before, her legs stretched out upon a chair, a rug round them, and a cup of tea beside her. She was smiling. Through the ceiling came the sounds of preparation above.

Her cheeks were flushed, but dully. Her eyes seemed part of the flushing, even as her hair seemed to have lost lustre. The fire was already laid in the grate, and he asked why it had not been lit. She murmured that she was not cold. Saying of course she must keep herself warm, he knelt and struck a wax vesta. The edge of the paper caught; but went out. He lit it again, elsewhere. The coal collapsed on the wood. A wisp of smoke arose and expired.

"As I thought," he said, "the sticks are laid all together, lying one way. Fire cannot breathe that way. Flame has to grow, like anything else."

"Perhaps the sticks are damp, dear."

"How can they be, I dried them myself on the kitchen range. Now look at the mess in the hearth. All your work wasted."

He was disappointed; he was so anxious that the fire should burn, on this special occasion, with the least trouble. How many times had he told her the correct way to lay a fire, and always with no result?

"I am so sorry, dear."

"Oh, I shall have it going in a moment, now."

He lifted the mass of charred paper, sticks, and coal from the grate, and put them on the black-leaded bricks of the hearth. His hands were grimed, displeasing. It was unfair; it was *wrong*. He went into the kitchen to fetch an old copy of *The Morning Post* from the pile neatly standing on the pot-board. While he was there Mrs. Feeney came downstairs, looking into the front room to tell Hetty that she would now set about getting tea for the master. "I'll fry the liver and bacon just right, I know how Mr. Maddison likes it, m'um."

Having washed his hands, Richard returned with the newspaper. He knelt down and after tearing off a single page, crumpled it before rending it into two pieces. These he placed on the iron bars of the grate. He crumpled more pieces, and placed them on top of the others.

"Like this, you see, the flames will have a chance to breathe through the paper. Now the sticks, the smallest first. Not too close together, but spaced. The next lot go across them, and the next lot across *them*. Now one match to touch off the paper, and the flames run up and through the little wooden house, just as they did in the Great Fire of London. No need for the poker fetish, 'to draw up the flames'."

Yellow flames bit, pine-wood crackled. He added two more sticks, making about a third of a farthing bundle of firewood bought at the grocer's. The flames of the resinous wood rose into the chimney, while he added selected lumps of small coal with the tongs.

"It's simple, you see, like all things done the right way."

"Yes, I see now exactly how to do it, dear. Thank you, so very much."

"How are you feeling now?"

"The pains are better, Dickie. Please don't take any notice of me, I shall be quite all right."

Mrs. Feeney came into the room, carrying a cup of tea on the Japanese tray. "Here you are, sir, all nice and hot, a good strong cup of tea will put you right. Now I think Mrs. Maddison should come with me, and get into bed. I've put a nice hot-water bottle for her feet, bless her. Then I'll see about your tea, sir. Feeney shall go up to the Jack, to get three pints of porter, and two gills o' gin, for Mrs. Birkett when she comes. Do you fancy some nice hot buttered toast and a boiled egg, m'um? Why, you haven't drunk that cup o' tea I made for you!"

"I will finish it now, Mrs. Feeney."

"But it's cold, m'um! Let me pour you a fresh cup, do!"

"May I have this cup, Mrs. Feeney, and you pour another for Mr. Maddison. He likes his on the weak side, isn't that right, Dickie?"

"Oh, I am not particular. It is most kind of Mrs. Feeney to help as she has done. You have this cup, dear, I can wait till I have my meal."

"It's no trouble at all, sir. I'm only too glad to be able to help, while I keep my health and strength, work never killed nobody, look at old Pooley over there, just come back from his rounds with his little ole moke. Have you seen its foal, m'um? It come last week, and it trots along of its dam happy as a prince."

Hetty, feeling suddenly better, turned her head and looked out of the window. There beside the patient jenny-ass, hitched by string and cracked leather to the barrow cart, stood the foal, not much bigger than a lamb on stilts. As she watched the foal began to suck, while Pooley and his granddaughter unhitched the donkey to lead it to its grazing on the land above the railway cutting.

After getting Richard's meal Mrs. Feeney departed, saying she must give her old man his tea and then send him off to the Jack.

No sooner had she departed when Richard asked about the capabilities of the midwife. What sort of person was this Mrs. Birkett? Visions of a villainous old frump out of a novel by Dickens came to him. Somebody staggering about and hiccupping, perhaps causing a death by her tipsy carelessness. Gin! What could Mrs. Cummings be about, to suggest, and even to recommend, such a personage?

Hetty, whose pains were increasing, lay there and heard only part of what was said.

After a while his agitation subsided; he ceased to rant; and went to stand over her, laying his hand on her forehead, which was hot, and damp with perspiration. There was no true sympathy in the touch, no communication: for he was thinking, Where is Mrs. Birkett? Why is she not available when wanted? What shall I do, if Hetty were to faint? Should she not be in bed?

The rhythmic spasms passed.

"I am better now, thank you, dear. Mrs. Birkett is quite capable."

Mrs. Feeney, having given her old man his tea, had gone round to see Mrs. Cummings. She wanted to borrow a waterproof sheet for the bed, for she had an idea that Mrs. B. might have gone to the Empire to see Albert Chevalier who was billed there that week with Little Tich and Marie Lloyd, two other big attractions. Mrs. Feeney was quite prepared to take Mrs. B.'s place, if that was so, until Mrs. B. came home.

But there was no need for it. Mrs. B. had only gone to the butcher's to get some pigs'-trotters for Sunday's dinner for Mr. B., a sewerman working for the Deptford Board of Works. To Mrs. Feeney the midwife said she would be round after she had had her tea. And having had her tea, and put on the trotters to stew in a large pot, Mrs. Birkett donned bonnet and cape, took her black bag, and went to the end house in Comfort Road.

Richard was to have further anxieties soon after the midwife's arrival; for when she had made her inspection of Hetty and sent her to bed, she went down to the kitchen and set about unpacking her black bag. The first articles to be taken from it were two enormous stockings, of the kind Richard had thought were worn by divers; they were thick and woolly, more than a yard in length, and the feet were well over a foot long. Whatever were they for? Then he recalled that Mrs. Cummings had once mentioned that the midwife's husband was a sewerman. Sewermen wore leather boots to their thighs, and these must be the under-stockings. Sewer stockings!

Mrs. Birkett hung the stockings over a chair-back, and placed the chair before the fire, remarking that they had been aired already, but every little helped, and it was as well to have them nice and warm when the little woman required them.

Although startled and alarmed by the thought of where such stockings must have been, Richard asked no questions; and deeming it proper to vacate the kitchen, he went into the parlour and sat before the fire as twilight dissolved the prospect outside, and the light of the street lamp cast a wan lace pattern on the wallpaper.

Try as he might to compose his mind, the image of the long loose woollen stockings would not be dismissed. At length, overcome by doubts of what infection the monstrous stockings might hold made him start up, determined to ask to what use it was intended they should be put. He went into the kichen, as Mrs. Birkett, a short stout woman with a big face, was going upstairs with a rubber sheet folded over one arm, a bed-pan in her hand. The stockings were still on the chair-back.

He regarded them with mixed fear and distaste. The gas-jet made the faint singing noise it always made when turned full on. This distorted the flame, making it too blue on one side, and therefore not the illuminant it could be when trimmed to the shape of half a yellow pansy by adjustment of the tap. He moved to turn it down, while dreading lest Mrs. Birkett take it as a slight upon her action in turning it full on. One never quite knew where one was with such people. Then he realized that she had come quietly down the stairs and was entering the kitchen. He was about to explain when she said conversationally:

"That's better. Some little things get on the nerves after a while, don't they? Not that they worry me, but I can understand how they might with some people. Your little wife is going to be all right, Mr. Maddison."

"I am sure she is, in your capable hands, Mrs. Birkett."

Turning her large grey face to him, she replied, "You won't forget my porter, will you? And the two gills o' gin? Feeney isn't to be relied on. It's hard work, you know, and in spite of what the teetotallers say, porter is the best stay-by for anyone doing this work. It nurses the strength, that we need to nurse the one in labour, and help her through, you see. Tea hasn't any body in it, refreshing as it is at all times."

"I think Feeney will be returning with it, Mrs. Birkett. I suppose it will take some hours yet, the birth, I mean?"

"You never can tell, that's the trouble. Some are quick, but with a first confinement it is usually long. I've known cases that took four or five days, and the mothers losing their little ones after all they've been through, too. 'The Lord giveth, and He taketh away.' But there, we must look on the bright side, and hope for the best, Mr. Maddison. Now if Feeney is relied on for my porter and gin, there's small hope of seeing him back before midnight. He'll be celebratin' till then."

Richard thought it best not to talk any further on the subject. Looking at him, she said. "You had a good long walk in the country, didn't you, with your little wife this afternoon?"

"Yes, perhaps she went too far, Mrs. Birkett."

"No harm done, the exercise did her good, and brought it on a bit early, that's all. Now don't worry, she's going to be all right, she's young and healthy."

Mrs. Birkett's glance went to the stockings on the chair. "I saw you looking at them just now. They're a great help, you know, when heavy labour comes on. Gives the little woman something to pull on, to ease delivery." Her voice became even more conversational. "They're washed in carbolic after every time used, only I can't answer for how recently the chair-back has been scrubbed, of course. Now I must get upstairs, and help walk my patient about, so don't worry if you hear footsteps overhead, will you?"

Mrs. Birkett was reassuring. She spoke quietly, in level tones with a pleasant intonation, as of one who had seen service in an ordered world. Mrs. Birkett had acquired her manner from an admired matron, trained by Miss Florence Nightingale herself, of St. George's Hospital, at Hyde Park Corner, under whom she had worked in her youth. Later she had been in the service of what she called the real gentry. And later still, she had become a certified midwife. Richard learned these facts later that evening, when Mrs. Birkett had departed to her supper. Mrs. Feeney said, "Yes, sir, she was under-nurse to the children of Parson the Honourable Legge, at St. Mary's Loosam, brother to the Lord of the Manor, and now Bishop of Lichfield."

"The Honourable Legge? Then perhaps that accounts for the stockings before the kitchen fire?"

Mrs. Feeney, always in good spirits, was glad that the master was cheerful. And when he had eaten his supper on a tray in the parlour, and was sitting by the fire with his feet up reading in his own father's journal on the subject of the decay of farming in England, Richard began to enjoy the adventure of becoming a father. The illusion was only in part aided by Raggett's stout, an empty bottle of which stood behind one of the aspidistra pots on the window shelf.

Chapter 29

RICHARD'S VIGIL

AT MIDNIGHT the splay of yellow light from the miniature iron turret of the lantern cast its soft radiance upon the bearded face and the slender hands intently working upon the three-legged table. Overhead footfalls had ceased. Hetty was lying sideways on the bed, while Mrs. Birkett took her second half pint of porter, laced with a little gin. Crooning *Kathleen Mavourneen*, Feeney had brought the bottles to the door shortly after ten o'clock, and on being given fourpence by Richard, he left cheerfully with the air of one who had a purpose in life—a return to the Jack.

Richard went into the kitchen shortly after one o'clock, to make a pot of tea. He put in an extra spoonful, and then went upstairs to the bedroom. With the nail of his index finger he tapped lightly on the door, and waited until it was opened by Mrs. Birkett.

"Ah, that will refresh Mrs. Maddison wonderfully, Mr. Maddison," whispered Mrs. Birkett at the door. "She is bearing up well, but I fancy it won't be for some hours yet before the water-bag falls. There are two stages you know, and the second may take a day, or even more. There is nothing to worry about, first babies usually take their time. Come in and talk to her, sir."

"Thank you, Mrs. Birkett."

"Now, if you'll excuse me, I'll attend to some things downstairs," continued Mrs. Birkett, in her serene tones. "Just you lie quiet, dear, under the blanket, and conserve your strength, won't you," to Hetty, as she went out of the door.

"Well," whispered Richard. "How are you feeling?"

"Quite happy, dear," she whispered back. "How are you?"

"Oh, I have been writing and reading. Can you drink some tea?"

"Yes, dear, it would be refreshing. You won't work too long, will you?"

By the light of the candle he saw her eyes darkly upon him. He put out a hand, and held the back of her hand. It was hot, and he felt it quivering. He took it, and stroked it between his cooler hands.

The reading of his dead father's journal had made Richard feel, at times, very close to him. This reassurance made him, in turn, feel calmer towards his living.

"It was a capital walk to the Pond, I did enjoy it. Such a wonderful trout you discovered—and that nice Austrian with the bear."

He put his hand on her forehead. It was clammy and hot. The dread phrase, *puerperal fever*, which he had read in a medical book recently, recurred in his mind. "I'll go and get the tea, I left it in the kitchen. Will you be all right if I leave you?"

"Quite all right, dear, don't you worry," she said, feeling his anxiety.

"No no, of course not. Things will be all right, I am sure."

"Yes, dear, of course."

She shifted under the sheet and blanket which covered her, and lay on an elbow. "How kind of you, dear, to think of the tea."

He went downstairs, and returned with two cups and a jug of milk on a tray.

"Let me taste it first. It may be too hot. Just a moment, I will add some milk. I left the pot with Mrs. Birkett."

"Thank you, Dickie." She sipped. "Oh, it is lovely!"

"Is it too hot?" he said. "Do not burn your lips, whatever you do. Blow on it! Why not! Have a good blow!"

She sipped, blowing slightly. "Ah, so very refreshing." She took another sip, sighed, and said, "I think I'll lie down now, Dickie." Her eyes closed, the line of her mouth compressed as she clenched her teeth against crying out.

He stroked her forehead, then as her knees arose under the bedclothes he went to the door, opened it, gave a timid look, and went down the stairs on his toes, to tell Mrs. Birkett in the kitchen.

Mrs. Birkett was pouring herself a second cup of tea. "It's often nearly as hard on father as on mother in these cases," she said tranquilly. "You must try and get some sleep, Mr. Maddison. She'll feel easier to know you are resting, and not worrying on her account. I don't think anything will happen before the morning so there will be plenty of time to let Dr. Cave-Browne know, although he does not go to church, being a Theosophist. But whatever the religion, a doctor likes to be told in good time. The dilating pains come and go sometimes for a day or more, as I said upstairs just now, and so we must be patient."

"If you wish to lie down, Mrs. Birkett, there is a bed made up in one of the other bedrooms. Perhaps if you left the door open—"

"There's no immediate change likely, so I think I'll go back to my house for awhile, but I'll return soon, for I don't like to leave my little mothers alone for too long. You must get some sleep yourself, you know, Mr. Maddison, then she won't worry about you."

When Mrs. Birkett had left the house Richard tip-toed up the stairs again, and peered round the open door, to see in candlelight the dark eyes watching him from the pilliow. Hetty had been praying. She took his hand and held it, and then, as he knelt by the bed she lifted his hand and pressed it to her cheek. She did not want him to be worried; she knew that a baby might be in the wrong position, and that forceps were sometimes necessary. She knew, too, that if the mother's life were in danger, they might have to—but she could not bring herself to think of it—it must not happen, she would endure all, so that it would not happen. With her senses acutely aware, she knew what Mrs. Birkett had been thinking when she had been feeling for the position of the head, and then listening for the heart-beats within. Never would she permit the forceps to crush the baby's head. Though not a Catholic, Hetty believed in the truths, as she saw them, of a religion which had drawn her instinctively during her convent-school days at Thildonck. It was one of her secret sadnesses that she had to keep her faith to herself, as Richard had more than once declared his disbelief in any religion.

Richard thought that she looked tired; perhaps she might be able to sleep awhile now.

"Mrs. Birkett has gone for some supper, and I shall be downstairs, with the door open, so do not hesitate to call out if you should require anything."

"Thank you, dear. Are you warm enough down there? Try and sleep, won't you? Take these rugs, I don't need them."

Richard crept away with one rug; and seated at the three-legged oak table once more, went on with the addressing of envelopes. Each name, as particularly requested by the stock-broker's clerk, had to have its abbreviation of *esquire*, a form of business flattery that went against the grain; but there, it was a changing world, with the power gone from the land to the money of the towns.

Richard had been deeply impressed by some of the entries in his Father's journal, lent to him by brother John, from the library at home. He had read certain passages several times already; he thought them revelatory: they presented Father in an entirely new light. In them the ruin of England was virtually prophesied. They were a *cri de cœur* from one whose love of the soil was deeply inbred!

When, towards three o'clock, Mrs. Birkett having meanwhile returned, he grew tired of addressing envelopes, he took the leather-bound volume off the table by the wall, and unfastening the brass lock with the key on his ring, opened it at the page marked by a wood-pigeon's feather, and read.

The wheezy cry of the partridge sounds across the untilled acres tumbling down to dock and burdock, thistle and corn-cockle, between the overgrown thorn hedges spreading with bramble and briar, where once the stooks stood mellowing in the wind and sun of August. Where is the rosy-faced countryman, who once with his sons and daughters set up the sheaves, and made the corn dollies with the first ears of wheat? Let us arise above the earth, and look down through the timeless air of history, and consider the sinister trend of today in the light of previous civilizations. From the land which is the mother of the race go the children to the towns, with their cheap food, foreign produce of peasants paid but a few pence a week to produce that food, which is bought by the financiers of the City of London, who virtually control the economies of those foreign countries, for their own profit. These financiers also control the exports of our factories, in which the rosy-faced countryman has gone, in a few years to lose his health and his stability of living, which before was balanced in natural work upon the soil.

A generation later the pallid workers in the slums have lost the true virtue of living, and the grime of their fœtid surroundings has penetrated their very minds, with their faces turned from the sun, and their bodies become as unwholesome as the bleached white bread deprived of all goodness of the wheat berry. A cancer of untruth eats into the minds of the pallid-faced townsman before the physical cancer absorbs what is left of his bodily living.

Richard sat back. Should he buy the house, which, although as yet unbuilt, he had been imagining off and on ever since he had stood on the track leading up to the school in the twilight, or should he take the bit between his teeth (as he put it to himself) and clear out to New Zealand or Australia, while yet he remained a comparatively young man, and start an entirely new kind of life with his wife and child, on two thousand pounds capital?

The footfalls overhead were beginning again. They were irregular; there were pauses; with sounds as of dragging feet. He breathed deeply, and uttered a low cry of despair. Pushing back his chair, he lifted the blinds, to see if the sky were lightening. It was still dark; the lamp shone steadily down the street.

> The black coat of the lost men of the towns is in truth an outward symbol of the nation's death. Black hair-dye, that palliative of fear and dread, must cover the grey hairs of the bread-winner after he is turned of forty, if his little ones are not to starve outside the tenements of the workers in factory and sweat-shop. The hand that holds the pen, that should be clasping the hoe, or the shovel in the cottage garden after the honest day's work is done, trembles when the age of forty-five is passed. It trembles while the great lords of Free Trade sit in their new halls and dispense their champagne and rejoice in the number of peers and peeresses who come to their tables, often to receive presents of gold and jewelled trinkets to put them in good mood for the advertisement banquet that follows.

Was that a cry overhead? Was it Hetty? A murmuring voice; shifting of the bed, as of brass rail being clutched for support. Silence. He read on, momentarily relieved by the silence.

> The sinister migration from the land to the towns, this spoliation of the true wealth of the nation, which is the health and strength of its people and the fertility of its mother soil, where will it end? Who will stay its downward rush upon the slopes of Gadarene? When will a prophet arise to lead the people back to their natural heritage, before the nation shall perish even as ancient Rome? Such a prophet will have to face, like David, not only the towering strength of Goliath, which is *laissez-faire* and the so-called inevitability of progress implanted

in the minds of the millions who cannot help themselves, but the entire power of the money massed in the vaults of the City of London. What fate befell even the Son of God, when He turned over the tables of the money changers in the Temple, we know from the sad reading of Holy Scripture. How much greater then, in this age of what the poet Blake calls the satanic mills, in this epoch of the inhuman machines of the money-minded, will be the massed cry for Barrabas against such a man who shall arise to lead the people back to health and Truth? When he arises it will be St. George for Merrie England come again, and though the broken temples of his brain shall be trampled under the cloven hoofs of the swine of Gadarene, future generations shall know him as a living saviour, and call him blessed.

The sweat had pressed wisps of Hetty's hair to her brow, she lay inert, breathing harshly, after the paroxysm had passed. Mrs. Birkett took a swig of gin and porter, to keep up her strength. Then sitting on a wooden chair, she folded her arms and leaned her head forward, closing her eyes for a respite.

Down in the room beneath Richard with a deep sigh read on.

The harlot curses in the shadow of the dock wall, and drops her unwanted child into the foul waters of the river; yet there is health and comeliness waiting for these lost city millions in the countryside which is the mother of the race. Once in the wheatfields of mighty Rome men laboured and built, and went forth to bring order and beauty throughout the world; but the towns grew with the riches of the few and the cynicism of the many, so that honest work and craftsmanship became debased, and the wheatfields shrunk and the desert came back and so inevitably Rome fell and only ruin told of its former health and virility. The very gold that is now in process of ruining England is the same gold that sapped the soil that fed the strength of Rome. The money changers have moved on, that is all—into the City of London.

This reference to the City made Richard hesitate. How could the City be in the wrong? The City was like—the Royal Family

—the ironclads of the Navy—Britain's supremacy throughout the world. But the next passage was the key to it.

> The idea of resurrection lies dormant, as the germ of the wheat berry in the mother soil, within the darkness of each of us in our daily circumstance; and each of us in our varying ways gives praise to the false idea which seizes new territories far away so that their riches may be transferred to the barren vaults of the mighty City of London, even at the cost of war, which follows what is called Trade behind the Flag. While the sighs of the soldiers dying far from the cottages and cornfields of their lost living mingle with the sighs of their brothers in the dark and narrow streets under the shadows of the factories of progress. And in passing these tombs of the living, let us bow the knee to the Lords of Free Trade, who are in process of disinheriting mankind from the earth.

Richard looked at the pile of addressed envelopes, each an esquire, an inheritor of manorial copyhold—a squire. What damned irony! Every one to be sent out with prospectuses for mining shares, for exploitation by those robbers and looters in South Africa! How many men like himself, able only by means of the strictest economy to save at the most a shilling or two a week—for a rainy day—a few pounds after several years—how many men had been tempted to risk those savings in what perhaps was a palpable swindle, but within the letter of the law, through those hundreds of thousands of envelopes!

> Let us consider for a moment the seven phases of the growth of the new aristocracy of Free Trade in the social sphere. First the *parvenu*, as we have seen, full of generosity and hospitality to his betters; then the candidate for Parliament, with expenditure of twenty, thirty, even forty thousand pounds on free coal, free blankets, "invalid" wine, and of course beer unlimited to guarantee the winning of the country constituency—"Such a wonnerful kind gen'elman he be, you!" Soon the knight in the New Year's Honours List, "for services rendered", the services being, of course, a thumping big cheque to the party chest. Better still, why not a baronetcy—or a jump (elevation, that is the term) to the genuine peerage—yes, a barony, for further services rendered—endowment for a hospital this time, accompanied,

of course, by a modestly anonymous donation—shall it be a hundred thousand pounds—to the party funds. Why stop at a barony? Money is pouring in from dozens of companies, some of them controlled by "banker's nominees",—again the admirable modesty of anonymity—for the exploitation of gold mining concessions—millions of shares issued on news of a heavyweight strike of a new reef in the Rand—news carefully propagated, of course, to produce the desired effects on 'Change.

So the gold shares are bulled, and sold on the top of the rise. Who buys them on the kerb, and in the House itself? The man in the street, the poor clerk with the dyed hair and the fiver carefully saved up for an emergency. And then, of course, the fall to a value not worth the paper the share is inscribed upon, after the cable that the reef has suddenly terminated in rock.

Why stop at a mere barony? A viscountcy is included automatically in an earldom, and provides a pleasing courtesy title for the son and heir at Eton. So the coat armour is issued under patent from the College of Heralds, and the noble family is founded—for a generation or two at least—the earldom of Gadarene established but for the plunge into the darkness of a nation's death, self-exiled from its native soil.

And so the little brown partridges, birds faithful and heavenly, shall inherit the earth from which man, like Lucifer, has fallen.

"Confound it all!" cried Richard, pushing the lists off the table. "This is the very last time I shall have a hand in that sort of thing!" and feeling for the moment as David confronting Goliath, he got up and helped himself to another bottle of Raggett's stout. Raising his glass to a new vision of his Father, he drank the black creamy liquid, while reminding himself to see to it that both bottles be replaced, as he considered they belonged to Hetty. Then opening the door he tip-toed upstairs, to tap gently with his fingernail. It was ajar; Mrs. Birkett came and opened it. "Just kiss her goodnight, will you, she is very brave, the dear thing. She is resting now, and in the morning I shall ask you to go to the doctor's, he will put things right. But don't worry, Mr. Maddison, by this time tomorrow you should be taking your afternoon tea together, all three of you."

Richard touched shyly with his lips the brow of a quiescent and strangely fragile Hetty, patted her shoulder with the least touch of his fingers, and tip-toed out of the room, carrying away an impression of a child lying there, silent in a strange world, a child wanting mother but not daring to say so. With a hysterical flutter in the throat he determined in the morning to cycle over and brave the hostility of Mr. Turney, in order to tell Mrs. Turney that he thought she ought to come. The parlour when he re-entered it seemed curiously empty, as though something had gone from it forever; the dark lantern casting its wavering wan light upon the envelopes on the table seemed but a childish thing; and sitting on the sofa, he put his head in his hands, and wept silently to himself, thinking that if Hetty were to die he would not know how to go on living.

Chapter 30

CONSUMMATION

AFTER AN uneasy doze on the sofa, Richard sat up at six o'clock, feeling frowsty. Immediately his heart sank; footfalls were still audible. He crept upstairs, after hurriedly combing his hair and beard. He tapped on the door apprehensively: to find Hetty being walked about the narrow space by the midwife, in an attempt to promote the bearing-down pains. She was too wan to speak to him at the moment, and he went down to the kitchen to light the fire and boil a kettle for tea. He had set the sticks to dry the night before, and soon flames were roaring in the chimney.

While he was washing his face and neck, the window being open, his name was called over the back fence. He saw Mrs. Feeney, who asked if she might come in and help get his breakfast, and anything else Mrs. Birkett wanted doing. While she was speaking he heard a familiar sound in the air above; and looking up into the sky when she had withdrawn her head, Richard saw that two swallows were perched upon a neighbouring roof-top. Surely this was in the nature of a good omen? The first swallows of the year!

When he had made himself presentable he went upstairs again and found Hetty in momentary relief. "The first swallows have come back! I saw a pair just now, twittering on a roof-ridge!"

She gave a groan, for the dragging flash of pain had transfixed her, whereby he was expunged.

Time dragged with the morning light. Refusing breakfast, Richard took his bicycle from the coal-cellar under the stairs and dusted it, preparatory to going to the doctor's. Was that a cry overhead? He listened with thudding heart.

The elementary core of creation's flame is pain. Hetty was now consumed. Mrs. Birkett saw the waters come away, that heavy labour was upon the mother. As the sun slanted down the road she put on the woollen stockings, while Hetty lay with her hands clawed upon the bedclothes, her eyes shut and her mouth clenched as she tried to think in prayer, against her inward screaming, of

Jeanne d'Arc in the fire. For Hetty's heroine was the Maid, whom Mère Ambroisine at Thildonck had often said was surely with the blessed Saints, and if Jeanne d'Arc could think steadily of Christ and His mercy while the first flames were blistering her flesh, she herself could endure these lesser pains, even the agony of thinking that by her delay she might be suffocating her baby. Mrs. Birkett pulled the stockings on and taking Hetty's hands she opened the fingers first of one hand, then the other, and guided first one hand, then the other, to a new grip upon the white worsted. But first she had to loosen again the fingers which had clutched her own unknowingly.

"There now, dearie, there now," she said in a level voice, "you try and pull yourself inside out, that's right, dearie, you pull like anything."

Half an hour later she said, "That's good, I can see baby's head now. It's got black hair!"

Some time later she was saying, "Push again, dear, push your hardest, then I'll be able to tell you the colour of baby's eyes."

At eight o'clock she opened the door and called to Richard, who came up two steps at a time, to be told to go for the doctor.

Five minutes later Richard was knocking at the door marked "Surgery" of the large house at the corner of Charlotte Road and the Hill. To his alarm he learned that Dr. Cave-Browne had just been called to another urgent case in Twistleton Road. The uniformed maid took his name and address, saying that she would give his message to the doctor as soon as he returned. Quivering with fear, Richard gave the girl a slight bow, then turned away and cycled back with the news for Mrs. Birkett.

"Then we must be patient, Mr. Maddison. She is being very brave, and doing her best, but the baby's head is very big. However, do not be alarmed, I've seen many more difficult cases in my time come through all right. Go you to fetch her mother, that will help, and perhaps by the time you return we shall have your son, or perhaps a daughter, to show you. Won't you eat the fried bacon Mrs. Feeney had prepared for you, you must keep up your strength, you know. It will help the little wife to know you are being properly looked after."

He ate his food, and set out along the high road up the Rise towards Berehill and the Crystal Palace leaden-hued but oddly glittering in patches; and breasting the high ground, descended to the woods and farms of Surrey, with the North Downs in the distance. He told himself many times that he must keep calm, and not think of how Mr. Turney would receive him: and if Mr. Turney blamed him for his daughter's critical condition he must on every account bear himself with restraint.

The sun was now becoming warm on his left cheek, but he scarcely noticed the morning, neither the weather nor that the surface of the road took a firm print of his tyres as he pedalled onwards, avoiding the damp depressions and muddy potholes of winter, which later on in the year would arise as dust from the fast wheels of gig and trap. So he came to Croydon, and turning down Cold Harbour Lane pedalled after his shadow while the sun on his back broke the sweat from his skin, and so eased a little the constriction of his thoughts. Through the villages with their red tiled roofs; past the fields of lavender and thyme, rosemary and aniseed, sage, marjoram, and comfrey among rows of other pot-herbs; and so to Cross Aulton and the pond mirroring the morning.

He got off the bicycle and walked slowly up the gravel sweep to the hearth-stoned steps, just as the coachman-gardener, the cook, and the new parlour-maid left the breakfast-room, where they had been kneeling in line on one side of the carpet while Sarah, Hughie, and his young brother Joey home from school kneeled on the other side during the reciting of prayers by Mr. Turney.

Richard walked up the steps and knocked on the door. The maid showed him into the morning-room. Mrs. Turney came, knowing at once by his face that it concerned Hetty. She waited while he made his apologies for the intrusion, and then asked news of Hetty. Thomas Turney came into the room and interrupted his formal account.

"How's Hetty? Is she in danger?"

"I do not think there is any grave danger, sir. But the midwife considers that the presence of Mrs. Turney cannot but be beneficial."

"Well, thank ye for coming, my boy," said Thomas Turney. "I appreciate your coming over like this. Joey, tell Jim to get the carriage ready. Now sit down and eat some breakfast, Dick, you must need it after your ride. Tell me what the doctor said."

"Dr. Cave-Browne has been out on another case, I gather, sir, but Hetty is in charge of Mrs. Birkett, a trustworthy person, trained at a London hospital."

"Well, we must get a doctor, eh Sarah? Hetty must have the best there is. How about asking Dr. Shillingworth to go over, eh? He's treated Hetty since she was a child, and knows her. What say?"

"If Hetty's present doctor has the case, I expect he will want to be asked first, Tom," said Sarah. "I'll go over and see her, and let you know, dear, when I return."

"I'll come with you. The drive will do me good. Now help yourself to some kidneys and gammon, my boy. Of course you're anxious, but when you've been through it as many times as I have, you'll learn there's no reason for undue worry. Now help yourself, sit down there, and enjoy the fire."

Richard sat uneasily at the table. The fire was hot on his back. Opposite to him sat Hugh Turney, the pallor of his face accentuated by his dark eyes and black moustache. Hugh was in pain; the day before he had been injected with a new drug. Sidney Cakebread had told the Old Man of Hugh's condition, and the father had gone to see his son, and taken him forthwith to have the best treatment for his illness in Harley Street. There had been no recrimination; beyond saying that if Hugh had confided in him from the first he could have saved him from quacks, Thomas Turney had not discussed the subject. Sarah was in the secret. It was understood by the rest of the household that Hugh was suffering from the effects of rheumatic fever, contracted from a damp bed in his shady London lodgings.

Richard thought that Hugh's manner was due to dislike of himself, and after drinking a cup of coffee, he got up and asked Mrs. Turney if she would excuse him, as he thought he ought to be getting back.

"Yes, dear boy," said Sarah. "We quite understand, and thank you *very* much indeed for coming to tell us. We'll bring a picnic basket, it is a beautiful day and will be over as soon as we can. Now do not worry, Hetty will be all right, I am sure." Sarah was concealing her anxiety.

Richard bicycled back the way he had come, and arrived home under the hour, to find that there had been no change. The doctor had not come.

Soon after he had got back he saw through the window the old man from opposite coming across the road with flowers in his hand. Richard went to the gate. Pooley held out a bunch of primroses, and another of bluebells. "For the lady," he said. Richard thanked him, and took the flowers indoors, putting them with water in a vase.

Not wanting the dark lantern to be seen, or the envelopes, when Mr. and Mrs. Turney should arrive, he hid the lantern on the top shelf of the kitchen cupboard and put the other things away in his black bag, including the volumes of his Father's writings. His hands were by now trembling.

Two carriages drove down Comfort Road within a few minutes of one another, shortly after half-past ten o'clock. The first was the doctor's. He said good morning to Richard and at once went upstairs with Mrs. Birkett. Richard waited below. The second carriage drew up behind the first, with Thomas and Sarah Turney. He went outside to meet them, and took them into the parlour. Thomas Turney tried to divert Richard's strained calmness of manner by telling him that in the anxious period before his eldest daughter Dorothy was born, he had made every good resolution under the sun, including control of a hasty temper, but good resolutions seemed to be about as valid as good intentions, he-he-he. Richard did his best to look amiable, while the attempt at ingratiation made him feel as remote from Mr. Turney as before.

After sitting silent for a few minutes, he heard the door above open. The doctor was calling his name. Richard turned to Mrs. Turney and said in a voice higher than normal, "Mrs. Turney, would you be so good as to see Dr. Cave-Browne for me, and hear what he has to say?"

"Yes, my dear, of course," replied Sarah. "Tom, go with Dickie and hear the birds singing in the field by the railway, will you? Don't go too far away, be within call."

The two men went out of the house, and walked about beside the railway cutting. Pooley stood by the jenny-ass suckling her lanky little foal. The old fellow touched his worn moleskin cap when they went to have a word with him. Thomas Turney cast an eye over the gravelly ground, with its stumps of cabbages and other brassica killed in the frost, and asked if he made it pay.

"Oooh, I gits by, sir, me an' th'old moke," replied Pooley, out of lips thin and blue in a hairless face. Even his eyebrows were gone, Thomas Turney noticed. He was about to ask him how he had lost his hair when Richard said, "Mr. Pooley brought in two fine bunches of flowers for Hetty this morning, sir. They are in water waiting to go into her room later, when I am sure she will send you her thanks, Mr. Pooley."

"That's very kind of ye, I'm sure," said Thomas Turney, feeling in his pocket for a shilling. "How old are you, d'ye mind telling me, eh?"

"I wor born in seventeen hunner an' ninety three, sir, an' I started wark at Slagrave farm by th'Randisbourne crow-scarin' when I wor five year hold."

"Then you must be more than a hundred years old, eh? Wonderful. How do you account for it?"

"An' I wor warkin' th' Gre't Fiel' o' Bridge Ause farm what is now a cem-etairy when Boney wor beat at Waterloo. I'm hold, you know, I ain't like a young'n no more, but I ken still wark."

"You've seen some changes in your time, eh?"

"I wor 'ere when there worn't no railway, 'twas all water i' th' cuttin', an' barges come along loaded wi' coal for as far has Crydon."

"You must have seen Noah when he came along this way with the Ark, eh, he-he-he?" chuckled Thomas Turney, giving him a crown piece, to the old man's delight and amazement. He spat on the big silver coin for luck, before putting it into the flap pocket of his corduroy trousers, which were covered to above the knee with buttoned buskins of the same material.

"Yar real gennulman, sir," said Pooley, anxious gratitude on his face, as he sucked his gums in excitement.

"Have a cigar," retorted Thomas Turney, giving him one from his brown leather case. "You're old enough to smoke, I hope? He-he-he."

At this moment Sarah appeared between the pillars of the doorway, and seeing the men on the grass, walked slowly towards them. Sarah was struck through with fear, but trying to maintain herself by prayer. The doctor wanted to see Dickie, to tell him what he had told her. During a pause in her darling's agony there had come from Hetty such an appeal that Sarah had broken into tears, despite all her resolution. *Don't hurt the baby, don't hurt the baby, don't hurt the baby, don't*——

Sarah had kissed the hot brow, and taken the small curly head, with its dear curve at the back, the familiar, eager head of her little child, in her hands, and laid her cheek against her daughter's. "God is with you, darling. He is watching over you, as He is watching over us all, and He wants you to have your little one in your arms, this beautiful spring day. Try hard, Hetty dear, try hard, trust the gentle Jesus, there are angels all around us, bringing their help for the little one."

"Is Papa here?" asked Hetty, in an easier moment. "Is Papa very angry with me, Mamma?"

"Why no, dear, of course not! Papa and Dickie have taken a nice little walk together. The past is forgotten, and forgiven."

Hetty turned her head and whispered, "Look after Dickie, Mamma, if I——"

Sarah held her daughter's hands, praying wordlessly. Then Hetty lying on her side under the sheet gave a riving cry; the white core of flame consumed all her senses; she was gone from the world she had lived in.

The midwife came into the room at the cry, and the doctor followed to open his black gladstone bag holding the forceps. The moaning cry began again, *Don't hurt the baby, don't hurt the baby*——

Sarah remained with Tom, while Richard returned to see the doctor. Dr. Cave-Browne said:

"Mr. Maddison, you will require your fortitude. Are you a Catholic?"

Unable to speak, Richard shook his head.

"There is no need for excessive apprehension, but all cases where instruments have to be used are of course fraught with the unknown. The pelvis is small in your wife, and the baby's head is large, and facing the wrong way. There is danger of asphyxiation of the child unless forceps are used, for your wife does not seem able to summon up that extra energy in the muscles that is required for parturition. Therefore I have to ask you to make a decision, which is, should it be necessary to imperil the life of the one to conserve the life of the other, which shall it be? As the husband and father, you must make the decision. There is not at the moment an urgency for this decision, but the need for it might arise in the course of the next few minutes; so I will leave you for the moment to think things over. You will forgive what may seem a professional baldness of manner, but it is my duty to speak as plainly as I can."

"Now *sursum corda*, my boy," said the elderly Dr. Cave-Browne, laying his hand on the younger man's shoulder. "I will come and see you again shortly."

As he came downstairs Sarah told an obedient Tom to remain outside. Then she said, in the front room, "Hetty is most brave, Dickie, fighting for her little one's life."

Richard tried to speak. To his remote surprise no sound came from him. Trying again, his thin voice asked if he might be allowed to see Hetty. Sarah replied that the doctor might allow him a moment, but they were very much occupied at such times, and did not like any relations coming near, as a rule. To herself she thought that very soon the doctor would be giving Hetty chloroform, in order to use the forceps. Sarah closed her eyes at the thought of the baby's head being crushed, should this be the only way to save Hetty's life. Poor little one, she could hear in her mind the husky *Don't hurt the baby, don't hurt——*. It was God's will. He was the only hope.

As in a dream Richard went upstairs again.

"Yes, by all means, my boy, it might help if you saw her, but it must be for a moment only."

He knelt by Hetty, all experience dissolving as he saw her beseeching eyes, and heard the muttered words, *Don't let them hurt the baby, don't let them hurt the baby, don't let them——*

"No, Hetty, no." His hand sought to hold her brow in reassurance. She recognised him.

"Don't let them hurt the baby——"

"No dear, do not worry."

"Don't let them hurt the baby——"

"No dear, I promise you."

"Don't let them——"

Mrs. Birkett was standing at the bottom of the bed. "Come now, father," she said, and led him out of the room.

"Doctor, may I have just one minute——"

Richard went into the little room, which he had fitted up with his butterfly cases and other mementoes of his life, including the whistle, cuff-band, and truncheon of special constabulary days. He closed the door, to think about his answer. He felt the silent rushing of time within the little square box of a room, with its cheap wall-paper creased in places by inferior pasting; he saw the small garden through the window, the broken fencing with the ivy creeping up, and a robin flying to its nest among the leaves. He turned back to the pale enclosed room, while he began to breathe faster, as anguish surmounted upon his life, dissolving him as the pale interior of the little room. He closed his eyes, hearing again the words of Hetty's prayer to him; and then, feeling himself riven by the terror of loneliness, he clasped his cheeks and his mouth lest he cry out. Hetty dead! How could he live then? His mind rushed out in wildness. What would they do to her, to save the baby? His mind recoiled upon itself from the stricture of such thought, and became vacant; and the vacancy became a calmness, as though he were no longer involved, but standing away from what was happening; and the calmness became the face of Father, the dream-like feeling that Father was holding out his hands to him, and saying *Don't let them hurt the baby*. Yes, yes; he must keep his word.

Before he knew what he was doing Richard went down on his knees and remained with head bent and hands covering his face while he breathed deeply to recover himself.

When, less than a minute after he had gone into the little room, he came out again, the doctor knew that he had been praying. The young man had the face of a ghost.

"Do not you worry, we will do our best."

"Please do nothing to hurt the baby." Anguished eyes stared into the doctor's face.

"We shall do our best to hurt neither, my boy. Now go for a walk, and keep up your heart. By the way, I heard that you have seen a Camberwell Beauty on the Hill; now tell me, is it true?"

"I—I—thought so, sir. But it was in the light of my lantern only."

"Of course colours are deceptive in lamp-light; but it is most interesting. We must have a talk about it another time——"

A cry came from the bedroom.

Richard went down the stairs, and out of the house, like one walking out of the world, for he thought that by keeping his word to Hetty he had thereby signed her death-warrant.

Theodora was about to enter at the gate, but seeing his eyes she fell into step beside him, and taking his arm, accompanied him along the uneven grass-grown mounds of the embankment, asking no questions, for she had divined at once what was happening.

Some way down the embankment they sat down, and he told her of the events of the morning, omitting Hetty's plea to him and his decision therefrom; and as he spoke Theodora held his hands, reassuring him, saying again and again, "It will be all right now, boy, I know it will." They walked on the embankment, while he told her that once it was a canal, and herons fished there.

When they returned the doctor's carriage was turning the corner into the high road. Sarah was crying with relief, as was Thomas Turney, while Mrs. Feeney smiled as she wiped her eyes on her apron.

"There, brother," said Theodora. "All is well, you see!"

A son had been born, weighing nearly nine pounds. The baby was shocked, and marked about the brow and face. Hetty had four stitches in her torn flesh.

While in the room downstairs the others were resting, Mrs. Birkett in the room above was finishing the last of the Raggett's stout, while Mrs. Feeney set about clearing up the newspapers which had been spread, and trampled, upon the floor. Mrs. Feeney was doing the cleaning-up, in a strong odour of carbolic.

Meanwhile the picnic basket, packed with good things, was waiting in the carriage. Thomas Turney suggested that they drive to a green field, and fortify the inner man. So the carriage drove to the foot of the Hill, while Sarah remained behind with Hetty. Jim the coachman drove the carriage up the slope towards the grammar school, while Thomas, Richard and Theodora walked over the grass. There near the summit rugs were spread, and while the horse cropped the grass, Thomas Turney opened a bottle of claret and filled three glasses.

"A toast," he said, after sniffing the wine. "To the baby, coupled with congratulation to the father!"

By the expression on his rubicund features, Thomas Turney was congratulating himself as well.

"A nine pun boy, good bone, a man of Kent, he-he-he—drink up, Dick, and let me fill your glass. Jim, help yourself to a bottle of stout, and keep an eye on the hoss."

It was the first time Thomas Turney had been in the neighbourhood. Afterwards, when Theodora had returned to Comfort House, saying she would like to help Mrs. Turney, the two men went for a walk upon the crest of the Hill.

Seeing the ewes upon the new growth, Thomas Turney remarked that it was more of a rural district than he had thought it to be. The ewes were lying down, their backs to the sun and the southerly breeze, while their lambs in groups played together, leaping and frisking their tails. "Mutton doesn't pay like it did," said Thomas Turney. "There is a future in the Argentine for a farmer with capital and enterprise. My advice to any young man today is to learn Spanish."

The view over the Thames, with the spars and rigging of ships in the docks of the north and south banks, made him remark a few moments later that British ships carried in their bottoms half the wealth of the world.

"Commerce, the future lies in commerce! In Free Trade! Farming is finished in England. Only fools put money into it now."

Richard made no reply.

"I was sorry to hear of your Father's death like that, my boy. D'ye know your Shakespeare, the Seven Ages of Man, eh? He has a phrase and a word for all the ills the flesh is heir to. First the puling infant, eh? You'll know all about that very soon! How did you like the ham we had just now? It's a York, a little too fat for my taste. I fancy they feed 'em on too much home-grown wheat up there in the North. The millers won't buy the soft, home-grown wheats any more, now the hard Canadian and Australian grains come so quickly. But for feeding pigs you can't beat barley for flesh and flavour."

"We used to finish off our pigs, for the house, on oatmeal mixed with only a little barley meal, for the last fortnight, Mr. Turney."

"Ah, they're good farmers where you come from, m'boy. But farming's finished in England, as I told you. You can't farm properly without a ewe flock, and mutton doesn't pay any more. Nor does wool. You can't compete, at wages of nine and ten shillings a week, against Argentine peons paid the equivalent of a few pence." He pointed to the yellow and red spars in the Thames-side docks. "And now that steam has ousted sail, and passage is quicker, it will further reduce the balance."

"What do you think of South Africa, Mr. Turney?"

"There's chances there, of course, like anywhere else. It's a scramble just now, for gold and diamonds, and clever ones get the pickings, like Barney Barnato. They're clever, the Jews, they work hard, they stick together; and arouse a lot of envy, from those who aren't prepared to match their wits and their industry. So there's a rising prejudice against 'em in some circles. Look at my silly boy Charlie, he's out on the Rand now, trying to make his fortune, by striking it lucky, as the current phrase goes. First he couldn't rest until he got to Canada, nothing interested him but Indians and the 'golden wheatfields of the West,' but after two winters loading muck on to sleds, and feeding bullocks, and then the spring rush to get the seed in, he gave it up. Before he'd properly started! Now it's all 'striking it lucky' on the veldt."

They walked past the square brick building of the grammar school. "What's this place? Grammar School! I learnt little at mine in Bedford. Now if they have the sense to drop Latin and teach Spanish grammar, it would be in keeping with the times. I hear you've left Doggett's, and gone into insurance. Are they paying you so well?"

"Oh yes, sir, quite well, thank you. There are chances, too, of going abroad, possibly so far as Hong Kong or Shanghai."

"Then you take a chance and go, my boy! There's a great future in the Far East. Tea, tin, rubber, and some talk of cotton, though Manchester laughs at that. Coolie wages will enable enterprising firms to undercut the home market. Mark my words. You seize the chance, if you get it, and go abroad, that's my advice. See the world!"

They came to the eastern crest with the prospect over Shooter's Hill and the low lands extending away into the Thames estuary. Thomas Turney's eye caught sight of scaffolding on the lower slope facing south from where they stood.

"Building started, I see. Isn't this one of the places going to be taken over by the London County Council? Let's go see what's going on down there, shall we?"

They walked down the track. At the bottom, where it joined Charlotte Road, they looked at the new notice board, advertising for sale the houses being built.

"Leasehold for ninety nine years, I see. Well, it's a pleasing site for a house, the sort of place I'd like to come to live when I retire, Dick. It's in the country, and yet conveniently close to the City. Good bricks, too, and that timber stacked there is Baltic spruce, the best. Let's sit down, shall we, then we can listen to the birds, and have a little talk about the future. I think I'll take off m' coat, it's warm now, ain't it, though they do say, 'Cast not a clout, till May be out'."

They sat on the wood for rafters.

"See the close grain, Dick? That reveals the slow growth, the endurance through those Finnish winters. It toughens the tree, and the resin acts as a bond, you see. The worm doesn't like resin, any more than it likes the tan in oak. If you notice, the worm only attacks the sap wood, never the core of oak timber."

Feeling less constricted, the younger man replied:

"There are several kinds of wood beetle, are there not, Mr. Turney? I used to see a long legged fly, or beetle, in the wood-stack at home, yellow and black it was. I think it hatched from a pupa in the wood, from the grub boring through. Then there was another kind of fly, an ichneumon, black and red, trying to probe into the cracks of the wood, with a long black whisk pushed down, sometimes an inch in length, the ovipositor. The ichneumon was seeking grubs on which to lay its eggs. The eggs hatched, and ate the grub when it had pupated, and instead of a yellow wood fly emerging in due course, out came an ichneumon fly!"

Richard's voice was a little strained as he spoke. He felt himself to be sweating under the arm-pits.

"Most interesting, my boy. I suppose with your father's passing, your brother will inherit the estate?"

"What is left of it, sir."

"He's a barrister, isn't he, so Sarah was telling me? How's he doing?"

"I've no idea, Mr. Turney."

Meditatively Thomas Turney's thoughts turned from money to his children, the other subject seldom far from his mind.

"Did ye notice Hughie's appearance this morning, Dick? Poor silly fellow, his intemperance has got him into trouble." He grunted. "The trouble is, young people won't learn from the experience of their elders. Now you're a steady young fellow, and tenacious, how would you like to come into the Firm? Eh? Don't answer now, think it over. Hughie don't care for the business, Charlie has gone off to follow 'is own line, Sidney—d'ye know Dorrie's husband?—is doing well in the wine trade, and Joey, now home from school for the holidays, is a good boy, but not particularly bright. Someone in the family ought to be in the Firm, someone steady and capable, to learn the business. Why, some family businesses have been goin' on for hundreds of years! You've got a son now, and he's my grandson. I shan't last forever, and between ourselves Mallard's a bit of a duffer, with a silly wife.

A man's wife makes all the difference. Well, think it over, it's interesting work, and takes you about. You're too much of a countryman to spend all your life on an office stool, Dick. With your gentlemanly appearance, you could do better for yourself than a clerk in an office, good as the Moon Insurance is. We insure with them, you know. Yes, machinery and stock-in-trade, close on forty thousand pun."

Thomas Turney closed his eyes for a minute or so; he felt tired. Then he pulled a watch from his fob. "Well, we must be getting back. I wonder what they are asking for one of these new houses? Property is likely to appreciate here, the land all round remaining open."

He dropped the watch back in his fob.

"Well, time we were moving, eh?"

"Yes, Mr. Turney."

Rooks cawed in the elms beyond the heaps of building materials. The noise was harsh in Richard's ears; the sunshine was brassy.

Chapter 31

SUMMER WEATHER

IN THE month of June, on a Sunday afternoon in the church of St. Simon Wakenham there was much suppressed excitement among the children of the classes taken by Mr. Crowley and his faithful assistant Miss Danks. After the Scripture a strange kind of baby was to be christened, and all the children were wondering how much of it they would see: a Donkey Baby.

During the Bible story, and the catechism, old Mr. Crowley—benevolent and gentle with white hair and whiskers, pale face and hands and eyes and thin red nose—was softly persuasive as usual in his attempts to make the children listen and look at him while he recounted, as he had recounted many times in his fifteen years in charge of the Sunday School, the story of how no more than a few slices of bread, and a number of little fishes caught in the Lake of Galilee, had been turned suddenly into hundreds of loaves of bread, and basket after basket of fishes, and all solely by the aid of prayer and blessing from on High. Strange things called miracles could still happen in the world, for God was everywhere, and could do anything He wanted to do in His Mysterious Way. But only if those here below had belief in Him, and faith, could miracles happen. Mr. Crowley's thin and throaty voice piped on, as it had during the years, in voluntary and devoted service to his beliefs.

When the story was over, a hymn was sung to the strains of the organ played, without pedal notes, by Miss Danks; and then a whisper of excitement went round the varnished pine-wood benches where the children sat and shifted, for Mr. Mundy, in surplice and stole, had come in from the vestry. It was just three o'clock, the time for the christening.

The vicar believed it to be a good thing for children to see a christening, and so the classes were permitted to stay behind and watch, provided they behaved themselves by sitting down and not standing up, and not talking during the ceremony.

Footfalls in the porch, a shadow past one of the leaded windows, Mr. Mundy with hands crossed walking to the door. The people were coming in with the Donkey Baby!

It was said that when the baby grew up it would have long grey fur all over it, and when it opened its mouth to speak it would bray. One of the older children, a girl, had heard that its mother had been frightened by a donkey just before the baby was born, and so the baby was covered with donkey hair and its ears were ever so long. Two doctors had come in their carriages when it was being born. The baby was to be taken away after the christening and would never be seen again, because such a thing would not be allowed to grow up.

As the people walked into the church, the mother carrying the baby in its long white christening gown, the children gripped the backs of the pine-wood pews and bobbed up and down, drawn by curiosity and only partly suppressed by obedience to the sharp whispers of Miss Danks. They hoped that when it cried, as most babies did when the water was dropped on them, it would at least go *e-aaw*, *e-aaw*!

But nothing happened. The baby, christened Phillip Sidney Thomas Maddison, did not even cry when Mr. Mundy took it, and, holding low the white bundle, dabbed water on the black-haired head with his fingers.

The children wanted to see the baby close-up. The girl who had heard that it was to be put away held up her arm for permission to speak to Miss Danks.

Miss Danks took the whispered request, passed it to Mr. Crowley, who on tiptoe at the suitable moment approached the font where the Vicar was speaking in his ordinary cheery voice to the parents, complimenting them on the good behaviour of the baby, and that they had got over the early difficult period of feeding so successfully.

Following the baby's birth, Hetty had been ill. The doctor had recommended regular feeding times for the baby, to get it into good habits. No feeding after ten o'clock at night. If the baby cried, it should be put in a spare room, to cry itself to sleep. "They start to play their tricks early, and cultivation of regular habits from the very first is the secret of a happy life. A baby should sleep from ten at night to six o'clock in the morning."

Alone in a room, among Richard's fishing rods and boxes of butterflies, the crying baby at times came near to throttling itself;

and the doctor, further consulted, suggested that it be given a bottle of warm water to suck, with a little dill-water added. Still the baby grizzled and wailed, heard by Hetty lying sleepless in the next room.

Unable to bear the crying of the baby, after the first few nights Richard insisted on taking upon himself the duties of a nurse. To pass the time he made a copy of his father's journals, with permission from his brother John. Night after night he sat at the kitchen table, holding the baby in the crook of his left arm while writing by the light of the companionate lantern. When the baby had its paroxysms he rose to walk the floor with it, desperate for lack of sleep, but always thinking of the baby, and of the need for Hetty upstairs to sleep.

From the first Mrs. Birkett and Mrs. Feeney declared that the mother's milk must be wrong. They recommended a wet-nurse. Richard set his face against it. He had heard of babies being infected with disease from foster-mothers. It was obvious that the baby was being starved, so cow's milk was tried, diluted with warm water and a little sugar added; but the baby was often sick afterwards, its frothy vomit sour with acid. At the end of the first month it had lost weight to eight pounds.

Other foods were tried, proprietary brands; but it did not seem able to digest them. At six weeks of age it still weighed but eight pounds. Night after night during the first three weeks of May Richard walked the oil-cloth of the kitchen floor with the baby, trying to soothe it, talking to it in a whisper lest Hetty be awakened. He changed its diapers, and dropped the soiled ones into the pail for washing at the end of the night. One morning he tip-toed to the front door and opened it, the baby awake but silent in his arms. The cold air of dawn passed down the street; the moon was sinking beyond the grass-grown heaps of earth raised on the embankment, and the dark outline of a donkey against the sky. He listened to the nightingales singing in the distant cemetery.

As he stood there, he looked at the baby in his arms, lying so quietly, all eyes and peaky face. Suddenly the baby smiled at him. He felt emotion, the tears came into his eyes, smarting with sleeplessness. He whispered to the baby. Dear little fellow, he had smiled at his father!

"Poor baby—there now—be a good boy, won't you—poor baby."

Later, when taking Hetty up a cup of tea, he told her about it. He was so pleased; he thought it was the turning point, somehow, in the baby's condition. When later that day Hetty told Mrs. Feeney, Mrs. Feeney said that is likely to be a wind pain, for babies did not usually smile until three months.

"Yes, Mrs. Feeney, but I don't think we ought to tell Mr. Maddison that, do you?"

"No, ma'am, of course not." Both women were pleased that he loved his little son.

Alas, there was no change in the condition. The baby's face became more puckered. No more smiles were detected during the weary nights in the kitchen. With eyes shut it screamed itself to feebleness; its paroxysms lasted an hour and more at a time. It lay as though dead afterwards, in waxen sleep. It stirred; it whimpered; its face puckered; again the feeble screaming, until it seemed to be choking itself, to the father's helpless distress.

One night in early June, after such a period, the baby seemed to quiver, to shake convulsively, and then to become inert. Richard stared piteously at it. Was it dead? Oh, why had Mr. Turney been the cause of so much unhappiness? Was there any connection between Hetty's long unconsciousness, after being struck like that, and the baby's condition now? Was it in a fit? What should he do? What could be done? Dr. Cave-Browne had said that all that could be done was to keep it warm, to keep to regular feeding times, and not to experiment with too many quack patent foods. Was it breathing? He opened his father's journal, took out the pigeon's feather, one of the downy breast-feathers, a smoky grey. He held it in the open mouth of the child. It did not stir.

His heart jumped. The baby was dead! But might not the pigeon feather be too stiff? The ring dove's feathers were so hard that they could resist a charge of shot, that was well-known: he must keep calm. There was an owl's breast-feather in another page, that would be the test!

It was a feather of *strix flammea*, the white owl; it had come from Skirr farmhouse, where the owls nested under the thatched roof. It was so soft and wavy that as he bore it between finger and thumb the white filaments were pressed by the air against his nail. He held it by the end of the thin quill under the baby's nose. It stirred, the filaments waved. Thank God, Oh thank God!

The baby lay, its head within an elbow, on his knees. He sat by the table, his sight too painful for reading or copying. He closed his eyes; rested the other elbow on the table, the weight of his head borne sideways on his left palm. The baby slept, one hand clasping the digit finger of the father's right hand. The clock ticked on the chimney-piece; afar off a cock crowed beyond the railway cutting. A mouse ran across the floor, unafraid of the motionless figure on the chair by the table.

Some time later Hetty awakened with all her senses directed to the kitchen below. Gradually it came to her that she smelled burning. Was it her imagination? She lay still, listening. All was quiet below. She had dozed through the night, on the edge of awakening, her body resting, but not her mind, which was linked with her baby's distress. She had prayed for strength to help Dickie and the baby, for a calm mind whereby not to upset him. Dr. Cave-Browne had said that she had a germ in her system, which made the passing of her water painful, and was the cause of her fever. She must keep warm, on no account must she walk about the room.

"Dickie!" she cried out, unable to bear the thought that the house might be on fire. The night-light burned palely in its saucer of water by her bed. "Dickie!" Her voice was feeble. She listened. There was no sound from below.

Shaken by fear, she cried out again. No answer. Perhaps he was unconscious upon the floor! She could smell burning more distinctly. Perhaps the baby had fallen on the kitchen stove. "Dickie! Please answer, dear! Are you there, Dickie?"

As in a bad dream she pulled herself out of bed, managing to put on her dressing gown. She got to the head of the stairs. She called his name again.

She walked down the stairs. It was a terrible dream: she was trying to pull herself along by the wall of the passage, swaying and almost falling. She got to the kitchen. A mouse ran across the floor. She saw Dickie seated by the table, his head fallen sideways. A lock of his hair was being singed upon the top of the lantern. The baby was asleep on his lap. Her relief was so great that she could not move; while the sight caused sobs to shake her.

Richard awakened to see her standing by him. At once he protested against her being out of bed, declaring that he was merely resting for a moment: and laying the baby in the armchair, he half-carried her upstairs, and put her back into bed. Afterwards he returned to the kitchen and considered what to do. It was nearly five o'clock: hardly worth while trying to sleep now; so he would wait until it was six o'clock, when it would be time to mix the baby its bottle, and make a pot of tea.

While waiting for the kettle to boil, he went into the garden, to breathe the fresh air of the early morning, and to look around his plots of growing vegetables and flowers. Afterwards, as he was filling his tub in the kitchen, for his morning sluice, there came a knock on the front door. Mr. Pooley stood there, holding a jug in his hand.

"For little maas-ter," he said, touching his moleskin cap. It was milk from the jenny-ass.

Mrs. Feeney came out of her gate at that moment. "You won't do wrong, sir, by warming it for the baby. Mr. Pooley is quite honest, Mr. Maddison. It's the softest milk there is, next to mother's milk, which Mrs. Maddison hasn't got, poor little soul. Just bring it up nice and warm, don't let it boil, and you'll see the difference if Master Phillip can keep it down."

Richard warmed some in a pot, and poured it into the bottle; then making sure it was not too hot, he went upstairs and told Hetty. He sat her up in bed, arranged the pillows, brought the baby, and she gave it the bottle to suck. It took the small amount, cried for more, took a second feed eagerly, and, its wind having been tapped up, it fell at once into a sleep, and remained like that until the mid-morning.

Thereafter, with regular supplies of ass's milk, the baby put on flesh, and soon was sleeping all night. The crisis was over. Hetty grew stronger, Richard became happier. In gratitude he gave Pooley his lucky crown piece, and never missed it, for always a warm feeling arose in him with the thought of the old fellow's action. He felt that at last his life was becoming stabilised: and about this time he entered into an agreement to purchase one of the new houses in the road across the Hill.

At ten weeks the baby smiled whenever its father's face looked down at it; and Richard considered that he and his little boy had an especial understanding between them. He would imitate country sounds for it, in regular succession—wood owl, rook, green woodpecker, plaintive whistle of kestrel—to the baby's (and the mother's) delight.

Seeing the baby smile at its father during the christening, the small girl who had enquired if it was going to be put away asked, after some hesitation, if they would be allowed to keep it?

"I hope so, dear," said Hetty. "He is ever so much better than he was. It was a miracle, I think, that we found the right food in time."

The children clustered round the baby, the white embroidered skirts of its gown swaddling its feet. The baby smiled at them.

"Oh, isn't it a dear? Please, may we look at its feet?"

Hetty folded back the cambric gown, which Mamma had given her, the one in which she herself had been christened, and showed the baby's feet, long and thin.

"He takes after his father," she said proudly.

"Then he's an ordinary baby, and not a donkey baby!"

At this Thomas Turney laughed. "I'm the donkey sometimes," he said. The children wondered what was meant by the old gentleman. He did not look like a donkey at all. They were absorbed by the baby.

"Oh, isn't it lovely, look at its tiny toes!"

Just before the party left the church Hugh Turney, who had scarcely spoken a word since greeting his sister and brother-in-law on arrival in the early afternoon with his parents, saw upon the face of Theodora as she spoke to Sidney a look which finally decided his hopeful-hopeless thoughts. His sister Dorrie saw the look, too, and hid her feelings of dread and fear under a gentle smile as she regarded the face of the baby. Her own infant, a daughter, was at home with the nurse.

They walked down the leaf-shaded Twistleton Road, and back to the house for tea, which Mrs. Feeney, in best gown and bonnet, had prepared. Hugh was rehearsing in his mind what he should say to make his excuses to avoid going in. He wanted to be alone, to walk and walk and walk, anywhere, nowhere. At the corner of Charlotte Road he said he was not feeling well, and would find his own way home. Before anyone could reply he raised his hat, and turned away.

After tea the others departed, leaving Hetty, Richard, and Theodora with the baby in the parlour. Theodora told them that she had made up her mind to fulfil an ambition she had until recently never thought to be able to realize: to sail in a ship through the Pillars of Hercules and along the Parthenopean shore by the Mediterranean Sea and so to the Aegean, to the isles of

Greece, and the wondrous places of the Odyssey and the Greek poets.

And she would see where Byron swum the Hellespont, stand by the grave of Keats in Rome, and tread Lerici's shore where the drowned body of Shelley was left by the sea, to be burned while Byron stood beside the funeral pyre and watched the coloured flames arising into the wild twilight. Italy and Dante, the painters of the Renaissance, the incomparable beauty of Rome! Theodora's voice was ecstatic as she spoke to Hetty beside her on the sofa, and bending over her godchild, she hid the tears of renunciation which she could not keep from her eyes.

"But before I go, you must come and have a holiday with me in my cottage. I shall not leave England until the end of the summer."

Theodora had taken a cottage for the month of July at Lynmouth in North Devon. It was, she said, a little fishing hamlet where Shelley had stayed nearly a hundred years before. How jolly it would be if Hetty and Dickie could come and spend their holiday with her during part of the time. She had written to invite John and Jenny, and perhaps such an opportunity for all six of them to be together might never occur again.

At first when Richard heard of the project he shook his head, saying that he did not expect to be given leave that year; but it so happened that the head of the Town Department the very next day asked him when he would care to take his holiday, and on learning that he was entitled to ten days, Richard asked if he might have four and twenty hours before deciding; and this being readily given, he went to see brother John in his chambers that evening. It was decided that they should go down together, all four with the baby, and join their sister in the second week of July.

So one morning they all met on Waterloo Station, the baby in a wicker cradle specially made, with two handles for carrying, by a basket-maker in Randiswell, from osiers grown on the banks of the Randisbourne.

Hetty had never seen Dickie so happy, he looked so young and handsome, she thought, dressed in his tweed coat and cream flannel trousers and waistcoat with the brown stripes, and his straw boater. He had brought one of his sea-fishing rods, and a greenheart fly-rod, for there were many trout in the torrential and rocky Lynn streams. Jenny had brought a luncheon basket, and since the baby was now able to take Neave's Food, there would be no difficulty in feeding him properly.

It was a romantic journey that sunny July morning. Beyond Salisbury and the Great Plain, beyond the fields and grey-stone houses of Dorset the country became new to them, and when in the afternoon the train drew into Exeter station, both Hetty and Richard began to feel the excitement of entering almost a new life. The baby behaved well, sleeping all the way, awakening to take its feed, heated over a small spirit lamp, as the train entered the valley beyond the cathedral city, with red fields and wooded hills over which the great hawks soared. A river ran at the bottom of the valley, sometimes approaching the train across level meadows, when they saw under steep banks its grey-green waters flecked with foam as the train thundered over bridges. Red cattle grazed in the meadows, or stood under oaks which threw their wide shade on pastures which seemed so very green, after the dull sooted grass of the Hill.

The train stopped at every station, beside little platforms where rambler roses grew with sunflowers, geraniums, and hollyhocks. Oil lamps with bulbous globes stood on wooden posts along the platforms. The river grew wider as the train ran westwards, past cider apple orchards and hamlets of thatched cottages with lime-washed walls. And at last they drew into the old port of Barnstaple with sailing ships tied to the quay beyond stretches of yellow sand, for the tide was out; and below the bridge wading birds ran and flitted among gulls and swans.

After tea at an hotel at the end of the High Street, with its Regency bow-windows and lamp with copper-oxide red glass fixed to the wall, they took their seats with half a dozen others in a coach with the name *Tally Ho!* painted on the sides. To the notes of a six-foot horn blown by the boy at the back they drove down one of the main streets and turned right-handed up another street to the Lynton road. The coach was large enough to take twenty passengers, so there was plenty of room inside for the travellers, with John and Richard sitting on the box beside the driver.

The drive up the valley was for Richard pure delight. The world he had known since he had left his old home had always been outside, never of, himself, for he had never become part of it, except at rare moments, such as the encounter with the Mundys on the Hill during the time of snow. That incidental intimacy had lapsed, owing to preoccupation with the circumstance of the baby, and Hetty being indisposed until recently. But now—riding on the box of the coach beside his brother John, and with the happy thought that there were nine whole days of freedom before him—Richard was fully himself. He wanted to utter a shout—he was on a coach going up to Exmoor, the wild and romantic country of the Doones, and Lorna, and mighty Jan Ridd!—for of course he had read *Lorna Doone* as a boy, as had all his brothers and sisters.

Four sturdy horses drew the coach north-eastwards at a steady trot along the winding valley route, above the meadows where a stream ran fast in its rocky bed, and overgrown by trees. The air became cooler as they climbed upwards, the road sometimes level, but gradually rising and often causing the horses to walk, the wheelers pressing against the leather tug-pieces drawing the traces attached to the swingle-trees, eager for their feed of crushed oats in the farm-yard stables at Loxhore, where a fresh team would replace the tired horses.

The coach turned left-handed at a fork in the road after they had been travelling a little under an hour, and entered a bend in the valley, with a wider view of green meadows and the trout stream winding through them, and wooded hills rising steeply to the blue and white sky.

Here the four horses began to show a greater eagerness, and were in a mild sweat when the boy raised the long copper horn and blew blasts on it, to announce their arrival to those in the farm just above the turn in the road. While the boy helped to unhitch the horses, the driver walked up to the farmhouse for a mug of cider, and after a word with Hetty and Jenny, the brothers took advantage of the interval to stretch their legs and being invited to take each some cider in a pink china mug, poured from a cloam pitcher, they accepted, and sipped appreciatively. It was sharp, pale yellow stuff: Richard finished his pot with determination, while thinking that this was the real drink of Devon; but the more realistic John, knowing its acid quality, managed to pour his unobserved into a patch of dusty nettles.

The team having been changed, and a fifth horse hitched on for the long climb upwards, the coach moved off, while Richard began to feel that he was swaying curiously: and jumping down, he followed on foot, and in a gateway leading out of the deeply sunken lane up which the horses were hauling the coach he leaned, unseen by the boy with the horn, over the top bar of a gate and vomited the contents of his stomach. The relief was instant; and feeling much happier, he hurried after the vehicle.

It was a long hill, rising to the crest into mellow evening light illuminating leagues of heather and stunted furze and acres of rush and white-tufted cotton grass, with a backward view of the blue tors of Dartmoor and the Cornish hills beyond the long headland of Hartland lying out into the Atlantic. Wonderful, wonderful!

The coach stopped on the crest while the fifth horse was unhitched, to return by itself; and Richard clambered up. Driving on at a good pace, the coach soon came to the crossroads of the Black Moor gate, and the road lined with beech hedges leading down from the heath. And now before them opened another marvellous view, of the northern coast with its heather hills ending precipitously above the Severn Sea. Over the water were the mountains of Wales, and the sands of the Gower coast.

The coach stopped at the beginning of a steep hill, while the boy, leaning the horn in the hedge, fixed upon the rear wheels the iron shoes, chained to the axle, which he called the drags. This locked the rear wheels, and with the horses pressing against the breechings, they descended the stony way, with its gutters cut deep by rain-storms. Richard, thinking of his father being dragged under similar wheels, was alarmed lest the coach slue sideways and overturn; but they reached the bottom safely, to notes of the horn, and at the sharp right-handed corner of the village the drags were taken off. What hills! Another horse was required, to help haul them up the steep hill leading between cottages and so out of the village. At the top they rested, while the extra horse was unhitched and ridden down the hill to its stable by the boy who had come up with it.

Then onwards, coming to yet another steep hill, with wooded coombes below, through the meads of which ran one of the feeders of the Lynn river. Again the drags; again the slow descent; and coming to the bottom of the coombe, the hot skids were removed and hung up, and with blasts of the horn echoing with the noises of water rushing over brown rocks and mingling with the clopping of hooves, the *Tally Ho!* entered the precipitous valley with its trees in shadow until far up the rocky hillsides their canopies met the line of the western sun.

There was one more stop, at the junction of the Lynton and Lynmouth roads. Here the passengers for the bay alighted, to see several small vehicles, like governess cars, each drawn by a shaggy moor pony, in line beside the road. Among them were other ponies, harnessed to low sleds on iron runners, for the luggage. And there, coming forward with pink cheeks to greet them, was Theodora.

While Hetty and her baby rode in a jingle, which she thought was the dearest little thing on wheels imaginable, Theodora with her brothers walked down the narrow stony way leading to the village seen below the trees. The descent was the most fearsome of all the hills they had met so far. The track was stony, and deeply rutted, with a sharp bend at the bottom, approached while the noise of waterfalls was loud in the air. Richard, apprehensive for his wife and child, walked behind the jingle, prepared at any moment to hang back on the combing and so save them from calamity, but the sure-footed pony was used to the gradient, and they arrived safely at the bottom by the bridge under which the torrent roared.

Richard looked over the parapet. Great smooth boulders, each of many tons in weight, lay in the bed of the stream. Indeed, they were the bed, around which the green and white water plunged on its way to the sea.

Cottages built of stone rising directly above the river marked the way down to the quay. The street lay on the other side of the waterside cottages, past their fronts, with doors and windows opening right on it, without any side-walk. Small shops were built on the other side of the street, and above them trees rose to the heights of Lynton.

The cottage Theodora had taken was near the quay, with its tower and lantern, wicker crab-pots and nets spread to dry on the wall, and boats moored below, each with its sentinel gull. The river lost itself in the sea beyond the bouldered shore. The cottage was thatched, and they reached it by a sloping path leading up from the street. There were three bedrooms, with latticed casements looking out over the sea and the great precipices of red iron-stone rising into Somerset across the bay.

For tea they had lightly boiled eggs, with delicious bread made from wheat ground in the mill up the valley, and baked in a cloam oven in the side of the open hearth. The oven was oval, like half an egg, masoned into the wall. Theodora explained that the oven was made of earthenware, and had a lid which fitted into the oval after the fire of sticks had been raked out, and the bottom of the oven cleaned by a bundle of wet rags tied to a stick. The cloam oven remained hot; and into it the dough shapes were put, the lid replaced. The result, as the owner of the cottage declared, was "butiful plumm bread, my dears."

Plumm it was—light, of an even texture, dissolving in the mouth with pats of salted butter made in a farmhouse on the hills above. After the eggs, bread and scald cream and honey—honey from bees which flew up a thousand feet to the ling and bell-heather of the moor above, returning with the sweetness of sun and soil and air.

Shades of Haybundle Street, and the white bread of the Golden Grain Company shops in the city . . . Richard could hardly wait to finish his tea—ending up with bottled whortleberries from the moor, delicious blue berries eaten with yellow crusty cream and shortcakes—and saffron cake for to fill up with—and there was plenty of ham if they were still hungry, said the good woman looking after them—"Don't 'ee deny your stummicks, my dears, there be plenty more out yurr if you'm hungry"—but the tide was nearly high and Richard could hardly wait to unpack his sea-rod and start fishing then and there from the end of the quay. Which he did, buying bait from a fisherman, and catching three good pollack as the sun was going down and all the colours of sea and cliff and sky were changing momentarily, and lights were shining brighter in cottage windows.

The days passed and the sun shone over the grey bouldered shore where they sat and talked, sometimes setting up cockshies of rusty can or tide-jetted wood, or paddling among the boulders; and when the sun was hot, Richard and John retired to put on blue-and-white ringed bathing suits, which covered their bodies to the neck, their arms to the elbow, and their legs to just below the knee, and thus clad they crept and slithered past boulders to deeper water where they might strike out, always mindful of the tides which moved swiftly up and down the Bristol Channel. They went fishing together up the glen, taking turns with the greenheart rod, and using three wet flies which disappeared in the foaming torrent and seemed to hook the small and lively trout of themselves. They saw dippers in the glen, small and sturdy white-and-brown birds which dived into the shallower flumes at the edge of the river, and holding on to pebbles by their feet, sought caddis flies and shrimps in the gravel. The trout were fried in bacon fat, and though white-fleshed, were pronounced to be of a most delicate flavour.

The days passed. It was calm summer weather, with no south-west wind to bring the rain. The nights were quiet, with only the sound of the sea in the open casement windows filling the restful darkness. The baby slept until dawn, which came golden down the Severn Sea; and when the sun was high it lay happily on its back in the shade of the wooden groin among the boulders of the shore, smiling to itself.

Within the cottage, when sitting on Hetty's lap, its head supported by her arm, it would stare at Dickie or John or Dora or Jenny in the most solemn way. Its head wobbled as it changed its stare unexpectedly from one to another, while its eyes, in the thought of its mother, were like those of a little mouse. In these moments it appeared to be sensitive to every word and movement of the face it watched. Once when Theodora, talking to Hetty when the others had gone out for a walk, suddenly wept, they both saw the baby's mouth to be drooping. Theodora smiled, and immediately the baby was smiling with her.

Theodora was telling Hetty that she would not be seeing her again for a year, perhaps more, and if she did not write often, Hetty would understand, would she not. Yes, said Hetty, her face gently reflective; then looking at Dora, she whispered "Honk!" which was the near-forgotten greeting of the Tree-frogs Club, and Dora replied with a scarce-audible "Honk!" The baby made a sound, too, which was more a little grunt than a honk; and with a laugh Hetty laid him over her shoulder, tapping the small of his back, until the baby made the same noise again.

In the morning Theodora was to depart by a ketch which, having unloaded its cargo of Welsh limestone pebbles for the lime-kiln, was sailing for Bristol with some cattle. It was due to arrive there two days before the schooner in which she had engaged a cabin was sailing for the Mediterranean. And at midday, on the rising tide, Theodora departed—an exile from love.

The four friends watched the two-masted vessel standing with full sails, out into the bay, where it met the plunging currents sweeping east round the red promontory of Foreland Point. A white flicker of a handkerchief on deck, and Theodora was gone.

"Well," said John. "I wonder when we shall see Dora again?"

They all knew that she was in love with Sidney; they all thought that she had done the right thing, indeed the only thing, by going away.

Richard and Hetty had but two more days left before they must depart, and take the afternoon train back to London from Barnstaple. Richard concealed his thoughts under an amiable and open countenance. He was happier than Hetty had ever seen him; he was an open air man, she knew now. He was entirely different from his former self. Hetty was happy, too; every part of her was given to the baby, and her affection towards Dickie was part of the joy she felt in her little son. And she had very nearly lost him, Little Mouse! They were soon going to move into their new house, with the beautiful Hill directly in front of it, and behind, an open field with rooks in a cluster of elm-trees. Oh, life was truly wonderful.

Richard was thinking that soon, ah soon, would be ended the games of chess and whist by candlelight of an evening; the walks up the long hill above the cliffs, two miles and more of it, to the county gate by the Blue Ball inn; the bathes of an early morning, fishing from quay and boat, the trout in the shadowy Lynn, the water-ousels on the rocks in the stream; and sun-lazy talks among the warm boulders of the beach, while on the flowing tide salmon leapt to meet the fresh water of the stream in the post-marked fairway. A wonderful holiday, he kept saying to himself, as though for reassurance against the dark thoughts of having to go back to London. A glance at Jenny, and his heart lightened. It was she who had made him feel so free, by her presence, by her way of talking to him, by her understanding, by her very *being*. So different from his feeling for Hetty, or anyone else he had ever known: it was higher than ordinary love. Just to be with her, to know that she was alive in the world, was all that he asked, secretly within himself.

At last the farewells were said, and the notes of the coach horn but a faint echo among the trees of the valley.

"You have a fine brother, John," said Jenny, as she walked down the steep track to the village below, hand in hand with her husband. "What a difference from the shy, haunted young man I knew before."

"I think he should have been a farmer, darling. He nearly went to join Hilary in New South Wales, but there, Hetty has her people here, and perhaps it would have been too hard a life for her."

They were staying on for another week, to make the most of the fine spell while it lasted; then they were moving their home from London to Rookhurst.

"Dear little Donkey Boy," said Jenny. "I would like a son of my own, your baby," she smiled, looking at John with bright eyes. "Then he could invite his cousin Phillip to stay with him, and go fishing in the Longpond. What shall we call our son, darling?"

"I think he should be called William, after his grandfather. You can, should you register him when I am away, hardly make a mistake of an extra 'l' in his name, as Hetty apparently did, with Phillip. Dick told me she said the swallows spelled it that way. *Phil-lip, phil-lip.*"

"I think there is something swallow-like about the child, you know, John. Hetty thinks of him as a Little Mouse, but did you ever see a mouse with blue eyes?"

"Well, did you ever see a swallow with blue eyes, Jenny? Or a donkey?"

"Yes! We had a donkey when we were little, with one brown eye and the other light blue, so there!"

Happily they walked down to the cottage.

The three were in their thoughts, as the sun shone over the valley, so they did not miss them overmuch; Dickie and Hetty and little Phillip were in their thoughts, part of their living—the contented living of two people who loved each other truly, being matched in mind and outlook. With them there was no regret, no feeling of loss. It was Richard who grieved, even as Hetty dreamed in secret, sitting in the train, the baby asleep between them, on the way back to London, in the summer weather.